⋆Futuristic Romance⋆

Love in another time, another place.

THE PRICE OF LOVE

"Even you must have your price."

"Yes, Marissa, I suppose I do," Brace growled, his voice vibrating with cold fury. "My freedom. I'd do anything for my freedom."

"And what about my needs? What about Cassandra's freedom?"

He eyed her, something snapping within him. Curse her for being the alluring woman she was in spite of it all! Let her just once feel some of the same frustration and confusion he felt!

"Well, there can be a price for that, too," Brace replied, as a challenge that he knew Marissa wouldn't dare take formed in his mind. "But have a care. You won't like paying it."

"Won't I?" she jeered. "And what could it possible take to buy a coward's backbone?"

His glance slid down the length of her body, and a bewildering mix of rage and lust flooded him. "Mate with me. Then perhaps I'll reconsider."

CRYSTAL FIRE

KATHLEEN MORGAN

LOVE SPELL ◆ **NEW YORK CITY**

To Alicia Condon, an editor with the courage and vision to take a chance on a new genre and give it her wholehearted support. You've allowed me to stretch, to soar, and to fulfill at last my heart's desire.

And to Anne Avery, a talented writer and dear friend. Thanks for keeping me on the "straight and narrow," which I have a tendency to veer off of at every opportunity. This book is so much better for your insightful and generous input.

LOVE SPELL®

November 1995

Published by

Dorchester Publishing Co., Inc.
276 Fifth Avenue
New York, NY 10001

Printed in the United States of America.

Prologue

"Aeiii . . . aeiii . . ."

The mournful keening swirled about the room, grating on Marissa Laomede's tightly strung nerves. Finally she could bear it no longer. She whirled about, confronting the huddled group of maidservants.

"Must you go on so?" Marissa demanded through gritted teeth. "It'll do Candra no good. Be silent, I say!"

"Pardon, Domina. We beg pardon," quavered one of the servants, using the feminine term of ultimate respect.

The old, scraggly-haired woman climbed to her feet. "We tried to protect our Holy Woman. Truly we did, but they were males—"

"Yes, males," Marissa interjected bitterly, "and none of you had the courage to go against them. You'd never defy a male, would you, no matter how cruel or unjust their cause? But these weren't even our kind. How *could* you let them take my sister?"

Tears spilled onto the old woman's cheeks. Her lips trembled. She sank back to her knees

7

and began to wail anew. The other women joined in.

Marissa grimaced and turned from them. They were all a pitiful, weak-spirited lot—typical Moracan females. With every sol rise she was more and more glad to no longer be a part of them. Yet it was still strange, after over nine long cycles, to be back. If not for Candra's psychic plea, a plea of terror and sheer desperation, Marissa would not be here now. Here, back home, a home no longer hers...

She had been but a girl of eleven cycles, standing on the threshold of womanhood, linked by a special love and bonding to her twin sister, Candra. Yet that very specialness was also the source of her painful exile.

Female twins were both an abomination and benediction on the planet Moraca. By ancient tradition, one twin was always born a Traveler, possessor of the rare genetic ability to mentally traverse and change the physical composition of solid objects. That ancient power, its true purpose shrouded in the mists of time, was revered. But, by that same tradition, the other twin must eventually be cast out to die.

Marissa shook off the haunting recollection of the morn when she was torn forcibly from Candra's embrace, the psychic pain of separation far worse than the physical one could ever be. The memories of the bitter sols and dark, lonely noctes tied to that stone post on Mount Desolat, of the cold, the hunger, had faded long ago. She remembered clearly only the moment the Sodalitas had found her.

The outcast warrior women had taken Marissa in, hidden her from the wrath of her people until it was too late to matter. And though the emotional link with her sister had never waned, Marissa had thought she had put the past behind her, had accepted the fact she'd never see Candra again. But this new, disturbing psychic disconnection with her sister...

It was more forceful, more painful than ever before, this certainty that Candra was now far from Moraca. For some unknown reason, a mysterious group of males had stolen her away.

Males, Marissa thought, her loathing once again burgeoning to full-fledged hatred. Males were the source of all chaos and cruelty. They were the law-givers, the ones who kept all females shackled by rules and traditions. *They* were the ones who had cast her out when it was finally determined that Candra, and not she, was the Traveler...

Tentatively, a bony hand touched her arm. Marissa's blue-green eyes swung to those of the old scraggly-haired woman.

"P-pardon, Domina." The maid offered Marissa a scrap of paper. "A male—their leader—left this. H-he said to give it to you. That you'd know what to do."

Marissa accepted the missive and scanned the flamboyant script. The words were simple

9

and few. Their cryptic meaning stirred an angry, fearful frustration.

Somehow, someway, she knew their bidding called her to a quest she was loath to follow—a quest that would forever change her and the comfortable life she had finally managed to build with the Sodalitas. And Marissa didn't like that. Didn't like it at all.

But what choice had she? Candra needed her.

She crumpled the note and shoved it beneath her domare-hide jerkin and into her tunic pocket. The male was correct. She knew what to do.

Her cycles with the Sodalitas had prepared her well. Once past puberty, Marissa had no longer been in danger from her people. It had then been safe to reveal her true identity, to come and go as freely as any other Sodalitas.

She had risen quickly through the ranks of the militant society to become one of its finest warriors. Her reputation had spread far beyond Moraca, and she'd been hired out successfully several times in the past few cycles, her fees handsomely fattening the Society's coffers.

No, she thought grimly, there was no doubt in her mind. She indeed knew what to do.

Marissa turned from the scene of impotent mourning and strode from the room, her purpose clear, her resolve hard. The single line, however, shimmered in her mind. With each step the message pounded through her skull, taunting her ... haunting her ...

Bring me Brace Ardane, it said.

Chapter One

Brace slammed against the rough stone wall. The air expelled from his lungs with a low, agonized grunt. For a fleeting instant he shoved back into the jagged rocks in an effort to remain standing, gasping desperately for breath. Then the pain surged through him. His legs buckled and he slid to the floor.

"Get up, Ardane," a harsh voice grated. "It's your choice, after all. Either recant or suffer the consequences."

Bright lights swirled before Brace's eyes in a dizzying kaleidoscope of color. Nausea roiled in his gut. And he hurt. Gods, he hurt so badly he wanted to scream. He struggled to rise, but the strength eluded him.

"Fool!" the man above him snarled. "Stupid, stubborn fool!"

A hand ensnared his hair. With a powerful tug, Brace was jerked to his knees. His head was wrenched back until he stared up through swollen, bleary eyes into the pitiless face of Mardoc, his newest jailer. Brace knew what was coming. He struggled futilely in his bonds but the beryllium shackles held.

12

"You'll not win this time, Ardane. The High King has finally tired of your obstinacy." Mardoc smiled. "Your past jailers were too soft, too kind. They didn't know how to 'persuade' like I do. But you'll not cheat me out of my five thousand imperials."

He bent Brace's head further back to a painfully awkward angle. "Well, what will it be? Will you recant your disobedience? Money is quite fine, but I gain equal pleasure in torture. Either way, I win."

Gazing up at him, at the cold, glittering light of anticipation in his eyes, Brace knew the man spoke true. There was nothing ahead but endless torment. And he was so tired, so weak, so very hungry after sols of near starvation. What was the point of going on? What had he ever hoped to prove?

With a grim smile, Mardoc raised his huge fist. Brace tensed, girding himself for the blow to come, but it did little good. Pain exploded in his jaw. The world splintered into blackness, then white-hot agony.

He wanted to die.

Mardoc released his hold. Brace fell forward, his gut in spasms, the gorge rising in his throat. He dry-heaved onto the moss flower-covered stones. Finally the nausea passed, but he remained there, doubled over, damp-faced and panting.

With a disgusted growl Mardoc kicked him hard in the side, sending him sprawling. The man walked over to a stool and sat down. A small, satisfied grin touched his lips.

"Thinking about things, are you?" he inquired coolly. "Well, I'm a man of infinite patience. Take a few secundae to mull it over. I know how hard these decisions of honor can be."

Honor. Was that what this was all about? Brace wondered groggily. Somehow, in all the pain, he'd lost track of that. Strange. He'd thought it but a battle of wills...

Honor.

Ah yes, he remembered now. That futile, foolish ideal that had inspired him to stand before the King's High Council over two cycles ago and defy the sentencing of his brother and their old teacher to death on the planet Carcer. That futile, foolish ideal...

But there was no honor left on Bellator. Indeed, there was no remnant of integrity or decency left in their entire Imperium of planets. The loss of the Knowing Crystal had seen to that. But that had been hundreds of cycles ago. And reality was now, in this stone-damp prison cell, in the hands of a man who sat but a few meters from him—watching, waiting.

Why did he persist in holding out? He must be mad...

Mad.

Ah, the doubts, the abject fear that word evoked! Terror shuddered through Brace. With a fierce shake of his head, he flung the feeling

14

aside. Gods, he mustn't allow it to take hold! Yet *wasn't* he mad, to fight such a losing battle?

The shimmering specter of madness was with Brace constantly now. The familial curse of House Ardane—that erratic scourge of insanity that had taken the life of his father when he was but a lad—had finally found him as well. It held more substance than the teachings of the old white robe, Vates, benevolent mentor to him and Teran. It held more reality than his years at the Imperial Academy, where Brace had eagerly gone to join his older brother when he'd finally come of age. It held more credence than the pride and honor inculcated there, the strict military obedience and unthinking discipline—tenets that had ultimately clashed headlong with those of their old teacher ...

And now? Now he was incarcerated in an impregnable Bellatorian fortress, condemned to life imprisonment unless he recanted everything Vates had raised him to revere. It would be so simple, so easy to say the words, to lie and regain his freedom. Yet he couldn't. He just couldn't.

Bitter despair welled in the depths of Brace's heart. He must indeed be mad ...

Movement caught the corner of his vision. He glanced toward Mardoc. The man rose, a cruel, familiar gleam in his eyes. Brace swallowed hard against the swell of dread.

"You're as stubborn as an elephas," his jailer growled.

15

Mardoc's fingers entwined in Brace's dark, shaggy mane, then tightened. Brace inhaled a shuddering breath. Ever so slowly, Mardoc pulled him back to his knees.

"Time for further convincing, is it?" With a sharp tug, he jerked Brace halfway to his feet, than rammed a fist deep into his abdomen.

Bright, burning agony engulfed him, his gut twisting, knotting around the blow. Brace heard himself, from deep inside a spiraling well, grunting out his distress. Then his legs went limp and he slumped, suspended in air by the powerful hand so cruelly gripping his hair.

The hand shook him and he flopped like a rag in the wind.

"Recant, Ardane!" Mardoc's voice demanded through the blur of sounds rushing through his head. "Recant and the pain will end!"

Recant. How hard could it be to open his mouth and speak the words? There was nothing left worth fighting for. No family, no friends. He was alone.

Alone.

Tell him, a tiny voice screamed. *Tell him what he wants to hear. Nothing is worth suffering such torment for. Nothing is more important than survival. Nothing . . .*

Again the pain smashed into him, splintering into layers upon layers of reverberating agony. He sought refuge in the blessed swell of darkness but it wavered, then slid away. Gods, he couldn't take any more!

I'll tell, he cried silently. *I'll recant. Anything. Just don't hit me again.*

Brace tried to speak, but the sounds would not come. Something deep within his throat blocked them. The word *coward* formed in his mind, growing in force until it echoed through his skull.

Shame flooded him. Was there *nothing* left then? No pride, no honor—no hope?

His heart pounded, clouds of darkness, then light, swam before his eyes. Brace swallowed hard, frantically. He *must* say the words. Now, before it was too late. Before . . .

Again Mardoc's fist connected brutally with Brace's gut. With a great whoosh of air, Brace fell forward.

Suddenly the pain was gone. Reality was now a place of pristine sweetness and gentle voices. It beckoned from just ahead. But was it the blessed oblivion of unconsciousness—or the more terrifying seduction of madness?

It didn't matter. Brace moved toward it with desperate abandon. There was truly nothing—on this world or beyond—worth remaining behind for . . .

Marissa nearly lost her grip as she pinched her nose against the Simian's foul stench. With a frustrated curse she gave up the attempt. Her fingers tightened once more in the greasy, matted fur of the huge alien who was methodically scaling the fortress's outer wall with Marissa on his back.

By the Crystal Fires! she thought in exasperation. For as much as she was paying him, he could at least have taken a bath!

She tried holding her breath in an effort not to inhale the Simian's rank odor. It only prolonged the inevitable. Marissa gagged when she was finally forced to breathe.

Things were *definitely* not going as planned. The task of discovering who Brace Ardane was had been relatively simple. The warrior planet of Bellator, by force of sheer military might, was the ruling planet of the Imperium. And everyone seemed to know the tale of Brace Ardane's defiance of Bellator's High King—and of his sentencing.

It had been relatively easy to discover Ardane's whereabouts, too. The problems began when Marissa learned he was in a Bellatorian prison out in the Vastare wastes. The fortress was said to be impregnable.

The tales had been quite accurate, Marissa thought with grim irony. She had discovered that disheartening fact shortly after transporting across space from Moraca to Bellator. Disheartening indeed . . .

At that moment the Simian's hold slipped. They dangled by one gangly arm for what seemed an eternity before he swung back and reestablished his grip. Marissa's eyes clenched shut after one quick glance below. Jagged rocks, interspersed with long, sharp stakes, lined the dry moat that surrounded the fortress. Suspended several hundred meters above the ground as they were, their impact, if they fell, would be agonizing—and fatal.

But there'd been no other choice. Careful study had revealed no way in save for the main entrance, and that required the use of hand imprinting. She'd tried getting one of the fortress guards drunk in the hopes of using his imprint to get her inside. The disgusting male had swilled a small fortune in Moracan ale, then passed out just short of the fortress.

Marissa had been forced to hire a Simian, the only being conveniently available capable of scaling the walls. Unfortunately, the highly intelligent, apelike species didn't come cheap. Her stash of imperials had dwindled to half by the time she'd paid for the guard's ale and the Simian's exorbitant fee.

That was yet another problem, once Marissa managed to get Ardane out of the fortress. She wasn't certain how long his gratitude for rescuing him would last. In the event it faded quickly, the money was to have been the added incentive. But her rapidly decreasing stash was losing much bargaining power.

Well, one thing at a time, Marissa consoled herself. She could always lie and promise him more later. And if force was necessary to "convince" this Ardane, so be it. She was quite competent in Empty Hand combat and the Simian's contract included the potential of strong-arm tactics. One way or another, Brace Ardane was coming with her.

At long last they reached the parapet and swung over onto the catwalk. A quick scan assured Marissa the sentry had yet to approach on his rounds. She settled the thick coil of rope they'd use for their escape more comfortably across her chest, then motioned toward the nearest tower. The Simian followed.

The imperials spent on the fortress guard hadn't been completely wasted. She *had* managed to glean the exact location of Ardane's cell from the male, and the safest means to approach it. Marissa now used this information to slip through the fortress and down into its subterranean depths.

The dank, dimly lit corridor outside the underground cells was eerily silent. For a horrible instant, Marissa wondered if the male she sought so determinedly was even alive. No one she'd questioned could say for certain, and it *had* been two cycles. What would she do if he were dead?

She knew who had Candra. The servants' descriptions of the abductors, combined with the Imperial Security Service's video files, had quickly identified the leader as the master criminal Ferox. Everyone on Moraca knew of that vile killer. Barely four cycles ago he and his army of renegades had invaded the capital and slaughtered over half the residents. The remaining half Ferox sold into slavery. The locals had yet to recover from the disaster.

But why had he taken Candra? The malevolent illogic of the act haunted Marissa. She had tried, time and again, to reestablish the psychic link with her sister, but each attempt had failed. For some reason, Candra was purposely choosing not to commune. It was the only answer. Candra couldn't possibly be dead.

As expected, the cell that was supposedly Ardane's was locked, the solid door of robur wood secured by a mechanism opened only by a key control. Marissa destroyed it with a hand laser she'd acquired for the purpose. Leaving the Simian outside to keep watch, she slowly shoved open the massive door.

Recessed lighting high on the walls dimly illuminated the cell. Marissa pulled a small light beam out of her tunic pocket and used it to more thoroughly scan the room. She found him lying face down on a crude cot, dressed only in breeches and boots, one arm dangling limply to the floor.

As Marissa crept toward him, he moaned, attempted to lift himself, then slumped back to the cot. Marissa frowned. What was wrong with the male?

She halted a few meters from him. "Ardane? Brace Ardane?" she whispered.

Brace fought to rise through his pain-bewildered haze. He could have sworn he'd heard a femina's voice calling his name. Gods, now, on top of it all, he was hallucinating!

"Brace? Brace Ardane?"

Curse it, there it was again! Had yet another

21

tormentor arrived to torture him? Two sols' reprieve since the last beating had been more than he'd dared hope for. But, perhaps, if he confronted the voice...

Brace inhaled a ragged breath. "G-go away," he groaned. "Haven't you done....enough?"

"Are you Brace Ardane?" Marissa persisted.

"By the f-five moons of Bellator!"

With a superhuman effort, Brace rolled over and shoved himself to one elbow. Behind the beam of light pointed at him he could barely discern a slender form.

He blinked hard in the sudden brightness. She remained. Inexplicably, it angered him. He much preferred her as a hallucination.

"Yes, c-curse you," he rasped. "I'm Brace Ardane. Now leave me...alone!"

Marissa sucked in a breath. Dark brown eyes, bloodshot and swollen, stared out of a pale face nearly unrecognizable in its bruised and bloated condition. One eyebrow was a clotted gash. His nose was broken.

Her gaze lifted briefly to long, black, unkempt hair before again lowering to Ardane's face. A ragged mustache and beard covered his upper lip and jaw, and dried blood caked his mouth. When he moved again to ease his awkward position, he grimaced and clutched at his abdomen.

Marissa's eyes swung to his torso. Large, purpling bruises covered his ribs and abdomen, the marks spread like so many continents upon a huge map.

By all that was sacred! Ardane had been beaten brutally—perhaps fatally so! All Marissa's hopes took a sharp, sickening plunge. She hadn't expected him to be in prime physical condition after two cycles in prison, but this? How was she going to get him out now? And what if he died in the attempt?

She moved to the cot and knelt beside him. "I am not here to harm you, but to rescue you. Will you come with me?"

"R-rescue me?" Brace blinked in confusion. "What are you ... talking about? There's no way out of this prison ... unless you plan to march out the front door. You're mad!"

"No," Marissa soothed, worried he might alert the guards in his rising agitation. "We'll leave by the walls, not the front door."

She made a quick decision. "I brought a Simian to carry you down. I ask again; will you come with me?"

His swollen eyes narrowed to glittering slits. "And why do you want ... to help me? Who are you, anyway?"

"My name is Marissa Laomede, of the planet Moraca. I need your warrior's skills in rescuing my sister. I can pay."

"P-pay?" Brace gave a strangled laugh, then stiffened in pain. "Gods!"

He glanced back up at her. She was dressed in a dark brown domare-hide jerkin, tan tunic and breeches, and tall, knee-high boots. A long, sheathed dagger was strapped to her right thigh, a thick coil of rope looped across her chest.

A mercenary warrior woman, Brace thought blearily, no doubt intent on using him for some harebrained quest. Well, two could play that game.

"As if I wouldn't pay *you* . . . to get me out of here," he croaked.

Relief filled her. "Then you agree? You'll help me find my sister?"

Brace nodded, the movement setting his head to pounding. "Yes, I'll help you. It's a small price to pay . . . for my freedom."

He paused to scan the room. "Where's this . . . Simian . . . of yours?"

Marissa gestured toward the door. "Outside. I'll get him."

She found the Simian squatted against the corridor wall, leaning forward on his long arms in a position of repose. Irritation surged through her. How in the heavens was he supposed to be prepared for the unexpected when he was all but asleep? Her question was answered by his immediate, agile leap to his feet.

"Our plans have changed," Marissa said, losing no time in getting to the point. "Ardane's too weak to climb down the rope on his own. You'll have to carry him."

The Simian replied with several quick hand motions.

Marissa made an exasperated sound. "I *know* that wasn't part of the original deal, but it can't be helped. Surely your strength is up to it."

Rapid hand movements again answered her, this time accompanied by a sly smile.

Fury flared in Marissa's blue-green eyes. "Why, you slime-ridden Arborian maladroit! How dare you demand more money after the outrageous sum you've already managed to extract from me? You're asking for nearly every imperial I possess!"

Her hairy companion shrugged casually, then gave a few more hand signals.

"T-take it or l-leave it?" Marissa choked.

She made a move toward the stunner in her pocket, then froze at the sharp warning in the Simian's eyes. Her hand fell away. Stunner or no, she hadn't a chance against the creature's superior strength and reflexes. And, as costly as he was, he was now Ardane's only means of escape. By the Crystal Fires, if it weren't for her sister she'd gladly leave that troublesome Bellatorian where he lay!

Curse it all! Her stash was nearly exhausted in just freeing that loathsome male from prison. And now, on top of everything else, he was too ill to immediately set out after Ferox and Candra. What else could possibly go wrong?

Even for a beast as large and powerful as the Simian, with Brace Ardane slung over his shoulder the climb back down the fortress walls was arduous and awkward. Once again on solid ground, things were not much better. Though Ardane tried valiantly to make his own way through the sleepy city, his steps were stumbling and slow. In exasperation, Marissa finally signaled for the Simian to carry him the rest of the way.

The alien deposited Ardane in the abandoned monastery at the edge of town. In the heavy darkness, the lights from the fortress perched high above on the hill gleamed so sharp and clear Marissa felt she could almost reach out and touch them. They were close, far too close, for any sense of security.

She rounded on the Simian. "You agreed to get us to safety. This is *not* where I hid the skim craft."

The hairy man-beast grinned, his double row of sharp, narrow teeth glinting in the moonlight streaming into the ruins. He made several sweeping movements.

Marissa sputtered in outrage. "P-pay you? Why, you ignorant sandwart! I'll not give you one single coin until you—"

"I suggest . . . you pay him," came a deep voice behind her. "He looks none too pleased . . . and. could easily take the money. One way or another."

She whirled around, her fists clenched at her sides. "And I suppose you'd stand there and let him do it, wouldn't you?"

Brace leaned back wearily against a half-fallen wall, bracing himself to keep from sliding to the ground. "In my current condition,

26

I'm afraid there's not much . . . I could do. But look at the bright side. He got us out . . . of the fortress."

"And then what am I supposed to do?" Marissa demanded, her keen glance assessing that he had little more to give. "You can barely stand, much less walk. Do you expect me to carry you all the way to safety? By the morrow, if not sooner, they'll discover your escape and come looking for you. Your freedom will be brief indeed, and I've already wasted enough time to have to start over again!"

"Your concern for me has been duly noted," Brace rasped. "But anger this Simian . . . and the rest will be academic. He'll simply murder us . . . then take your remaining imperials in the bargain."

For a moment all Marissa could do was stand there and glare at him, battling with a sense of futility. Ardane was right, curse his arrogant male hide.

The admission did little to soothe her emotions. As weak and hurting as he was, he was already proving most provoking and argumentative. What would he be like once he was well? Uneasiness skittered through her. Was *nothing* about this quest going to go smoothly?

Marissa forced herself to relax. "Here, take your money," she muttered, glowering at the Simian.

She slipped the pouch of imperials from about her neck. It was an easy enough task to separate what remained from what was owed.

Fifty coins were counted out and the rest handed over to the big alien.

He took great care in ascertaining that the proper amount remained in the pouch, then nodded his acceptance. Momentarily, dark, beady eyes considered the money in Marissa's hand. With a small hiss, she whipped out the stunner and aimed it at him.

"Don't even think about it, you greedy bag of hair!" She made a waving motion with the gun. "Now, get out of here before I lose what little gratitude I have and take it all back!"

With a smirk and a shrug of broad, bony shoulders, the Simian turned and loped off into the darkness, his rank odor lingering on the nocte air. Speechless with rage, Marissa stared after him, all but forgetting the man behind her.

"You certainly have a way ... with the hired help," Brace drawled finally.

He lowered himself to the ground and, with an exhausted sigh, leaned back against the wall. "This promises to be ... a most interesting ... partnership."

Marissa wheeled around. "Spare me your sarcasm, Ardane! We're in the gravest danger and I'm the only one capable of doing anything about it. So if you can't offer anything constructive, don't offer anything!"

"You're right, of course." He exhaled a deep, shuddering breath and closed his eyes. "I beg pardon. What would you ... have me do?"

Marissa's lips curled in disgust at the sight

of him sitting there on the ground, his battered body barely able to maintain an upright position. Males, she thought. So quick with words, with so little of substance to back them.

"There's nothing *you're* capable of doing at the moment, and you know it," she muttered. "Just—just stay right where you are. I'll be back."

Marissa strode off into the nocte.

Brace watched her leave, then once more closed his eyes. Gradually he became aware of the chill air. What monate of the cycle was it anyway? Late autumn most likely. And winter soon on its way.

He shivered. Even that tiny movement set his tortured muscles to aching. Brace groaned aloud. He was cold, he hurt so badly he wanted to die, and now he was saddled with a sharp-tongued little femina who seemed to have taken an instant dislike to him.

And yet, she'd specifically sought him out to rescue her sister. He tried to sort through the muddle in his head, but it was too much. What he needed now was rest. To rest and replenish what little strength he could—until she returned.

Some time later, a firm hand shook him awake. With a grunt, Brace jerked upright, momentarily disoriented. The action sent a sharp spasm of agony through him. He groaned, clutched his abdomen, and fell back.

Slowly he forced open his eyes, his bleary

gaze sweeping the scene. It was near sol rise, the nocte sky tingeing to faint gray across the flat expanse of the Vastare wastes. By the five moons, where was—

"Wake up," an irritated feminine voice demanded. "It's nearly morn and we must be on our way before we lose the advantage of darkness."

Brace blinked, then attempted to refocus. The little Moracan femina towered over him, her piquant face twisted in exasperation. He blinked again, then attempted a smile. It failed miserably as his swollen features rebelled. He groaned again. Gods, he felt worse now than he had last nocte!

"I am at your call, *gentle* femina."

He made a move to climb to his feet, and the effort stimulated a paroxysm of coughing. For a long, heart-stopping moment, Brace couldn't catch his breath. His abused abdominal muscles clenched, twisted. He wrapped his arms about himself in a futile effort to control the pain.

That made it worse. He doubled over and began to retch.

In spite of herself, Marissa experienced a small twinge of pity. There was no time for any of this, but reality being what it was, they weren't going anywhere until he was ready. With a weary sigh, she knelt beside him and tilted back his head. He was pale and clammy-skinned.

She lifted a domare-hide flask of water to his

lips. "Here, drink, but in small sips. It'll ease that cough."

Her voice softened. "And then we *must* be on our way."

Greedily Brace swallowed the proffered water, then shook his head, the action dejected and despairing. "I-I haven't the strength," he gasped. "Leave me. Get away before it's too late."

"Foolish male. I'm not going anywhere without you. I told you before—I need your help in rescuing my sister."

Marissa allowed him one more swallow before recapping the flask and slinging it over her shoulder. "Now, if I get you to your feet, can you make it to the skim craft over there?"

"S-skim craft?" Brace lifted his head to scan the enclosure. "You . . . you really have a skim craft?"

"Yes," she muttered wryly. "I stole it earlier. I'm no fool; that was part of my plan from the start. And desperation makes one quite resourceful."

She slid her hands around his chest and looked her fingers behind his back to aid him in standing. "Now, enough of the explanations. It's past time we were out of here."

Out of here. Exhilaration surged through Brace, fueling, for a few secundae, his meager supply of strength. With Marissa's help, he struggled to his feet and staggered the short distance beyond the ruins to the small skim

Kathleen Morgan

craft. He sank down in the passenger's seat with an exhausted sigh.

Marissa climbed in beside him, flipped a few levers, and punched in the preflight commands. The engine whirled to life. She glanced over at Brace. He'd begun to shiver again in the cool, early morning air. Marissa sighed and programmed in the force field bubble.

With a low hum the field encompassed them, effectively shutting out the chill breeze. Marissa returned her attention to the craft's control panel and punched in the take-off command. The relative wind-breaking abilities of the bubble would have to do until they could reach her stash of supplies in the distant mountains. With that, she forgot Brace Ardane and concentrated her efforts on getting them away from there.

As the craft rose in the air and headed off into the desert, Brace slowly opened his eyes. The rising sun bathed the little Moracan's features in a lavender-rose light. Her long, curling chestnut tresses glinted with a sparkling halo, and the faintest glimmer of a smile touched her lips. He was struck with the surprising realization of how lovely she was. A lovely, mouthy little bundle of trouble . . .

Utter exhaustion flooded him with the force of a surge tide. Brace groaned and promptly lost consciousness.

Chapter Two

They ran out of fuel just short of the mountains. Angry expletives, rather than the sudden lack of engine noise, woke Brace from a deep, dreamless sleep. He forced his gritty eyes open a crack. In the light of a setting sun, Marissa stood beside the skim craft with arms akimbo.

A renewed string of curses failed to elicit any fresh life in the machine. She strode over to Brace.

"We'll have to walk. Are you up to it?"

He shot her a weary smile. "I'll have to be. I'm just grateful the skim craft...got us this far."

His glance moved to the flask hanging at her side. "A swallow of water might help, though."

Silently Marissa handed Brace the container and watched him drink. He was a strange one, she mused. If the tales regarding the cause of his sentencing were true, what kind of male would submit willingly to imprisonment over some nebulous principle of honor? An impractical waste of time and energy, to her thinking—especially in an Imperium such as theirs.

Self-preservation was all that mattered. Only a fool thought otherwise.

She scanned him. Incarceration had done little to mar his splendid physique. True, he was thin, but his tall, broad-shouldered form was indicative of vast power and awesome virility. A warrior's body—and just what she needed. It would take time—time she was loath to spare—to build him back to his former strength, but Marissa had little choice.

Her eyes narrowed. What did he look like beneath his unkempt, filthy appearance and bloated face? She shoved the question firmly aside. He'd serve his purpose whether handsome or ugly. In the end, all that counted was that Ferox was willing to trade him for her sister.

A grudging pity lanced through her. Better that she'd never involved Ardane in this. Things would have been so much simpler without him. But there had never been any choice. Rescuing Candra was all that mattered, even if it required sacrificing this male's life in the bargain.

Brace lowered the flask after several deep, satisfying swallows. Noting her close scrutiny, he arched a quizzical brow.

"What's wrong now?"

"Nothing. Nothing at all." Marissa held out her hand for the flask. "It's time to be going, but first I need to bury the skim craft in the sand. There's no sense in leaving a trail."

He climbed out. Noting his trembling weakness, Marissa sighed. She didn't dare let Ardane squander a bit of his meager strength, not if they were to make it to the safety of the mountains.

"Sit and rest while I hide the craft." She gestured toward a spot several meters away.

"I...I can help."

She rolled her eyes. "You're in no shape to risk additional exertion. Besides, I'm not helpless, so spare me the masculine heroics."

His mouth lifted in a swollen, lopsided grin. "I noticed that, sweet femina."

"I'm *not* your sweet femina! This is a business arrangement and nothing more."

He studied her for a long moment. "You don't like men, do you?"

"No," came the flat reply.

Brace shrugged and headed to the spot Marissa had indicated earlier. "Well, I suppose deep affection," he threw over his shoulder, "was never a prerequisite...for a 'business arrangement.'"

She snorted in disdain, then moved back to stand beside the skim craft. Leaning over, Marissa punched down a small blue button on the control panel and held it in.

"Stand back," she ordered. "This will only take a few secundae."

With that, Marissa released the button and jumped away. For a moment, nothing happened. Then, with a high-pitched whine, the skim craft began to vibrate and sink slowly beneath the sand.

Brace's features twisted in a wry grimace. "I see you managed to steal a military skim craft. They're the only ones equipped with a burrowing mechanism."

"So, what of it?"

"The theft of a Bellatorian military vehicle of any kind means an automatic death sentence. You'd have done well to steal a civilian skim craft. Then, if you were caught, you'd have only lost the first three fingers of your right hand."

Marissa rolled her eyes. "A small consolation, to be sure."

She paused. "Any additional helpful comments, or can I finish covering the craft?"

"None for the moment, sweet femina."

Her mouth tightened briefly, then she turned back to the skim craft. A half hora later they were again plodding toward the mountains, their progress slowed by the deep sand and Brace's unsteady gait. After several stumbles, Marissa was forced to lend assistance to keep him upright.

She moved to his side. "Here, hold on to me."

He eyed her proffered arm. "Are you sure you want me touching you? I'm filthy and stink to high heaven, not to mention being a disgusting man."

Marissa shot him an icy glance. "I'll do my best to ignore your shortcomings. Now, no more talk."

"As you wish, gentle—" He paused at her frigid glare. "As you wish, *Domina*."

She quirked a slender brow, then slung his arm over her shoulder and grasped him about the waist. Once more they began their staggering journey.

Several horas of agonizing, faltering travel brought them to the foothills. Near the end, Marissa had half-carried the exhausted Brace. Only his indomitable will, she admitted grudgingly, could have brought him as far as it had. For some strange reason that realization unsettled her.

A cave in a nearby hillside caught Marissa's eye. She deposited Brace beside the nearest convenient boulder and went to ascertain if the cavern was uninhabited.

Returning, Marissa squatted beside him. He was spent and she dared not push him further. She touched him lightly on the shoulder.

He glanced up. "Yes, Domina?"

"The cave seems safe enough." Marissa climbed to her feet. "Come, but a few secundae more and you can take your rest."

Brace crawled to his hands and knees. For a long moment, she thought he'd never rise. Then, unsteadily, he pushed to a kneeling position and lifted a hand.

"Help me."

The simple request sent an odd tremor through Marissa. She grasped his hand. Even her added strength was barely enough to get Brace to his feet. Several meters inside the cave, his knees buckled. There was nothing

Marissa could do but ease his way to the ground as gently as possible.

"I-I'm sorry," he rasped. "I j-just couldn't go on."

"It matters not." She slipped the water flask from her shoulder and laid it beside him. "About a half sol's journey into these mountains I've stashed some supplies. Once you're stronger we'll head out for them. In the meanwhile, there's a village nearby. You can rest here until my return."

"It wouldn't be wise to alert anyone . . . to our presence. This is Bellator, after all. They would only . . . turn us in."

"I'm quite aware of mindless Bellatorian ways. I'd only planned on appropriating a little food and clothing to get us through the nocte."

"Stealing, you mean," he corrected her huskily.

A reluctant smile teased her lips. "Stealing, then. What does it matter? It accomplishes the same purpose."

Brace exhaled a deep breath and closed his eyes. "That it does. Good fortune, then . . . until your return."

Marissa rose. "Good fortune indeed," she muttered.

Good fortune. What a strange concept, she mused as she left the cave. Neither of them had profited by an overabundance of that in their lives. And now, thanks to the mysterious actions of a felon from yet another world, their fortunes had taken an even more unfavorable turn.

Against both their wishes, they were compelled to join forces. Two outcasts, Marissa thought grimly as she headed into the mountains; two adversaries—on a dangerous, uncertain quest ...

By the time Marissa returned, Brace was stiff with cold. He sensed rather than heard her arrival. Even when the familiar light of a perpetual-flame box finally illuminated the cavern, Brace didn't move.

He sat hunched over, his arms wrapped about his draw-up knees in an effort to conserve his rapidly waning body heat. His total concentration centered on controlling the fierce, wracking shivers. It did little good. His battered muscles seemed locked in endless, agonizing spasms.

Gods, Brace marveled through his half-conscious haze, what further forms of torment could there be?

A thick blanket settled about his shoulders, then Marissa knelt before him, tucking the heavy covering more snugly in place. Brace continued to shiver, immersed in his pain.

She eyed him. It was cold, even in the cave, and Ardane was dressed only in boots and lightweight breeches. Curse him for his weakness! They should have easily reached her stash of supplies this nocte, and the warm, phoca-fur coats she'd brought along for the both of them.

But that was hardly the priority now. With his lack of clothing and in his battered condition, Ardane was in imminent danger of death. She must warm him quickly.

Her small hands slid beneath the blanket and began massaging his arms. He groaned at the firmness of her touch.

She knew she was causing him terrible pain, but resolutely kept on. His eyes clenched shut, his teeth gritted, but he didn't stop her. The effort seemed profitless, though. Ardane's shivering continued and he leaned forward weakly, his head falling to rest upon her shoulder.

The action, so trusting, so needful, struck an answering chord in Marissa. She stroked his shaggy mane in an unconscious gesture of comfort. Suddenly there was no hated male before her, just another being in great want of assistance.

Gently Marissa shoved Ardane away, steadying him by the shoulders. "Lie down, atop the blanket."

"W-why? W-why do you w-want me to l-lie down?" he asked through chattering teeth.

"You need the warmth of my body. I'll lie beside you and cover you with the other blankets." Marissa pushed at him impatiently. "Now, no more of it. Lie down."

Brace complied at once, rolling over on his side and opening his arms to accept Marissa's lithe young form. After a few secundaes to arrange the two other blankets, she settled next to him.

Her nose brushed a hair-roughened expanse of pectoral muscle. The scent of his sweat and blood-tainted skin was too much for Marissa. She gagged and twisted her head away.

"Ugh!" she cried. "How foul can one be? You smell worse than a-a subterranean slime weevil!"

"I-I'd imagine s-so," Brace agreed unsteadily. "B-but let's n-not f-form any p-premature opinions. O-once I've h-had a b-bath, I clean up q-quite nicely. Y-you just m-might find me m-more to y-your l-liking."

"And the Crystal Fires will freeze solid before that sol dawns! I told you before, I loathe—"

He tucked the edge of a blanket between him and Marissa, then gently but firmly pulled her head back down to lie upon his chest. Already the warmth of her softly curved body was thawing his numbed limbs.

"Yes, I know. You l-loathe all men. And I'm s-sure there's a legitimate reason for your f-feelings..."

"My reasons are my own."

Brace smiled and shifted her more comfortably against him. As bruised and exhausted as he was, as stiffly as she lay next to him, it was still *so* good to have a woman in his arms. It was the first time in monates he'd felt any peace. His eyelids lowered in drowsy contentment.

"Tell me, M-Marissa," he prodded huskily. "Partners work best if they u-understand each other."

"I'd rather not speak of it. It—it is personal and you wouldn't understand. No male could ever understand the pain of unfair exile and subjugation."

Piercing brown eyes lifted, ensnaring Marissa in their bleak, haunted depths.

Don't I understand? they seemed to ask. *How can you look at me and deny the suffering of my own unfair imprisonment? How can you say I don't understand?*

It was too much to comprehend, now, pressed so close to Ardane, as weary as she was. Marissa lowered her eyes, unable to face him. The rhythmic rise and fall of his broad, densely furred chest did little to ease her confusion. Reluctantly she dragged her gaze up to his.

"Tell me, Marissa," he urged, his voice low, seductive. "I want to know."

Marissa.

Strange, but the sound of her name on his lips didn't anger her, though his audacity in using it should. And the delicious sensations of his hands, lightly stroking her arms, befuddled more than her body. She had to put an end to this. Perhaps if she told him, it would satisfy his curiosity and he'd leave her alone. Perhaps then he'd be silent and just go to sleep ...

Marissa inhaled a steadying breath. "I am a Sodalitas," she began, by way of explanation.

"A Sodalitas," he repeated thoughtfully. "I understand now. You're part of that outcast group of female Moracans sworn to despise all males. A band of malcontents, are they not, dedicated to undying celibacy? With that attitude, one wonders how you manage to reproduce yourselves."

His words were like a slap in the face. She should have expected such a response from a male.

"The Sodalitas are *not* dedicated to undying celibacy!" Marissa snapped. "We have our needs and reproduce ourselves quite adequately, if and when we wish to. Males do have their purpose. We just don't allow ourselves to be either physically or emotionally enslaved by them.

"And we are *not* malcontents," she added fiercely. "How would you like to be compelled by law to a life of virtual servitude, your only purpose obedience to another?"

"Even in my current sorry state, the thought of a beautiful femina at my beck and call possesses a certain attraction. Could you not find some male to love enough to make such a life pleasant?"

"*Never!*"

The horror in Marissa's voice gave Brace pause. "You've never known the love of a man, have you, Marissa?"

"Love a male? Relinquish your independence, for the sake of some crazy emotion, to one whose only wish is to control you?" She

43

shook her head. "No. It's insanity and I'm not mad."

"A sweet madness, indeed," Brace murmured, "but one shared by both partners. If there is subjugation, it's a willing one and only of the heart. Love does not force itself, nor place one above the other. It's an emotion of equals."

"Easy for you to say," Marissa muttered, "when *you* have nothing to lose and everything to gain."

She moved to free herself from his grasp. "But enough of this. You are quite evidently warmed and have no further need of me. Let me up."

Brace gazed into her eyes, eyes that sparkled like blue-green jewels in the flickering light. Was she mad, to think that after two cycles without a woman he had no further need of her? If he weren't so weak, his body bruised beyond bearing, he'd be sorely tempted to disabuse her of her naïveté. Not that he'd ever take Marissa against her will, but, ah, to savor just a few moments of pleasure . . .

With a deep sigh, Brace released her. Marissa scrambled over to a large cloth bag, carefully avoiding his gaze. She began to sort through its contents.

He shook his head and smiled. "The fruits of your little foraging expedition?"

"But of course."

"You've a decided talent for thievery. Is that

yet another skill acquired from your little gang?"

Marissa's head lifted. Glittering bits of ice riveted on him.

"Perhaps it would be wise if we kept our past lives to ourselves from now on. We obviously cannot seem to have a friendly discussion about personal matters, and I don't want dissension to hamper the true purpose of our ... 'arrangement.'"

Gods! Brace thought. He'd been a fool to antagonize the little Sodalitas, as helpless, as dependent as he still was upon her. He might be out of prison, but he was far from safe. What had gotten into him?

Unwaveringly, Brace returned her gaze. "I'm sorry, Marissa. I misspoke a moment ago. I, too, have no wish for dissension between us."

"It matters not," she muttered, grudgingly accepting his apology. She returned to rifling through the bag. "Go to sleep. I'll have a meal prepared when you awake."

A meal. The image of a fat, long-eared lepus roasting over a fire, its juices dripping and popping in the hungry flames, filled Brace with heady anticipation. His mouth watered. To be able to sleep in peace, then wake to a hearty meal of crisply browned meat ... Ah, it felt so good to be pampered!

He closed his eyes for just a moment. For just a moment, and it was all the encouragement his exhausted body needed. He promptly fell asleep.

* * *

Brace's nostrils twitched as a savory smell wafted past. He moved restlessly, mumbled a few incoherent words, then settled back to sleep.

The scent would not be denied. It teased and tantalized the fringes of his consciousness. Brace grumbled louder and turned toward the smell. His eyelids lifted.

A fire two meters from him crackled merrily, a small, thick black pot on a crude wooden frame suspended above it. Marissa knelt before the fire, stirring the pot intently. For a long, drowsy moment, Brace watched her.

She must have found a pool to bathe in while he slept, for her unbound hair fell in damp waves far past her shoulders. The moisture made the riotous tumble of hair seem darker, with a deep rich hue like polished robur wood. He let himself imagine how soft and full her hair would be when dry. Like dark, shimmering bronze flowing over his fingers . . .

Brace swallowed a savage curse. He was mad to let her delicate beauty seduce him into a course of action not in his best interests. He might be woman-starved, but he had yet to be led by his loins. He'd never had to in the past—females always flocked to him. And they would again, just as soon as he freed himself of this determined, fiery-tongued little she-devil and made his way to a safe haven.

Word of honor or no, she was a fool not to imagine that a desperate man would promise anything, then think nothing of going back on it. Yet, to break his word...

Shame lanced through Brace. Gods, to finally fall so low as to surrender his honor—that deepest, most precious part of him. But he was just that desperate.

Recapture was out of the question. Another imprisonment would surely mean his death. In light of that brutal reality, what did a few words matter? But the little Sodalitas didn't need to know that just yet.

He needed a plan, some way to escape her and set out on his own. First, though, he'd have to allow his body time to mend, to rebuild his strength with food and rest. That would necessitate allowing her to care for him with no intention of repayment. Another emotion, faintly reminiscent of guilt, drifted across his mind. Brace shoved it fiercely aside.

He owed no man, nor woman, loyalty. Not now. Not ever again. With each monate that had passed, locked in that filthy, stagnant cell, with each blow that had slammed into his body, Brace had been forced to relinquish yet another remnant of his humanity. There was nothing left him now but a primal need to survive. No one—nothing—mattered more than that. He didn't *dare* let anything matter more than that.

In the end, his betrayal of her wouldn't surprise her. She despised all men, thought them capable of little else anyway. Why should he bother to disabuse her of such a dearly cherished conviction? It served both their purposes.

Brace smiled grimly. How the mind could twist anything to suit its needs! With a grunt of pain, he levered himself to one elbow and cleared his throat.

"What are you cooking in that pot?" He lifted his head slightly in an effort to peer inside. "A stew perhaps?"

Marissa grimaced at the hopeful note in his voice. She turned.

"A *vegetable* broth."

Brace frowned. "No meat?"

"None. I'm a vegetarian."

"Well, *I'm* not."

She arched a slender brow and smiled. "I'm afraid you are this nocte."

He fell back with a groan. "I need meat if I'm to regain my strength, not some . . . some putrid vegetable water."

"When did you last eat?"

"I don't know," he grumbled. "Maybe two, three sols ago."

"And you think your stomach could handle a slab of greasy meat? You'd heave it back up five secundae after you'd wolfed it down. Vegetable broth is what you need. On the morrow, if you've tolerated the soup, I'll allow you some fruit."

"*Allow* me?" Brace propped himself back up and glared over at her. "You're not my nursemaid, to *allow* me to—"

"I am most precisely that, you ignorant

sandwart," Marissa interjected angrily. "You're no good to me if you don't heal. When you're better, feel free to go out and slaughter every animal on this despicable planet—and eat them all! In the meanwhile, permit me to care for you in the manner I see fit."

Brace groaned and fell back again. "By the five moons! You're the most infuriating femina I've ever met!"

"And you're the glorious light of the Imperium!"

Marissa lifted the pot off the fire and set it between them. Picking up two spoons, she offered one to him.

"Get up and have some soup. Since you don't want my 'nurse-maiding,' I'm certainly not going to feed you."

He shoved himself to a sitting position, his own anger muting some of the pain of his protesting muscles, and sullenly accepted a spoon. For a while he watched Marissa eat, his stubborn pride warring with his ravenous hunger. Practicality finally won out. After all, Brace consoled himself, the sooner he regained his strength, the sooner he could go out and hunt for real food. He dug into the pot of soup.

Sometime later, his stomach pleasantly full of what had been surprisingly tasty for a mess of vegetables, Brace lay back with a sigh. At the sound, Marissa looked up from her task of sand-cleaning the pot. She shot him an inquiring glance.

Brace chuckled wryly. "As much as I hate to

admit it, the soup wasn't all that bad. You're quite a cook, considering the circumstances."

The unaccustomed praise unsettled her. "It was a tasteless mess," Marissa mumbled. "Your hunger made it seem better than it was."

He stared at her until she couldn't bear it. "What? Why are you looking at me like that?"

"Why must you throw an honest compliment back in my face?" he asked quietly. "Why can't you judge me by my own actions, rather than by the actions of others?"

"And what makes you think I'm not judging you by your own actions?"

"Because I've done nothing to deserve your disdain. If you were honest, you'd admit that."

A myriad of emotions flashed through Marissa. He was right, curse his righteous male hide! He'd been aggravating; at times even arrogant, but so far he'd never failed to treat her as an equal.

Never, save for that moment he'd held her pressed close to him ...

The memory sent a surge of heated blood rushing through Marissa, blood that churned chaotically until it rose to flush her face. She'd never felt that way before. More than anything else, that realization angered her. It was male domination at its worst, and she'd not have it!

"You mistake yourself if you think to play upon my sympathies," she retorted. "Your actions are indeed what I react to. You are nothing but a blustering, arrogant male, constantly demanding, endlessly hampering my quest. And all these questions!"

Marissa made an irritated sweep of her hand. "Content yourself with regaining your strength so we can get on with the rescue of my sister. It'll more than satisfy me."

"Well, it won't satisfy me."

The flat warning gave Marissa pause. She searched his face, finding his anger.

Exasperation filled her. What now? Would this infuriating male *never* be placated?

"Then what will it take?" she ground out. "What will finally satisfy you?"

What indeed? Brace wondered. There was no reason to prod her like this, to force revelations that, in the end, would only make his betrayal of her the harder. Better he continue to consider her the mouthy, self-sufficient little she-devil she made herself out to be. Better not to delve too deeply, to pluck at her barely contained vulnerability hovering just beyond that veil of determined purpose.

Better for the both of them.

"I need to know more about the particulars of this quest," he forced himself to say.

Stick to the reason for your rescue, Brace lectured himself. Keep it impersonal. Keep her thinking you mean to help while you buy time.

"And what would you know?"

"To begin with, why was your sister abducted?"

She laughed and shook her head. "You had to start with the hardest question of all, didn't you? Well, I don't know why Candra was abducted. She was singled out, though, for the males took no one but her."

Brace frowned. "And there was nothing special about her? Nothing that would motivate her abduction?"

Color flooded Marissa's cheeks. She must tell him, she supposed. Would a Bellatorian hold a revulsion for multiple births as her people did?

She returned his stare unwaveringly. "We are identical twins, and Candra is a Traveler. That is all that is special about her."

He cocked his head. "A Traveler, is she? I've heard of their strange powers. Only female twins possess that ability."

Brace paused, his eyes narrowing. "But it's said that on Moraca both twins never live to adulthood. One is always cast out to..." A dark, unfathomable look flared in his eyes. "That's why you're a Sodalitas, isn't it, Marissa? Because you were the twin without the powers. The useless one. The one cast out."

She couldn't seem to free herself from his visual hold. What *was* it about his eyes? What were the emotions that darkened them to deep, bottomless black?

Pity? Disgust? Amusement?

"Yes," Marissa replied. "I was the one cast out. The one sacrificed to appease our laws and lawgivers."

She met his gaze squarely, refusing to cower from the truth, from the unrelenting reality of her existence. She'd dealt with her fate long ago and would never allow a male to make her feel bad for it again. She knew her true worth— what little there was of it.

"And those lawgivers were males," Brace finished quietly. "That's why you hate us, isn't it?"

Blue-green fire flashed in her eyes. "For that and your subjugation of our women! Yes, that's why I hate males! Now are you satisfied? Have you heard enough?"

"No, Marissa. I'm not satisfied."

His deep voice was rough. The rasping sound skittered down her spine. It made Marissa tingle, then fill with a languorous warmth. Fiercely she shook off the unfamiliar feelings, fearing their power.

By the Crystal Fires, was this how males influenced women then? By heated glances, deep, silky voices, and mesmerizing words? Well, she would have none of it!

"Then what?" Marissa snapped. "What more would you know? I tire of this inquisition."

He regarded her steadily. "You claim not to understand why your sister was abducted. Do you perhaps then know who abducted her and where he took her? If not, I fear this quest of yours is doomed from the start."

"I'm aware of that." A defensive edge crept into her voice. "Though I have yet to determine where he has taken Candra, I do know the male's name."

"And?"

Marissa hesitated. Here it comes now, she thought. If this doesn't drive him away, nothing will. She wet her lips and, for a secundae, couldn't quite meet his eyes.

Uneasiness coiled in the pit of Brace's stomach. "Marissa?"

With a sigh, she forced her gaze back to his. "The man who abducted my sister is known to all. He is a vile criminal who roams the Imperium at will, wreaking havoc and destruction."

She paused to inhale a steadying breath, then forged on. "The male's name is Ferox."

Chapter Three

Surprise slashed through Brace, then sickening horror. Ferox. Marissa planned to find and take on Ferox. Did she truly know the futility of such a quest? She had to; she was a Moracan. They, of all the peoples of the Imperium, knew the depths of Ferox's depravity.

Concern for her filled him. Soon she'd not even have his assistance. But perhaps it was better that way. Without him, Marissa would be forced to reassess the wisdom of her quest. Reassess and admit it was hopeless. Yes, Brace assured himself, in the end he was doing her more than a kindness—he was saving her life.

"Ferox, eh? Nothing small about your undertakings, is there?" he drawled with feigned casualness. "And how do you propose we approach this? Ferox is not only armed with every imaginable weapon, but also leads a large force of felons."

Marissa forced herself to return his steady gaze. She'd anticipated an angry lecture, if not outright rebellion. His unexpected coolness unnerved her more than she cared to admit.

How calm would you really be, Brace Ardane,

she retorted silently, *if you knew Ferox wanted you? And that I have only to deliver you?*

Guilt stabbed her, but Marissa flung the traitorous feeling aside. She dared not allow him to weaken her resolve. Candra's welfare would always matter more than his. It had to. Their twinhood bound them to life itself.

"I haven't quite formulated a plan as to how to take on Ferox," Marissa admitted, turning her unsettling thoughts to a more immediate topic. "A lot will depend on where he's at and what his own plans are. But, first things first. You must regain your strength before we head out to Tutela, the closest interplanetary transport station. Once there, we can hide out in disguise until we acquire enough money to replenish our supplies and determine Ferox's current location. Then we'll transport there."

"Why are you doing all this, Marissa?" Brace asked softly.

He leaned forward, impaling her with an intent pair of dark brown eyes. "You're far too practical for such an act of mercy, especially when the services of loathsome males are as easily acquired as tossed aside."

Possible replies raced through Marissa's mind and, for a moment, panic churned them all into a confusing muddle. Then she calmed, forcing a smile to her lips.

"Only a desperate man would go after Ferox, and I thought you'd be the most desperate. There was nothing for you where you were. At least now there's some hope."

"You think so?" Brace gave a bitter laugh. "And is my desperation enough to overcome an army of bloodthirsty criminals? I am only one against many, after all."

"You are a great and powerful warrior, renowned for your courage and resourcefulness in battle."

"I *was* a great and powerful warrior," he corrected her grimly. "But that was two cycles ago." His expression turned bleak. "I tell you true, Marissa. I'm not sure what I am anymore."

He really believes that, Marissa realized, seeing the doubt, the fear smoldering in his eyes. But how could that be? He was a male. Males never wavered in their self-assured conviction that the universe revolved about them, that they were omnipotent in thought and deed. But that look in Ardane's eyes . . .

Once more Marissa's confidence faltered. Before, everything had been so simple, so clear. Rescue Ardane and somehow trick him into going with her to Ferox. Trade him for her sister, then turn and walk away. So very, very simple.

But was Ardane even up to the task? She had thought she'd only have to contend with a physically weakened male and his reluctance to cooperate, especially after he discovered who had abducted Candra. But now—now Marissa realized that the wounds of his imprisonment ran deeper than the flesh, slicing through to his very soul. And she didn't know how to deal with that.

She climbed to her feet and stoked the fire, then retrieved the little black pot.

Brace frowned. "Where are you going?"

Marissa glanced over her shoulder. "To get water for your bath. I can't abide another moment of your stench. If we're to sleep in close quarters, it's time to see you clean."

Without another word Marissa strode from the cave, the pot tucked under her arm. Brace stared after her for a long while, an uneasy memory nibbling at the edge of his mind. He'd seen the apprehensive look that had flitted across Marissa's face when he'd admitted his self-doubts.

He regretted telling her that. It wasn't just the foolish revelation of his shameful weakness. What if she decided he wasn't worth further time and effort? What if she left him here? He couldn't survive without her—at least not yet.

Even more troubling was the knowledge that he didn't want the parting until *he* was ready for it. But why? Was it just instinctive male possessiveness for a female, slipping past his newly constructed determination to think only of himself?

Brace chuckled grimly. Old habits die hard, but die they must. From now on he'd have to guard more closely against the pretty little Sodalitas. And separate from her as quickly as possible.

He watched the fire while yet another unsettling thought eased into his mind. Marissa had said she'd chosen him for his warrior's abilities. Warriors, in times such as these, were easily had. There were a lot simpler and safer ways to acquire an accomplice—and Marissa was not a fool.

No, Marissa was not a fool and neither was he. For some mysterious reason, she needed him above all others. Marissa indeed had a plan. And that plan entailed a lot more than she was yet willing to reveal . . .

The fire was blazing by the time Marissa returned. Her glance moved to Brace's before skittering away.

"You need to undress," she announced as she once more hung the pot over the flames.

"Well, I can't do it by myself."

Marissa's eyes swung back to his.

Calmly Brace returned her gaze. "I haven't the strength to get my boots off, and I'm not sure about my breeches, either."

Her eyes narrowed. "No games then. I'm not in the mood."

"No games, Marissa. I promise."

With a deep sigh, she moved to his feet and grasped his right boot. After a prolonged struggle, it slipped free. She laid it aside and proceeded to remove the other. When it was free, Marissa eyed him. "Cover yourself with the blanket and pull your breeches down as far as you can. I'll help the rest of the way."

Brace managed to get his clothing down to

mid-thigh before his protesting muscles rebelled. He fell back.

"That's it," he gasped. "That's all I can do."

Gingerly Marissa reached beneath the blanket until her fingers brushed his bare leg. She
jerked reflexively at the touch of his hair-
roughened skin, then forced herself to grasp
the bunched-up cloth. With a quick tug she
pulled his breeches down to below his knees,
then grasped the bottoms and had them off.

The realization that he was naked beneath
the blanket filled her with a strange excitement. She had never been so close to an unclothed male before. Yet, why should it
matter?

Her imagination was working overtime.
Raina, leader of the Sodalitas and Marissa's
mentor, had frequently chided her about her
inclination to dream. "Life is hard, people even
harder," Raina had once told Marissa. "Expect
little and you'll never be disappointed." Yet
here she was, alone in a cave with a naked
male, unaccountably stirred and confused by
his presence. Hoping, dreaming—for what?

For degradation and domination, that was
what! Self-disgust filled Marissa. Fool! Stupid,
loin-crazed fool! That was all it was—the mating urge. Despite all attempts to forestall it, it
was bound to strike her sooner or later. Moracan females were a hot-blooded lot, driven
ultimately by the same primal instincts as
were the males. It was also the reason they

were so easily controlled. But that would never happen to her. *Never!*

She climbed to her feet and strode to the fire. For a long moment Marissa battled with her roiling emotions. Her gaze lowered to the hungry flames devouring the little pile of wood. Red-gold and hot, the fire rose and fell in erratic bursts.

Sparks scattered in the air to flicker and die in the thin tongue of smoke that wafted gently upward. Her eyes followed the sooty trail. It wound its slow, sinuous way toward a large opening, the smoke curving as it slipped past a ledge jutting high in the cave.

Stars twinkled brightly through the ashy haze. As Marissa gazed upon their familiar light, an anguished thought lanced through her.

Somewhere out there, on some Imperium planet, Candra waits for me. Waits, and wonders where I am.

Her eyes lowered as the pain of that realization swelled in her breast. *Candra, sweet sister, why won't you answer?* she cried silently. *Why now, when you need me most, do you shut yourself off from me? And do you truly understand the extent of our danger?*

"You're strangely pensive," Brace intruded softly. "Do you care to talk about it?"

Marissa blinked in surprise. His audacity never ceased to amaze her. With an emphatic shake of her head, she forced herself back to the matter at hand.

"No," she gritted out. "I—I am just tired, that's all. Let's get on with your bath. Then we can both get some sleep."

A lazy grin spread across his face. "Have at it, then. I but await your pleasure."

Marissa grimaced. "You overvalue yourself, to think I find pleasure in this."

She stooped to rummage through the bag, extracting several rags and a small container of cleansing sand. Grabbing the pot of simmering water, Marissa returned to Brace's side.

He eyed the articles she carried. "You're a thorough little thief, aren't you?"

"A matter of survival," she muttered. "My nose couldn't take much more of your filth."

Marissa opened the container of cleansing sand and moistened a rag in the water. "Now, be quiet and let's get on with it."

Brace's mouth twisted in a smile, but he remained silent. Marissa moved first to his face, gently soaking the blood-clotted brow until it was clean and the wound exposed. She frowned. The jagged cut wasn't deep, but would leave a scar.

"That bad, eh?"

Marissa shook her head. "No, not really. I only wish I had a needle and thread to sew your eyebrow closed. It would heal better that way."

"A most pleasurable consideration, to be sure."

She ignored his obvious lack of enthusiasm

and returned to her task. His face was soon cleansed, but the washing did little to improve his overall appearance. If nothing else, the bruises now stood out more prominently, dark purple and glaring. Gently Marissa blotted his face dry.

Next she turned to his chest and torso, then his arms and back. The feel of his flesh, so warm and alive beneath her fingers, roused totally unexpected but quite stimulating sensations. Marissa clamped down on the foolish reactions and forged on. Brace tried to help as best he could but he hurt too badly for any prolonged effort.

Marissa ended up giving most of the bath. She wondered at her efforts to spare him pain, thinking she pampered him overmuch, then rationalized them as just another attempt to conserve his strength.

Finally she moved to his legs, halting her efforts halfway up his thighs. She handed him the rag.

"Here, it's time you finish this."

He arched a quizzical brow. "Why? You were doing so well."

She exhaled an exasperated breath. "Curse you, Brace Ardane! I am *not* going to wash your male parts!" She grabbed his hand and shoved the rag into it, then turned away. "Now do it and get it over with!"

Brace chuckled and finished his bath. Then he tossed the rag over by the pot.

"All done. You can turn around now."

The amusement in his voice was not lost on Marissa. She rounded on him.

"Why do you persist in taunting me every step of the way? I saved your life, curse you! If nothing else, I deserve some consideration for that."

He grinned at her, swollen features and all. "Has anyone ever told you how pretty you are when you're angry?"

She gaped at him with slackened jaw, an expression of incredulity on her face. Then renewed anger surged through her.

"Why, you big, blustering—"

"Loathsome male?" Brace supplied innocently.

"Yes," Marissa hissed. "That's *exactly* right."

She grabbed his breeches and shoved them into the pot of water.

"What are you doing? Taking out your anger on my clothes?"

She shot him a quick look. "There's no sense going to all the trouble of a bath if you put filthy breeches back on, is there?"

"No, I suppose not. But that means I must sleep unclothed. How do you feel about lying next to a naked man?"

Marissa froze. "Put that thought from your mind. I have no intention of sleeping next to you."

"Oh? Do you plan to get up every hora or so and stoke the fire then? If not, this cave will soon be quite cold. And in my fragile condition, I need all the warmth I can get."

She scowled, then returned to her fierce scrubbing of his breeches. "Fine," she gritted through clenched teeth. "That's fine with me. But if you lay one hand—"

"I'd never force you to do anything against your will, Marissa. Can't you trust me in that?"

His voice was deep and rich. It caressed her, mesmerized her. Marissa struggled to free herself.

"Trust you?" She shot him an angry look. "And since when has that been a prerequisite for our 'arrangement'? I only want your cooperation."

She pulled the breeches from the pot and wrung them out, spreading them on a nearby rock to dry. Then Marissa returned to Brace's side.

"Keep yourself wrapped in that blanket." She grabbed up the other two blankets. "I'll cover us with these."

Brace shrugged. "As you wish."

He moved over to make a spot for her before the fire. "Come to bed, Marissa."

She glared down for a moment more, then lowered herself to lie beside him. Settling the blankets over them, Marissa scooted up against Brace's backside.

His masculine scent, musky and warm, rose to her nostrils. It was surprisingly pleasant. She hadn't thought a clean male could smell so good. But then, there were a lot of things she hadn't realized about males.

"Rest well, sweet femina," he murmured drowsily.

"I am not your—"

Marissa halted. Oh, what was the use? He was the most stubborn, arrogant male she'd ever met. And also the most disturbing.

She sighed. "Rest well."

And regain your strength as quickly as possible, she added mentally. *The sooner we're on our way, the better. And the sooner I can be rid of you. Once and for all...*

Brace jerked from a deep sleep, his heart pounding, his body bathed in sweat. He'd been back in prison, with Mardoc brutally, relentlessly beating him until he screamed from the pain. Screamed on and on until he finally spiraled down into an endless maw of madness.

With an effort, Brace shook the horrible memory aside. Strange that never once in the cycles of his imprisonment had he experienced such a dream. Perhaps it was the newness of his freedom, a freedom he still found hard to accept. Or perhaps, just perhaps, it was the madness working its insidious way into the deepest recesses of his mind...

He shoved himself up and glanced around. Where was Marissa?

His sleep-thickened gaze swept the cave. No sign of the little Sodalitas. With a deep sigh, Brace fell back.

Marissa must have wakened earlier and set out on another foraging expedition to the village. But how long had she been gone? There was no way of knowing. And if something had happened . . .

Brace cut short the thought. It was pointless to consider going out after her. His strength wouldn't be equal to any extended journey, much less attempting a rescue.

He did feel markedly better, though. The long rest, combined with last nocte's nourishing if meatless food, had done wonders. His glance sought out Marissa's booty bag. There should still be some fruit left . . .

A sound behind him—faint, but unmistakably a footstep—brought Brace up short. He jerked around, but it was already too late. A fist slammed into his jaw. A scattering of stars exploded before his eyes. He gasped, inhaling a rank, heavy scent.

Simian!

The sun was setting behind the mountains before Marissa made her weary way back to the cave. What a long sol it had been! The foraging trip to the village had required more time than she'd planned, thanks largely to the numerous skim craft searching the area.

The Bellatorians were looking for them, that much Marissa knew, and she'd been forced to hide countless times. She hoped no one had discovered Ardane in the cave. One way or another, they'd have to head out this very nocte. To remain a moment longer would guarantee Ardane's recapture.

She prayed he'd rested well this sol, regained some of his strength. He'd need it for the difficult climb through the mountains. Luckily, three of the five Bellatorian moons would be full this nocte. Their brilliance would more than adequately light the way.

Marissa shifted the heavy pack of booty to her other shoulder. Thank the Crystal Fires she'd been able to steal as much as she had. She now possessed another water flask, journey bread, dried fruit, and more vegetables and seasonings for trail soup. And, because she knew a male would require it, a small supply of meat sticks. Ardane would be ecstatic.

A faint odor wafted by as she neared the cave. Marissa's steps faltered. The scent came stronger, ranker. Her nose wrinkled. It reminded her of something . . .

She crept closer. The smell was overpowering now. Marissa froze. Simian. It was the stench of a Simian!

A quick leap and she was hidden behind an outcropping of boulders. She peered around a large stone. Had the beast seen her approach? Marissa scanned the mountainside. Where was he? The answer struck her with the force of a blow. He was in the cave with Ardane. He had to be.

Marissa laid down her pack, her thoughts racing. There was no way of knowing how many were actually in the cave. She had smelled one Simian, of that she was certain, but what if he was accompanied by Bellatorians? How would she overpower them all?

She scanned the cave. No sign of activity, but Marissa knew a frontal assault would be foolhardy. She considered smoking them out by setting fire to the bushes that grew in dense profusion near the cave's entrance, then discarded the idea. In Ardane's weakened state the smoke inhalation might be fatal before it drove out his captors, not to mention the possibility of the smoke drawing more skim craft to the area.

Frustration spiraled within her. How, by all that was sacred, was she to get into that cave and take Ardane's captors unawares?

Smoke.

Of course. Grim determination swelled in Marissa. She'd climb in through the cave's smoke hole. From her vantage point high overhead, she could hide in the rocks and assess the situation. A dangerous ploy, but the only chance she had.

She skirted the cave and made her way up the mountain to the vent hole, then leaned over cautiously and peered down. A ledge jutting below obscured most of her view. Marissa sat back and waited for the nocte to fall.

As twilight settled over the land, a fire was lit within the cave. Thin curls of smoke drifted up through the large opening. She cursed silently. So much for sneaking in under the cover of darkness.

Digging through her pack, Marissa extracted

the water flask and a rag. After thoroughly wetting the cloth, she tied it over her nose and mouth. It was the best she could do to help herself breathe through the smoke. She secured her stunner in an easily accessible pocket and rechecked the dagger strapped to her thigh. Then Marissa once more leaned over the hole.

There'd be about a two-meter drop straight down before she reached the ledge that jutted over the cave. From there she could make it all the way down. The climb looked precarious, but there was indeed a chance—if she was quiet and very careful. And at least this climb wasn't as high as the one from Ardane's prison had been.

Marissa scanned the scene below for one last time. She caught a glimpse of the tall, hulking form of a Simian as he glided by. Her gaze followed until he disappeared from view. Hopefully, he was the only one she'd have to deal with. She eased her way off the edge. For a heart-stopping moment, Marissa dangled over the cave.

Smoke stung her eyes and she clenched them shut an instant before she released her grip. Marissa fell for what seemed an eternity. At the last moment she opened her eyes and landed with lithe grace. She flattened herself against the stone floor and waited for some response from below.

There was none.

Ever so carefully, Marissa scooted over and looked down. She saw Ardane leaning against a far wall, unbound, chewing on a piece of dried cerasa fruit. There was no sign of anyone else except the Simian.

Relief, then confusion, swept through her. Ardane was alive. But why was he lolling down there without an apparent care in the world, rather than bound like the captive he should be? Was it a trap to lure her in? Well, there was only one enemy to deal with—and he had made a fatal mistake.

From the care the alien was taking with his captive, it was evident he intended on taking Ardane back alive. Recalling a Simian's love of money, Marissa knew there must have been a ransom offered for Ardane's capture. The Bellatorians seemed determined their countryman serve out his sentence to its fullest extent.

Marissa's hand crept to her stunner. Would even the highest setting be enough to stun a Simian? There was only one way of finding out, but she'd have to get closer. The alien was still out of firing range.

It took a long while to climb farther down, as utmost care was necessary. Simians were renowned for their acute hearing. Marissa thanked the long horas Raina had spent teaching her stealth techniques. They stood her in good stead now. At long last, Marissa moved into stunning range.

The Simian had resumed his place at the fire and was rummaging through the cloth bag she'd stolen the sol before. He growled in frustration at the lack of food in the sack and

71

scowled at Ardane. The creature made a few quick hand motions Marissa couldn't see.

Ardane shrugged. "I told you before. The little Moracan went out to find more food. She should be back soon."

Marissa choked back a gasp. What, by the Crystal Fires, was Ardane doing? He'd all but given the Simian her exact time of return. Uneasiness wound about her heart. Had he betrayed her to the alien? And if so, why?

Her resolve hardened. It didn't matter; nothing had changed. Once she took care of the Simian, the Bellatorian was still coming with her. The only difference was that now he too seemed to play a similar game of deception.

The Simian made a motion of disgust and tossed aside the bag. With a sigh, he leaned back against the cave wall. His action gave her a clear shot. Marissa aimed the stunner and fired.

For a terrible instant she thought the small gun had failed to function. Then the alien jerked and a glazed expression spread over his face. He slumped forward.

"By the five moons—!" Brace sat upright, his glance lifting until it met Marissa's.

He grinned. "Bring any food?"

Marissa climbed down the rest of the way. "Ever appreciative, aren't you?" she countered irritably, squatting before him.

She pulled the rag down off her face. "Some sol I'm going to grow weary of rescuing you."

"And did I look like I needed rescuing?" he inquired mildly.

Marissa glared down at him. "No. And why is that?"

"In the interim between your departure and return, this Simian and I have come to an understanding." Brace smiled grimly. "Seems my uncle has offered a bounty of five thousand imperials for my capture. Rodac decided to cash in on the opportunity."

He chuckled. "You can't help but admire his single-minded pursuit of wealth."

"Rodac?" Marissa stared at him for an incredulous moment. "By the Crystal Fires, how did you find time to make his personal acquaintance?"

"He looked familiar, and when I questioned him further, I discovered he was the same Simian you'd hired to rescue me. After several military assignments on their planet of Arbor, I still have some difficulty telling them apart. It seems he'd planned from the start to make money in freeing me from prison, then dragging me back for the reward."

Brace grinned up at her. "I might have to give that novel career opportunity some serious consideration."

"Are you m-mad?" Marissa sputtered in outrage. "How can you sit there, in danger of recapture, and admire that foul-smelling, underhanded—"

She unsheathed her dagger and moved toward the Simian.

73

"Wait." Brace grabbed her arm. "He's of far more value to us alive than dead."

"And have your brains turned to a pile of mush? He can't be trusted. That much is apparent by how quickly he turned on us. I'm only surprised that hulking bag of hair let us get this far before coming after us."

"Think about it, Marissa," Brace replied. "His strength will be useful in traversing these mountains. How long and far do you think I'd be able to travel before I gave out? We've got to get away from here before someone else finds us. Rodac is the only one who can help us do that."

"No." Marissa shook her head firmly. "I don't trust him and never will." *And I don't trust you, either,* she thought. "It won't work."

"It *will*, Marissa. He agreed to help us, for a price, of course, but one I can easily meet. And I risk far more than you if I fail. Remember that."

Her gaze met his. *Ah, Ardane,* she thought. *If you only knew the full extent of what I risked.* Yet, in spite of it all, the look burning in his dark brown eyes was so intense, so compelling, that Marissa found her resolve melting. Curse him! He could very easily betray her, yet she almost believed him. She turned away.

"Marissa," he prodded, his voice deep and rich. "Trust me in this. I know what I'm doing."

Exasperation filled her. They'd both regret this decision. She just knew it!

But Ardane spoke true. They needed help desperately if they were to escape these mountains. For the time being, her wiser course was to use the Simian and wait for Ardane to misstep. And never, ever, lower her guard against either of them.

She resheathed the dagger. "Have it your way, you stubborn male. But if you're wrong and we live to regret it, I'll never listen to another thing you say."

Brace grinned, a broad, devastating expression filled with relief and boyish gratitude. Marissa's heart did a somersault. Then, with a fierce scowl, she turned away.

Curse Brace Ardane, she thought. From the start he'd been nothing but trouble. And the trouble he stirred with these new, exquisitely disturbing emotions frightened Marissa most of all.

Ah, curse him and the ill-fated quest that had forced them together. Curse him for the eventual pain she knew he'd cause her. And curse Ferox most of all—for forcing them both into this morass of lies and deception.

Chapter Four

With hard resolve, Marissa quashed her fruitless lamenting and turned to eye the Simian's prone form. "I had no idea a stunner worked so well on a beast that size. But then, I did set it on high."

"An advantage that might stand us in good stead."

She forced her gaze to meet his. "You spoke of coming to an understanding with this creature. Are you planning on sharing it with me?"

At the bluntness of her question, Brace grinned. "Ever the diplomat, aren't you, Marissa? Have you given any thought to entering politics? Your verbal skills far exceed—"

"Enough, Ardane!" Marissa snapped. "I'm tired of your clever banter. Either tell me why this Simian agreed to let you go, or—or I'll slit his throat and be done with it!"

Brace laughed and held up a hand. "As you wish, *gentle* femina." He paused to glance around. "Did you bring any food back with you? I can easily talk while I eat."

Marissa rolled her eyes. "All you males think

of is food. But I left my bag outside." She made a move to rise.

"No, Marissa." A big, gentle hand stayed her. "That's not *all* we males think of. But I imagine food is all you're willing to share."

Her blue-green gaze met his.

In the fire's flickering glow, Brace's dark eyes danced with golden lights. His look was smiling, almost teasing, but beneath it hovered a deeper message—intense, disturbing, and hungry.

High color swept Marissa's cheeks as she frantically considered and cast aside half a dozen responses. There was no reply she hadn't given before. She twisted free of his grip.

"I-I'll be back with the bag." Marissa fled the cave.

Brace was waiting when she returned. Marissa lowered herself beside the fire and extracted parcels of journey bread and meat sticks.

"Here, content yourself with these." She tossed Brace two packages.

He arched a dark brow and unwrapped the food. At sight of the meat sticks, he smiled. "Thank you, Marissa."

His rich-timbred voice slid over her, soothing her jangled nerves. She smiled, then caught herself. "You had it in your stubborn head you'd never recover without meat. I simply gave you what you wanted."

A smile quirked Brace's mouth. He bit into a meat stick, savoring the texture and tangy flavor of the highly seasoned food. Intense pleasure filled him. Brace swallowed, then sighed.

"Are you sure you wouldn't like to try one?" he asked, offering her a meat stick.

Marissa choked down the gorge that rose in her throat. "No. No, thank you."

Brace noted the sudden pallor in Marissa's face. With one last, longing look, he set aside the meat stick and took up a slice of the thin, crisp journey bread.

"I'm still awaiting your plan for the Simian," she said.

He paused to swallow the bite of journey bread. "It's quite simple, really. I made him a better offer."

"Oh?" Marissa arched a slender brow. "And how did you manage to come up with something valuable enough to appease a Simian? Have a stash hidden somewhere?"

"In a sense, yes. I know where a cache of Imperial treasures are held here on Bellator. There's an air duct that will get us inside the building to the treasure rooms, once I've disabled the alarm system that guards it all."

"Sounds a little too easy."

Brace grinned. "It's a very sophisticated system. I just happen to have been around when it malfunctioned and was able to catch a glimpse while it was being repaired. The Imperial Academy prepares you for more than war, you know. The majority of my academic studies were in mechanical technology."

"How convenient. I still find this all too easy."

"Well, there *are* a few guardbots about, if it's action you're wanting. Of course, once the alarm system's deactivated, it does hamper the 'bots' communication with each other. Not as even a fight, but the best I can provide."

Marissa shot him an exasperated look. "I thought as much. Now tell me, how did you 'happen to be around' when the system was repaired?"

Color spread up Brace's neck to flush his face. "I led several military expeditions to other worlds to 'appropriate' many of the treasures now housed in the Repository. I was delivering some of the booty one sol when the repairs were being done."

Marissa stared at him for a long moment, then gave a bitter laugh. "You've had quite a full life at the expense of others, haven't you, Ardane? I'm amazed your High King would have ever thrown such a valuable asset into prison!"

"Obedience can only go so far," he muttered. "Even I had my limits."

Disdain twisted her lips. "But how can that be? Limits to unthinking, unwavering obedience? Why, that's unheard of in Bellatorians! Your people recognize only one possible motive for disobedience—cowardice." Marissa's eyes narrowed. "Were you a coward, then, Brace Ardane? Was that your crime?"

"Careful, femina. My imprisonment is not the issue."

"Isn't it? Don't I deserve to know whether my partner in this quest is a coward or not?"

Even as she spoke, Marissa knew she shouldn't be taunting him like that. Assurances of his courage would settle nothing. Lies came too easily to most Bellatorians. Only actions would prove the truth of the matter. Yet the realization that Ardane was probably as mindlessly cruel as the rest of his kind was as unsettling as the contemplation of his cowardice. Either way, Marissa was strangely disappointed.

And it had *nothing* to do with her conception of him as a person, she was quick to assure herself. All that mattered was her quest. Ardane's true value would always be as trade for Candra's life.

Yet, in spite of her best intentions, Marissa couldn't help one last little dig. "Well?" she prodded. "Are, or are you not, a coward?"

Her taunt sliced through Brace, laying open that old wound of his imprisonment. A coward. Gods!

Scorching fury flared in his eyes. "You *dare* question my courage? Then why not call the whole thing off? Surely you've no need for a coward on your precious quest?"

His challenge drew Marissa up short. Why had she goaded him in such a stupid, mindless manner? Her foolish reaction to the possibility of his cowardice now threatened Ardane's continued participation. She must calm him, and quickly, or risk losing everything. *Everything*.

Her eyes lowered. "I—I beg pardon. It was my—my anger at hearing of more Bellatorian offenses that drove me to lash out at you."

She glanced back up at him.

He graced her with a thunderous glare.

"Why were you imprisoned? Can't you at least tell me that?" she asked, managing a tentative smile.

"And why do you care?" he growled.

"Partners work best if they understand each other," Marissa replied softly. "And besides, I've decided you're not as loathsome as I first imagined."

Her reluctant admission teased a slow, grudging smile. Brace's anger faded.

"My brother," he finally sighed. "I was imprisoned because I dared stand up to the Bellatorian High Council and defy their sentencing of my brother."

"Your brother? What did he do?"

"While on a military assignment to the planet Agrica, Teran refused a lawful order to slaughter a helpless village. For his 'cowardice' he was condemned for life to the prison planet of Carcer."

"But no one survives more than six monates on Carcer," Marissa exclaimed, "and you've been in prison over two cycles now."

"Oh, I realize he's dead," Brace admitted, a bleak look in his eyes, "but whether alive or dead, his punishment has no further bearing on my sentence. Unless I recant my disobedience and publicly beg forgiveness before my uncle, King Falkan, my fate is no less final than his. If not for your timely rescue I'd have soon been dead from torture—or have lost my mind."

Understanding, and a wondering respect, flared in Marissa. "That's why I found you starved and half-beaten to death—because you stood up for your brother."

Silently Brace returned her gaze.

A soft smile touched her lips. "You're no coward, Brace Ardane. A stubborn fool and unrealistic dreamer, perhaps, but no coward."

A dreamer once, he thought, *but no more*.

"Careful, Marissa," Brace warned. "Your back-handed compliments threaten to overwhelm me."

Her mouth tightened in exasperation. "Don't misconstrue my meaning, Ardane. I meant no compliment. It was a simple statement of fact."

"Oh, I understand . . . I think."

Marissa frowned. This male was becoming one of the most disconcerting—

She pulled her thoughts back to the safer topic at hand. "So, where is this treasure trove you spoke of? If the Bellatorians stole it from others, I've no qualms about liberating a little for ourselves."

"The Repository is located in a town called Olena, a short detour from Tutela. Think about it, Marissa. Not only will this gain us Rodac's cooperation in getting us through the mountains, but, by also dangling the temptation of acquiring some of Ferox's fabled wealth, I've assured his continued participation in the rescue of your sister."

Renewed anger surged through her. "Nothing was said about his accompanying us on our quest!"

"No, but Rodac has invaluable skills, not to mention his brute strength. And we need all the help we can get."

Marissa's thoughts raced. Another participant would only complicate her eventual betrayal of Ardane—a betrayal that was fast becoming difficult to contemplate. Curse him for revealing that act of courage and integrity, and all because of his love for his brother! She didn't want to know that. But then, why had she asked?

She shook her head. "No. I neither want nor need him on our quest. You are sufficient."

"And I thank you for yet another compliment," Brace muttered. "But either Rodac comes along or I don't."

"What?" Marissa cried. "You promised! You gave your word!"

"I gave my word to help you," he replied, struggling to maintain a calm tone. "But I never agreed to not seek extra assistance along the way. Whatever I do, have I not fulfilled that promise if my actions result in the rescue of your sister?"

"Yes, I suppose so," Marissa acknowledged.

"But why must it be that stinking, treacherous, money-grubbing Simian? I'll tolerate his presence until Tutela, but no further. That's fair enough, I'd say."

"No, Marissa." Brace's dark eyes bore into hers. "That's *not* enough. This is a suicide mission. Make your choice and make it now."

Her anger grew. Curse him! In his own way Ardane was as treacherous as the Simian. But why should that surprise her? He was a male, after all.

Yet, in all fairness, she had no right to condemn him for the same intentions she'd had from the start. This quest had always involved deception and coercion. They were necessary evils if she were to lure him into Ferox's trap— a trap that would most probably result in his death.

But the admission still changed nothing. Whatever it took, she must continue to use him. In the end, Candra's and her own continued survival were what mattered, not her foolish pride or sense of guilt.

Marissa gave a bitter laugh. "I don't see that you've left me much choice. If I want you, I have to take along a smelly alien. But tell me now. Have you any other surprises in store?"

Something flickered in his dark eyes, then Brace shook his head. "No, nothing that wasn't decided long ago."

"Good."

She reached for the bag and withdrew a parcel of dried cerasa fruit. Unwrapping it, Marissa tossed a few pieces to Brace, then scooped up a handful for herself. She tore off a bite of the tart, chewy fruit.

"Then it's settled, once and for all."

Brace's mouth drew into a hard, ruthless line. "Yes, once and for all."

He quashed the brief flare of remorse at his deception, an unpleasant feeling that was rising more and more often of late. Marissa only half knew what he was planning. Once he'd seen her stash replenished by looting the Repository in Olena, and Rodac committed to his anticipated quest to relieve Ferox of some of his ill-gotten goods, Brace intended to leave her.

The little Sodalitas would be furious, but there'd be nothing she could do. He'd be well on his way, transporting across space to some secret hiding place. Then Marissa would be more than grateful for the Simian's aid.

It was all he could do for her, all he *dared* do. Yet the thought of turning his back and walking away filled Brace with a strange regret. He had never willingly betrayed another. This fledgling self-concept as liar and deceiver, born of the past two cycles in prison, fit like a new pair of boots. Tight, uncomfortable, rubbing him raw in all the wrong places.

But there was *nothing* in this twisted, demented Imperium worth fighting for. Nothing save his own survival. He'd been forced to learn that harsh reality, and now it was all that mattered—not some wide-eyed, alluring little spitfire blithely calling him to a hopeless quest. A hopeless, stupid, fatal quest.

Brace grabbed his meat stick and tore into it savagely, ignoring Marissa's look of revulsion. At that moment the Simian stirred. Both turned toward him, grateful, each in his own way, for the distraction.

Though Rodac was not in the best of moods thanks to his post-stunning headache, they traveled all nocte to avoid detection and reached Marissa's stash by early the next sol. In the rapidly dropping temperatures the extra supplies were a godsend, especially the two long, hooded phoca-fur coats Marissa had thought to pack.

An early snow blanketed the craggy summits, and the frigid wind whistling through made it seem even colder. The chill weather appeared to have little impact on the densely furred Simian, but even with the added protection of their coats the journey through the rest of the mountains was miserable for Marissa and Brace. Both heaved silent sighs of relief when they finally reached the relative warmth of the flatlands.

Each nocte of travel, Brace required less and less of Rodac's assistance. By the time they arrived in the vicinity of Olena, the only remaining signs of his brutal beating were fading yellow bruises and his slightly flattened, still broken nose. If not for the dreams of prison that haunted him each nocte of their journey,

Brace would have felt almost back to normal. But those dreams . . .

They set up camp outside the small town in a thick stand of trees and made final plans for entering the Repository. As they talked, Brace busied himself scraping off his beard with a primitive shaving stone.

"There's really no need for all of us to enter the Repository," he said. "You'll stay outside and keep watch, Marissa."

At mention of her name, Marissa jerked her gaze up to Brace's eyes. As she'd watched his dark, dense beard fall away, revealing the clean, square lines of his jaw, she'd found herself pleasantly torn between the beard and the smooth-shaven face. Was there nothing about this male that wasn't fascinating? Marissa wondered, as she struggled to recall what the tall Bellatorian had just said.

Her brow wrinkled. "Keep watch, you say?" She shook her head emphatically. "No. Once we enter the Repository, speed is of the essence. Most guardbots I've come across are not only sneaky, but armed to the teeth. And three going through all that booty will be far quicker than two.

"Besides," Marissa muttered, shooting the Simian a scathing glance, "two pairs of eyes keeping watch on him is far wiser than one. Once he gets his hairy paws on all that loot, I wouldn't put it past him to turn on us."

"He won't turn on us, Marissa," Brace sighed, pausing in the scraping of his upper lip. "He gave his word, and the Simian code—"

"—of honor is second only to Bellator's," Marissa finished mockingly. "Yes, I know, Ardane, and that's exactly why I want to go along. Now, no more of it. My skills are quite sufficient to the task, and I *will* accompany you."

Brace shot Rodac a long-suffering look. The Simian merely rolled his eyes and shrugged his shoulders, then resumed his braiding of a long coil of rope from the supply of sturdy funis vine he'd gradually acquired during their journey.

"Have it your way, then," Brace growled in disgust. He resumed his shaving. "You will anyway."

Marissa's chin lifted. "And why not, Ardane. It *is* my quest. And that makes me the leader, does it not?"

The shaving stopped and dark eyes glared over at her.

"Well?" she prodded. "Doesn't it?"

"Of course, *Domina*," Brace drawled. "Most certainly, and I am but your humble servant."

She snorted in disgust. "And the Crystal Fires will freeze solid before that sol dawns!"

Brace eyed her for a moment more, then laughed. "Be honest, Marissa. You wouldn't like me docile and obedient, and you know it."

Surprise flitted across her face. Then she shook her head.

"You don't know what I like and don't like,

Ardane, and that's the way it'll remain. I don't care if you approve of my decisions just as long as you cooperate."

"Yes, Domina."

"Ardane!" Marissa warned, noting the cynical quirk of his mouth.

Brace laughed and resumed his shaving.

He was taunting her again. But that wasn't half as unsettling as Marissa's reluctant admission that he could so easily get to her. Or that she almost enjoyed the tension it produced between them. Angrily she flung the realization aside.

Enjoyed talking and being with a male? It was impossible, insane! Yet a reality nonetheless.

Once again that strange apprehension shivered through Marissa. Her emotions were spiraling out of control, filling her with a hungry, aching need. Though she'd never lain with a male, Marissa recognized the feelings. A need for a male—this male.

It confused her. Marissa was too honest not to admit that. It confused and frightened her, yet beckoned to her all the same. For a fleeting moment, she wondered how Ardane felt about her. Then she quickly turned her thoughts to less upsetting things. Like the impending foray into Olena.

The trio crept into town at sol set. Aside from the Repository situated there, Olena was little more than a guild center for Bellatorian tradesmen and essentially went to bed when the shops and offices closed. The Repository lay in the center of the sleepy town, a squat, circular building of four stories.

They made their way to the alleyway behind the Repository. As Marissa watched with rising unease, Rodac uncoiled his rope.

She turned to Brace. "I hate heights, but, one way or another, this time I'm climbing up on my own. My stomach couldn't take another secundae pressed against that malodorous Simian."

"We're just as foul-smelling to them."

"Oh, really? Perhaps you meat eaters are, but there's no stench from fruits and vegetables."

"And what do you think, Rodac?" Brace turned to the Simian. "Do vegetarians smell better then meat eaters?"

The alien's gaze flitted from one to the other, as if he were considering the question. Then he rolled his beady eyes and turned away. With a quick twist of his wrist, Rodac circled the rope above his head. When it fed out to the proper length and speed, he hurled it upward.

The rope ensnared one of the roof's crenelated edges. With a practiced tug Rodac settled the loop snugly in place, then turned to Brace. Brace grasped the rope as high as he could and began a swift, hand-over-hand climb. Once he was safely on the roof, Rodac gestured toward Marissa.

With a small grimace, Marissa stepped up. Her journey to the rooftop was considerably slower and a lot more nerve-wracking, but she soon joined Brace. A few secundae later Rodac was there, silently hauling in the rope behind him. After stowing the coil beneath a water storage cylinder, the trio lowered themselves through the air duct to the level below.

A quick check confirmed there were no guardbots about. With a few skilled manipulations of a nearby control box, Brace deactivated all alarm and communication systems. Then he turned to Marissa.

"Well, Domina? We await your command."

She nodded. "Remember to take every level in a systematic fashion. Only when all rooms have been searched will we proceed to the next level. Take only items of high value that are easily carried. Understood?"

Brace and Rodac nodded.

"Good." Marissa waved them ahead of her. "Let's go."

The next hora was spent in a fruitless search of the fourth floor, a level apparently utilized for the storage of ancient texts and manuscripts. What a wealth of knowledge, Marissa mused as she sifted through piles of vellum and ornately gilded tomes, hidden away from an Imperium long starved of learning. And how ironic that Bellator, well-known for putting little store in things of the mind, was now possessor of most of the few remaining books left in the Imperium.

Some sol, Marissa vowed, she'd return and relieve this Repository of a lot more of its ill-gotten gains. The Sodalitas, at the very least, would appreciate some of these books—

The deep bass hum of a guardbot's anti-grav plates brought Marissa up short. She swung around, her blaster waist-high, her trigger finger ready. A 'bot stood in the doorway, its green scan beam slowly surveying the room.

She ducked and rolled aside, firing point-blank at the guardbot. The sound was loud and abrupt in the sudden silence. It brought a light, rapid tread of footsteps in her direction.

"Marissa!"

Brace slid to a halt behind the guardbot's shattered remains. His sharp glance took in the pile of twisted metal, then Marissa's calm countenance as she slung her blaster back onto her shoulder. He grinned, then signaled her onward.

With one last, regretful look at the manuscripts stacked about the chamber, Marissa followed Brace. There was a job to be done, she reminded herself, and the room of books was now a thing of the past.

The third floor consisted of ceremonial weaponry acquired from virtually every royal house in the Imperium. Jewels encrusted the ancient shields, helmets, and swords wrought of precious aureum and argentum metals, all glittering with seductive brilliance in the flickering light of perpetual torches. Marissa paused to pry some of the larger stones free, then added them to the growing stash in her bag.

In a room of gems on the second floor, on a miscellaneous pile on a back table, a narrow, ornately gilded box caught Marissa's eye. On its cover was engraved the form of Aranea's famed mutant weaving spider. Marissa picked up the container and flipped open its lid.

Inside lay an ancient scroll, yellowed and brittle with age. More secrets of the ancients, Marissa thought wryly, and closed the box. She made a move to return it to the table when a sound behind her drew her up sharply.

Another guardbot! She wheeled about, her hand moving to her blaster—and froze.

An old man, gray-bearded and dressed in long white robes, shimmered before her. He smiled, his expression gentle and kind. Marissa's throat constricted.

Either she was having a hallucination or the Repository was haunted. She clamped her eyes shut for a brief moment, then snapped them open. The old man remained.

"Take the box, child," he murmured softly. "You'll need it later—for the quest. Take it, child."

"Wh-who are you?" Marissa choked out the words. "What's your—?"

He began to disappear even as she spoke, fading away as quickly as he'd appeared. Marissa blinked. Had she really seen the old man? She glanced down at the box in her hand.

Though made of precious aureum and inlaid with several fine stones, it was not overly impressive when compared to the fabulous wealth scattered about the room. Still, old man or no, there was something about it . . . With a shrug, Marissa tossed it into her bag.

Three horas and a platoon of destroyed guardbots later, they departed the Repository through the same air duct, their booty bags suitably laden. Olena was soon left behind, after a brief detour to acquire a supply of fresh food from the various shops. The trip into town had been surprisingly successful, and the trio celebrated with a lavish banquet of stolen victuals.

Afterwards, Marissa spent the last few horas before sleep sifting happily through the contents of her bag. She came upon the box with the embossed Aranean spider and once again flipped open its lid. She unrolled the scroll carefully. The writing was unintelligible though vaguely familiar.

With a frustrated sigh, Marissa rerolled the ancient vellum and returned it to its case. Need it indeed, she thought in irritation, harking back to the words of the strange old man. The only thing she needed was the money the aureum box would sell for. The scroll itself was of little value, save perhaps for tinder.

Marissa tossed the box back into her bag and resumed her intent rifling through the rest of her booty. Brace, meanwhile, stared gloomily into the fire, planning for the moment he'd reveal his plan to leave her—and battling the mixed emotions that that contemplation stirred. And, high in a tree above them, Rodac snored away, his own bag of riches clutched to his hairy chest.

They reached Tutela in another sol, arriving in the early afternoon. After taking a room over a tavern, the trio went their separate ways to comb the city for any word of Ferox, not meeting again until sol set. Marissa was the last to return. She was not pleased with the news.

"Nothing?" she demanded. "You found nothing about Ferox?"

"He seems to have disappeared for the time being," Brace called from behind the room's dressing screen, where he was changing into the new clothes he'd bought with some of his stash. "Until he decides to resurface, there's not a lot we can do about it."

"But I haven't the time—"

"There's little choice," Brace interjected. "Now I suggest—"

Marissa rounded on Rodac. "And you? Are you sure you heard nothing of use? You *are* capable of some simple spying, aren't you?"

The Simian's lip curled in a sneer and he made a move toward her. Brace stepped from behind the screen.

"Why not head down to the tavern?" he suggested to the tall alien, slipping between Rodac and Marissa. "We'll join you shortly, after Marissa's had a time to calm."

"Calm?" There was an edge of rising fury to her voice. "I'm warning you, Ardane. Don't patronize me!"

Brace motioned Rodac toward the door, then turned to Marissa. He waited until the door clicked shut before replying.

He might as well tell her now. She couldn't get too much more agitated. Brace pulled over a chair. "Marissa, sit down."

She glanced briefly at Brace's long-sleeved dark blue tunic, laced up the front, and his snug-fitting black breeches, tucked into shiny new black boots. Her gaze lifted to his face, and she gave a start of surprise. He'd had his nose fixed as well.

Marissa grimaced. If he thought some new clothes and a rapidly improving appearance gave him the right to order her around...

Her chin lifted in a mutinous angle. "No. I don't want to sit down."

"Marissa, sit," came the soft, definitive command.

She eyed him for a moment more, considering further defiance, then decided it was pointless. With a disgruntled sigh, Marissa strode to the chair and sat down.

"Yes, Ardane?" she inquired silkily. "And how may I serve you?"

He chuckled. "You're mistaken, Domina. It is I who am the humble servant, not you."

"Thank you for reminding me. I forget so often of late."

Gods, Brace thought, she was so beautiful sitting there, the setting sun bathing her in a nimbus of golden light, her chestnut hair a riotous tumble about her, her striking eyes flashing a seductive challenge. He would miss her, he realized belatedly, miss the clash of wills, the fiery interchange, the hope for something more between them.

A hope that would be quashed forever in the revelation of his betrayal. But there was no other way—and he *had* provided for her the best he could. He swallowed hard and forced himself to go on.

"I once asked you if I would have fulfilled my vow if my actions, whatever they were, resulted in the rescue of your sister. Do you recall your reply?"

"Yes. I agreed. Now, what are you getting at? I grow weary of this game."

"I enlisted Rodac's aid for two reasons," Brace admitted, moving right to the point. "One was to get us through the mountains to Tutela."

Marissa saw the guilt smolder in Ardane's eyes and flush his face. Her apprehension grew. Finally she could bear it no longer.

"What?" Marissa demanded. "What is the other reason?"

For a fleeting instant regret flared in Brace's eyes. Then his expression hardened.

"I go no further on this quest of yours. Rodac is your partner now. And either you learn to work with him—or head out alone."

Chapter Five

Marissa stared at Brace for a long moment. She'd expected this, she struggled to remind herself. Yet his betrayal still hurt.

"So, how long have you been plotting this?" Marissa forced herself to ask.

Brace squared his shoulders for the battle to come. "I never meant to get involved in this hopeless quest. You'd do well to give it up, too. Your sister is probably dead by now."

"Believe me, she's alive. I'd know if she wasn't."

"Well, it doesn't matter. I'm not going with you."

"You gave your word."

"The word of a desperate man."

"You mean, the word of a coward!"

Brace's jaw went taut with rage. "Don't start, Marissa."

She moved until she confronted him face to face. "And why not, Ardane? Aren't you man enough to face the truth? The truth that you're a spineless coward and liar?" Marissa snarled, hating herself, even as she spoke, for the liar she was as well. "But even a coward can be bought. Even you must have your price."

"Yes, Marissa, I suppose I do," Brace growled, his voice vibrating with cold fury. "My freedom. I'd do anything for my freedom."

"And what about my needs? What about Candra's freedom?"

He eyed her, something snapping within him. Curse her for throwing one of his deepest fears into his face, for taunting him, and for being the alluring woman she was in spite of it all! Let her just once feel some of the same frustration and confusion he felt!

"Well, there can be a price for that, too," Brace replied, as a challenge that he knew Marissa wouldn't dare take formed in his mind. "But have a care. You won't like paying it."

"Won't I?" she jeered. "And what could it possibly take to buy a coward's backbone?"

Brace's glance slid down the length of her body, and a bewildering mix of rage and lust flooded him. "Mate with me. Then perhaps I'll reconsider."

She stared at him, stunned.

"Well, Marissa?" Brace prodded. "Surely the price isn't too high? Not for the life of your beloved sister?"

"You despicable slime worm!"

His eyes narrowed to icy slits. "Why should your sacrifice be any less than mine? I gave up everything to save my brother, and it all but destroyed me. Now, here you stand, demanding the only thing I have left—my life. Surely that deserves some token sacrifice on your part?"

Brace's voice lowered to a rasping whisper. "How deep does your love for your sister really go, Marissa? Deep enough to endure the indignity of mating with me?"

Marissa's hand moved to the dagger sheathed on her thigh. "G-get out of here!" she cried, nearly choking on her rage. "Get out before I kill you!"

He gave a harsh laugh, then backed away. "Take some time to think about it, femina. I've seen how you've looked at me when you thought I wouldn't notice. I'd wager you need the mating as much as I."

The dagger barely missed his head as it sank into the door frame. Brace turned and left the room.

Mixed emotions assailed him as he strode the length of the hall and down the stairs. Gods, what had he been thinking, to taunt her like that? It had been crude, cruel, and so unlike him. And why had he offered his services if only she'd mate with him? No female was worth his life!

What would he have done if she'd taken him up on his offer? Mate with her? The consideration held a strong, if disconcerting, appeal. After all, he'd been without a female for over two cycles, and Marissa, mouthy defiance and all, most definitely stirred his desires. But to use, and then turn his back upon her . . .

For all his newly heightened sense of self-preservation, Brace couldn't stoop that low. He was already having enough trouble hardening his heart to Marissa and her plight. He was already having enough trouble accepting the man he'd become.

Gods, Brace thought with a surge of disbelief, what had he been thinking a few secundae ago? He had to get away from that little Sodalitas, and soon, or she'd manipulate his emotions to her own ends after all!

The crowded chaos of the tavern was a welcome relief from his troubling thoughts. Brace melted into the mass of sweating, jostling bodies, inhaling deeply of the scent of well-aged Moracan ale and smoky cannaba weed hovering over the room in a thick, heady cloud. By the five moons, could anything sound or smell as rousing as a noisy, rabble-filled tavern?

Brace wedged into a spot at the bar and studied the counter top of well-scarred robur wood as he awaited his mug of ale. The various hues of the grain swirled and mingled in deep, intense gradations of color. Rich, vibrant—like the shimmering bronze of Marissa's hair.

With a fierce shake of his head, Brace rejected the swell of feelings evoked by that memory. It was over, dead between them, before there'd ever been a chance. Dead, as well it should be.

His mug of ale slid down the counter to strike his arm. He gripped its metallic coolness and lifted it to his mouth. A long, deep, satisfying draught of the spicy brew did a lot to calm his highly charged emotions. Brace emptied the contents and ordered another.

Gradually a warm lethargy settled over him. He turned to eye the tavern occupants, his second mug in hand. Rodac was sprawled in a corner booth across the room, three empty mugs neatly lined up before him on the table. In his leathery hand he clasped a fourth.

Brace frowned and leaned back against the bar. Simians weren't known for their ability to hold their liquor. Even from across the room Rodac's movements appeared sluggish, his eyes glazed. Brace muttered a silent prayer that the alien would pass out before some foolhardy soul decided to pick a fight.

Snatches of conversation floated by, snaring his wandering attention. And all the talk seemed to have a similar theme.

"The Knowing Crystal ... finally discovered on the planet Carcer ..."

"... some Aranean princess and a criminal found it ..."

"... Ferox had it all along ..."

At the mention of Ferox's name, Brace stiffened, his mug halfway to his lips. A strange premonition washed over him. His heart began a dull, heavy thudding.

"... and now she's Queen of the planet Aranea, and Teran Ardane's her lord."

Brace shoved through the crowd toward the voice's owner, his mug still clenched in his hand. He grabbed the startled man by the front of his tunic and pulled him close.

"Ardane. Teran Ardane," Brace demanded. "What has he to do with the Queen of Aranea?"

The man reared back, a look of puzzled amusement on his face. "Where have you been this past monate, not to have heard the tale of their rescue of the Knowing Crystal? Locked away in prison?"

Laughter erupted at the man's mocking question. Brace scowled. His grip tightened and he pulled the man up to him until they stood eye to eye.

"I've neither the time nor patience for your twisted sense of humor," he snapped. "Now, tell me the tale or I'll—"

"Th-the Knowing Crystal was stolen by the criminal Ferox and hidden away on the planet Carcer until Queen Alia joined forces with Lord Ardane to rescue it. Lord Ardane was a criminal at the time, you know, condemned for an act—"

"I know what his crime was," Brace was quick to silence him. "All I want to know is where is Teran Ardane now? Here, on Bellator?"

"No," the man hurried to reply. "He's on Aranea. Once again Ferox has stolen the Crystal, leaving the Queen critically wounded. It all happened only a few sols ago. That's where you'll find Lord Ardane, attempting to set right the calamity."

Teran—alive and on Aranea. It was almost more than Brace could comprehend.

Then a sudden thought struck him. *It all happened only few sols ago ...*

What if it were a trap? The tale tied in nicely with the time of his escape, and Bellator might stoop to anything to recapture him. Even this.

Well, one way or another, he meant to transport to Aranea and ascertain the truth. He'd just have to take care in the process.

Gradually Brace became aware that all eyes were riveted on him. With a lopsided grin of apology, he released his captive and smoothed down the front of his tunic.

At that moment a string of curses, followed by a guttural growl, erupted from the corner booth. Rodac sprang across the table at two men, sending them tumbling to the floor. In a confusing melee of fur and clothed bodies the trio rolled across the tavern, fists pummeling, legs flailing.

Brace sighed and handed his mug to the nearest bystander. Rodac, even in his drunken state, could easily handle two men, but there was always the chance that others might decide to join in. Simians, thanks to their fabled mercenary habits, weren't all that popular in the Imperium. And the last thing Brace wanted was to get involved in a full-fledged brawl.

He strode to the tangle of bodies on the floor, pulling first one, then the other man off the alien. "Get out of here," he snarled when each made a threatening move toward him. "I'm saving both your scrawny necks, whether you've the sense to realize it or not."

Rodac climbed to his feet to glower behind Brace. The other two men pondered their options, then grinned drunkenly, shrugged, and backed away. Brace turned to Rodac.

"You need to sleep off that ale." He motioned toward the door. "Come on. Let's find you a nice tree to curl up in."

Two rows of sharp Simian teeth gleamed in the dimly lit tavern. Then, without protest Rodac strode off, Brace following. Into the dark coolness of a starlit nocte they went, Rodac listing at times but always managing to remain precariously upright. Neither spoke until they left the city and reached a dense stand of trees.

My thanks for your assistance back there, the alien's hands motioned unsteadily, requiring all Brace's powers of concentration to interpret the message, *but I could have easily handled those two.*

"I know that," Brace replied. "But you're too valuable to risk injury in some petty fight. Besides," he drawled, a smile quirking his lips, "partners look out for each other."

The Simian scowled. *The only thing that binds us is money. Remember that, Bellatorian.*

Brace grinned. "That's a crock of barsa dung and you know it."

In his own way, Rodac hid his true feelings just as poorly as Marissa. But then, Brace reminded himself wryly, after several military tours on Arbor, he did know Simians better than most.

He gestured up at the trees. "Will you be safe up there, considering your, er, well-lubricated condition?"

Your concern is heart-warming, Rodac's hands waved, making Brace a little dizzy keeping up with them, *but I'm as at home with heights as you are on the ground.*

With that, the big alien turned and made his unsteady way to a tall tree. Despite his inebriated state, he made the lower branches in one agile leap. Rodac climbed as far as the leafless limbs would bear his weight, then settled into a tight curl in the crook of two stout branches. Soon a sonorous snore drifted down to Brace's ears.

As he made his way back to the tavern, Brace mulled over the events of the past several sols. What had begun as a simple attempt to use Marissa to survive had quickly burgeoned into a complicated, emotion-fraught, commitment-laden undertaking. Now, not only did he have a disturbingly beautiful, man-hating little spitfire to deal with, but a money-grubbing suspicious, and smelly alien as well. What else could go wrong?

A heavy sense of foreboding settled over him. He had to get to Teran. Somehow, someway, Brace sensed that the theft of the Knowing Crystal and Marissa's quest were closely entwined. And only his brother would have the answers.

106

But how, by the five moons, could he convince Marissa to come along? The sudden realization that he even cared if she came with him drew Brace up short. He'd already informed her their former agreement was severed. He didn't *need* to take her with him to Aranea. And yet . . .

With an angry shake of his head, Brace once more strode toward the tavern, no longer quite so certain what he'd do when he once again confronted Marissa.

Marissa paced the confines of the small room, the shouts and bursts of raucous laughter from the tavern below doing little to calm her ragged nerves. What, by all that was sacred, was she to do about Brace Ardane? She *had* to get him to Ferox—that much was clear. But must she now find a way to force him, and if so, how?

She had money aplenty, thanks to the first bag of Repository booty she'd cashed in earlier that sol. Surely a burly male or two could be bribed to drag the treacherous Bellatorian along. And it would certainly eliminate the need to consider his earlier offer—that loathsome suggestion to buy his services by mating with him.

Yet, as revolting as it had first appeared, she was tempted, nonetheless, to take him up on the offer. A perverse part of her wanted to call his bluff and watch him back away, while another secret part hoped he wouldn't. But that was only her foolish heart slipping past the cycles of hardened logic, Marissa reminded herself angrily.

No male would ever want her for herself. She was an outcast. The rejected half of a twin birth. A freak of nature.

He wanted only to enslave her body. And wasn't that exactly why she'd made the decision to join the Sodalitas—because they'd always known the truth about males and had sworn never to allow them that opportunity?

But why not use Ardane as well? Marissa asked herself, struggling past her innate fears to force a more practical bent to her thoughts. For all his underhanded ways, he was a physically attractive male, far more so than most she'd encountered.

And the mating urge, that curse of all Moracans, called stronger every sol, heating Marissa's blood, clouding her mind. Why not experience the act for once in her life? Why not have one nocte of sheer physical pleasure?

She wanted no child from the joining, though Sodalitan law allowed children as the ultimate motive. She'd *never* bear children. But if she were the one to use *him*, and kept her head while he was losing his, she'd be the one in control, not he. There was no submission in that.

Yes, Marissa resolved, her mind made up at last. All this unrequited desire on both their parts was muddying the waters. Better to have the physical release behind them and get on with the quest.

But could she trust Ardane to keep his word, once he'd had her body? In the end, *that* was the true issue, not her loss of maidenhood, nor fear of domination. Males were the ones who had traditionally placed such value upon virginity in yet another of their ploys to control women. That motive, in itself, lessened any worth it might ever have had for Marissa.

But Ardane had already broken his word once. What was to stop him from doing it again? All considerations of the mating urge aside, there was far, far too much at stake for her to fail in her rescue of Candra.

Marissa paused, her mouth twisting in a wry grimace. Indeed, what *would* Ardane do if he knew *all* the reasons for her quest?

Footsteps echoed down the hall, moving closer until they halted outside her door. In a rush of fearful anticipation, Marissa brushed the question aside. An issue of more immediate concern rose to confront her in that instant of decision. She had no choice. She must give Ardane what he asked and take the chance that he'd keep his end of the bargain. But how, by all that was sacred, did one seduce a male?

Recalling the actions of the alley walkers who frequented all towns and cities, Marissa quickly fluffed her hair, pinched her cheeks, and wet her lips. Mating was but a battle of a different sort, with the body as weapon, and the ultimate goal to conquer with pleasure rather than pain.

Pleasure, Marissa repeated to herself. Make Ardane feel pleasure. Drive him mad with desire until he cannot think straight. Then the battle will be won ...

Ever so cautiously, Brace pushed open the door and peered around it, half expecting the dagger to again come hurtling at him. The room was dark, the only light that of the five moons spreading a large circle of illumination on the floor directly inside the window. Marissa stood there, her face in shadow.

"Come in, Ardane," she beckoned softly. "There's still the matter of a quest to be settled."

He stepped into the room and shut the door. "Yes, I've news—"

"Not now."

Marissa strode across the room to stand before him. Her arms lifted to entwine behind his neck and she stretched on tiptoe to press close.

"I've decided to accept your offer."

For the longest moment Brace couldn't breathe, the air trapped in the sudden constriction of his chest. The scent of Marissa, fresh and clean as a rain-washed meadow, filled his nostrils, befuddling his mind. She moved even nearer, flattening the soft mounds of her breasts into his body.

Desire, hot and sudden, tore through Brace like a raging conflagration. Everything narrowed to this moment and the tantalizing woman pressed so close.

With a tormented groan, Brace captured Marissa's lithe young body, pulling her yet tighter to him. His head lowered and his mouth opened hungrily over hers, moving with fierce, wild abandon. He touched his tongue to her lips, coaxing them apart, and was inordinately gratified when they did. His tongue plunged between them in one bold thrust, to entwine with hers in a sweetly primitive dance. Ah, Gods, she tasted so good!

As her quivering lips parted for his probing tongue, a knot of pure sensation exploded in Marissa's belly. She'd been ready for the touch of his body when she'd first approached him, but nothing had prepared her for the riot of emotions his mouth and tongue now worked upon her. She gasped with startled pleasure and pulled back, gazing up into smoldering eyes.

"Ardane," she whispered. "I—"

"Brace. Call me Brace," he coaxed, his voice deep and husky. "We're far past the point of formality."

"Brace, please," Marissa breathed. "I'm not so sure—"

"That this is right?" he finished for her. "I'm not, either, but then again, I'm not so certain I care. I need you, sweet femina. Let me love you."

Before she could reply, Brace covered her mouth with his, moving with fiercely seductive tenderness, shaping and fitting her lips to his. He deepened the kiss with consummate skill until Marissa's body quivered with a pleasure so exquisite it was almost painful. By the Crystal Fires, never had she imagined the mating urge to be so powerful! She felt like tinder consumed in a blazing inferno, with Brace Ardane's powerful body the flame, kindling hers to a rising frenzy.

His hands roved over her, gliding down her torso to clasp her slender waist, then lower to pull her hips more fully into his. He pressed against her belly, his shaft thick and hard. It stirred something deep inside Marissa, something hot, primal. She ground her hips into his and heard him groan, long and low and so very male in his need.

"M-Marissa. Femina, if you only knew what you do to me!"

"Don't talk," she whispered. "Show me. Touch me."

It wasn't her speaking, she thought from some distant corner of her mind as Brace's head lowered to the full swell of her breasts. This was some other woman, wild and wanton, controlled totally by the man before her. She whimpered when his mouth captured her nipple through the fabric of her tunic and suckled it. She clutched his head to her breast, threading her fingers through his dark, shaggy mane, unthinking, uncaring, surrendering . . .

Surrendering!

Fear, like an onrushing surge tide, shot

through her. It couldn't be happening! It couldn't—but it was! All the former, most logical reasons for permitting this act were swept away in the reality of the moment.

She was allowing herself to be shackled to a male, accepting, nay, *begging* for domination—just as eagerly, as mindlessly as the other females of her planet. She who'd been taken into the Sodalitas and taught the ways to avoid that ultimate humiliation, including the surest way of all: to renounce the joining of flesh!

Yet the hot, agonizing pleasure he wrought with his mouth upon her breast, his teeth gently working her nipple, was hard to deny. She wanted him.

The mental anguish swelled to excruciating proportions, until Marissa thought her mind was being torn from her body. She was a coward, a disgrace to her sisters, for she hadn't the strength, the courage to fight past this aching, unbearable heat.

From somewhere deep within a cry rose, spiraling past her constricted throat to find voice in a sob, then another and another. Like waves crashing upon the shore to die in the ebbtide, the force of Marissa's battle pounded through her, a battle she won in her emotional withdrawal, and lost, in the fear that kept her from discovering a new freedom in surrendering her heart.

The tears began to pour, hot and humiliating, from her eyes. Though she tried to turn, to hide them, Brace wouldn't allow it.

"Marissa. Sweet femina. What is it?"

"I-I can't," she wept. "Please ... don't m-make me."

He cradled her face in his two large hands, smoothing away the tears with gentle swipes of his thumbs. "Hush, femina," he soothed. "I won't make you. You know that. I'd never do anything to hurt you."

Brace pulled Marissa to him, gathering her up to carry her to the bed. Tenderly he laid her down and lowered himself beside her, cradling Marissa's tremor-wracked form next to his, fiercely quenching the fires that still raged within his own body. Fires that burned for her, stirring needs that, for a time more, must remain unrequited. As the nocte crept on, through starlit blackness to graying sol rise, Brace remained with her, soothing away her tears, softly murmuring her name.

Marissa opened her tear-swollen eyes to gaze upon a glorious sol. Sun streamed in through the window to puddle in golden brilliance on the floor. An awareness of the city, already awake and bustling, grew with each staccato burst of sound. She moved, arching like some feline in a languorous stretch—and felt a body next to hers. Marissa froze.

Memories of last nocte, of hot desire and fevered caresses, rose to mingle and then clash with the shameful recollection of her tears.

114

She'd never allowed herself such an indulgence since that sol of her banishment. Not even all the times she'd suffered deprivation or injury, not even when she'd learned of Candra's abduction. Yet, last nocte, in the arms of a male no less, they'd flowed with the most disconcerting ease.

Had it happened because she'd pent them up so tightly all these cycles? Or was the cause more insidious, and due to the seductive powers of a male over a female?

Marissa turned toward Brace, determined to confront him and conquer at last the debilitating doubts. He slept on, relaxed and unguarded in his slumber. In spite of her resolve to remain indifferent, Marissa's heart softened.

She lifted a hand to his face and, with a gentle fingertip, examined him. The bruises had all but faded. The swelling had disappeared. His features were once again etched in sharp, striking relief.

There was an arrogant jut to his finely chiseled chin and jaw. His well-shaped lips were full and sensual. A hard, ruthless face to be sure, aggressively virile and, Marissa admitted with a small shiver, outrageously handsome as well.

Why hadn't she noticed that before? Had she been too engrossed with the demands of her quest, or had she managed to deny the disturbing realization until now?

Yet another memory insinuated itself into her mind. Brace, holding her last nocte in the strong embrace of his arms. The warmth of his powerful body, the soothing sound of his voice as he endlessly murmured her name. She'd felt so safe, so comforted—so very wanted.

Fear shuddered through Marissa. Brace Ardane's growing effect upon her was more than she'd ever bargained for, an effect that would surely only increase with time and close contact. After last nocte, she'd be blind as well as stupid not to realize that.

And now there was the added burden of forcing him to come along on the quest. There was no other recourse. When her tears had ended their lovemaking, she had failed to pay his price.

Well, she could always sedate him into submission, Marissa consoled herself. She'd search out those drugs this very morn. In the meanwhile, she would shield her heart against him—until the sol she led him to his doom.

Hot tears once again filled her eyes. Angrily Marissa wiped them away. No more. No more! She rolled off the bed and strode to the window.

The narrow, winding streets and alleyways of the ancient city of Tutela spread out before her, crowded with throngs of people going about their business. Below her, shops, filled to overflowing with exotic wares from all over the Imperium, burst with colorful variety. The trading at each was fierce and heavy.

Tutela, Marissa mused, remembering a girl-hood lesson on the video tutor, was one of the

Imperium's major crossroad cities with its famous trade center and large transport station. A transport station she must soon use, once she'd ascertained Ferox's whereabouts.

Again Marissa turned inward, opening herself to any sound, any stirring—and called to Candra. As before, there was no reply.

Frustration welled within. How, by all that was sacred, was she to track her sister's abductor if Candra refused to help? Did Candra think to protect *her*, by preventing Marissa from finding Ferox? If so, her sister was a fool.

With a sigh, Marissa walked to the bed and shook Brace awake. He cocked open one sleepy eye.

"Get up," she ordered. "We've work to do and the sol's half gone."

Marissa turned and went to pack their bag of supplies. Behind her, she heard Brace rise from the bed and move toward her. She tensed.

"Marissa," he rasped in a sleep-thickened voice, his hands clasping her shoulders. "About last nocte."

She jerked free of his hold and whirled about. "I—I don't want to talk about last nocte. You said you were leaving me, and that's that!"

Brace shook his head. "No, it isn't. I learned some disturbing things last nocte—not only down in the tavern, but up here as well. Before I make any final decisions regarding your quest, we need to take a short detour to Aranea."

Kathleen Morgan

"Aranea?" Marissa's eyes narrowed. "Why this sudden change of heart? Surely our brief interlude last nocte wasn't enough to satisfy you. And it certainly won't ever happen again!"

His gaze dipped to the rounded fullness of her breasts, jutting softly against her sleep-rumpled tunic, then back to her face. Gods, for a fleeting moment when he'd wakened he'd thought last nocte but a dream—sweet, hot, and oh, so thrilling. Thrilling, in the surprising ardor of Marissa's response.

She had stirred him as no other woman had done, with her vulnerability, her courage, her fire. And, as he held Marissa last nocte, Brace had known, with a piercingly sweet insight, that he had to have her.

"Are you so certain of that, femina?" he asked softly. "Do you deny your response to me?"

His heated glance ignited a river of molten excitement that coursed through Marissa's body. Hot color flushed her cheeks.

"No, I don't deny it," she gritted out the admission, "but I meant what I said. It won't happen again!"

"What are you so afraid of, sweet femina? I meant you no harm, only pleasure—for the both of us." Brace took a step toward her. "Let me show you, finish what we began last nocte."

"No!"

Marissa backed away. The fight ebbed from

118

her in one debilitating rush. If he should press his advantage just now...

"No. I can't bear any more. Please, just let it be."

Brace studied her for a long, impassive moment, then sighed. "Have it your way—for the time being. But mark my words, Marissa. This is not settled between us."

"Fine," she agreed nervously. "But, for the time being, there are matters of greater import to deal with. And I ask you again. What made you change your mind?"

"It appears my brother is alive and somehow involved in the recent rescue, then second theft, of the Knowing Crystal. And it seems Ferox is involved as well. That's why we must journey to Aranea to learn more."

"Aranea, the spider planet?" Marissa's brow wrinkled in puzzlement. "Is Ferox to be found there?"

"I don't know. But my brother is, and I must first seek him out."

She shook her head. "Later. There's no time for side trips while my sister's life hangs in the balance."

"And I say we must first seek out Teran. He's sure to have knowledge of Ferox. Listen to reason, Marissa. I do not ask this lightly."

"You do nothing lightly, do you," she stormed, "except when it comes to giving your word? How do I know this isn't just another one of your tricks? Curse you, Brace Ardane, I'm sick of your games!"

"And what are my games compared to yours, Marissa?" he countered, a dark, dangerous glint in his eyes. "Part of that game, though you've yet to share it, includes me, doesn't it? Do you think me so stupid I haven't figured that out yet?

"That's exactly why you'll come with me to Aranea, isn't it?" Brace ground out in sudden, triumphant realization. "Because you need me—and only me—for this precious quest of yours!"

He pulled her to him. "It's true, isn't it, Marissa?"

"You're mad!" she snapped. "I told you before. It's your warrior's skills—"

"Little liar," he cut her off huskily. "You're not very good at lying, either."

Brace motioned toward the bag she'd laid aside. "Get on with your packing. We leave for Aranea within the hora."

She glowered at him for a long moment, then walked back to her bag. She had no choice. If Aranea was where Brace wanted to go, she must follow. But if he asked for one more thing . . .

"And what of your friend Rodac?" Marissa shot over her shoulder. "Where is he?"

Brace grinned in sudden remembrance. "Still sleeping off his Moracan ale in some tree, I'd wager. I'll fetch him while you finish packing. Meet us at the transport station in a half hora."

"We'd do better to leave him behind. I fear your trust in that alien is sadly misplaced."

Brace chuckled. "As yours is in me, sweet femina?"

Marissa quashed the momentary surge of exasperation—and guilt. "Yes, most assuredly, Brace Ardane. Most assuredly."

The transport technician pocketed the transport fee and shoved the power lever forward on the control panel. Multicolored lights flashed on the console. A buzzing pervaded the room as Marissa, Brace, and Rodac faded slowly from view.

The last sight Marissa had was of Brace, one corner of his mouth twisted in a devilish smile. He was baiting her again, she thought, but this time she sensed it was to take her mind off the transport process. Wanly Marissa returned his smile, but it was already too late. Brace was gone.

She followed quickly, her mind whirling chaotically through the dark, sharp coldness of space. Marissa felt splintered, her soul torn from her body. The buzzing softened to an undulating hum, then rose in volume until the pulsations reverberated through her skull. By the Crystal Fires, the pain!

A moment later it was over. They materialized in a transport chamber in the Aranean capital, and quickly departed the station. It was twilight in Araneum. Swathed in dark cloaks, the hoods pulled low to hide their faces,

Brace, Marissa, and Rodac made their stealthy way toward the royal palace where the Queen and, hopefully, Teran, would be found.

The palace was huge. Combined with the extreme care required to evade the guardbots prowling the halls, it was several horas before they discovered the sleeping chambers. They crept into each one until, by process of elimination, they found the Queen's. Two ladies-in-waiting snored loudly in the antechamber. In the cacophony, it was an easy task to slip past them.

Queen Alia slept alone in a huge bed, her breathing the deep slumber of drugs. Her auburn hair was a riotous tumble about her, her beautiful features pale and marred by an ugly bruise on one side of her face. A slender forearm peeked from beneath the covers, a bandage covering the limb from wrist to elbow.

Standing over her, Brace frowned. Where was Teran, her reported lover, and what exactly had happened to injure the Queen? An uneasy presentiment snaked about his heart. Things were fast becoming too complex.

He stifled an impulse to waken the sleeping woman and ask where Teran was. The possibility that this was all some elaborate plot to recapture him must still be considered. Brace signaled his companions out of the room and into the shadowed corridor.

Marissa drew close. "What next? Must we search every closet and corner in this cursed palace before you're finally satisfied? Your brother isn't here!"

"Yes, *every* closet and corner, if that's what it takes," he whispered back. "I know he's here. I can feel it."

"So, now you're psychic as well," Marissa grumbled, but allowed Brace to take her arm and lead her down the hall.

The nocte had pinkened to sol rise before they finally found Teran, in a book-lined library, slumped over an open volume and sound asleep. Brace stood for the longest time gazing down at his brother.

At the loving expression on his face, tears once again stung Marissa's eyes. She quickly blinked them back. The visible manifestation of the depth of Brace's love moved her as no realization of his terrible sacrifice the past two cycles ever had. And at that moment she knew, though he uttered not a word, that Brace felt it had all been worth it.

Would she feel the same once Candra was safe again? Would the terrible price she'd ultimately pay be found worth it at that moment of their reunion? It had to. It just had to.

Brace moved to his brother's side and hesitantly touched his shoulder. "Teran," he rasped. "Wake up."

Teran mumbled something unintelligible, then lifted his head to slowly take in the trio standing there. They gazed back silently.

Joy flared in Teran's gray eyes. A broad smile spread across his handsome, bearded face—a face several cycles older than Brace's but so reassuringly similar. Marissa couldn't help but smile in return.

"Brace," Teran whispered, his gaze riveted on the tall man standing beside him. "Is it really you, little brother?"

"Yes, Teran. It is I."

With a low cry, Teran was out of his chair and clasping Brace to him. "Thank the Crystal you're well! I tried to find you, but they said you'd escaped. I didn't know where to look after that."

"Well, I dared not advertise my whereabouts," Brace muttered dryly. "Uncle Falkan had half of Bellator out looking for me."

"That's all over, Brace. You're a free man."

Brace gave a bitter laugh. "Somehow even that doesn't make things right. I don't know if I can ever forgive him for what he did to us." He paused. "And Vates. How is Vates?"

A bleak look flared in Teran's eyes. "Our old teacher died on Carcer."

"By the five moons!" Scorching anger emanated from every pore of Brace's body. "Yet another evil deed to thank the King for! Curse his narrow-minded, righteous old hide!"

"The loss of the Knowing Crystal has twisted us all, in one way or another."

"Not *all* of us," Brace snapped savagely. "There was no wiser, nor kinder, nor gentler man than Vates. He was our friend and father—the only one we ever truly knew. He didn't deserve to die on Carcer!"

Teran sighed. "No, he didn't and I mourn him still. But he felt the sacrifice was worth it, in this battle to regain the hearts and minds of all the people. And that battle is now ours."

He eyed Brace closely. "Trust me. The healing will come. It took a time for me to make peace with my feelings for Uncle Falkan, but I finally understand—and forgive. But we can talk about that later." Teran cuffed Brace affectionately, on the side of the head. "For now, little brother, it's enough we're together."

Brace gave a shaky laugh, the tension ebbing in a great, body-draining rush. He returned the playful gesture.

The depth of emotion and shared history behind their actions reminded Marissa of the special relationship she'd once had with Candra. She turned away, once more feeling the outcast.

"Marissa."

She hesitated, schooling her features to impassivity, then turned to face him. The two men had parted and Brace stood there, his hand outstretched. Deep in his dark brown eyes burned a gentle understanding.

Marissa raised her hand and accepted his. He smiled and pulled her to stand before his brother.

"Teran, this is Marissa Laomede, my rescuer and one of my partners." Brace turned to Marissa. "And this is my brother, Lord Teran Ardane, of the Royal House Ardane of the planet Bellator."

Marissa inclined her head. "I am honored to meet you, my lord."

Teran glanced from one to the other, and a dark brow quirked in amusement. "I am honored, and grateful as well, Domina, for what you have done for my brother."

His gaze moved to the Simian who stood nearby, waiting patiently. "And who is this?"

"My other partner. He is Rodac, from the planet Arbor." Brace chuckled. "He, too, was instrumental in my escape from prison, though Marissa might have other thoughts as to his true usefulness."

"I am honored and grateful as well to you then, Rodac," Teran said, offering his hand.

The alien eyed the bearded Bellatorian for a brief moment, then moved closer to clasp arm to arm in the traditional Imperial greeting. Teran's nostrils flared at the rank scent that engulfed him, but his smile never wavered. Releasing his grip, he motioned for them all to sit at the table while he brought a flask and cups from a nearby sideboard.

"Here, let us drink to your two friends and your safe return," he said, pouring out four cups of uva wine. "And then we'll talk, for I sense there's more to your visit than filial affection." Teran raised his cup. "To the Knowing Crystal and its safe return. And to the Imperium, that has yet to fully comprehend the Crystal's true power."

Brace frowned, then emptied the contents of his cup.

Marissa eyed the two men, then quickly swallowed her own wine. A frisson of uneasiness shivered through her. More and more of late she kept hearing of that mythical Knowing Crystal. And she didn't like how it seemed to be insinuating itself into her quest. It complicated things.

"What happened here?" Brace demanded as he set down his cup. "I've heard tales you found the Knowing Crystal and now Ferox has it once more. And your Queen looks like she's been through a terrible battle."

"You've seen Alia then, eh? And when was that?"

Brace flushed. "We first thought to find you with her—in her sleeping chamber."

Teran smiled. "Normally that would be true, but I couldn't seem to get to sleep this nocte. The events of the past sols have been eating at me." He chuckled grimly. "It's true enough, the tales of Alia's and my rescue of the Knowing Crystal. We were painfully naïve, though, imagining that our only problems lay in restoring the Crystal's reign over the Imperium."

Anger tightened his features. "I was gone on a mission to Agrica when Ferox returned. He destroyed the Crystal's pedestal of power in an attempt to steal the stone. Alia must have sensed the danger to the Crystal, for she arrived just as the pedestal exploded. The impact nearly killed her.

"Ferox left her lying there, hurt and bleeding," Teran muttered, "and escaped with the stone."

"But Queen Alia lives," Brace said.

"Yes, but Ferox still has the Knowing Crystal. And I cannot leave Alia until I'm certain she's fully recovered. She carries our child."

"She is your mate, then?"

"In all but ceremony. We were to be life-mated a few sols ago." Teran paused to eye Brace intently. "But enough of Alia's and my personal problems. You spoke of Marissa and Rodac as your partners. Partners in what?"

Brace glanced at Marissa. "Tell him."

She met Teran's scrutiny. "Ferox abducted my sister."

Gray eyes narrowed. "And what is so special about your sister for Ferox to seek her out?"

"We've yet to fathom that ourselves," Brace interjected, "save for the fact she's a Traveler."

"A Traveler?" Teran frowned. "So, Ferox has the Knowing Crystal and a Traveler. A most unsettling combination. I don't like it. Don't like it at all."

He gestured toward the ancient volume still lying open on the table. "In the sols since Alia's injury I've had time to explore this library. There are some very old, and disturbing, books here. Books long unread, books that speak of the Crystal's origins—and more of its powers."

Teran rose and strode over to gaze down at the hearth fire, his shoulders tense with some strong emotion. "The Knowing Crystal has always been revered for its benign aid to the

Imperium, for fostering peace and prosperity. And the chaos into which all planets of the Imperium were cast when the Crystal was first stolen those hundreds of cycles ago was blamed solely upon its loss."

He wheeled around to face them, his eyes tormented and bright. "But I'm not so sure the Crystal was ever benign, not after what I've discovered in those books, not after thinking things through. If what I suspect is true, everything we've believed all these cycles was nothing more than a cruel hoax!"

Chapter Six

"It's time we spoke of your own special Crystal powers," Teran began later that sol after his brother had taken several horas of sleep.

Brace shot him a sharp glance as they walked through the autumn-colored palace gardens. "Crystal powers? What, by the five moons, are you talking about?"

Teran paused to wave at Alia, recuperating in the fresh air and sunshine up on her bedchamber balcony, before replying. "In the sols of the Knowing Crystal's creation, certain bloodlines were genetically manipulated to commune with and control the stone. Alia's family has always been known for those powers—the Certares were the original Crystal Masters on Aranea. And much later House Ardane's bloodlines, thanks to a rebellious great-grand-aunt of Alia's who followed her heart rather than the law, were also imbued with those same powers."

Brace frowned. "Then why, if all our family are Crystal Masters, haven't I ever heard of it?"

"I'm not so certain all are Crystal Masters. It seems that only some of the more inbred

Ardanes possess the intensity of powers to commune." Teran paused. "And, in answer to why you haven't heard of the powers before, apparently the knowledge of the gift was buried all these past cycles of chaos after the Knowing Crystal's loss—and not discovered again until I joined Alia to rescue the stone. The Crystal and its Crystal Masters have a longer and more complex history than we ever imagined."

"I'd always thought its origins were relatively simple," Brace said. "Wasn't it commissioned by an ancient Aranean king, to serve the Imperium as a resource unit in the development of judicial codes? What's so complex about that?"

"Nothing. The problem is how complex and dangerous the Knowing Crystal has become after all these cycles, worming its way into our lives until most are now all but incapable of thinking on their own."

Teran halted, turning to face his brother. Deep concern furrowed his brow. "And the danger only grows worse. I've discovered the Crystal gains its power from sentient beings— feeding on their emotions."

Brace's gaze narrowed. "Go on."

"When our emotions are calm and passive," Teran explained, "the Knowing Crystal functions in a benign and helpful way. But when the feelings fueling it are intensely strong— whether negative or positive—the stone can become quite aggressive and even go awry.

131

Strong emotions also seem to speed up its evolutionary process. Over the cycles, in the battle for its possession, the Crystal has gradually developed self-awareness, an ability which ultimately led to the need to protect itself by further expanding its powers."

Brace pondered that for a few secundae. "It all falls into place now," he said, "In the process of expanding its powers, the Knowing Crystal encouraged the Imperium to abdicate its moral judgments and decision-making abilities. After that, the weakening of society was inevitable."

His mouth tightened into a grim line. "And it's a lot easier to control weakness than strength."

Teran nodded. "Exactly. Man, once the master, is now becoming the slave. Yet perhaps the greatest threat is that the Knowing Crystal is still evolving and no one knows exactly where that process will lead."

"Well, it seems obvious to me where the process will lead," Brace muttered. "The Crystal intends to gain total control—by taking over our minds. It's a simple matter of self-preservation, with a limitless source of power—human emotions—as the prize."

"Perhaps, little brother. Just perhaps." Teran indicated they should resume their walk. "One way or another, I'm convinced we're gradually losing control of the Knowing Crystal."

"Your research appears depressingly thorough," Brace observed. "Has it also revealed how we're to combat this growing menace?"

His brother sighed. "From all I've read, only a Crystal Master has any chance against the Knowing Crystal."

"At the rate the stone is evolving, how long will that ability last?"

"I don't know."

"Teran, this doesn't bode well." Brace paused, then inhaled a resolute breath. "You're going to need all the help you can get in the battle to come. Teach me to be a Crystal Master."

A sense of relief filled Teran. He motioned to a stone bench warmed by the slowly fading sun. In the horas while Brace had slept, Teran had thought long and hard about what part his brother would play in the drama unfolding before them—and how to get him to commit to such a monumental and dangerous task. After what Brace had suffered in the past two cycles, Teran wouldn't have blamed him if he'd turned his back and walked away from what lay ahead.

But Brace was as much an Ardane as he, his fierce, familial pride tempered by the deep sense of honor imbued by their old teacher, Vates. In times such as these, the combination of such attributes allowed for few options. No, Teran thought with a grim sense of foreboding, he needn't fear that Brace would run from what lay ahead. He could depend upon his brother—to the very forfeiture of his life.

"The main talent of a Crystal Master is the ability to attune one's mental wavelength to the Knowing Crystal," Teran began as he sat down beside Brace, "and influence it to do one's bidding."

"No small talent, if the stone's powers have become even half what the tales would have them be," Brace muttered.

"Yes," his brother agreed, "and what better reason for Ferox to so avidly covet the Crystal?"

"The man is a scourge upon the Imperium! It's time he's permanently removed."

"I had the chance to kill him once," Teran said, a faraway look in eyes.

"But you didn't."

"No, I didn't. It would have negated my Crystal powers." Teran turned to Brace. "Once your powers come to fruition, you can never kill again without destroying forever your ability to commune with the Knowing Crystal. The intense emotional effort required to take a life severs the psychic link between a Crystal Master and the stone. Remember that, little brother."

Brace gave a wry laugh. "Ah, that certainly simplifies things! I can't kill without losing my powers, yet I'm committed to a quest that requires Ferox's death."

"And do you imagine your Crystal powers aren't tied to the rescue of Marissa's sister?" Teran inquired calmly. "Think about it, Brace. There's a sinister sequence to everything Ferox has done of late. First, he regains possession of the Crystal, then abducts Marissa's sister. Next, Marissa seeks you out, of all the men in the entire Imperium, to enlist your aid. You, who have Crystal powers—unrecognized, but powers nonetheless. What Ferox wouldn't give to get his hands on an untutored Crystal Master and bend him to his will! Think of it—total control of the Imperium through the minds of the people!"

A muscle jumped in Brace's jaw. The unvoiced doubts that had plagued him since he'd first realized Marissa's unique need for his services formed in his throat. But to put words to his worst fears . . .

He forced the question through gritted teeth. "Are you implying Marissa is in league with Ferox?"

Teran saw the pain flare in his brother's eyes. They're already bound by more than a quest, he thought. Just as he and Alia had been . . .

He shrugged. "She may unwittingly be in league with him, but I'm certain that, one way or another, your participation fulfills Ferox's ultimate goal—to possess not only the Knowing Crystal but a Crystal Master as well."

"And Candra?"

"She may be just a pawn to lure you to him, or her own skills may also be integral to his master plan."

"Then we must beat him at his own game!"

Teran smiled grimly. "I don't have all the answers, little brother. For the time being, I

135

fear there's little we can do except teach you of the Crystal. The rest will depend upon Ferox."

"Gods!" Brace leaped to his feet to pace restlessly, his fists clenched at his side. "After two cycles in prison, do you know how sick to death I am of being at another's beck and call? Isn't it enough I've got my hands full with a femina who may intend to betray me, not to mention a Simian who's constantly at odds with her? Curse it! Why did I allow myself to be drawn into this insane quest?"

"Somehow I doubt there's ever been any choice," Teran replied. "Besides, it's past time we discovered the real truths behind the Knowing Crystal and its ultimate purpose in the Imperium. We dare not tarry much longer if we're to have any hope of stopping it."

Brace gave a rueful laugh. "Do you realize what you're saying? It's not enough to take on Ferox, but we must also battle some indestructible, omnipotent computer unit as well!"

"Nothing created by man can be indestructible or omnipotent," his brother pointed out, a thoughtful expression darkening his face. "There has to be a way to destroy it, if need be. Besides, now that Alia's recovering, I plan to accompany you on your quest." He grinned. "With two of us against it, the Knowing Crystal won't have a chance."

"For a Crystal Master, you suddenly seem bent on the stone's destruction."

Teran eyed him. "What do you think, after

all I've told you? Has the Knowing Crystal *ever* been our friend?''

"You toy with me, Teran. I don't know what to think anymore.''

His brother climbed to his feet. "Well, no matter what the stone is, the only known way to control it is through Crystal powers. You must learn to commune with it, Brace. It's our only hope.''

He motioned Brace to follow him. "Come, there are books I would share with you and the time for your training grows short. The Crystal calls you even now.''

Puzzlement twisted the younger man's face. "What are you talking about? I hear nothing.''

Teran sighed. "No, you wouldn't yet. You must first be sensitized to the Crystal's call. And it's past time we began.''

He strode off back toward the palace, leaving his brother to stand there in rising frustration. What, by the five moons, was happening to him? Brace wondered. The quest. The Crystal calling. Ferox's master plan. The danger to the Imperium.

It was more than he could fathom—or ever wished to. And he definitely didn't like the growing sense that he was once again losing control of his own fate. Didn't like it at all. With an angry curse, Brace headed after Teran.

Marissa woke a little after mid sol. A maid-servant waiting in the antechamber was immediately at her side. The woman offered

Marissa a lustrous green dressing gown to cover her nakedness, then escorted her to the bathing room where a warm mineral bath had been readied. With a contented sigh, Marissa slid into the bubbling water, luxuriating in the exquisite sensations. The servant applied a floral-scented soap to Marissa's hair and began to scrub it gently.

It was so good to be pampered, to have her every need seen to, Marissa thought. Her life would have been very similar to this if she'd never been cast out. Instead, it was filled with hardship and deprivation. And the quest that loomed before her had suddenly assumed even greater consequence than before.

Her thoughts drifted back to sol rise when they'd found Brace's brother. The Knowing Crystal stolen, Queen Alia nearly killed, and their quest now of Imperium magnitude. An eerie premonition shivered down Marissa's spine. Somehow, someway, this was all inextricably linked with the reason Ferox wanted Brace.

Marissa had always wondered why Ferox had specifically asked for Brace Ardane in exchange for Candra. In the past, she'd brushed it off as some personal vendetta. But now there appeared to be a more sinister, wide-ranging purpose. And she was as much a pawn as Brace and Candra.

The consideration angered her. No one, and especially no male, was going to manipulate her life! The sooner she learned more of Ferox's motives in this whole sordid mess, the sooner she could devise a plan to circumvent him.

Suddenly the maidservant's ministrations seemed too slow and irritating. Marissa tolerated her bath until her hair was washed and rinsed, then motioned the woman away.

"Please prepare my clothes while I finish bathing," she requested. "Then I'd like to meet with Lord Ardane and his brother."

"The two lords asked not to be disturbed," the woman replied. "Our Queen, though, has requested your presence as soon as you're ready."

Frustration filled Marissa, then she quashed it. There'd be time enough later to speak with Teran and Brace, and Queen Alia was as good a source of information as any.

She nodded. "Then please help me prepare for the Queen."

Marissa paused. Her warrior's garb was pretty shabby apparel for an audience with royalty. She glanced up at the maidservant as she hurriedly scrubbed herself clean. The woman was dressed in a simple gown of pale yellow.

"Would it be possible to borrow a garment from you?" Marissa began. "I wouldn't care to go before your Queen in my own poor clothes."

The woman smiled. "There's an ample selection of fine apparel in the large closet in your room. And once you're dressed, I'll prepare your hair." She studied Marissa for a moment. "The bright blue gown, with matching flowers in your hair, would be perfect. It would bring out those striking eyes of yours."

Marissa rose from the bath. "The gown sounds fine, but absolutely no flowers. I'm not a frivolous girl skipping through a garden, intent on pleasing some male. I just want to appear before your Queen with some semblance of dignity."

"As you wish, my lady." The servant wrapped Marissa in a large, warmed towel as she stepped from the bath.

A half hora later, garbed in the most sensuous-feeling gown she'd ever worn, Marissa was ushered into the Queen's bedchamber. She glanced down at herself, inordinately pleased with her appearance. The bright blue gown shimmered about her, flowing loosely from her shoulders to expose a tantalizing glimpse of cleavage and a long expanse of slender arms through the wide slit in the full, narrow-cuffed sleeves. Aside from the thin, jewel-encrusted chain belted about her trim waist, the gown was simple, elegant—and made Marissa feel surprisingly beautiful.

She shook the uncharacteristic emotion aside and forced her attention back to the Queen of Aranea. Alia was propped up in bed on several large pillows. She smiled and waved Marissa to a plump-cushioned chair set beside the bed.

"Welcome, Marissa," the Queen said. "Come, sit beside me and we will talk."

Marissa walked over to stand beside the

chair and bowed. "I'm honored to meet you, my lady."

"Alia. Please, call me Alia," the auburn-haired woman replied. She extended a slender hand in greeting, an ornately jeweled ring of sovereignty sparkling on her middle finger.

Marissa accepted Alia's hand, squeezing it briefly before releasing it.

"There is much that binds us, I think, besides the two important men in our lives. I'd like to be friends." Alia motioned to the chair. "There's no need for formality. Sit, Marissa, and be comfortable."

Marissa studied Alia as she lowered herself into the chair. The Queen was beautiful, with pale ivory skin, rich honey brown eyes, and luxuriantly curling flame-dark hair. She was also several years younger than Marissa.

The look in her eyes, though, was just as steady, just as sure as the one Marissa bestowed upon her. *She, too, has been tempered in the forge of life,* Marissa realized with surprise. *She, too, has known hardship and danger.* And, similar coloring aside, for some inexplicable reason the Queen reminded her of her best friend, Raina.

Respect and a growing sense of kinship welled in Marissa's breast. Perhaps they could indeed be friends.

"What is it you would know?" she began. "I'd be pleased to tell you what I can, but my own experiences are probably mundane in comparison to your rescue of the Knowing Crystal."

A smile of remembrance warmed Alia's eyes. "I found more than the Crystal on that quest. I discovered myself and my one true love. Things I think you, too, will find on yours.

"Strange, isn't it," she mused, suddenly pensive, "that each quest for the Crystal seems to require both a man and a woman—and the strength of their love—to have any hope of success. There's some wonderful mystery to it all, but it's truth, nonetheless. Keep that in mind, Marissa, when things seem darkest."

Marissa frowned. "Brace and I are partners and nothing more. I'm a Sodalitas and despise males. I would certainly never allow myself to love one. Especially one such as Brace Ardane!"

"Strong feelings, even hatred, can be but a mask for deeper emotions. And, no matter what you say, I still think you were predestined to join." Alia paused. "It is good that you are brave and resourceful. Ferox's evil is not a simple thing. He's a very complex, seductive man, with motives that go beyond the mere desire for power."

Her eyes clouded with memories. "There's more than a simple schoolboys' rivalry between Ferox and Teran. Yet, though I well know the source of Teran's enmity for Ferox, I've never truly understood Ferox's hatred for Teran. It's so . . . so bone-deep and soul-rotting.

And there's something disturbingly familiar..."

With a tiny shudder, Alia refocused her attention on Marissa. "Well, be that as it may, Brace will need a woman like you at his side for what lies ahead."

"First Lord Ardane, now you!" Marissa burst out in spite of herself. "Ah, lady, I grow so weary of these cryptic statements, as well as of everyone wanting to involve themselves in my quest."

"It has never been just your quest, Marissa." Alia smiled. "And that frightens you, doesn't it?"

Marissa couldn't quite meet Alia's gaze. "I— I don't know what you're talking about. If everyone would just keep out of it..."

"Teran has told me that Ferox has your sister as well as the Knowing Crystal. We can assume Ferox wants Brace, who possesses the powers to be a Crystal Master, as well. Think about it, Marissa. Is this quest really so simple, or just yours anymore?"

Wide, blue-green eyes swung back to Alia. "What do you mean Brace possesses powers to be a Crystal Master? Nothing was ever mentioned about that."

"Why would one brother possess such powers and not the other? It's passed by blood, not talent."

"By all that is sacred!" Marissa lowered her face to hide it in her hands. "I just want my sister back. That's all. Why must everything be so complicated? I curse the day I met Brace Ardane!"

"What are you afraid of, Marissa?" Alia prodded softly.

"Not the dangers, if that's what you're implying," Marissa replied hoarsely, lifting her head to glare at Alia. "It's just...everything else."

"You mean Brace."

"Yes. I mean no!" Frustration twisted Marissa's face. "Oh, I don't know what I mean! I'm a warrior. I've faced hardship and danger, yet nothing, *nothing* I've ever experienced has frightened me like *he* has! I want to run, turn from him before it's too late, but I can't. I *need* him to rescue Candra. There is no other who can do it!"

"Let me help you, Marissa," Alia soothed, leaning forward to touch her arm. "I, too, once feared my feelings for Teran. I, too, had to fight past the doubts and fears to find my true self— in loving him. Let me help you sort through your feelings for Brace."

"How do you know so much about what's between Brace and me?" Marissa asked suspiciously. "Did the Crystal tell you?"

"No." Alia smiled. "Perhaps it's just because I've been through it myself. Perhaps it's just because fate frequently calls two kindred souls together." She shrugged. "Do the reasons really matter?"

For a fleeting moment indecision wavered in Marissa's eyes, then a hard, shuttered look descended. "My feelings for Brace Ardane aren't the issue here. The rescue of my sister is. The Knowing Crystal is not my quest. Please, lady, let's talk of Candra, or talk of nothing."

Alia eyed her for several secundae, then sighed. "As you wish, Marissa. Your heart isn't yet ready for other things. But hear me, and hear me well. You'll be forced to face your feelings for Brace sooner or later. The quest has no hope of success if you don't."

"Concentrate, Brace. Clear your mind of all thoughts, all questions, and trust. Trust!"

From a distant place Brace heard Teran's voice, deep and intense, urging, encouraging. He inhaled a shuddering breath and willed himself to relax. Sweat beaded his brow and his muscles trembled with weariness, but he struggled on.

They'd been at this for over three horas. The first hora had been spent in the rudiments of Crystal power and how to achieve union. Those lessons had been difficult enough, but the practice itself had been grueling.

To unlearn what you had once learned, to empty yourself and take nothing into those hidden, uncharted recesses of your being and patiently wait to be filled by some unknown entity, was a terrifying, nerve-wracking experience. It was also too submissive for Brace's proud spirit.

"You're fighting it again," Teran's dispassionate voice once more intruded. "Trust; submit. Call to the Crystal; then wait."

Frustration welled in Brace's heart. Teran didn't understand. As much as both desired it, there wasn't a trace of Crystal powers in him—his brother saw only what he wanted. There was no point in going on. It was hopeless!

"Relax, little brother. Do it for me, for the Imperium."

With a deep inward sigh Brace tried again. Perhaps it was the utter exhaustion, but this time the resistance ebbed out of him. Peace flowed in to fill the void, pervading Brace with warmth and joy. And suddenly the deep silence was no more.

A sound, faint yet lovely, drifted through his mind. The sensation was so fleeting that Brace wondered if he hadn't imagined it. Then it came again, this time accompanied by a feeble glimmer of light. Brace concentrated all his strength on remaining open and pliant. Fresh sweat beaded his brow to trickle down the sides of his face.

The light grew, found substance. The Knowing Crystal! Wild, fierce elation flooded Brace. The Knowing Crystal!

"Yes, little brother," Teran said. "Now go. Join with it. Commune."

For a brief moment Brace hesitated. Commune? Join? The utter trust of such an act gave him pause. What if it consumed him, took over his mind? He couldn't . . . he just couldn't.

"Come, little brother. I'll go with you. There's no danger for a Crystal Master."

In one great leap of faith Brace's mind joined with Teran's, hurtling past the boundaries of conscious control toward a blinding light. Hurtling, spinning, falling—

A loud, discordant sound shot through his brain, finding voice in sharp, imperative words. *Not Teran*, it said. *His time is over. I want you, Brace. Only you . . .*

Both men broke contact simultaneously. Their eyes met in stunned surprise. Wracking tremors shook Bracc's body and his breath came in ragged gasps. Teran squatted before him and gripped his arms.

"It's enough for one sol, little brother," he said, struggling with his own shock at what had just happened. "The morrow's soon enough to try again."

"Wh-what did the Crystal mean?" Brace rasped. "Why only me? I—l don't understand."

"I don't either, but there's time later to ponder it all. In the meanwhile, let's get you to your bedchamber. You look exhausted."

Brace allowed Teran to pull him to his feet. "Yes, I am."

Slowly the two men made their way down the long corridor to Brace's room. Once inside, Brace collapsed across the bed. Teran stood beside him for a long time, concern furrowing his handsome face.

There was something amiss here, he

147

thought. The Knowing Crystal had never refused to commune with him before. Had his powers diminished, or could the stone only commune with one of them at a time? But that wasn't possible. He and Alia had communed jointly several times in the past and never experienced any difficulty. What made this instance so different? What was the Knowing Crystal trying to do?

Teran stared for a time longer at the form of his brother, sprawled in boneless exhaustion upon the bed. Uneasiness snaked through him. Brace and Marissa's quest was rapidly becoming one of unsettling difficulty and dire dangers. And Brace, a fledgling Crystal Master, was hurtling toward it all—virtually unprepared for what lay ahead.

The room was dark save for the soft, soothing glow that bathed Brace's face. He awoke to bright light and a sweet, melodious sound emanating from the brilliant stone hovering before him. Brace smiled dreamily.

He reached toward the stone, needing to join, when another sound intruded. It was a masculine voice, low, familiar, and filled with a tormented anguish.

Brace, it moaned. *Beware. Beware.*

Confused, Brace jerked back his hand. Who was it, and what was he warning against? The Knowing Crystal?

But that couldn't be—the Knowing Crystal was a Crystal Master's friend.

Or was it?

The mournful voice rose in volume, moaning and pleading. *Beware. Beware.*

The Crystal's light sharpened. The stone gleamed oddly, growing in size. Its once pleasant voice hummed irritatingly, turning louder, discordant.

Fear shot through Brace. The Crystal. It was turning on him!

He wheeled about and fled, pursued by the flashing stone—and by the loud, mournful voice. Down dark, endless corridors he ran, the terror rising, his heart slamming within his chest. And still they pursued him.

The stone grew closer, the voice's wailing louder. Mindless panic filled him. Was there no escape? No way to evade the horror that threatened to consume him?

His breath came shorter now. He couldn't go on. It was over. Over . . .

Brace stumbled, fell. He clawed wildly, grasping for something, anything, to pull himself back out of the yawning pit, but it was too late. He was going mad!

A cry of stark, nameless terror rose to his lips. He screamed, again and again, then tumbled downward into a maelstrom of blinding light and deafening sound.

"Brace? Brace, wake up!"

Through the swirling tumult, Brace heard a voice. It was soft but nonetheless commanding, drawing him from the madness of his dreams. He struggled upward, out of the fetid, smothering mists.

The sweet voice came louder now. A sweet, gentle, loving voice ...

"Curse you, Ardane! Wake up before I slap your eyes open!"

Once again Marissa shook Brace by the shoulders. Cold fear gripped her heart. By the Crystal Fires, would he never wake up? What vision held him so tightly, so horribly, that his frightened voice had carried through the walls of his room to hers next door?

His rich brown eyes opened slowly, meeting hers. For a moment confusion clouded his gaze, then his eyes focused.

"F-femina?" The word was choked out through a constricted throat. "Wh-what's wrong? What are you doing here?"

Relief flooded her. Marissa leaned back.

"You were dreaming and your shouts would have soon wakened the whole palace. I thought to slip in and gag you to silence." She moved to scoot off the bed.

Brace levered himself to one elbow. His hand stayed her.

"Don't go. Please."

Her gaze narrowed. She'd never seen him quite like this, sweating, shaking, with a haunted, wide-eyed look. And that anguished need that threaded his voice ...

She should leave him—and quickly—but something stopped her. An instinct born of time immemorial flooded Marissa. Brace

150

needed her physical presence to soothe away the dream terrors, a need she could well understand.

With a sigh, she gathered Brace to her. His dark head found its place upon her breast, his body, a comforting haven within her arms. He groaned and moved yet closer.

They sat there for a time, Marissa stroking his hair, until the last of his wracking tremors eased. Then she moved, attempting to slip away. He gripped her tighter.

"Brace," Marissa murmured. "It's time I was going. We both need our rest."

"You smell so good," he rasped. "So fresh, so clean . . . so female."

Uneasiness curled within Marissa. "Brace, let me go."

He gazed up at her, his glance suddenly dark and smoldering. "What are you afraid of, femina? There's nothing wrong with holding each other, enjoying the closeness of our bodies. And *you* came to me, took me into *your* arms."

Marissa twisted free. "You always find some way to place a lustful connotation on everything I do, don't you? Even to the simple kindness of comforting your dream terrors. You sicken me!"

Brace grabbed Marissa before she could get away, wrestling her down to the bed. For a long moment he leaned over her, fighting to pin her hands above her head. Finally Marissa stilled and glared defiantly up at him. Beneath the thin veneer of anger, however, Brace saw her uncertainty—and fear.

"Marissa," he whispered thickly, "I meant no offense. I only tried to point out the innocent pleasure there is in holding each other. And the fact that you must feel something, to come to me and offer comfort. It wasn't an act of a femina who loathed me."

She averted her eyes. "You are a valuable asset."

A callused hand captured her chin, guiding her eyes back to his. Reluctantly Marissa met his gaze.

"If I kissed you now, I'd wager I'd prove those last words wrong."

She stiffened. "Don't even think it."

His glance lowered to her lips. "You have the most beguiling mouth. Full, and red, and soft as the petals of an arosa flower. And when I kiss you deeply, you taste like—"

"Don't!"

He quirked a dark brow. "Don't what, Marissa? Are you afraid to hear what you do to me? Afraid it will stir those same feelings in you? And, worse still, what those feelings might lead to?"

His hot glance moved over her, slowly, thoroughly, igniting a feverish heat wherever it went. Marissa swallowed hard as his gaze came to rest on what her parted bedrobe revealed.

The full mounds of her breasts were half exposed, the vee of the open garment plunging low to her belly before the cloth finally joined again. Marissa cursed her stupidity in not securely belting her bedrobe before leaving her room. But there'd been no time when Brace's cries had called her.

Now the slightest movement might expose her completely. The realization sent a tremor of excitement through Marissa. Another move and she'd reveal her nakedness to his hot, hungry gaze, her body to his mind-numbing, marauding mouth . . .

Marissa's lids lowered and she felt the desire engulf her. She wanted him. Oh, how she wanted him!

His hand released her chin to trace a searing path down her neck and chest until it reached the satin valley between her breasts. With slow, deliberate strokes, Brace's finger outlined the firm flesh, slipping beneath the cloth to ease the robe off first one breast, then the other. Marissa shivered as the cool air washed over her, tightening her nipples to hard little nubs.

Brace smiled and lowered his head, his tongue lightly laving one pouty rose tip before taking it into his mouth. Marissa gasped as he began to suckle it. Unconsciously she writhed beneath Brace, one thigh brushing his groin.

She tensed at the touch of him, at the thick shaft straining his breeches. Reality flooded back with a frightful, piercing clarity. If she didn't stop this he'd take her. Take her, and she'd willingly, nay, eagerly, let him.

Confusion whirled through Marissa. *Should* she let him?

"B-Brace," she moaned. "Please. Oh, please..."

Were those indeed her words, her voice groaning out a need she could barely admit even to herself? Begging him, like some pitiful, weak-spirited woman?

She was a Sodalitas, a warrior. She should demand her release and, if he refused, fight him for it. Anything but lie here so passively, melting at the very sight of him and the image of what he intended to do to her.

But she hadn't the strength save to whimper piteously in his arms. "Don't. Please don't, Brace."

He released her and leaned back on his haunches.

"What are you so afraid of?" Brace demanded in a savage whisper. "Your feelings?"

Marissa clutched her bedrobe shut, then violently shook her head. "No! I'm just afraid what you'll do to me!"

"Little liar. When will you face the truth?"

She propped herself up and glared at him. "The truth is nothing more than I don't *want* to feel anything for you. Why won't you just leave me alone?"

"And I say you don't know what you want, except to drive me mad!".

Brace climbed from the bed to tower over her. "You want me, Marissa," he growled.

"Why do you fight it so? I won't hurt you. I'll go slow, be gentle with you. Your needs matter as much as mine."

At the raw emotion in his voice, something softened in Marissa. He hurt, was as tormented and confused as she. Suddenly her own desires didn't matter anymore. All she wanted was to comfort him, to make him happy.

"Yes, Brace," she breathed on an agonized whisper, "I do want you. But this is all happening too fast. I—I need more time. Will you give it to me?"

A beautiful smile spread across his face and the anger eased from his big body. "All the time you need, sweet femina."

Silence laden with unspoken feelings settled over them. Finally Brace could stand it no longer.

"Come." He offered his hand.

"Where are we going?"

"I haven't eaten since last nocte and I'm starving. Come with me to the kitchen."

For an instant Marissa hesitated, then accepted his hand. He led her out of the room and into the chill, darkened corridor, away from the heated emotions of the past few moments.

There were still decisions to be made, frightening decisions. Marissa admitted that at last. But she could not make them just now, and not alone. However much she might protest or

155

pretend it was not so, she was joined with the man beside her. Joined not just by the hand she now clung to, but heart-to-heart. Joined as inextricably as their fates had always been.

Chapter Seven

Marissa watched Brace for a time, marveling at the amount of food he was capable of consuming. After half a roast fowl, a small loaf of bread, and a large slab of domare steak she'd finally had enough. She rose from the table and strode across the kitchen to the stasis field, an electronic system of preserving food by maintaining its static balance.

He grinned at her as she returned to the table. "You must be getting used to my carnivorous habits. You don't look quite so green this time."

Her mouth twisted wryly. "Amazing what one can learn to endure, isn't it?"

She shoved a bowl of fresh berries and another of sweetened cream across to him. "You need something more than meat in your meal. These will help balance your diet."

"You think so, eh?"

"Well, it can never totally compensate for all the toxins you've just finished pouring into your body, but if it begins to educate your tastes..." Marissa picked up a plump, ripe

157

berry and swirled it in the cream. "Here, have a bite. See if I'm not right."

Brace's lips parted to receive the fruit. Her fingers brushed them as she popped the berry into his mouth. A jolt of pure electricity coursed down Marissa's arm. His lips were so soft, so full, and the memory of that nocte in the tavern room rushed back with disconcerting force. She jerked away, nervous, unsettled.

"Th-there's something I'd like to speak of, if you'd care to talk about it." She forced the words out through a tightly constricted throat.

He smiled lazily, quite aware of her discomfiture—and just as pleased. "Oh? And what is that?"

"Your dream. What frightened you so?"

Brace's expression darkened, then he shrugged, evading her intent scrutiny. "A typical dream terror, nothing more. I was being chased."

Marissa frowned. "I think not, Brace Ardane. You were locked so deeply in that dream I feared I'd never wake you. Something had you in its power, and you barely escaped."

His gaze swung to hers. The look in his eyes was suddenly wild and haunted.

"I—I'd rather not talk about it."

Once more he evaded her gaze, reaching for a berry which he proceeded to consume.

"Has it anything to do with our quest?" she persisted. "If it has, I must know, for the consequences affect me as well."

"Your concern moves me deeply."

"I didn't mean it that way," Marissa hastened to explain, her voice softening. "Ultimately, anything that affects you affects our quest, but no one deserves to suffer like you suffered in that dream."

Brace covered Marissa's hand with his. His dark eyes met hers, and for the longest moment he just stared, until Marissa wondered if he'd ever speak.

Then he sighed. "The Knowing Crystal. First it seemed my friend, benevolent and warm. Then a voice intruded, warning me of it, and the Crystal turned hostile. It began to chase me, hovering behind me in the air, until I could run no further. Just as I started to fall into some horrible, yawning chasm, I awoke."

As Brace spoke a fine sweat broke out on his brow and, once more, he began to tremble. He lowered his head to hide the terror he knew must lurk in his eyes, struggling to master himself. Gods, even speaking about it seemed to evoke the same sense of helpless horror. Brace wondered if he'd ever be able to sleep again.

"And what did it mean, that dream of yours?" Marissa prodded gently.

She almost wished she hadn't asked him about the dream terror, but somehow sensed it was vital she know. He'd needed her this nocte, and might again.

Brace shook his head. "I wish I knew, Marissa. It was probably a passing thing, stimulated by my earlier efforts to commune with the Knowing Crystal. Perhaps it was just hard for my mind to let it go."

"Perhaps." She paused. "You spoke of communing with the Knowing Crystal. Is that what you and your brother were doing earlier this sol?"

"Yes. Teran was trying to teach me to join with the Crystal."

"And were you successful?"

Brace hesitated. How much of his powers should he reveal? Despite the relationship growing between them, a tiny part of him still questioned her ultimate motives. She had yet to satisfactorily explain why she needed him for her quest—and that need could well be tied to his Crystal powers. He decided to tread lightly.

"I'm not so certain I possess Teran's talents," Brace began carefully. "The training will take time."

Marissa frowned. "How much time?"

"I don't know."

"Brace, we can't stay here much longer."

"Yes, Marissa. I know. I'll speak to Teran on the morrow."

His gaze dipped to her hand. Slowly he threaded his fingers through Marissa's.

Her eyes followed, drawn by his heated touch. Such strong, capable hands, she thought, studying the long fingers that merged into taut, vein-studded skin with its sprinkling of dark hair. Her glance moved up, past his wrist to his forearm, bulging with muscle and sinew beneath the rolled up sleeve of his tunic. Such powerful, capable arms, she mused; such strong, beautiful hands . . .

With a start, Marissa jerked her gaze back up to Brace's. A hot flush flooded her face. He'd been watching her, knew her thoughts. And she was far from ready to share so much.

Marissa nervously, disengaged her hand from Brace's clasp. He smiled. Then, never breaking his gaze, Brace reached for a berry, swirled it in the cream, and lifted it to his mouth. Marissa watched in fascination as his strong white teeth bit into the succulent fruit, saw his lips close around it and draw it into his mouth. A strange lassitude flooded her.

A smear of cream at the corner of his mouth caught her eye. Without thinking, Marissa captured it with the tip of her finger and brought it to his lips.

"Here," she murmured huskily. "Clean up after yourself."

Dark, dense lashes lowered as Brace dipped his head to her hand, but through their shielding screen his gaze burned molten hot. His lips parted, touching her, and then his tongue emerged to lick the cream away. His warm, moist tongue, his firm, dry lips . . . slipping down to capture her finger and draw it into his mouth.

Marissa's eyes widened. Her breath caught in her throat. And still Brace continued, laving the slender digit, suckling it until her eyelids lowered in heated pleasure. He took Marissa's hand then, his lips moving to her palm, where he alternately planted velvet kisses and playful little nips.

She watched him, struggling to fathom the rapidity with which her feelings for Brace Ardane had changed. When had it happened? Something had definitely thawed when he'd agreed to give her time, to go slow and be gentle with her. And that wonderful smile when she'd finally admitted she wanted him!

But somehow Marissa knew he'd begun to insinuate himself into her heart long before this nocte. His integrity in standing up for his brother had stirred her respect and admiration. His stamina and courage in enduring two long cycles of torture and imprisonment filled her with awe. And his renowned warrior's prowess—and animal magnetism—were seduction itself.

Yet it was his lighthearted teasing, innate sensitivity, and thoughtful concern that drew her most of all. He was unlike any male she'd ever known. She felt safe with Brace . . . cared for . . . needed. Almost as if he were her other half.

It was madness to think such things, Marissa realized, struggling to rise out of her dreamy haze, but the ecstasy of his hot, wet mouth threatened to rob her of the last vestiges of reason. It was *so* hard to fight him—and she no longer wanted to.

Marissa began to tremble, sharp little spasms that shot to the core of her being. Her eyes followed the movement of his dark head. He was making love to her, she thought languidly, making love with just his mouth upon her hand. What would it be like to actually mate with him?

She licked her lips unconsciously, rosy lips, swollen with her rising desire.

The door to the garden opened in a frigid blast of air. Marissa jumped, jerking her hand from Brace's clasp. In that same instant Brace leaped to his feet, turning to face the intruder. His eyes locked with those of Rodac.

The Simian stood there, bleary-eyed with sleep, an irritable growl rumbling in his throat. He made a few quick hand movements.

Brace lowered himself back to his chair, his body still taut with his now dampened passion. His glance met Marissa's. Her eyes were overbright, her breathing ragged.

A grim satisfaction flooded him. Good. She'd been as roused as he.

"I'm sorry we woke you," he said, forcing his attention back to Rodac.

To calm his still pounding heart, Brace proceeded to pour out three mugs of hot, sweet faba and shove one across the table to the Simian, another to Marissa. "I'd forgotten you were sleeping in the garden or we wouldn't have turned on all the lights."

I tried my best to ignore them, but between the brightness and all the noise you were making . . .

"Noise, eh?" Brace grinned at Marissa, then gestured toward the table. "Are you hungry?

163

There's plenty of food, and since you're awake, we might as well talk. There are new plans to make, and this is as good a time as any."

Rodac eyed the food spread out on the table, then nodded. He proceeded to consume everything in sight.

Marissa rolled her eyes. What a pair of ravenous beasts! Half of the quest would probably be spent watching them hunt meat to appease their appetites.

Finally the Simian leaned back in his chair. After a loud belch, Rodac motioned to Brace.

"Time for another nap in the trees, is it?" Brace inquired. "Well, I'll try to make this quick."

He glanced at Marissa. "The quest has become a bit more involved than the simple rescue of Marissa's sister. The Knowing Crystal is also in Ferox's possession. We must now rescue it as well."

Rodac swung forward in his chair, his small eyes narrowing. *That makes things a lot more serious—and dangerous.*

Brace took a swallow of faba, then nodded. "I agree. We're all in a lot of trouble. Will you still help us, knowing this?"

Arbor is in as much trouble as Bellator. I'll help.

"And how much extra will that cost us?" Marissa remarked snidely.

The alien's gaze swung to hers. *Only your word to keep that smart little mouth of yours shut. Can you afford such a price?*

Marissa reddened with anger, and it was all Brace could do to keep from choking on another mouthful of faba. Only after he'd stilled his fit of coughing did he speak.

"Well said, Rodac," Brace agreed laughingly, then turned to Marissa. "Could I also buy into that little deal? It would be worth a small fortune to me as well."

Marissa's lips clamped shut and she glared over at him. "Stop picking at me and I may just agree."

She rose from the table. "And as for you, you hairy bag of bones," she snapped, shooting Rodac an icy glance, "this sudden act of Imperial unity doesn't fool me for a secundae. I still don't trust you!"

The Simian stood in one fluid motion, eying her for a long moment. Then, slowly, he relaxed and smirked. Without another word, Rodac ambled out the kitchen door and back into the garden.

Brace exhaled a deep breath, then went to shut the door. "You really ought to watch that tongue of yours, Marissa," he chided as he returned to the table. "Simians can be quite short of temper, especially where their honor is concerned."

"Honor," she muttered. "And when has a Simian ever known honor? I'm sorry, Brace. I still don't trust him."

"Well, I suppose things like trust take time—for all of us." He offered his hand. "Come, we

165

need to get to bed. It will be sol rise soon and we've a lot of work ahead."

She hesitated before taking his hand. "How much longer, Brace? How much longer before we head out? Candra needs me."

A smile of understanding touched his lips. "I know, Marissa. I'll speak to Teran. It won't be much longer. I promise."

"Another sol. No more. That's all we can spare."

Fleetingly his keen eyes caressed her, then he nodded. "Another sol. No more."

"One more sol?" Teran stared at his brother in stunned incredulity. "You're giving me just one more sol to prepare you? You're mad, Brace! This quest is of too great a magnitude to rush into haphazardly, to learn as you go."

"There's a young femina's life at stake here, Teran," Brace replied calmly. "Teach me the rudiments. My mind is set."

"By the five moons!" Teran cursed. "If you think I can so easily teach you the rest along the way—"

"It doesn't matter. You're not going. The Crystal refuses to allow your participation— and you know it," his brother offered quickly. "We've spent the past two horas in attempting a joint communing and the stone won't permit you in. The quest is mine now. Accept it, big brother."

Teran shook his head. "I can accept it, but

I don't have to like it. Something's wrong. Very wrong." He paused, a deep frown creasing his brow. "I wonder if Ferox has already used that little Traveler. If she somehow managed to get inside the Crystal and reprogram it . . ."

"All the more reason for haste. Time is of the essence now. Whatever powers I gain in tarrying here may soon be useless if Ferox has manipulated the Crystal."

"You're right, of course," Teran muttered, "but the danger of sending you out half-tutored is just as great." He sighed. "There seems little choice, though. I just don't want to lose you so soon after having found you again."

Brace smiled. "Nor I, you."

"The little Sodalitas. She's integral to the eventual success of this quest. I feel it strongly, as does Alia."

"Of course she is," Brace began. "It's Marissa's sister, after all, and there's that psychic link—"

"No, I mean her relationship with you. Though she lacks Crystal powers, the strength of her love for you is vital to this quest. It will aid you in your search for the Knowing Crystal—and the inevitable outcome of that search."

"You speak in riddles," Brace growled. "Marissa doesn't love me. And the possibility of that ever happening is virtually nonexistent." He shot his brother a dark, shuttered look. "Why should it matter, anyway?"

"Love has always been a force to be reckoned with. It has a mysterious power of its own, to stir the heart, to compel one past the limits of logic and physical ability. And it's a force the Knowing Crystal will never fathom. For all the Crystal's wondrous powers, in the end it's only a machine."

"A machine that seems to have turned on us long ago," Brace muttered. He shook his head. "You speak of emotions that only muddle the head when you need clear thinking most of all. And I say that's an interference, not an advantage."

"It can be at times," Teran agreed. "But love can also stir one to great things. Why do you think you finally agreed to Marissa's quest?"

Brace's jaw went taut. "Madness most probably. Lust most certainly. She's a fetching little morsel, once you get past her smart mouth."

His brother threw back his head and laughed. "Now that's the most brainless reason I ever heard for risking your life!"

"Maybe so, but it's a lot safer than loving a femina like Marissa. Leave it alone, brother."

Teran's expression sobered. "I'm not trying to force feelings that aren't there, Brace. I just want you to use all the advantages you have. You'll need them."

"Well, I'm telling you—love isn't one of them!" Brace exhaled deeply. "Now, time is short. Shall we resume my lessons?"

Gray eyes studied him. "As you wish." Teran

rose and retrieved a small, fragile volume. "There's something in here I want to share with you," he said as he carefully turned the ancient pages. "It has to do with the Crystal's range of communication. It extends surprisingly long distances and even has the ability to physically affect the body through its impact on the mind.

"This book speaks also of a special box," he continued, "comprised of some alien metal that can block the Crystal's power when the stone is enclosed within it. If Ferox has managed to get his hands on this container, the task of tracking the Knowing Crystal through your Crystal powers may be difficult indeed..."

Later, after the supper meal, they met once again in the library. Marissa sat next to Brace with Alia at the head of the table and Teran on her right. Rodac sprawled several chairs away, considerately downrange from everyone's sense of smell.

"There's some information I would share," Alia began without preamble. "Information vital to your quest."

"The only information needed is where to find Ferox and my sister!" Marissa interjected heatedly. "As important as this Crystal learning supposedly is, enough time has been squandered. Do you know where Ferox can be found?"

"He is on Bellator."

Brace frowned. "Bellator? Where? And why?"

Alia shook her head. "I don't know why. All I can tell you is that I saw a scene of an ancient monastery high in the Carus Mountains just before the Crystal's pedestal exploded and Ferox stole the stone away. It was the monastery of Exsul."

"And what did it mean, that vision?" Marissa demanded. "Is that where Ferox went?"

Alia regarded her. "Yes."

"How can you be so certain Ferox is on Bellator?"

"I just am, Marissa."

"And you expect us to transport back to Bellator, travel across the planet and into the mountains, just to see why you had a vision of some monastery?" Marissa rose from the table. "By all that is sacred, I'm so weary of wasting time!"

"Do you have any better idea of where to find Ferox?" Brace growled. "If not, sit down and be quiet!"

She rounded on him. "Ardane, don't give me orders. I've had about all I can take of you, too!"

Brace glared at Marissa. A muscle twitched in his jaw at the effort it took not to snap back at her. He knew that the burden of responsibility for her sister weighed heavily, that the forced inactivity of the past sols ate at her.

"Marissa, sit down," Brace said, his voice softening. "Please."

Her mouth opened. For a moment he thought she'd resume her attack. Then Marissa sighed and sank back into her chair.

"I'm sorry," she muttered. "Please, Alia, continue."

"I understand, Marissa," Alia said. "Truly I do."

Her gaze slowly scanned the assemblage before coming to rest upon Teran. Their eyes locked.

"And I would not send you on a false trail for all the lost learning of the Imperium," she began again. "Yet I feel very strongly that something vital to your quest awaits at Exsul. Trust me. You *must* go there first."

"Trust you?" Marissa's eyes echoed the rising anguish in her voice. "I'm used to taking charge, not sitting back and being passively directed by people I barely know and have no reason to trust. By the Crystal Fires, do you know how hard this is for me?"

"And do you think you're the only one who feels that way?" Brace demanded. "I don't like this any more than you—this dependence on others, the need to trust, to go blindly forward. And the hardest task of all, sometimes, is trusting you!"

She recoiled at that, as guilt and then a sharp, stabbing pain shot through her. The haunting realization, firmly shoved to the back of her mind of late, once more lifted its ugly head. He was right not to trust her. In the end, it would be his doom.

Marissa sighed. "Then we all have our battles, don't we?"

He gave her a long, meaningful look. "Yes, I suppose we do. And sometimes I wonder if either of us will come out the victor."

Teran cleared his throat. All eyes riveted on him.

"Well, some of your battles are still to be fought along the way." He grinned at Rodac. "They may need a peacemaker."

The Simian smirked and motioned his reply.

"What do you mean, that'll cost us extra?" Marissa cried, her voice rising in irritation. "You'd just better stay out of this if you value that money-grubbing hide of yours!"

"Marissa," Brace warned.

Teran chuckled. "I almost wish I were a little pack rodent so I could ride along and eavesdrop on you two. It would be most entertaining."

"Maybe so," Marissa grumbled, "but our arguing hardly gets much accomplished."

"My point exactly," Brace said. He turned to Alia. "Is there more? If not, I'd like to get some rest. The morrow will come soon enough, and there's a quest to begin."

"No more, Brace," Alia replied, "save that I caution you to remember Ferox is a crafty foe, and his enmity toward Teran will easily extend to you. He'll show no mercy."

"The feeling is mutual," Brace muttered savagely. His gaze locked with Marissa's equally fierce one. "Isn't it, femina?"

* * *

She found him later that nocte drenched with sweat. His fists twisted in the sheets as he writhed in the throes of another dream terror. The bed cover, bunched between his taut, outspread legs, barely covered Brace's nakedness. For a secundae, Marissa's gaze skimmed his big, hair-roughened body. Flat planes of muscle and rigid bands of sinew sculpted his chest. In the light of the room's perpetual torches, his abdomen gleamed in tight, rippling waves that ended in a groin . . .

Marissa sat down beside him and pulled the cloth up to cover his lower body. "Brace," she called, grasping him by the shoulder to shake him, "wake up!"

He twisted and turned, moaning piteously, flinging the bed cover aside. Marissa quickly flipped the sheet back over him. By all that was sacred, he was a big male—in every way!

She shook him harder. "Brace, wake up! It's only a dream. Wake up!"

A guttural cry tore free from Brace's lips. He arched up from the bed, agonized, straining, but his eyes remained closed, his mind far away.

Panic curled within Marissa. He was caught in the throes of a dream terror that would not release him. She'd heard tales of people who never escaped—who fought the terror until the physical stress of the experience drove their hearts to explode. If she couldn't free Brace . . .

Fleetingly she considered going for Teran

173

but realized his help might come too late. By the looks of him, Brace couldn't hold on much longer. How long had he been dreaming before she finally heard his cries? She *must* wake him!

Marissa gathered his sweat-slick body to her, cradling his damp head against her pounding heart. "Brace, Brace," she implored. "Come back. Come back to me. Fight it, whatever it is. Don't leave me. *Please!*"

He struggled, jerking hard in her embrace. Marissa clutched him all the tighter. She strained against him, willing all the strength she possessed to flow into him, to encompass his heart and mind with the essence of her being.

And, ever so slowly, his struggles eased. His moans ceased, his breathing evened. Dark, tormented eyes fluttered open.

"M-Marissa?"

She would not let him go. "Yes, Brace?"

"I-I heard you call me. I followed your voice out of the darkness." He choked back a sob.

"It's over now," she murmured as she began to rock him back and forth as a mother would her child. "You're safe."

He clung to her, fighting the tremors that wracked his body. "I-I'm sorry to be so weak. I've just never experienced anything so horrible before. Not even those two cycles in prison terrified me like these dreams have." He shot her a wild look. "Am—am I finally going mad?"

"No. No," Marissa soothed. "Why would you think that?"

"M-my father," he gasped. "He died of his madness. And . . . it runs in my family . . . on the male side. Ah, by the five moons, Marissa! Has it finally taken hold of me, to now reach even into my dreams?"

"Brace, don't distress yourself—"

"There were times in prison when the pain and despair became so unbearable I—I almost thought I was losing my mind," Brace went on as if he hadn't heard her. "The madness beckoned to me—a place of bright, sweet oblivion, of gentle voices and loving friends."

He inhaled a ragged breath. "I almost succumbed several times, only to find it had been unconsciousness calling me instead. But with each experience I felt I drew a little closer . . . that it was only a matter of time."

"Brace—"

"I thought I'd finally escaped it when you freed me from prison," he continued, "but now these dreams! Gods, Marissa. What am I to do?"

"They'll ease," she murmured, stroking his head. "Just give it time. It's the stress of your imprisonment still haunting you, and the wearying efforts of the past sols. You'll be better soon enough. Once we set out on the quest in earnest . . ."

He sighed, a heartrending sound. "Perhaps so."

Brace glanced up at her. He managed a

weak, lopsided grin. "These dreams do have their advantages. Two noctes in a row now, they've managed to get you into my bed."

She graced him with an arched brow. "You are the most incorrigible male I've ever met!"

He chuckled. "I'd rather call it enterprising." His expression sobered. "Will you stay with me, Marissa? Hold me?"

"I...I'm not so sure that would be wise."

"Please, Marissa. I want to be near you, nothing more. I promise."

The look in his dark eyes was imploring, filled with a gentle yearning that stirred something deep within Marissa. Longing—for his arms around her, for the comforting warmth of his big male body—engulfed her, and she knew she could no more refuse him than she could herself. It was unwise, dangerous, but she suddenly didn't care. And it was just one nocte after all. Just one dark, terror-ridden nocte.

"Yes, Brace," she breathed, "I'll stay with you, but only until you're asleep. Now, close your eyes and rest. We've a long, difficult sol ahead of us."

"Thank you." He pulled her up against the hard length of him.

She held Brace for a long while, until he finally drifted off to sleep. His horrible revelation stirred Marissa's own doubts and fears anew. She had told him it was only the effects of his long imprisonment that still ate at his mind. Yet, after hearing of his father's fate,

Marissa knew her words were little more than meaningless assurances, meant only to ease Brace's torment.

Frustration rose to entwine about her heart. For every step Marissa took to secure the success of her quest, yet another obstacle was thrown in her way. And the shimmering specter of a blood-borne insanity seemed the most awesome obstacle of all—an enemy from within that threatened to destroy a man whose value gained greater and greater significance with each passing sol.

Her heart full of bittersweet emotions, Marissa rose from the bed, covered Brace against the nocte's chill, and returned to her room.

Chapter Eight

They made their farewells early the next sol in the lavender light of a false dawn. As Alia stood beside Marissa in the transport chamber, Teran embraced his brother.

"Take care," he said, his gray eyes moist with emotion. "And if you need me, send a message and I'll be there as soon as I can."

"You've work enough here," Brace replied huskily. "I'm only rescuing a stone. You have the task of setting right the entire Imperium."

With a deep sigh, Teran released him. "Neither of us can succeed without the other, and your mission is far more dangerous than mine. My thoughts will be with you, little brother."

Brace smiled. "As will mine with you." He turned to Marissa and extended his hand. "Come, femina. It's time we were on our way."

Marissa glanced at Alia. "Farewell," she whispered, "and thank you for everything."

Then, with Brace, she joined Rodac on the transport platform. With a whir, a transparent circular shield lowered to encompass them.

A few secundae later, they materialized in another transport room. Before them stood an entourage of richly garbed males. Marissa blinked in confusion, for once without a ready word.

Brace broke the silence with a low curse, then grasped Marissa's arm and led her off the platform. They halted before a tall, regally clad male who stood in front of the others.

"Marissa," Brace growled through clenched teeth, "this is King Falkan, my uncle."

Her startled gaze swung from Brace to the other man. There was a strong resemblance in the piercingly dark eyes, high cheekbones, and squarely chiseled chin. Yes, she thought, they were indeed family—a family torn apart by inhumane laws and unthinking obedience.

She bowed low to the man who was ruler of Bellator and, by sheer military might, the Imperium.

"My lord." Marissa straightened to look him straight in the eye.

A faint smile hovered on the King's lips. He rendered her a slight bow.

"I am honored, femina."

"Why are you here?" Brace's words, clipped and cold, slashed through the gathering.

King Falkan tensed, his eyes narrowing. With an obvious effort, he forced himself to relax. "Teran notified me of your impending arrival. He explained the seriousness of your quest and asked that I offer whatever assistance you might need."

"I need nothing from you!" Brace snarled. "Nothing, save you leave me in peace!"

Though he tried to hide it, pain fleetingly twisted King Falkan's face.

"Brace," Marissa hurried to interject, "have a care. There is much your King could do for us. We need fresh supplies, and a skim craft or two would greatly speed our journey."

Brace whirled on her, his expression raw, anguished. "And would you have me accept assistance from a man who condemned Teran to death and me to a life of endless torture? Would you ask me to now heap even further humiliation upon myself by begging for his help?"

She returned his searing gaze. "For the quest, for the rescue of my sister and the Knowing Crystal, yes, I'm asking you to accept whatever assistance is offered. Pride can never be the issue where others' welfare is concerned. You know that, Brace, no matter how painful it is to accept."

He shot her a seething glance, then turned to his uncle. "We leave within the hora. Two skim craft and fresh supplies would be appreciated."

The King's mouth tightened. He motioned to a man, who immediately hurried away. Falkan then gestured to another man, who handed him a sealed letter. He offered it to Brace.

"And what's this?" Brace demanded suspiciously.

"Instructions for the abbot of Exsul. It's past time the real truth be known."

"What truth? By the five moons, you speak in riddles!"

"All will be revealed at Exsul," King Falkan replied softly. "I only hope it's not too late."

Brace took the letter and shoved it into his tunic pocket. "Fine. I won't trouble you further. Now, if you'd direct us to our skim crafts ...?"

"Brace. Wait," Falkan began, his words halting. "Teran and I have talked a lot in the past sols, and I begin to see the mistakes I've made. Can you, too, find it in your heart to understand—and forgive?"

"Never, do you hear me?" Brace rasped. "I'll *never* forgive what you did to Teran and me—your own nephews! And Vates! You killed Vates! Don't even imagine, much less ask it!"

The look in the King's eyes hardened. "Young, proud fool! Do you think the decisions of responsibility are always so black and white? That family matter more than the people's welfare? You've a lot to learn."

"Perhaps so," Brace snapped, "but it won't be from you. Now, have we your leave to go?"

"Go, get out of here before I change my mind!" the High King choked. "And, ultimately, may your quest accomplish more than the rescue of the Crystal. I pray it also broadens your heart to compassion and forgiveness. That, in itself, is a worthy undertaking."

Brace eyed him for a brief moment more. "Sorry, Uncle. I've already got more quests than I can handle."

Without another word, he turned and strode from the transport room, Marissa and Rodac close behind.

As the two skim crafts flew along, the rolling land surrounding the Bellatorian capital of Rector rose gradually to tree-studded foothills. Marissa and Brace took the lead, with Rodac bringing up the rear. By mid sol they were well into the higher elevations, climbing toward the first craggy summits of the huge, snow-capped mountain range.

It was a glorious sol, cool but sun-gilded, the sky an intense, cloud-strewn blue. For a change, they kept the force-field bubble down. Marissa threw back her head as they sped along, reveling in the sun on her face, the wind whipping through her tumbled, chestnut mane.

After all that had transpired earlier, the intensity of Brace's reaction to his uncle, the growing danger of their quest, the doubts and uncertainty, she marveled that she could now feel so carefree, so relaxed. It was totally illogical, and most likely unwise, but she couldn't help herself. And what could it possibly hurt—to forget all the unpleasantness for a brief moment and take a bit of pleasure where she could? Moments such as these were certainly few and far between.

She glanced behind her. Rodac followed stoically, guiding his craft with consummate ease. She was grateful he'd chosen to bring up the rear. Otherwise the headwinds would have deluged them in his rank scent.

There were fleeting moments every now and then when Marissa wondered if he wasn't actually doing things, like staying downwind, out of consideration rather than accident. A disturbing consideration, to be sure, that there might be some trace of kindness in the lanky, reticent Simian.

But then, why should that surprise her, Marissa thought, returning her attention to the man sitting beside her. She watched for a moment as Brace expertly guided the craft over a tall outcropping of rock. Then Marissa leaned back with with a sigh.

Who'd have ever imagined that her feelings for Brace Ardane could have changed so dramatically? Yet they had, and she was still struggling to deal with the consequences. She eyed him for a long moment, then cleared her throat. "Your dream last nocte. You never said what it was about."

Brace shot her a quick glance before resuming the delicate task of maneuvering the skim craft through the rocky crags. "It was the Knowing Crystal again—and the voice. I know now whose voice it was."

"And?"

. "My father's. It was my father's voice. I haven't thought of him in cycles. And to hear his voice now in these horrible dreams!"

"You said before that the voice was warning you against the Crystal. If that's true, then it's understandable why it would be your father's voice. He loved you and would want to protect you."

"I hardly knew my father," Brace ground out. "He died when I was but five cycles old. Vates was the real father to Teran and me. And now he, too, is dead."

"I'm sorry, Brace. It's hard to lose someone you love."

"Well, no matter. I'm not usually in the habit of baring my private sorrows."

A note of defensiveness tinged his voice. That, and a fierce pride. How alike they were, Marissa marveled, from their common experiences of pain and rejection to their resolute determination in the face of life's difficulties. Yet, for both of them it was all a facade. Beneath the steely exterior lay a deep, aching need—for love, acceptance, and peace.

"Do you have any idea why you'd be hearing your father's voice again, then?" she prodded gently. "And what significance the voice might have for our quest?"

Brace shook his head, puzzled. "None whatsoever. Just like everything else about this cursed quest so far!" He shot her another quick glance. "Doesn't it bother you that there's so very little we know regarding this mission and how we must eventually accomplish it? You're a warrior, too, Marissa. Admit it. This is about the most foolhardy way to approach something there ever was."

"I agree, Brace. And sometimes it terrifies

me, that unknown. I wonder if we'll survive, much less succeed."

"I don't want anything to happen to you, Marissa."

There was the merest catch in the dark register of his voice. She turned to view Brace's taut, rugged features. His eyes remained riveted on his piloting of the skim craft.

And I don't want anything to happen to you, either, Marissa thought. A sudden, wild impulse to tell him of the deadly plot in which she was a key player swept through her.

But the impulse died as quickly as it had arisen. There was no need to reveal something that might never come to pass. Too much was at stake. Too much still lay ahead. And too much was still to be learned about their quest—and a man named Brace Ardane.

Besides, Marissa reminded herself, there was always the possibility that she could win back her sister and still not betray Brace to Ferox. He didn't deserve to be handed over to that heartless slime worm like some bag of goods.

"Nothing will happen to *any* of us," Marissa forced herself to say, fervently hoping her brave words would indeed come to pass. "It will just take time to discover what information is still lacking, that's all.

"But we'll succeed," she added, trying to inject some lightness into the increasingly somber conversation. "We can't help but succeed. It's written in the stars."

A wry grin quirked the corner of Brace's mouth. "Written in the stars, is it? Really, femina, you're becoming quite the little optimist. To what do you attribute this radical change in yourself?"

She grinned and tossed back her windblown hair. "Oh, I don't know. Perhaps it's the glorious weather. It's hard to stay glum when each sol suddenly seems so fresh and new, and life's so full of opportunities."

"And would I perhaps have had some influence upon your new point of view?"

"Would you like to have?"

By the Crystal Fires, Marissa thought as she graced him with a long, considering look, he is such a handsome male! With that arrogant set to his jaw and those dark, high-bred features...

And his mouth, so sensuously tender, so finely chiseled...

A small shiver coursed through her at the memory of his lips gliding down her palm, and his tongue, hot and moist upon her fingers. With a great effort, Marissa wrenched her thoughts from their increasingly heated reverie.

"Well, would you?"

He chuckled. "You're also becoming quite the little tease."

Marissa grinned. "Yes, I suppose I am. Now, answer my question, Brace Ardane."

"Yes, Marissa," his deep voice rumbled. "I would indeed."

"Good." She settled back in her seat with a satisfied sigh. "Then I just might let you."

They rode awhile in companionable silence, clearing the first summit to plummet down toward a snow-covered valley. Far below, a frozen alpine lake glistened in the fading sun, a blue-green slash of ice in the land. The Monastery of Exsul lay in the foothills. As they headed toward the lake for a landing, another thought insinuated itself into Marissa's mind.

She again glanced at him. "Brace?"

He smiled. "Yes, Marissa?"

"Both Teran and Alia alluded to some special enmity with Ferox. What happened to cause it?"

"It all began at the Imperial Academy. Ferox was a gifted student there, convinced he was destined for greatness. For some reason, however, he fixated on Teran as his obstacle to success. Their rivalry became an obsession with Ferox, an obsession that ultimately destroyed his promising military career when he was caught cheating in his final year. He left the Academy in disgrace, eventually turning to a life of crime."

"I'm well aware of his cruel raids on the planets of the Imperium," Marissa muttered grimly. "He was particularly brutal with Moraca."

"That may have had something to do with the fact that Teran's first love was a Moracan. Her name was Darla. In the course of systematically sweeping his destructive way through the Moracan capital four cycles ago, Ferox came upon Darla and abducted her. He raped her brutally, over and over, until she escaped him in the only way she could—through madness."

"And what became of her?" Marissa asked, dreading the answer, knowing that Candra's fate could well be the same.

"Eventually Teran rescued her, but by then it was too late. She was terrified of all men and, inexplicably, of Teran most of all. Darla finally killed herself by leaping to her death."

"And do you think that's what Ferox plans to do to Candra? Rape her and drive her insane?" Marissa whispered, forcing words to the horrible fear.

He glanced at her, then commenced a circular landing pattern beside the lake. "I don't know, Marissa. I'd wager that Ferox took Candra for an entirely different reason—vengeance—though the end result might be the same. If he manages to gain control of the Imperium, he'll certainly destroy Teran in the process."

"Alia said there was more than simple rivalry between Teran and Ferox," Marissa murmured thoughtfully. "That his hatred was bone-deep and soul-rotting."

Brace shrugged. "That may well be. I never met the man myself. He had already been dismissed from the Academy over a cycle before I arrived."

The skim craft touched down with a soft bump.

Marissa sat there for a few secundae, pensively silent, as Brace proceeded to shut off the machine. Then she turned to meet his dark, glittering gaze.

"What is it, Marissa?"

"My sister's plight seems so insignificant in light of the threat to the Imperium's welfare. Yet her safe return means everything to me."

"I know that, femina. We'll rescue her."

"But what if it comes down to her or the Knowing Crystal?" she demanded. "What will you do then?"

"Is there a choice?" he countered quietly. "For either of us?"

Marissa bit back an anguished sob. "No, Brace. We must both do what we feel is right."

The stone walls of the abbey loomed before them in the fading rays of sol set. After pausing to ease the stiffness from muscles cramped by the long journey, the trio headed up the small hill toward the monastery gate.

An ancient porter, his tonsure gleaming dully in the dimming light, slid open the heavy viewing grill in the thick, robur-wood door. "May the Crystal reign," he began by way of greeting. "And how may we serve you, my sons . . ." The monk hesitated as his gaze took in Marissa. ". . . And, eh, daughter?"

Brace stepped forward. "I have a letter, for the abbot's eyes only, from King Falkan."

The porter squinted at Brace. "A letter, eh?

For the abbot's eyes only, eh? Pray wait here, my children."

The grate closed and the old porter could be heard hurrying away. Brace turned to Marissa and Rodac.

"Well, I guess we just do as the old brother said."

"And what's that?" Marissa asked.

He grinned. "Wait."

A half hora later they heard the sound of several pairs of sandaled feet shuffling back to the gate. Once more the grill slid open. The man who greeted them this time had a face that was weathered but sharp with authority.

The monk's eyes scanned them. "I am Abbot Leone. Who is the one with the message from the King?"

Brace again stepped forward. "It is I, Father."

"Then let me have it."

"And what is this?" Brace demanded, arching a dark brow. "No 'Welcome, children' or 'Would you like a place to rest and something to eat'? Only 'Let me have the letter.' Strange hospitality, I'd say, for three weary travelers."

The abbot had the good grace to flush. "Times are dangerous and we can't be too careful who we take in. If you'd but show me the King's royal seal on the letter, I'd be glad to offer the hospitality of my poor abbey."

Brace pulled the letter from his tunic pocket. The imprinted seal was barely discernible in the fading light, but it was enough to satisfy the abbot. The little monk stepped back, motioning toward the door.

"Open the gate," he commanded, "and let our most welcome guests in."

Rodac snorted in disgust before following Brace and Marissa into the monastery. The door was closed and quickly latched behind them.

Brace looked around. They stood in a small outer courtyard, red-tiled and immaculate. The crumbling stucco that coated the inner walls, however, bespoke better times and former wealth. There seemed no place in the Imperium, Brace thought with a touch of irony, that hadn't been affected by the catastrophic loss of the Knowing Crystal.

The abbot extended his hand. "The King's letter, if you please."

Brace gave it to him.

The old man unrolled the small scroll and scanned it avidly. He glanced up once, directly at Brace, his gaze intent and searching. Then he resumed his reading. Finally the abbot re-rolled the letter and tucked it up his sleeve. "Your name, my son?"

"I am Brace Ardane, of the House Ardane, and nephew to the High King," Brace began. He gestured to Marissa and Rodac. "And these are my friends, Marissa Laomede and—"

"I am honored to meet all of you," the abbot hurried to interrupt. "But time is short if I'm to fulfill the King's request."

Kathleen Morgan

The little man motioned for them to follow. "Come with me, if you please."

Brace grabbed the abbot's arm. "And what is so important that you cannot observe common courtesy? My companions are as important as the King's letter. And I wasn't finished with the introductions."

Abbot Leone paled, then reddened. "My apologies, my lord," he stammered, suddenly mesmerized by Brace's fierce glare and threatening stance. "But a man is even now dying, and if we don't hurry you may never have the chance to speak with him.

"Not that there'll be much to understand," he muttered as an afterthought, "considering the poor soul is quite mad."

Brace's grip tightened on the abbot's arm. "Are you telling me the King instructed you to introduce us to a madman?" A cold, controlled rage at his uncle grew within. "By the five moons, I swear I'll—"

"This is no ordinary madman," the old man interjected, impatient to be on his way. "He was sent here twenty-five cycles ago at the express wish of the King, his madness a secret shame and blight upon the House Ardane."

He paused.

"Go on," Brace urged, his jaw setting in stone as a fearful premonition washed over him. "Finish your tale."

Marissa stepped up beside him, her hand moving to take his arm. "Brace," she murmured, overcome with the same horrible presentiment, "perhaps it would be better—"

"No!" His steel-edged reply cut her off in mid-sentence. *"Let the abbot finish!"*

The little monk's wide-eyed gaze swung from Marissa back to Brace. He swallowed convulsively.

"Go on, Father," Brace growled.

"There's little more to tell," the abbot said. "I think you've already guessed. The madman who has been locked away all these cycles at Exsul is the Lord Ware Ardane—the High King's younger brother—your father."

Chapter Nine

Wild cries reached them as they hurried through the monastery. Finally, just outside the room from which the terrible sounds emanated, the small group halted. The abbot's gaze met Brace's.

"I am sorry you must see your father like this after all these cycles," the old man began. "Until five sols ago he was quite healthy in body, if not in mind." He shook his head, puzzlement furrowing his brow. "But ever since that last visitor, his condition has deteriorated rapidly. I made a serious mistake in allowing the man in. I realize that now."

Brace gripped the abbot's arm in a clasp of iron. "What man? Who was he?"

"He said he was your brother, Lord Teran Ardane. At the time it seemed quite plausible, since he evidently knew your father, as well as said he was sent by the King. So I let him in."

"What did this man look like?" Brace demanded hoarsely.

"He was tall, blond, and very striking in appearance. He was dressed in black and wore a govern collar. I knew the tale of your brother's

194

sentencing to Carcer, and that he wore a government collar because of it, so that fit in as well." The abbot paused. "He *was* your brother, wasn't he?"

"No," Marissa interjected. "Your visitor was the master criminal, Ferox. Your description fits that of the one given of my sister's abductor."

Her eyes met Brace's and an anguished look passed between them. Then Brace's gaze swung back to the abbot.

"What was the purpose of Ferox's visit with my father?"

"I—I don't know. He said he wished to be alone with Lord Ardane. I thought he was his son . . ."

Brace inhaled a shuddering breath. "I wish to see my father." He moved toward the door.

"Brace."

He halted and turned to Marissa.

"Let me go in with you."

Bleak eyes stared down at her and she saw the inner battle raging within. Then he sighed. "As you wish, femina." Brace motioned to the abbot. "I am ready."

The holy man nodded and unlocked the door. Brace squared his shoulders and strode through, Marissa following. Behind them, the door closed softly.

A man writhed on a low cot in the far corner, moaning piteously. A tremor wracked Brace's big frame, and Marissa gripped his arm in a gesture of support. He glanced down at her, his smile wan.

Gently freeing her hand, Brace turned, then made his way across the room.

"Father?" he rasped as he sank to his knees beside the cot. He touched his father's shoulder.

Ware Ardane stiffened, then flung himself around to face his newest visitor. Bloodshot eyes stared out of a ravaged, bloated face. He squinted, struggling to focus.

"Ferox!" he croaked. "So, you've come back to finish off what little is left of me."

"No, Father," the younger man whispered. "I'm Brace. Your son Brace."

Dark eyes, the same shade as Brace's, slowly scanned his face. For an instant Brace thought he saw recognition flare, then his father's eyes clouded.

"N-no," the older man groaned. "It's not possible. It's just another trick to get me to reveal the secret. But I won't. I won't."

Lord Ardane cried out, arching upward in the throes of an excruciating pain. His fists clenched in the sheets as if to hold him to the bed. Sweat poured from his body.

With an anguished sound Brace pulled his father to him, cradling him in his arms. "Father," he whispered. "Father . . ."

How was it possible, he wondered, to have been separated all these cycles and still feel such strong emotions for the man he now held? He'd thought they'd died long ago, buried beneath a thick layer of pain and longing for the father he'd hardly known.

Brace glanced down at him. The powerful frame was thin and wasted—the once handsome features haggard and aged beyond his cycles—but still belovedly recognizable. Brace blinked back a hot rush of tears.

The madness of the Ardanes had driven his father to this. For a fleeting moment, Brace couldn't help but see himself lying on that bed, his father's fate his own. The thought made him sick—sick to the marrow of his bones. He inhaled great gulps of air to tamp down the nausea.

Gradually the old man's pain passed. He slumped against his son. For long secundae Brace clung to him, as Lord Ardane's breathing slowly evened. Finally his father pushed back.

"Your brother. Teran." The light of lucidity returned to his eyes. "How is he?"

"H-he is fine, Father," Brace replied, his voice still ragged. "He co-rules now with the Queen of Aranea. And in several monates you'll be a grandfather."

Lord Ardane's mouth lifted in a tremulous smile. "A grandfather. And you, Son. Have you no children of your own to tell me about?"

Brace shook his head. "I've yet to life-mate."

"A pity," the older man sighed. "And your precious mother—how is she?"

Pain flooded Brace at the memory of how his mother had died, brokenhearted at the life-

Kathleen Morgan

sentencing of her two sons. Now, knowing the horrible fate of her husband, Brace understood his mother's secret anguish and what their sentencing, on top of that, had done to her. He damned the cruel destiny that might yet destroy them all.

"I hurt her in so many ways," his father rambled on, recalling Brace from his bitter thoughts. "With my unfaithfulness when I was first betrothed to her and the problems that followed, and then when the madness finally overtook me." He sighed. "She deserved better than I ever gave her."

"She loved you, Father. Always."

Ware Ardane smiled, and Brace caught a heartrending glimpse of the man he used to be.

"I know, Son. I know."

As if beckoned by a newer, more harsher memory, the older man's expression darkened. "Ferox came to visit me. He carried the Crystal in a strangely shaped box and opened it when I refused his offer. Ah, the pain then, the blinding light and shrieking noise!"

"What did Ferox want from you, Father?"

"He wanted me to key the stone, to use my powers in his service." Lord Ardane gave an unsteady laugh. "As if the Knowing Crystal would ever permit that!"

"What do you mean?" Uneasiness slid through Brace. "Wouldn't the Crystal allow you to commune with it?"

Ware Ardane laughed, grimly this time. "Not after I learned of its true essence all those cycles ago, and the insidious evil it had wrought upon us all. And, ever since Ferox left, it's as if the Crystal's turned on me with an even greater v-vengeance."

He turned to gaze up at Brace. "It's *his* revenge, I'd wager, after all these cycles. For the wrong he thinks I did him. Because I never . . .

"There's something you and Teran should know about Ferox," his father gasped, his fingers gouging into Brace's arm. "Something kept s-secret for far too long—

"*Ah!*" His face twisted in pain, and once more Lord Ardane arched back in agony.

Brace struggled to hold onto him, but his father's strength was suddenly too much to contain.

"Marissa!" he cried. "Help me!"

Instantly she was at his side, flinging herself across the lower half of Lord Ardane's body while Brace held down his chest and arms. The old man jerked beneath them, flailing and writhing, his cries shrill. Bloody tears poured from his eyes onto the bedsheets. Finally the struggles ceased. He lay there, unmoving.

His father's breathing was barely discernible. For a frantic moment Brace thought him dead. Then Lord Ardane's eyelids lifted.

"S-son?" he whispered, so softly Brace wondered if he'd only imagined the word.

"Yes, Father?"

"Beware the stone."

"Why? What is its true essence, its insidious evil?"

"Ah, Brace," Lord Ardane moaned. "If I tell you, the stone will turn on you as well, drive you to madness. It's the only way it has to protect itself against a Crystal Master."

Brace's eyes lifted to Marissa's. Their gazes locked and a moment of piercing insight arced between them.

"Brace," Marissa whispered, seeing his features harden with a fierce resolve. "Don't."

He smiled, but it never quite reached his eyes. "There's no other choice. There has never been. I must know."

"Tell me, Father," he urged. "Tell me the truth about the Knowing Crystal. I must know it all if I'm to prevail against it."

Eyes filled with an encroaching madness gazed up at him. "In the past," his father gasped, "the stone could only function under the direct control of a Crystal Master. But no more. To maintain itself, it now seeks to dominate us...body and mind. It seeks...total power! Beware, Brace. Beware!"

"Is that the secret then, Father?" Brace demanded. "Is that all?"

"Th-the secret?"

Confusion clouded Lord Ardane's eyes. For a panic-stricken moment, Brace thought he'd once more lapse into madness.

Then his father shook his head. "Part of it, perhaps. But the true secret is the Crystal's vulnerability. There are pools on the planet Moraca—*Ah Gods!*"

Once again the agony shuddered through his

father, increasing in intensity with each passing secundae. Lord Ardane jerked spasmodically, his cries of anguish rising to fitful, piercing screams. He choked, he gagged, then blood gurgled up from his throat. A glazed look spread across his face.

"Father!" Brace cried. "No!"

Beneath her grasp Marissa felt the old man go slack and knew the end had come. She released him and leaned back to gaze at Brace.

He gathered the limp form of his father to his chest, rocking him back and forth. And, though his face was turned away, Marissa knew that Brace wept, his broad shoulders shaking with the depth of his grief. She stepped away from the bed, not knowing what else to do or how to comfort him. Stepped back to watch silently, feeling helpless, confused, and very sad.

Brace wept on, his heart laid open, the anguish of all those wasted cycles slicing through him again and again. His father, condemned to a life of shameful exile, to madness made all the worse because a lucid mind broke through at times to taunt and torment him. His father. Found at last—and now lost to him forever.

"Father, Father," Brace whispered brokenly. "What am I to do? *What am I to do?*"

Blood pounded through his brain, filling it with a loud, rushing sound until he thought his head would explode. And within that surging wall of noise, a tiny voice cried plaintively, "Beware the stone. *Beware . . .*"

* * *

They buried Lord Ardane the next sol in a forest of shaggy sempervivus fir near the frozen alpine lake. As they stood beside the grave mumbling numb-lipped prayers in unison with the abbot and his monks, a frigid wind blew down from the mountains.

A winter storm was definitely brewing, Marissa thought grimly as the first large flakes began to fall. Better they remain another sol or two in the relative shelter of the monastery and determine the full severity of the impending weather than set out immediately as Brace had earlier decided. To be caught up in those snowy peaks when a blizzard hit . . .

The abbot drew alongside them as they departed the gravesite. "A moment more of your time, my son." He laid a firm but gentle hand on Brace's arm. "Alone."

Brace halted, then glanced at Marissa. "I'll meet you and Rodac back at the abbey."

She eyed him closely, then nodded and slogged on.

Brace turned to the abbot. "What is it, Father?" he forced the question through a pain-choked voice. "What more could there possibly be?"

"The tale of how your father came to find the Knowing Crystal."

"H-he found the Crystal?" Brace fought his way up out of the misery that had enshrouded him since his father's death. "But how? It's been lost for over three hundred cycles, until

202

my brother and Queen Alia discovered it on Carcer. When and how could my father have happened upon it?"

"You were but a small lad when the Lord Ardane was sent out on a secret military mission to Moraca. Though I wasn't privy to the details, in the course of the expedition your father somehow came upon the Knowing Crystal." The abbot shrugged. "Perhaps he was drawn to its hiding place by his inherent, if then unrealized, Crystal abilities. Your father was always a brilliant though unstable man. Even untutored he would have been sensitive to the Crystal's call.

"It doesn't really matter. What matters is that the Lord Ardane saw the stone for what it truly was—an evil, manipulative force bent on total control of the Imperium."

"And my father fought its powers, didn't he? Tried to destroy it?" Brace muttered. "Then the Crystal, to protect itself, turned on him, attempting to drive him mad."

Abbot Leone nodded. "Yes. Somehow the stone must have divined Lord Ardane's weakness, played upon it to push him over the edge. And, most tragically of all, no one would believe your father when he returned raving of the Knowing Crystal and its perils. As the madness progressed, he became dangerous. Finally your uncle was forced to banish him to our abbey—for the protection of your family as well as to prevent your father's dire predictions from inciting a panic."

"Did no one attempt to return to Moraca and find the Knowing Crystal? To try to discover if what my father had said was true?"

"No, my son," the abbot replied sadly. "No one really believed him. They thought him mad, after all."

"Curse King Falkan! He betrayed his own brother, condemning him to a life of exile and shame, without lifting a finger to vindicate him or validate his story." Brace's hands clenched at his sides. "If he had, perhaps the Knowing Crystal could have been stopped long ago and my father's madness halted. But instead he died, screaming in agony, an innocent victim of the cowardly indifference of others. Gods, how I hate them all!"

"There's little time left for hatred, my son," the abbot chided gently. "Though no one went back to validate your father's story when he first returned from Moraca, it's evident that Ferox eventually put it all together. I'd wager his search once more led to the Knowing Crystal. It has long been rumored that he was looking for something very special when he swept through the Moracan capital four cycles ago, massacring half the population."

Brace's mouth grew taut with rage. "The Knowing Crystal, perhaps?"

Abbot Leone nodded. "It seems the most probable set of circumstances for his acquisition of the stone." He sighed. "But that is no longer of consequence. There's a mission to be completed, an Imperium to save. And you are our only hope."

"And scant hope at that," Brace replied bitterly, "already half-mad, with no more defense against the wrath of the Knowing Crystal than my father had."

The wind swirled around them in a sudden frigid blast of air. The abbot shivered, pulling his thick gray cloak more tightly to him. He motioned them back down the road to the abbey.

"Take heart, my son," the old man said. "A father's weakness is not always the child's. Unless, of course, you choose to make it your own . . ."

Marissa sought, Brace out as soon as he returned. "Well, what now? What do we do now?"

His features were tight and drawn, but a fierce determination burned in his eyes. "We depart within the hora."

"There's a storm on its way," Marissa began. "It would be wiser—"

"In one hora's time, do you hear me, Marissa?" Brace said through gritted teeth. "I'll not waste a moment longer in pursuing Ferox. He must pay for what he did to my father!"

"But we still have no idea where to find him," she protested. "And to plow through the mountains with a storm building is madness!"

He riveted her with a bleak, anguished look. "That, too, may indeed come to pass, but I don't intend to delay another moment. Vengeance for my father can't wait.''

Marissa grasped his arm, halting him. ''Brace, Ferox will be seen to, your father avenged, but you can't risk our lives by traveling through the mountains in a storm. Skim crafts don't function well in blizzards. If they fail up there, then where will we be? Use your head!''

''Tutela was on the other side of these mountains. And the abbot informed me there was a travelers' hut halfway there, one that the monks ensure is always well supplied. If the storm gets too bad, we can head for it. One way or another, I intend to transport to Moraca as soon as possible. Somehow, I know that's where Ferox is headed.

''Besides,'' he added, glancing down at her, ''the pools that can destroy the Crystal are located there.''

''And which pools are those? Moraca has thousands of them. Which one was your father speaking of?''

''I don't know, but I'm sure we'll discover that answer when we get to Moraca.'' He jerked his arm from her grasp, his look hard and implacable. ''Now, are you with me, or not?''

There was no swaying him, Marissa thought, not now, not in the tormented frame of mind he was in. She'd just have to risk the storm. If Brace ever needed her, he needed her now.

"Yes, Brace," Marissa sighed, "I'm with you."

She turned to Rodac, who had drawn up behind them and was waiting patiently. "And what about you?" she asked. "Will you continue on with us, knowing the possible consequences?"

The Simian eyed her for a moment, then motioned with his hands. *You'll freeze in these mountains a lot quicker than I will.*

"And I'm sure you'd be overjoyed to see that happen," Marissa muttered.

Rodac smirked and gave a small shrug.

Fortified with fresh supplies, the trio set out an hora later. As the skim craft sped along, the winds grew in strength. They buffeted the lightweight crafts so viciously that flying soon became a dangerous undertaking. Countless times they were nearly slammed into rocky outcroppings as they wove upward through the mountains, until Marissa wondered at Brace's judgment in continuing on.

She wanted to say something, to offer comfort and to ease that strained, anguished expression from his face, but knew it was useless. His dark eyes were shuttered, his mouth drawn into a ruthless, forbidding line. Marissa had never seen Brace like this, so distant, so unapproachable. And she didn't know how to reach him. That realization frightened her most of all.

The snow began to fall heavily, until it became near blizzard conditions in the gusting winds. Visibility dropped. And still Brace flew on—until a snow-shrouded outcropping of rock finally halted their progress.

For a time, Marissa sat there, the craft's nose buried in a snow drift, stunned but unhurt. The pounding of Rodac's huge fist on the door finally jerked her back to the present. She turned to Brace, who sat there stone-faced, his hands clenched in his lap.

"Brace, are you all right?" she shouted above the din, the bubble doing little to mute the howl of the storm.

He nodded.

Marissa grasped his arm. "Then come," she yelled. "We need to find shelter and wait this out."

"And where do you suggest we find shelter?" he yelled back. "There's not a cave nor hiding place in sight. And we've still a ways to go to reach that hut."

"By the Crystal Fires, Brace Ardane!" Marissa cursed. "We'll find something. We have to. We can't stay in this craft."

Angrily she punched a finger at several buttons on the control panel. The lights flickered, then faded.

"See? All the life support systems are gone!"

With an exasperated growl, he disengaged the bubble and climbed out. "Well, let's get on with it then. Sitting here much longer will only freeze us to death."

"A piercing bit of insight," Marissa muttered as she scrambled out to stand beside Rodac.

He was already prepared for the inevitable journey, a huge coil of rope settled across his chest, a blaster slung over a shoulder. He smirked down at her.

Marissa chose to ignore him. She glanced around. The blowing snow allowed only brief glimpses of the surrounding mountains. The glimpses were enough, however, to warn of narrow, rock-strewn paths and sheer precipices.

"Well, femina?" Brace demanded. "Which way is it? Up or down?"

Marissa shivered and clutched her phoca-fur coat to her. By all that was sacred, it was cold! She shot Brace an irritated glance. He was baiting her. She refused to play his game and instead scanned the mountains.

"If we can get over that next peak, we should be able to see the lights of Tutela," Marissa mumbled through lips already stiff with cold. "And, from the map of these mountains, I believe that the travelers' hut lies just below this next summit."

"You *believe*?" Brace gritted, struggling with his rising sense of guilt over getting them into this. "For all our sakes, you'd better be more certain than that!" He motioned them forward. "Come on. Let's head out before we freeze on the spot."

We wouldn't be in danger of freezing at all, Marissa thought furiously, *if you hadn't been so thick-headed about setting out in this weather to begin with! Males!*

As they trudged along, however, Marissa's exasperation subsided quickly into the more immediate concern of fighting her way through the wind and snow. The going was treacherous, the ice layer beneath the snow pack slippery, the hidden rocks painful obstacles that bruised and lacerated her hands and legs when she fell. Soon, however, Marissa ceased to feel anything.

Her limbs grew numb, heavy. She stumbled. More and more frequently, Brace or Rodac were forced to help her back to her feet. Finally Brace grasped her about the waist and began to lead her up the mountain.

She squirmed in his clasp. "Let me go. I can walk on my own."

Brace's grip tightened. "Of course you can, femina. It's I who need the support."

"Liar."

He shot her a searing glance. Marissa's heart twisted in her chest. Beneath the fur hood and snow goggles, his face was pale and ice-coated, his eyes pained, weary. Oh, so weary and filled with an anguished regret.

Forgive me, they seemed to implore. *Forgive me for getting you into this*.

She tore her gaze away and struggled on beside him. There was no strength left to feel anything—neither fear, nor anger, nor forgiveness. All her efforts were centered on the next step, the lifting of an unfeeling leg and planting it just a little farther forward, the movement of a numb, exhausted body.

The wracking cold tremors had ceased a while ago. Now Marissa felt nothing. Nothing save a growing need to sleep. She fought against it, well aware of its fatal consequences.

The biting, blinding snow whirled around them. Marissa stumbled, her legs collapsing beneath her. Brace hauled her back up.

"Walk, Marissa," he rasped, gasping for air in the icy, breath-grabbing wind. "Don't you dare give up on me!"

"I'm so tired," she moaned. "Just let me rest for a little while."

"The quest getting too tough for you, is it, femina?" he growled mockingly. "Need a strong man to take over, do you?"

He shook her, his strong fingers gouging into her side in an effort to stimulate her to action. She cursed and pulled away.

"I can last as long as you—you ignorant sandwart! Don't you *dare* patronize me!"

Brace managed a frozen grin. "Then get on with you. The hut's just up ahead."

She followed his pointing finger. Through the blowing flakes Marissa could barely make out the outline of a small structure. She blinked, not daring to believe it wasn't just another rock outcropping. But no, it was definitely different, its shape more angular and defined.

The hut!

Elation filled her, warming her blood, propelling her forward. "Come on!" she cried.

With stiff, awkward steps, she turned and staggered up the mountain.

"Marissa! Wait!" Brace shouted, noting in a frozen instant the narrow path she was headed for—and that half of that path was nothing more than a thick overhang of snow.

But, even as he leaped forward, it was too late.

She stepped upon the snow-packed ledge and it gave way beneath her weight. With a strangled cry, Marissa toppled over the precipice and disappeared in a surging flurry of white.

"Marissa!" Brace roared and rushed to the ledge, edging out as far as he dared. "Gods, Marissa, answer me!"

The howling winds snatched his breath away, muting his cry to a strangled croak. He swallowed his despair. Where was she? And was she even still alive?

A firm grip settled on Brace's shoulder. He leaned back from the ledge and glanced up.

She's gone. Accept it, Rodac motioned.

Brace climbed to his feet. "Never, do you hear me? I won't accept that without proof!"

He grabbed at the rope the Simian carried and began to tug it over his head.

Rodac's hand stayed him. *What madness is this?*

"I'm going down after Marissa."

Rodac's grip tightened. *It's too dangerous. More snow could give way and you'd both be lost.*

Brace met his gaze. "It's a chance I'm willing to take."

The Simian eyed him for a moment longer, then wearily shook his head. *Better I go down for her. My climbing skills are more suited to the task.*

Gratitude flared in Brace's eyes. "Thank you."

The tall alien shrugged. *Don't delude yourself, Bellatorian. It's for the money, and nothing more.*

"I don't believe that, Rodac."

A smile curved the corner of the Simian's mouth, then was gone. He slipped the coil of rope off his shoulder and began to unfurl it, tossing one end to Brace.

Tie the line to that big boulder over there to anchor it.

He waited until Brace had the rope secured, then carefully eased out onto the ledge. The snowy overhang bore his weight well. With an agile leap backward, Rodac disappeared.

Brace crawled over to peer down the length of taut rope. The snow had quickly hidden the Simian from view. After a time, the rope went slack. Brace waited, not knowing what had happened to Rodac or if he'd managed to find Marissa.

Horrible possibilities assailed him. She could have fallen further than the span of the rope's full length and Rodac couldn't reach her. She could be buried in some snow bank, hidden from view. Or, worst of all, Marissa could already be dead, her body smashed and broken upon the sharp rocks far below.

Gods! Brace thought in a burgeoning, impotent fury. Why had he forced them into this? Why had he allowed his emotions to overcome his warrior's judgment? And what if he should lose her?

The questions tore through him again and again. Brace groaned. To lose Marissa. To never again see that piquant little face smiling up at him, or flushed with angry frustration at his playful needling. Or watch that dreamy, passionate light flare in her eyes when he kissed her. Why now, just when he was finally beginning to admit the depth of his feelings, did he have to lose her?

Anger grew, to roil within like a hot, scorching firestorm. His life was crumbling around him—his father dead, the specter of madness rising to taunt him, a dangerous quest tied to a stone of power that threatened to destroy them all—and now Marissa.

Time seemed to drag on and on as Brace peered down into the whirling snow. The wind surged around him. His body grew heavy and numb. Drowsiness nibbled at the edge of his consciousness.

With a low curse, Brace moved a little, tensing and flexing his muscles to force some warmth into his body. He couldn't remain here much longer, immobile, exposed to the full brunt of the storm. Not without freezing to death.

Rodac, blessed with that thick fur coat of his, could stay down there for a long while. And it might take time, horas even, to find Marissa. But what choice had he? If he left, they might never make it up, and in these subzero temperatures time was of the essence.

No, there wasn't any choice. He'd wait until their return, or die in the attempt.

The rope moved, then grew taut again. Brace leaned over to steady it with both hands. Hope filled him, sending a warming surge of blood to his half-frozen limbs. He peered down, straining to see, but the snow was too thick.

Finally a dark body loomed from the whiteness. It was Rodac. Slung over his shoulder was a smaller, slighter form.

Relief coursed through Brace, followed quickly by anxious questions. Was Marissa still alive? Was she injured?

As Rodac neared, the overhang began to shudder. Gods, Brace thought, not now! He leaned over.

"Rodac, the ledge is weak! It can't bear all our weight. Hand Marissa up to me!"

With one powerful hand maintaining his grip upon the rope, the Simian lifted Marissa up to Brace, who pulled her to him and scooted back, well clear of the ledge. A quick examination found her alive, but cold and unconscious. He shrugged out of his coat and wrapped her in it.

Brace crawled back to help Rodac. The snow-packed overhang shuddered again.

"The ledge is weakening," he shouted down to the alien. "I'll get back and you climb up as fast as you can. It won't hold either of us much longer."

He returned to Marissa and took her into his arms. As he anxiously watched the ledge for Rodac to appear, Brace tried to rub some warmth into Marissa's arms and legs. At last a large, leathery hand reached over the ledge, grasping about for the rope.

Relief flooded Brace. Rodac was almost to safety.

Just as Rodac tried to swing a leg up over it, the ledge disintegrated. Rodac's grip on the rope slipped and he reared backward. The ledge fell away.

"Rodac!"

Releasing Marissa, Brace scrambled as close to the newly formed ledge as he dared and peered over. The empty rope swayed wildly below, its end disappearing in a thick blanket of snow.

"Rodac!" Brace cried, his anguished voice snatched away by the howling storm. "Rodac, answer me!"

Suddenly the wind died. Brace strained for any sound. There was none. The world that surrounded him was cold, white, and deathly silent.

Chapter Ten

The wind quickened, rising to a fearful wail. Thick gusts of snow swirled around Brace, engulfing him in a cover of white. The sky darkened as the distant sun slid behind the mountains. The nocte was fast approaching. Soon, he wouldn't be able to find his way.

Time was of the essence. He and Marissa would surely freeze to death if they spent an unprotected nocte out in the wind and cold. Brace had two choices—either go down the rope and make a quick search for Rodac, or leave him behind and concentrate his efforts on getting Marissa up to the hut. Two choices, and no matter which he decided, it virtually guaranteed someone's death.

Brace's fists clenched in impotent rage. Gods, how could he make such a choice? It was so unfair, so cruel! But choose he must.

With a vicious curse, he edged back and climbed to his feet. If he hadn't been injured by the fall, Rodac's chances of survival were far better than Marissa's. Brace *had* to get her out of this wind and warm her, or she would surely die.

The trek up to the little hut was treacherous and exhausting. Even with Marissa slung over his shoulder, having both hands free did little to ease Brace's way. He slid and slipped with nearly every step, tearing through the cloth of his breeches to gash the half-frozen flesh of his legs until he ceased to care. After a time, the center of Brace's universe narrowed to the sight of the hut and the automatic forward movement of his legs.

Blessedly, the little dwelling was unlocked. Brace staggered in, shoved the door closed, then sank to his knees. The sudden absence of wind made the interior seem warm in comparison. He laid Marissa down and slumped beside her, relief draining his last reserves of strength. For a long while Brace remained there, until reality prodded him to action. He had to get Marissa warmed.

Brace crawled to his knees and glanced around. As the abbot had said, the hut was indeed well stocked for mountain travelers. There was a large pile of firewood stacked beside the hearth, not to mention a crude wooden table and two benches that could also be used for fuel if the need arose. A small bed, laden with quilts, sat against the far wall. Across the room was a pantry filled with freeze-dried food and cooking and eating utensils. With a little melted snow and the heat of a fire, it would be a simple enough task to prepare a meal.

Brace uttered a silent prayer of gratitude, then made his way to the pile of wood and gathered an armload for the fireplace. His own circulation began to return—sharp, piercing little needles of agony. He bit back a groan at the excruciating pain and concentrated all his efforts on the task at hand.

With the aid of a tinder box he found on the mantel, Brace soon had a small flame going. He fed it for a short while, coaxing it to a more sturdy fire before turning to the task of caring for Marissa.

After pulling her as close to the fire's warmth as he dared, he stumbled over to the bed on pain-stiffened legs and grabbed the quilts. Dragging them back, Brace proceeded to divest Marissa of her ice-coated clothes and wrap her in the quilts. He then stripped off his own garments and crawled into the quilts with her. Marissa's smooth-skinned young body was cold and limp against his own cool flesh, but Brace knew he'd warm quickly enough to share his own body heat with her.

The soft mounds of her breasts with their chill-hardened nipples pressed against him, and her downy woman's mound brushed his thigh. Brace grimaced wryly. He finally had Marissa where he wanted her, and could do nothing about it. And when she wakened and discovered their lack of clothing, Brace imagined he'd quickly experience the fullest extent of her wrath.

But he wouldn't mind, if only she were unharmed and well. There seemed so little he could do anymore, about anything. At least

Marissa's full recovery would ease a little of the pain of that realization.

Brace began to massage her body in an attempt to aid the returning circulation. As he did, he gradually uncovered Marissa to examine her for injuries. A large purpled bruise graced the left side of her forehead. The rest of her looked undamaged, but there was no way of ascertaining if she'd suffered internal injuries until she regained consciousness.

She moved in his arms and moaned. Brace tucked the quilt back up around Marissa and increased his efforts to warm her.

"Ah!" she whispered and stirred more forcefully.

Her lashes fluttered open and she gazed up at Brace. For a long moment, confusion clouded her blue-green eyes.

Then the pain of her warming limbs flooded her. "By all that is sacred!" Marissa groaned.

She bit into her lower lip and lay there, fighting against the agony until it subsided. She moved then, to snuggle close to him.

"B-Brace?" Marissa breathed. "What happened?"

"The ledge crumbled and you fell. I carried you up to the hut."

Marissa raised her head and glanced around. "We made it. Oh, thank the Crystal!"

Brace's expression darkened.

Fear shot through Marissa. "Brace, what's wrong?"

"Only the two of us made it, Marissa."

She scanned the room. "Rodac. What happened to Rodac?" A note of panic threaded her voice.

"He went down to rescue you. When he tried to climb up afterwards, the ledge broke under his weight."

Her eyes widened. "Did the fall kill him?"

"I don't know."

"What do you mean, you don't know?" Her fingers gouged into Brace's arms. "Didn't you go down to see?"

"It was getting dark, there was still a difficult journey to the hut, and I didn't know how badly you were injured. I made a choice, Marissa."

She rolled on her side, turning her face from him. "Curse that big smelly alien," she choked. "He didn't even like me!"

"Actually, I think he was getting to rather enjoy your little interchanges." Brace pulled her back up against him. "Are those tears I see? For a money-grubbing Simian no less?"

"And what if they are?" she sniffed. "I'm entitled to my personal sentiments, no matter what your opinions to the contrary!"

He nuzzled the damp, tangled hair that lay against her neck. It smelled like the hauntingly sweet, herbal bractea.

"And would you have wept if it had been me, rather than Rodac, lying at the bottom of that cliff?"

Marissa turned back to face him. "Perhaps."

She lifted the quilt to cover her shoulders and stiffened.

"What is it, femina?"

"I—I'm naked a-and so are you!"

"It seemed the most expedient way to get you warm."

"Well, I'm warm now." Marissa shoved to a sitting position, clutching one of the quilts to her. "You can move away."

Brace levered to one elbow. "Marissa, I didn't do anything but warm you."

"I—I'm sure you didn't," she replied nervously.

She eyed the broad, hair-roughened chest, rippling abdomen, and powerful arms that lay exposed above the quilt. By the Crystal Fires, Marissa thought with a small frisson of excitement, but he was muscling up quite nicely. And then, with another frisson—this time of fear—she realized those same muscles spoke as well of his awesome strength.

But he'd never force himself upon her. Marissa knew that now, trusted him. And the fear she'd felt but a secundae ago was not for her physical, but for her emotional safety.

In his own way Brace Ardane was a dark, dangerous animal, stalking her with that virile body of his, with his hot, hungry eyes. It stirred something in Marissa, something equally primal and darkly dangerous. Something that both attracted and repelled her.

She glanced around, searching for some ex-

cuse to change the subject. Her eyes alighted
upon the pantry.

"I'm hungry," she announced loudly.

Brace laughed. "I could have sworn that was
my line."

"Not this time." Marissa rose to her feet,
swayed unsteadily for a moment, then grabbed
at the mantel for support.

After a few secundae, she tucked the quilt
securely about her and glanced down at him.
"Are you coming?"

He eyed her slender shoulders and ivory expanse of chest exposed above the quilt. Her
smooth flesh gleamed in the flickering firelight.
Brace remembered how soft she'd felt against
him, how her breasts had—

With a superhuman effort, he shoved the
stimulating thoughts aside. This wasn't the
time nor the place for a tender interlude. Gods,
it was torment enough how full and heavy his
loins already felt! She was right to divert the
subject before things got out of hand. And, now
that he thought about it, he *was* starving.

Thankfully, there was dehydrated meat,
which Marissa grudgingly made into a stew
with several containers of dried vegetables and
some seasoning. Brace watched her as she
cooked over the fire, admiring the sleekly cur-
vaceous form that even the bulky quilt
couldn't hide, his ardent glance skimming the
sensuous undulation of flesh over bone.

Strange, he mused, that no woman had ever
seemed as beautiful or preciously dear as Mar-

issa. Strange how strong the protective possessiveness flared. And how he wanted her,
wanted to join bodies and share the ultimate
ecstasy.

Fleetingly, Brace wondered if he weren't falling in love. He quickly quashed that as ridic-
ulous. When it came to women, Marissa, with
her sharp little tongue and warrior's aggres-
siveness, was hardly his type. And yet, in so
many ways, she was all the woman he'd ever
need.

Marissa turned at that moment, the pot of
stew in her hand. At his heated look, a small
frown wrinkled her brow.

"What? What's wrong now?" she asked.

Brace sighed and shook his head. "Nothing,
Marissa. For all we've been through, all the
hardship and sorrow we've shared, nothing
could be more perfect than this moment—and
the simple pleasure of just being with you."

Her eyes widened. Then she squared her
shoulders and strode to the table.

"You're hallucinating from hunger," Marissa stated, placing the pot on the table between them.

She dished him up a healthy serving. "Eat.
You'll soon feel better."

He grinned and dug into his food, not pausing for another word until he'd polished off two
platefuls of the savory stew. There, with a sigh,
Brace leaned back from the table.

"You are by far the best trail cook I've ever
had the pleasure of traveling with. Once we've

rescued the Knowing Crystal and your sister, and taken care of Ferox, we really should team up for another quest or two. Ones with more hope of monetary gain, of course."

Marissa rolled her eyes. "Ah, yes. We'd make a wonderful team. Once we learned to agree on things."

"We agree on quite a lot already," Brace pointed out.

She arched a skeptical brow. "Oh, do we now?"

He gazed at her for a long moment. "You know we do, Marissa."

Brace sighed. "I just regret we had to meet this way, in the midst of such terrible danger and hardship. And I'm sorry for making it even worse, with my lack of judgment in dragging you into the mountains in such bad weather. I lost Rodac and nearly lost you as well."

"You were distraught over your father's death and wanted revenge. I can understand that."

Brace lowered his head. "I'm a warrior. There's no place for the luxury of emotion when one goes to battle. Not if one wishes to survive, at any rate."

He lifted pain-glazed eyes to her. "I'm afraid, Marissa. There's something wrong with me, something gnawing at my insides, and I don't know what to do about it."

Marissa rose and walked around to sit beside him on the bench, taking his large, callused hand in hers. "Whatever it is, I'm here for you,

Brace. Both Alia and Teran said this quest required both of us for success. The longer we're on this mission, the more convinced I am of the truth of their words."

"And can you rescue me from madness?" he demanded bitterly.

Her grip tightened. "You're not going mad, Brace."

"Aren't I? My father died of his madness, and I told you before that I nearly went insane while in prison. I fear I've inherited his weakness, a weakness the Knowing Crystal sensed. Perhaps it's just a matter of time before the stone turns against me as well."

"Any man would doubt his sanity after what you've been through. And this madness you fear in yourself could very well be just the influence of the Knowing Crystal. Your father claimed as much himself. That the Crystal might turn on you and drive you insane if you knew the secret. And now you know."

"Know what?" He gave a scornful laugh. "That the stone is vulnerable, and that some special pools on Moraca are tied into that? I hardly think I'm much threat to the Knowing Crystal with that little tidbit of information. At least not enough for it to turn on me."

He paused, frowning.

"What is it, Brace?" Marissa asked. "What's wrong?"

"I suddenly remembered Alia's words, when she told us of the vision of the monastery at Exsul. At the time, it seemed the vision must have come from the Knowing Crystal, at the moment of its theft. Almost as if the stone were trying to lead us to where Ferox was heading next, to aid us in its rescue. But now, now I'm not so sure . . ."

"Sure of what?"

Brace's gaze swung to meet hers. "Why would the Knowing Crystal willingly reveal the location of my father, a man who knew its terrible secret? It's not logical."

"Maybe it didn't willingly reveal it. Maybe at the moment it was wrenched from its pedestal of power, the stone went awry and transmitted information it couldn't control."

He considered that for a moment. "Perhaps. I hope that was all it was. And whatever the reason, it was definitely to our advantage."

"Yes, perhaps it was . . ."

Brace noted her thoughtful look. "What is it, Marissa?"

"Something your father said—or almost said—that still bothers me."

"And what's that?"

"Something about Ferox. Something you and Teran should know. 'A secret kept for far too long' . . ." Marissa shook her head. "What do you think he meant?"

"Who knows?" Brace shrugged. "Probably just another shocking revelation of Ferox's cruel and power-crazed life."

"You're probably right. And in the total scheme of things, what does one more past atrocity matter? It can't get too much worse.

In the meanwhile," Marissa said, rising from the table, "it's time we both took our rest."

He arched a dark brow. "And what do you suggest the sleeping arrangements be?"

"We've both slept close before. A spot beside the fire seems the most prudent. That way we'll be able to feed the flames whenever they begin to die."

"I could keep you very warm, Marissa."

"Yes, I imagine you could." She repressed the smile his hopeful words elicited. "But I didn't mean *that* close."

Brace sighed. "No, I didn't think you did. But it was worth a try."

He grasped the quilt about him and strode to the bed, returning with the extra quilts and two pillows. "Here, let's make a pallet and get some rest."

A half hora later Marissa was sound asleep. Brace lay there for a time, listening to her breathing. Watching her. Wanting her. Wanting her and fearing she'd never return his need.

She felt something, he admitted grudgingly. Her heated response in Tutela and again on Aranea was not that of a woman insensitive to him. But there seemed an impregnable wall of reserve about her, a rigid self-control she never let her emotions slip past. And he didn't know how to break through it.

With a despairing sigh, Brace rolled over onto his back, pillowing his head atop his hands. He gazed up at the cobweb-strewn rafters for a long while, listening to the storm.

Outside the snug little hut the winds howled with a ferocious intensity, the dismal sound mirroring the bleak, bitter pain that had twined about his heart.

Smothering blackness consumed him. Brace tumbled downward into an endless pit of deafening cries and clutching hands. Hands that clawed at him, tearing at his flesh until he was one huge, gaping wound. He watched as his life's blood gushed away.

He fought back, screaming out his rage and frustration, but to no avail. The blackness dragged him down as his body weakened. Brace knew the end was near.

There was no hope, nothing left but surrender. Surrender—to eternal oblivion, to the haunting vision of madness—and join his father.

Yet in that last moment before total submission, a voice called to him. Instantly Brace recognized it. Marissa, the woman he loved. The woman he'd never win. But a woman to whom he owed a debt and the fulfillment of a quest, terrible and dangerous though it was. With the last of his strength Brace fought back, seeking union with the voice that was his final link to sanity.

He awoke, gasping, drenched with sweat. Awoke—to find himself in Marissa's arms.

"By the Crystal Fires, Brace Ardane!" she sobbed. "I'd thought I'd lost you for certain this time. I couldn't reach you no matter what

I did. What are we to do? Ah, what are we to do?"

Brace turned into the comforting softness of her woman's body and groaned. "I—I don't know, femina. Gods, I don't know anything anymore! Just hold me. Hold me until the terror passes."

She bent her head and kissed his pale, clammy forehead. "For as long as you wish. Forever, if that's what it takes."

He lifted his face to hers. "I'm so sorry, Marissa. You need a strong man on this quest, and I'm rapidly falling apart. Better if I'd been the one to die, rather than Rodac. He'd have been of far more use than I."

"Hush, hush," Marissa soothed, stroking back his dark, damply matted hair. "You're all I need. You're the strongest, bravest man I've ever known. And I'm *so* glad I found you."

She gazed down into his beautiful, measureless eyes, saw his anguish and torment— and knew, in that piercingly sweet instant, that she was lost. The last vestiges of distrust and animosity faded. Her heart went out to him, and a woman's instinct to comfort, in the age-old ritual of mating, filled her. Marissa's head lowered, and her lips softly, tentatively brushed his.

He tensed for the briefest of moments, then, with a shuddering sigh, opened his mouth hungrily over hers. When she didn't draw away, Brace deepened the kiss, touching his tongue to her lips, coaxing them to open. When their soft fullness parted, he slid his tongue gently between them.

As he began to explore her mouth, pleasure spiraled through Marissa. Brace's hands caressed her, and when he moved to lie atop her, the hard strength of his body, pressed so intimately against hers, brought Marissa to vibrant life. She arched up to him, her hands wildly stroking the thickly muscled shoulders and taut planes of his broad, crisply furred chest. Ah, to finally touch him was heaven itself!

His hands left her to fumble with the quilt that covered the lower half of his body. In one sweeping movement Brace lifted himself and pulled it away, then lowered to once more rest upon Marissa.

She felt him then, even through the bulk of the fabric still covering her. Felt his sex pressing at the junction of her thighs, thick, hard, and straining. Marissa's hands slid down Brace's body, past his narrow waist and hips to grasp his roundly muscled buttocks and pull him more tightly to her.

He rubbed against her, in a rhythmic motion that imitated the mating act. The action stirred a rising excitement within Marissa, filling her with fire and a wet, unbearably aching heat. She lifted her hips, joining him in the dance.

"Marissa," Brace groaned. "Sweet femina. I need you so badly! It's been such a long, long time."

"Then take me," she whispered. "For this nocte I am yours."

He stilled, then lifted his head to gaze down at Marissa. His dark eyes impaled her.

"And for all the rest of the noctes of our lives?"

Inexplicably, an image of Brace bound and beaten with Ferox standing over him filled Marissa's mind. Nausea welled inside her. She must tell him. He'd understand and find some way through it all. There could be no hope of anything between them until she did.

"The future is so uncertain," she began. "And there's something I haven't told you about the quest—"

He silenced her with a gentle finger. "Later, Marissa. I was wrong to press you. There's time enough to bare the secrets of our hearts, to make plans for the future." His hand cupped the underside of a softly rounded breast. "But for now, it's enough to seal our fates with the joining of our bodies."

Before she could protest, Brace's mouth came down upon hers, fierce, hard, and utterly uncompromising. Marissa struggled against him, desperate to have the issue of her betrayal settled, but the seductive onslaught of Brace's lips and probing tongue soon drove all rational thought away.

He ran his hands over her breasts, teasing her nipples through the fabric until she tingled with anticipation. She whimpered, squirming beneath him. His fingers freed the quilt, flinging it aside to bare her to his gaze. For a long moment Brace stared down at Marissa, his glance hot, searing.

"You're so beautiful, femina," he whispered huskily. "The most beautiful, lushly rounded woman I've ever seen."

He trailed a finger lightly down the curve of her ribs to the narrow indentation of her waist, before finally following the sensuous flare of her hip. "And your skin," Brace murmured. "Like the finest of Tenuan serica cloth . . . so smooth, so warm, so alive."

Her eyes raked his powerful male body. "And you're the most beautiful man *I've* ever seen. I want you, Brace Ardane. I want you so badly I ache with it."

She pulled him into her, pressing his hard, throbbing shaft against her woman's mound. "Join with me. Please!"

Brace grinned down at her. "Ever the impulsive little warrior, aren't you? But once again you must learn patience. I mean to pleasure you like none other before we finally join."

Marissa flushed, averting her eyes.

"What is it, femina?"

She forced herself to meet his gaze. "Th-there has been no other. I'm a maiden."

A fierce, possessive joy surged through Brace. Tenderly he stroked her face.

"Do you know how happy that makes me, to hear you're a maiden? To know I'll be the first?"

"A typical male emotion, I'm sure," Marissa

233

muttered, still uncomfortable with this new possessiveness in Brace. She didn't know whether to be glad or angry. Was that what this mating urge was all about—a bittersweet confusion?

Brace kissed the tip of her rose, then her eyelids and temples. "Typically male, eh? Well, perhaps . . . but perhaps not. Would you mind sharing me with another woman?"

"I'd cut her heart out if she so much as touched you."

He grinned. "My point exactly."

Her lashes fluttered down onto her cheekbones. "But I—I don't know how to pleasure you."

"Then let me show you."

Taking her hand, he guided it down the muscled length of his body until her fingers spread against the warm, softly furred flesh of his groin. Brace trembled at her touch as her fingers grazed his sensitive skin. Then, with a deeply inhaled breath, he brought her hand to lie over his blatantly aroused manhood, curling her fingers around the thick erection.

"Rub me," he whispered in a low, constricted voice. "Stroke me," he pleaded as he guided her hand up and down his shaft. "Yes, that's it, femina. Ah, Gods, it feels so good!"

Brace arched upward as she worked his turgid flesh, throwing his head back to reveal his thick, strong throat, thrusting his sex even more forcefully into her hand. His eyes clenched shut. His face turned dark and strained with his arousal. A groan, low and guttural, slipped from his lips.

Gods, Brace thought, he was so hard he hurt, so swollen he felt near to bursting. It'd been too long, over two cycles without a woman, filled with long noctes aching with need, and now to have one as sensuous and beautiful as Marissa, lying naked beside him, stroking his—

With a grunt of desperation Brace moved to straddle her, a knee on either side of her hips.

His mouth lowered to hers, the kiss long, deep, and drugging. It left Marissa limp and pliant in his arms, save for her continued stroking of his sex. She marveled at the feel of him, his shaft hard, his skin so soft and smooth. And to think he would soon enter her with it, plunge it deep inside . . .

The thought both thrilled and frightened her. She expected pain. Like all Moracan females, Marissa had received the usual maiden's lessons on the act of mating. But it wasn't the pain that frightened her. It was what the penetration symbolized—all she'd ever been raised to abhor. Submission, domination, passivity. To become, at long last, the weak, docile female she'd always despised.

Marissa was nearly overcome with the impulse to turn away, to put a halt to the act they were rushing so headlong toward. But with one glance at Brace's face, at the hot look of passion which she sensed must mirror her own, Marissa knew that flight was impossible.

Whatever ultimately happened, they were meant to join this nocte. Whatever their fate, it had inexorably led to this.

And a single joining did not make her his mindless handmaid for the rest of her life. She chose this as freely as he, and there was nothing submissive in that decision. Listening to his ragged breathing, seeing the rising need in his eyes, Marissa knew that Brace was as much a slave to the delicious ecstasy as was she. If there were submission and domination, then both of them felt it equally. Equally—in this gloriously sublime act between male and female.

As he moved to suckle her nipples to taut, thrusting little peaks, Brace pulled her more snugly beneath him, until his throbbing shaft pressed a hairbreadth from the moist heat of her womanhood. His hand slipped over her softly rounded belly. He lingered over the silky curls guarding her femininity before sliding down into the velvet cleft. Marissa gasped when he found the nub at the top of her sex and began to rub it. Instinctively, her thighs parted to grant him greater access.

"Brace!"

"That's it, femina," he rasped. "Open for me. Let me see you, touch you there."

She moaned, writhing beneath him. An unbearable tension, a searing heat built within her. If she didn't soon find release ...

"Ah, please. I can't take any more," Marissa

cried on a sobbing breath. "Please, Brace. Please!"

At her pleading words something shattered inside him. In one quick motion Brace pulled her hand away and moved between her outspread legs. Grasping her buttocks, he lifted her up to him until his big, wet tip touched her secret place. For the space of a sharply inhaled breath, he hesitated, then drove himself into her with one quick, deep thrust.

Marissa arched back, her mouth opening in soundless agony, an agony that passed in an instant. She felt full, stretched wide with the length and breadth of him, consumed by the fierce heat of his hard male body. She lifted her hips toward Brace in an instinctive feminine move, and he grabbed at Marissa desperately, halting her.

"Not yet. Gods, not yet, Marissa!"

A secret smile curved her lips. He was as near his breaking point as she was hers. And her power to dominate him was as great as his to control her. The realization filled Marissa with a curious, soaring sense of elation.

But she lay there obediently beneath him, quite still, savoring the ecstasy to come. Finally, with a trembling sigh, Brace began to move.

His strokes were slow, languid, gauging her readiness with the greatest care. Her response soared rapidly past his. She whimpered and arched, wrapping her long legs around his hips, pressing her plump wet flesh against his rock hardness. His pace quickened, the rhythm of his thrusting shaft becoming hard, fast, and deep. His tongue plunged into her with the same probing intensity.

And Marissa matched him, thrust for thrust, kiss for kiss, as their ardor flared to a brilliantly searing inferno. She stroked his back wildly, urging him on, clutching at his taut buttocks. Her breasts, achingly sensitive, were crushed against his straining chest. Ah, but she was on fire, her body ready to burst into flame! She couldn't fight it any longer, couldn't . . . fight . . . him!

With a strangled cry, Marissa surrendered to the hot, agonizing pleasure. She spiraled upward into a shimmering, rarefied place, carried to an intense self-awareness and vibrant freedom. Freedom—where she'd thought there'd only be enslavement. Freedom—and the man in her arms had brought her there.

He laughed hoarsely, the sound full of male triumph, then groaned and thrust deeper. Brace's momentum increased, becoming sharp, desperate. He sucked in a breath through clenched teeth, then arched back, his body taut like a bow. Trembling spasms shook his body and, with a low cry, he spewed himself into her.

And all the while Marissa held Brace in her arms, murmuring words of encouragement, urging him on, until he finally collapsed atop her.

They lay there for a time, their sweat-sheened bodies pressed together, Brace still within her. Marissa's mind whirled, moved by the exquisite act she'd just experienced, thrilled at Brace's ineffable tenderness—and twisted by guilt at her continued deception.

On the morrow, she vowed, just as soon as they both awakened, she'd tell him of Ferox's demand. It was the very least she could do, after the intimacy they'd just shared. For the first time since that sol she'd been abandoned on Mount Desolat, Marissa allowed herself to hope for some semblance of a normal existence—an existence that now included a man to love.

Perhaps Brace really *did* want her for the woman she was, perhaps he really *did* care for her despite her being an outcast. Though it had been her first mating, Marissa sensed there'd been more than mere lust involved. The things Brace had said, the look in his eyes, the way he'd touched her—everything spoke of a deep, abiding affection.

No, it wasn't fair nor honest to hold back further secrets, Marissa decided drowsily as she snuggled against Brace's hard-muscled form. Not from a man like Brace. Not in the face of what they'd worked so hard to achieve.

On the morrow the final barriers would fall away. The trust, the sharing would be complete. Then they'd resume the quest, their future bright with hope and, perhaps—just perhaps—even love.

* * *

Kathleen Morgan

Something nudged Marissa, intruding on the warm, comforting thickness of slumber. She grumbled sleepily, then snuggled back against the hard body she lay beside. Distantly, Marissa knew it must be Brace. Her hand moved languidly to stroke his crisply furred, thick-muscled chest.

A touch, more sharply insistent, prodded Marissa again. Mild irritation pricked at her. She was so tired. The nocte had been filled with repeated, equally passionate bouts of lovemaking. Couldn't Brace let her rest just a few horas more?

Her eyes flickered open to gaze at him. He was still asleep, his breathing deep and even, his handsome features relaxed. Marissa frowned. It wasn't Brace after all. What had wakened her then?

Something hard, impatient, jabbed her backside. She froze, then turned slowly. Cruel, glittering eyes stared down at her. Marissa's hand moved, digging into Brace's arm.

Brace grunted in pain. "By the five moons, Marissa!" he growled in a sleep-hoarsened voice. He propped himself on one elbow. "There was no reason to claw at me so. If you're hot again—"

His voice faded as his gaze took in the hard-eyed man dressed all in black, a govern collar that marked him as a criminal of the prison planet Carcer about his neck. Surrounding him were ten or fifteen others, all with blasters

240

pointed down at them. Brace tensed, ready for battle.

"Don't try it, Ardane," the tall, blond man in black snarled. "You'd never have a chance."

Ferox's gaze turned back to Marissa, appreciatively taking in the sight of her half-exposed breasts and the slender curve of her bare arms and shoulders. At his heated perusal, Marissa jerked the quilt up to cover her.

He smiled. "You're as lovely as your sister, though you do seem to possess more fire than she.

"Well, sweet femina, will you lie abed all sol?" Ferox made an impatient motion. "Get up and dress. There's still the rest of our agreement to fulfill."

Brace's glance shot from Marissa to Ferox. "What agreement?"

A dark blond brow arched in pitying amusement. "Didn't you know?" He chuckled. "Well, I suppose not. She'd have never gotten you to trail behind her otherwise—and right into my hands."

Hot, gut-twisting rage flared within Brace. He grasped Marissa by the arm.

"Marissa?"

"Unhand her, Ardane," Ferox snapped. "Haven't you figured it out yet? She was always on my side from the very start. And you, as much a love-besotted fool as your brother, allowed a woman to betray you."

Chapter Eleven

Brace stared at Marissa as comprehension dawned. Then he grasped her arm in a viselike grip and pulled her to him.

"Are his words true?" he demanded tautly, savage fury flaring in his eyes. "Did you plan to betray me all along?"

Marissa choked down the gorge rising in her throat. "For a time, yes," she whispered. "He wanted you in exchange for Candra. But I meant to tell you. I tried to last nocte."

Pain and disbelief darkened his eyes. Then Brace's expression hardened into one of cold loathing. With a curse, he released her, flinging her arm aside as if burned.

"And was our mating just another of your ploys to lure me into Ferox's clutches, to trick me into trusting you?"

Tears filled Marissa's eyes. "No . . . never. Never that."

"Come, come," Ferox intruded bemusedly. "This is all quite sweet and tender, but I've neither the time nor patience for a lovers' spat. Get up and get dressed, Ardane. And don't try anything stupid."

Brace eyed Marissa with a lingering stare. Then, with a bitter twist of his mouth, he rose and began to dress. Marissa watched him with anguished longing. Her gaze slid down his body, admiring his impossibly wide shoulders and the play of lithe brawn across his broad chest and back, the whipcord muscle and sinew of his powerful thighs and buttocks. He was so beautiful . . . so magnificent, and he'd never be hers again.

In the end, her intentions to tell him all didn't matter. Reality was now the hard-eyed man with his murderous band of followers. Reality was now that Brace was a captive— just as Ferox had always intended—and she had betrayed him by omission just as surely as if she'd planned it all along.

When his boots and breeches were on and his tunic laced together, Brace was bound hand and foot with beryllium shackles. He never once resisted. Fleetingly Marissa wondered if his submission was more from the shock of her betrayal than from the overwhelming odds. Whatever the reason, his eyes, burning with disgust, never left hers.

"Now it's your turn, my pretty femina," Ferox's smooth voice prodded, wrenching Marissa from her misery. "Time for you to get dressed."

She shot him a disbelieving look, hoping against hope he was jesting in his intent to have her rise from the bed naked and dress before them all. He wasn't. His glittering stare was tinged with a lustful anticipation, as were those of his men.

Nausea twisted her stomach into a tight little knot. By all that was sacred, to have to bare her body—!

"Shall I have a few of my men help you, femina?"

The thought of strange male hands upon her moved Marissa to action. With a disdainful toss of her head, she rose from the pile of quilts, proudly naked.

"No, I think not," she replied haughtily. "I'm quite capable of dressing myself."

Hot, hungry eyes followed her every movement as Marissa proceeded to dress. Her face flushed and humiliation rose to choke her, but she refused to cringe or fumble hurriedly with her clothes. There was little left her in this moment of shame—for her nakedness as well as loss of Brace's trust and affection—but she still had her dignity. No one would ever take that away.

At last she was dressed. Her glance snared Brace's as she defiantly lifted her head. An expression of excruciating distaste and cold indifference smoldered in his eyes.

Marissa faltered, cut to the quick. Didn't he care that all these men had seen what she had given only to him? Had their mating meant that little?

She hid her pain behind a mask of cool neutrality as a storm of emotions roiled within. She deserved his anger, his distrust, but she didn't deserve the utter loathing—not after the nocte they'd just shared. Not unless . . . not unless Brace Ardane had finally gotten what he'd sought, and now had no further use for her!

Confusion flooded Marissa. But how could that be? Had she been so blind, so driven by her own lust, not to have seen it until now?

By the Crystal Fires, it was too much to consider at a moment such as this! Marissa turned to face Ferox. He grinned wolfishly back at her.

"Not so happy with your lover anymore, are you? Well, no matter. You're exquisite. Once I've finished with Ardane, I must do us both a favor and mate with you." He glanced at Brace. "After him, I dare say you'll find me quite impressive."

"You flatter yourself!"

Ferox quirked a brow. "Really, femina? You're such a little tease. But then, perhaps that's what makes you so desirable."

He motioned toward her. "Escort our compatriot out. It's past time we were on our way."

The storm had subsided, the cold winter winds having finally scoured the mountain clean of the heavy clouds. Outside, the midmorning sun shown, bathing everything in sparkling, pristine light. It was a fairy land, from the white-capped summits to the thickly laden trees—silent, serene, and beautiful.

But in the face of such bitter captivity and the painful realization of Brace's utter disdain, the scene only served to sicken Marissa. It was irony of the cruelest kind that her heart should feel so ugly and twisted, when just outside the little hut lay such breathtaking beauty.

It was life mocking her once again, Marissa decided glumly. Reminding her, in its brutally inexorable way, that she would never deserve nor have any lasting happiness.

She shot Brace a furtive glance. He, it seemed, was as doomed as she. Indeed, there'd never been any hope for either of them.

They loaded Brace upon a crudely wrought litter and carried him down the mountain to the skim crafts. In the largest of the crafts, he was pushed roughly to the back and wedged between two guards. He never once looked at Marissa. His gaze was riveted straight ahead, his features hard and frozen.

As Ferox led her to his skim craft, Marissa glanced at Brace one last, fleeting time. He was so handsome, Marissa thought achingly, and those eyes . . . eyes that could soften with tenderness until they glowed with an ineffable light. She'd once thought there'd been something special there for her, a deep affection, a caring. She'd been wrong. As wrong as her plan to betray him had always been.

Marissa turned away, the old hard, familiar shell settling back around her heart. Nothing mattered but her sister. She had to believe that—it was the only way to survive, to go on. Time to forget about Brace and his eventual fate. Time to turn all her efforts to rescuing Candra.

* * *

They headed across the mountains to Tutela, arriving under cover of darkness. It became quickly apparent that their ultimate destination was the transport station. A sleepy technician was soon roused. This time, there was no mention of the usual transport fee as the man was forced to program the interplanetary gates to Ferox's destination—Moraca. Then, with an armed guard left behind to make sure that the entourage arrived safely, Marissa and Brace transported across the Imperium with Ferox and his men.

New skim craft were awaiting them at the receiving station on Moraca. Marissa had a brief glimpse of Vitreum, the Moracan capital, before being whisked away toward the distant mountains. She wondered where they were headed and if Candra awaited at the end of their journey. The possibility that she might soon be with her sister filled Marissa with a combination of anticipation and dread—anticipation at seeing her beloved sister at last, and dread at what she might find had happened to her.

She shot Ferox a furtive glance. If he'd laid even one finger on Candra, Marissa vowed she'd kill him in the most painful of ways.

They flew for over half the nocte, until they were well into the mountains' fastness. Sol rise was just pinkening the sky when the skim crafts began their long, gliding descent. They circled in ever lower passes, landing on a broad outcropping of rock adjoining a cave on the sheer face of the mountain.

With anxiously beating heart, Marissa climbed out of the craft. Ferox held her back when she made a move toward the cave.

"Allow our guest to enter first," he commanded. "It's the hospitable thing to do, wouldn't you say?"

Marissa's glance was scathing. "And have you treated my sister as hospitably?"

Ferox chuckled, but the sound was hollow. "She's quite safe, femina. A Traveler is far too valuable to mistreat—at least until I've utilized her powers to the fullest. Afterwards..." He shrugged. "Afterwards, I'll savor her charms just as thoroughly as I plan to savor yours. Then, when I tire of you, I'll give you both to my men."

You'll be dead long before that sol rises, Marissa thought savagely. She turned her attention to the guards who were pulling Brace from the skim craft.

He stumbled and fell to his knees. The guards snickered, not offering assistance as Brace struggled to rise. His shackles gouged into his wrists until they began to bleed, while those about his ankles prevented much movement of his legs. He fell several times in his attempt to stand, and still the guards stood there, cruel grins on their faces.

Anger flooded Marissa, but she refused to consider its source. She turned to Ferox.

"Are we to wait out here all sol while your men are entertained at Ardane's expense?"

"Careful, femina," her blond companion drawled, "or your concern for our prisoner will drive me to jealousy. And that could go very badly for him."

"You mean to kill him in the end anyway," Marissa snapped. "What does it matter what I say or do?"

"Very little," Ferox admitted. "He's the brother of my lifelong enemy, you know. I intend to make his death slow and exquisitely painful. And every excruciating secundae of his torture will be projected back to Aranea for Teran to watch—until his brother dies, screaming for mercy, before his very eyes."

A cold emptiness filled Marissa. She didn't care. She didn't *dare* let herself care. All her efforts must be directed to freeing Candra and escaping Ferox's evil clutches. Yet the thought of leaving Brace to such cruel torment tore at her heart. There must be some way to free him as well, if only she could devise a plan.

Marissa knew now that there'd be no simple trade, Brace in exchange for Candra. As she and Brace had suspected all along, Ferox had a definite purpose for her sister. A purpose Marissa had yet to discover, but the wait wouldn't be long now.

She watched as Ferox signaled to his men. They yanked Brace to his feet and began to drag him forward. Then, grasping her arm, Ferox led Marissa behind them. Into the dark mouth of the cave they went, taking narrow, twisting turns until they were deep inside. At last they entered a large, brightly lit chamber.

Marissa scanned the room for sign of Candra. She wasn't there.

"Where's my sister?" she demanded, rounding on Ferox. "You've got Ardane. Now give me Candra."

He stepped closer until their bodies were a hairbreadth apart. "You want to see your sister, do you?" A perfectly formed finger raised to stroke her face. "A kiss might help arrange that."

Nausea roiled through Marissa. The thought of kissing those smugly leering lips was almost more than she could bear. Yet just to see Candra and ascertain that she was safe and well was worth almost anything.

She lifted her face to his. "If it's a kiss you want, take it and be done."

"Ah, and that's how it's to be?" Ferox chuckled. "A sacrifice on the altar of filial loyalty. No, sweet femina. I'll accept nothing less than a passionate offering on your part. We wouldn't want Ardane to get the wrong idea, would we?"

Marissa glanced at Brace. He was standing across the chamber, ensconced between two burly guards. His hot gaze, however, was riveted upon them.

Ferox wishes to twist the dagger of my betrayal yet deeper in Brace's heart.

The realization sickened her. By the Crystal Fires, would it never end?

"Well, femina," Ferox drawled, "isn't your sister worth a brief moment of intimacy? Take a chance—you might be pleasantly surprised."

"And I say again, Ferox. You flatter yourself," Marissa muttered, forcing her attention back to him. "You're dead behind that handsome face, and I'm not particularly fond of kissing a rotting corpse."

Fury exploded in the blond man's eyes. "You'll pay for that, my *sweet* little femina. Now, kiss me and make it appear like I'm your long-lost lover, or you may never see your sister again!"

Marissa inhaled a deep breath and lifted on tiptoe to press against him. Her arms entwined about his neck. Clenching her eyes shut, she kissed Ferox.

At the first brush of her lips, he pulled her into him until she was molded to the full length of his hard-muscled body. Marissa struggled to put some space between them, but he only tightened his grip until she could barely breathe. She signaled her submission by relaxing in his arms, and he loosened his hold slightly.

His firm, sensual mouth slanted over hers, urgent, almost desperate. That realization startled Marissa. In spite of herself, she felt a fleeting stab of pity. There was *something* about him, something smoldering beneath his outward layer of cruelty—a tiny vestige of humanity, a need. Ah, if only she could reach it, find a way to fan it back to life!

Then a hot, wet tongue was prodding for entrance, shattering Marissa's brief, hopeful bout of compassion. When she refused, he pulled back to whisper, "Let me in—or else!"

With a sobbing sigh, Marissa did as commanded. He plunged into her then, kissing her with hard, brutal passion, bruising her lips as he slammed them against her teeth. His hands slipped down her back to grasp her buttocks, rocking his thick erection against her. Muttered comments and suggestive laughter from the guards reached Marissa. She thought she'd die from the shame.

At last Ferox released her. "You're a hot little piece," he observed loudly. "But, until our business is finished, I must regretfully deny myself the pleasures of your lush body." He crooked her under the chin. "You can wait, though, can't you? I'll make it worth your while."

His cold glance impaled her, demanding a response. Marissa forced herself to nod, despising herself for the action.

Ferox gripped her arm. "Come then, my pretty femina. Allow me to escort you to your sister."

He led Marissa across the chamber, passing directly before Brace. Something drew her gaze to his. He glared back at her, his eyes black with pain—and a raw, primal anger. It squeezed the breath from Marissa's lungs, this sharp, sudden realization of his instinctive response to another male possessing her.

He still wants me, she thought. *He still cares!*

Wild joy surged through her. There was yet hope, if only she could regain his trust. Their gazes locked for an instant more. Tears filled Marissa's eyes. Then Ferox was leading her away, toward a tunnel angling off from the far end of the main chamber.

Save for the flickering light of perpetual torches, the narrow passage was dark. They walked for a short time. Finally Ferox paused outside a sturdy door. Retrieving the key control from his pocket, he unlocked the door and shoved it open.

With a mocking gesture, he indicated the room. "You've a half hora, no more. Then we'll *talk*."

A slight movement within caught Marissa's eye. She squinted in the dim light, struggling to make out face and form.

"M-Marissa?" a sweet, oh, so familiar voice quavered from the darkness. "Is it really you?"

With a low cry Marissa ran to Candra, engulfing her in a fierce embrace. "Yes. Yes, it's really me, Nuggin," she, breathed, falling back on her old term of endearment for her sister. "By the Crystal Fires, I feared I might never see you alive again!"

Marissa leaned back to critically study her. "You *are* all right, aren't you?"

Candra chuckled and clasped Marissa back

to her. "Quite all right. Have you come to rescue me?"

"After a fashion," her sister replied dryly.

Trusting eyes lifted to hers. "Though I feared for you, I knew you'd come," Candra murmured. "You were always the strong, resourceful one. My sister, Marissa Laomede, the famous warrior."

Bitterness filled Marissa. There was nothing particularly strong or resourceful about her now. Instead, thanks to Ferox, she felt helpless and violated. Just like all the other women of her planet.

A sudden thought struck her. For all his wounded fury at what he saw as her betrayal of him, Brace had never made her feel as degraded or common as Ferox had. Never, not even in those moments of greatest anger and disdain. She knew now that those feelings had been but a shield to hide his deeper emotions.

Brace had always treated her as all equal, encouraging her when she dared reach beyond her fears, gently chiding her when she didn't. Brace, the tender lover and faithful friend— and the man she, in the end, had unwillingly led into the clutches of a slime-rotted fiend.

With a violent shake of her head, Marissa flung the heart-rending memories aside. This was no time to be weakened by sentiment. Candra came first. Perhaps later, when her safety was assured, there'd be a chance to help Brace.

She stepped back from her sister. "We must talk fast and quietly. Do you have any idea why

Ferox brought you here, what he wants from you?"

"He told me very little." A fretful tone tinged Candra's voice. "He's been hateful, keeping me looked up in this damp, dark cell all this time, and my only visitors the ones that brought me food, a bath, or fresh clothes. I thought you'd never get here. Yet, at the same time, I didn't want you to come."

"Is that why you refused to commune with me? Surely you heard my call?"

Candra sighed. "Yes, I heard you, and it nearly tore my heart out not to answer, but somehow I knew we were safe as long as we were apart. As fearful as Ferox is, I knew he'd never harm me. For some reason, he needs me too much to do that. Just as he seems to need you."

"It's not me he wants," Marissa muttered. "It's the male I brought with me."

"Ferox mentioned something about you bringing someone, someone with special powers. Is this male the one?"

"Yes."

"Good," Candra responded happily. "Ferox said I must help this male with a very special task, and then we'd be free to go. When can we begin, do you think?"

"On the morrow, probably."

Marissa's thoughts raced. They had only one more nocte to formulate a plan. And she needed desperately to learn more of this mountain fortress, its exits, how well it was guarded, and the best route to make their escape by.

Let Candra think that Ferox meant to free them once he was finished with her services. There was no purpose served in distressing her. As much as she loved her sister, Marissa had always known that Candra was too gentle and sheltered to ever be more than a hindrance on this quest. It was up to her to handle things, and make certain Candra didn't get hurt in the process. It was the only way to ensure both their lives.

"Do you know any way out of here, besides that sheer cliff entrance?" Marissa asked.

Candra's smooth brow wrinkled in thought. "I once heard the guards talking outside. They mentioned something about a back way, through a tunnel off the main chamber."

Marissa recalled at least five, if not six, tunnels leading from the main room. "Which tunnel, Candra? I need to know exactly which one!"

"Well, you needn't be so sharp about it. It's not as if I were given free access here!"

Frustration filled Marissa. Had it come to this, that she was reduced to snapping at her own sister? Yet, how, by all that was sacred, was she going to obtain the freedom, much less unobserved opportunity, to examine all those tunnels? Well, at least there *was* another escape route—*if* they could only find it in time.

"And have you heard anything about how

many guards there are, and where they're stationed?"

Candra shook her head. "They hardly talk to me, you know, and I've never had a head for numbers at any rate." She studied Marissa. "I'm not much help, am I?"

"It doesn't matter," was her sister's glum reply. "We'll figure out something."

"I'm sorry, Marissa. I always depended on you to make the decisions, didn't I?"

"There was no need for anything else in those sols," Marissa hurried to assure her. "And there would never have been if I hadn't been cast out."

They exchanged an anguished, heartfelt look.

"You took my soul, my happiness with you when you left. Ah, Marissa, it's been so long since we last embraced!" Candra exclaimed, again hugging her sister tightly. "I always worried about you, though you soon sent word you were safe with the Sodalitas. And in my heart and mind you were always near, until that sol when Ferox abducted me."

She shuddered in remembrance. "He took me all over the Imperium, it seemed, before finally returning to Moraca. He had a strange stone in a box with him, which he used against an old man who refused to help him."

"You were there when Ferox visited Lord Ardane?"

"I don't know what the old man's name was, and I was never in the room with them. All I recall is that after Ferox was with him awhile, the old man began to scream. Then we left. Ferox sent me here and he stayed behind 'to wait for someone.'"

"That must have been us."

"It was indeed."

Both women whirled around. Ferox stood in the open doorway, a cynical grin twisting his face.

"Come, Marissa," he said, motioning her forward. "You've visited long enough. Time for our talk. You'll see your sister again on the morrow."

"Please, my lord," Candra pleaded. "Could she not spend the nocte with me? We've had so little time—"

"Come, Marissa!" he repeated stonily. "No more trouble, or your sister will pay!"

Immediately, Marissa stepped forward. "I am at your command, *my lord*."

"Don't mock me, femina!"

She answered her captor with a sardonic arch of her brow, then brushed past him into the tunnel. Ferox grabbed her as she started back toward the main chamber, jerking Marissa to a halt.

"Time for our little talk, my pretty femina." He smiled as he began to lead her in the opposite direction. "And we have *so* much to discuss."

Marissa considered attempting to make a run for it, but a quick scan of the guards posted at short intervals down the corridor quashed that idea. Better to lull him into a false sense of security and bide her time, she decided. Gritting her teeth, Marissa allowed Ferox to escort her down the tunnel to yet another room.

The small chamber was a surprise. Lushly appointed, it held a couch and two chairs positioned before a quaintly wrought stone hearth lit by the smokeless flames of a perpetual fire. Vibrant tapestries covered the wall, making the chamber seem more like a snug little room than a cave. A low, ornately carved chest stood against one wall and on it was a tray set with a flask and several cups. A large bowl overflowing with cerasa fruit and uva berries sat nearby.

Ferox motioned for her to sit while he strode to the chest. "Care for some Moracan ale? I greatly prefer its rich tang to that of wine."

Marissa shook her head. "No. No, thank you."

She glanced about the room, distracted by the strange, sweet scent that lingered in the air. A small brazier stood in one corner, the sensuous curl of smoke rising from a single glowing coal. Incense, she thought. But laden with what—a hypnotic, a mind probe, or even worse, a lust inducer?

That last possibility sickened her. By all that was sacred, she couldn't bear that! She just couldn't!

Marissa whirled about to face him. "What's

in that incense?" she demanded. "If you mean to drug me—"

"Calm yourself, femina." His voice was low and strangely soothing. "It's nothing more than a scent to take the edge off the stone damp."

"Then put it out!"

The corner of his sensuous mouth curled, then Ferox strode to the brazier and poured a dollop of his ale on the coal. With a snap and a sizzle, the smoking incense was extinguished.

Ferox turned. "Satisfied?"

Marissa nodded warily.

"Good. Now, please," he said with a sweep of his hand, "sit down."

Reluctantly, she complied, then watched as Ferox took his place across from her. He sipped his cup of ale and eyed her.

The room closed in as Marissa sat there, the air becoming heavy, smothering. The tension grew and it was all she could do to mask her rising anxiety. Her fists clenched in her lap.

He was studying her like some specimen on a lab plate, she thought in rising anger, like some predator contemplating its prey. And there was nothing she could do but wait for the first strike, then fend it off as best she could. Her warrior's instincts sharpened, readying for battle, yet the attack, when it finally came, was from such an unexpected quarter that Marissa was momentarily taken off guard.

"Your sister is terrified of men."

She stared at him, speechless, unable to fathom his meaning or intent. Was he implying that someone had raped Candra? But that couldn't be! Candra would have told her. Or would she? There'd have been nothing either of them could do about it, and Candra might have meant to spare her.

Fear rushed in to chill the very marrow of her bones. Then came the hot surge of rage.

"What did you do to her, you slime-rotted fiend?" Marissa cried, leaping to her feet. "If you or any of your men laid one hand on my sister, I swear I'll—"

Ferox held up a placating hand, chuckling all the while. "Ever the rescuer, eh, Marissa? Well, calm yourself. No one has touched her. I value her special talents too highly to mar them in any way."

He paused, visually ordering her to retake her seat. When she finally did, he continued. "I was but making an observation. I just find it very odd how you two can look so much alike, yet be so opposite in character."

He set down his cup to temple his fingers beneath his chin. "She's so timid, so gentle, so afraid of her own emotions and you ... well, you're a refreshingly strong and vibrant woman."

Unease coiled within Marissa. Ferox was leading up to something. She forced herself to sit there and wait.

The secundae ticked by. Gradually Ferox's expression transformed from one of avid interest to that same haunted, almost vulnerable look he'd had just before he kissed her. And still he said nothing. The anticipation grew, clawing at her tightly strung nerves until Marissa thought she'd scream.

"Ardane's very lucky," his deep voice suddenly sliced through the heavy tension. "Very, very lucky to have a woman like you to love and nurture and protect him. Just like a mother..."

Marissa blinked in surprise. There was almost a pensive note to his words, words that suddenly appeared fraught with a deeper, darker meaning. Realization flared to life, fanned by her desperation into a wild flame of hope. Perhaps Ferox did indeed have a chink in his armor—and perhaps, just perhaps, it had something to do with his mother.

Well, she had nothing to lose. Marissa wet her lips.

"You loved your mother, did you? Want to find a woman just like her?"

"Wh-what?" Ferox nearly strangled on the word, a stunned look on his face. Then his handsome features softened. "Yes," he breathed. "She was the most beautiful woman I've ever known."

"What happened to her?"

The door slammed down on his loving memories. Ferox's face hardened, resuming their familiar, shuttered look. "She's dead."

The flatness of his reply startled her. "I—I'm sorry."

Marissa hesitated, her thoughts racing. She had to get him to open up, to again reveal that fleeting moment of vulnerability, if she were to have any hope of influencing him. But how?

"You're a very attractive man," she ventured carefully. "Some sol you'll find a woman to love you like she did."

His harsh bark of laughter reverberated through the room. "No. It's too late."

"Too late? Why?"

He shot her a smoldering glance. "Don't play games with me, femina. You know as well as I that my life is on a set course. I long ago made my decision. And I won't stop now until I've won control of the Imperium and mastery of the Knowing Crystal."

He shook his head fiercely. "There's no time left for tenderness, for love. Indeed, there never was . . ." His eyes darkened with some fleeting memory. "I almost had it once. I almost won my mother's love."

Excitement coursed through Marissa. Here was her chance, if she could just win his trust!

"You *almost* won your mother's love? Didn't you always have it?"

"No. Never." Once more his features hardened, and his voice lowered to a harsh whisper. "I was always perfect, from the moment of my birth, and still she rejected me. Rejected me, just as my father had. But he didn't matter. I never knew him. It was my mother I wanted."

He glanced up. Marissa was struck by his

expression of childlike innocence—and the deepest anguish she'd ever seen.

"I tried all those cycles to win her love, to be worthy of her," Ferox continued softly. "And I almost succeeded when I entered the Imperial Academy and became its finest student. She noticed me then. As I reaped honor upon honor in my early cycles there, I finally realized that only the very best would ever be good enough for her—and that I had finally achieved it."

Bitterness transformed his face and voice. "Then Teran Ardane came. He stole my glory, my honors. Just as greedily as he'd taken everything else of value in my life. Then, my mother turned from me forever. Turned from me—and straight to Ardane."

His voice changed, becoming shrill, peevish. "She told me she wanted him, was in love with him, but I knew the real truth. She'd been obsessed with the Ardanes her whole life. Teran was but another chance to achieve her dream. And she was still a very beautiful, very desirable woman, even twenty cycles his senior.

"But still he rejected her. Can you b-believe it?" Ferox nearly choked on the words. "Ardane rejected my mother's love—the love she'd never given to me! He had what I would never have, and tossed it aside as if it were of no value! I hate him most of all for that!"

As she listened, horror rose in Marissa. She understood now the full extent of Ferox's lifelong enmity toward Brace's brother. In the end, Teran, however unintentionally, had taken everything from Ferox. From boyhood on, the fatherless Ferox's entire self-concept had been tied into pleasing his mother and winning her love. Then Teran had entered the picture and not only bested him academically, but had also easily gained the only thing Ferox could never have and so ardently sought—his mother.

It was all so tragic, an utter waste of a brilliantly talented life—a life now twisted to such evil, maniacal intent. And the intent, she realized with a sinking feeling, ran too deep to ever be turned from its inexorable course of self-destruction.

Marissa lifted her gaze, a gaze filled with compassion. "I'm so sorry."

Fury exploded in Ferox's eyes. "I don't want your pity! I don't want anyone's pity!" A crazed, haunted expression contorted his face. "They all guessed, you know. That my mother never loved me. That I was only half the man I was born to be. And they laughed at me behind my back."

He inhaled a tremulous breath. "But they'll not laugh much longer. Soon I'll be ruler of the Imperium and master of the Knowing Crystal. *Then they'll never laugh at me again!*"

The blond head suddenly dipped; the broad shoulders slumped. "My mother won't ever laugh at me again, either," he whispered in that eerie, little-boy voice.

The sound sent a cold prickle down Marissa's spine.

"She laughed one time too many, that sol I went to her and begged her one last time to love me," Ferox said. "And I . . . I finally killed her for it."

Somehow Marissa had known what was coming. It seemed the inevitable culmination of his unfortunate, twisted life. Yet his mother's murder hadn't exorcised Ferox's personal demons. It had only turned him from one violent path to another. And only death would end his tormented madness.

"I sicken you, don't I?"

The harsh rasp of Ferox's voice sliced through Marissa's rising despair. She forced herself to meet his steely gaze.

"No, you don't sicken me. What you've done, allowed yourself to become, sickens me. Your mother, the father who rejected you, are the ones at fault. Not Teran Ardane. Not the Imperium."

He howled with laughter, the sound wild, frightening. "And you *presume* to judge me? You, who have been cheated out of your own birthright—and had to watch another, far less worthy person, claim it? I thought better of you, Marissa. Thought that you, of all people, would understand."

"I—I'm trying to understand. Truly I am."

"Are you, Marissa?" Ferox shrugged. "Well, no matter. In the end, only one thing is of any import. Obedience."

266

She swallowed hard and returned his half-mad gaze. "Then why tell me this, if all you want is obedience?"

"We are partners now, my sweet little femina. And I *will* have your cooperation, your understanding—and your love." His eyes narrowed to glittering slits. "You *do* love me, don't you, Marissa?"

There was something in his voice, in his eyes that boded ill if she denied him what he asked. And there was far too much at stake to quibble over a few meaningless words.

Marissa wet her lips. "Yes, I love you."

He smiled then, and it was heart-stoppingly beautiful—and disconcertingly familiar.

"Good. I knew you wouldn't fail me. Now, there's one last thing I need from you, to ensure the success of tomorrow's undertaking."

A vague uneasiness snaked about Marissa's heart. In that fleeting moment when Ferox had smiled, he'd reminded her of someone. But who?

She forced herself to reply. "And what's that? What do you want from me?"

"I want Ardane primed to cooperate. It'll save us all valuable time." He paused to take one last swallow of his cup, then again set it aside. "It's all quite simple, really. I want you to regain Ardane's trust and affection this nocte, so he'll be more amenable on the morrow."

It was Marissa's turn to laugh. "You're mad.

267

After what's happened, do you seriously think he'll ever trust me again?"

Ferox rose from his chair. "Prove your love for me, sweet femina. Regain his trust—in any way you can. You won't regret it."

He offered her his hand.

Marissa eyed it warily. "Where are you taking me?"

"Why, nowhere but to Ardane. He's sure to be lonely this nocte. It's the perfect opportunity for you. And you do want to please me, don't you, Marissa?"

She stood, her fists clenched at her side. By the Crystal Fires, how much further must she debase herself?

"Yes, more than anything, I want to please you," Marissa cried, nearly strangling on the lie. "That, and win Candra's freedom!"

Ferox motioned her forward, a bitter, knowing look in his eyes. "Then you have the perfect opportunity this nocte—working the ageless deceit of a woman's love."

Brace shifted his position on the hard stone floor, but it did little to ease his discomfort. The rocks dug sharply into his back, and his arms, electronically secured in the beryllium shackles to the wall above his head, were already growing numb. The cell was dark, damp, and cold. Brace envisioned a long, miserable nocte ahead.

A nocte without much hope of rest, with plenty of time to replay the brutal recollection of Marissa's betrayal. He'd thought he'd known her, thought he'd begun to win her heart, if only a little. Her passionate response during their mating hadn't been that of such a calculating woman.

He'd been a fool. A love-besotted fool.

Perhaps that was what hurt most of all. He had given Marissa his love, with all the tender ardor of his heart and body if not yet his words, and then watched her toss it aside—as if it were an insignificant thing—and run to Ferox's arms.

Brace groaned and closed his eyes. How could Marissa find anything to care about in a man such as Ferox? What manner of woman was she really? He had never known her. Never...

Hollow footsteps thudded down the tunnel. Brace listened dispiritedly until they paused outside his cell. The lock clicked and the door swung open. Brace turned.

There, her face shadowed in the dim light, was Marissa. Beside her stood Ferox. Brace tensed.

"What do you want?" he rasped. "Haven't had your fill of gloating?"

"A lifetime would never be enough!" Ferox snarled. "As you'll soon see. But a doomed man is entitled to one last nocte of comfort, and I knew you'd want to spend it with the femina. Renewing old friendships, reminiscing about passionate encounters—"

"Get her out of here!"

Kathleen Morgan

Ferox shoved Marissa forward. "Go to him, sweet femina. Soothe his tired brow, and any other part of his body that may need comforting. He wants you, even if his pride won't allow him to admit it. And it'll be the last nocte he'll ever have with a woman."

Brace watched Ferox exit the cell. A pained, angry frustration churned within. Curse the man, but he was right. Even in light of Marissa's betrayal, he desired her still. Even now, his body ached for her. If she came to him, touched him in any way, Brace feared he might shame himself and beg her to kiss him, hold him—love him.

He fought back against the tender feelings and hardened his heart. He had to, or he was lost.

"Whose little idea was this—yours or Ferox's?" Brace demanded.

Marissa winced at the icy contempt dripping from his words. "Ferox's."

"Couldn't face me, eh? Strange, I never thought you a coward. But then," he growled, "I never thought you such a sneaking little conniver, either."

"I didn't mean to betray you!"

"Liar!"

She moved to his side, sinking to her knees. "You must believe me, Brace. I meant to tell you last nocte, but you wouldn't let me. And then, just before we fell asleep, I vowed to myself to tell you on the morrow. But when we awoke, Ferox was there."

270

"How convenient for you."

"Curse you, Brace Ardane!" Marissa cried, stung by his bitter sarcasm.

He riveted the full force of his anger upon her. "Have no fear, *sweet* femina. I've been cursed since the first moment I met you, and most likely will to my dying breath. But take heart. Neither of us will have to suffer the other's presence much longer. Ferox will see to that!"

A harsh sob wracked her slender frame. "I don't want you to die! I—I love you!"''

Marissa's breath caught in her throat. What had she said? How could she reveal such emotions? But the words, now uttered, must be faced. And, as the secundae passed, the enormity of her admission failed to lessen, nor the searing truth behind it.

She did indeed love Brace, but when or how it had happened was yet a mystery. At this moment, it didn't matter anyway. Only one thing mattered—convincing him.

A soft, wondering smile curved her mouth. "I love you."

"And do you think I care?" he demanded cruelly. "I've seen how freely you give your 'love.' I don't want anything you've shared with Ferox!"

"I've given him nothing!"

"That kiss a short while ago told me differently."

Marissa sighed. "It wasn't what it seemed.

He threatened to harm Candra if I didn't kiss him. And he did it solely to anger you."

Brace remained silent, his gaze hard, his mouth stubborn.

"It worked, too, didn't it?"

He didn't answer.

She scooted closer until her knee pressed against his muscular thigh. The simple touch sent a tremor of awareness through Marissa. She inhaled a ragged breath.

"Ah, Brace, what can I say or do to prove I never meant to betray you—or at least never after last nocte? Before, I admit that had been my plan. What choice did I have? He wanted you in exchange for Candra."

"And nothing matters more than your beloved sister. You needn't say more, Marissa. I understand completely."

"It's never been that simple, Brace," she replied softly. "It's always been more than just Candra. My life was in as much danger as hers."

His eyes narrowed. "Go on."

"From the moment of birth the tie between twins is powerful. By the time they reach puberty, however, an even more forceful bond, a life-link, has been forged. It binds one to the other so strongly that when one twin dies, so does the other. That's why my people always cast out the non-Traveler twin to perish before the onset of puberty. It's the only way to save the twin of value."

"And now it's too late?"

Marissa nodded. "It's been too late for cycles."

As the full implication of her words struck him, Brace's resolve to steel himself against Marissa wavered. If her words were true, she'd had good reason to keep so much from him. For Marissa, this quest was truly one of life and death. And could he blame her if she'd felt that the lives of her and her sister were of more value than his? What would he have done if the tables had been turned, and his and Teran's lives had been at stake?

Anger surged through him. It wouldn't have mattered. He'd have fought as strongly for Marissa as he would for his and his brother's life. He loved her too much to do any less.

That realization hurt most of all. No matter what she'd proclaimed earlier, Marissa didn't love him enough to do the same.

A fierce resolve filled him. He could forgive her betrayal because it had meant her life, and join again with her on the quest to save her sister, but he could never again trust her with his heart.

Once more, the look in Brace's eyes froze to brittle iciness. "You still could have confided in me. We could have worked out some plan to thwart Ferox and still preserve both your lives."

"Yes, perhaps so," Marissa admitted, "but there was so much at stake and I didn't trust you for a long while. You knew that. And by the time I did, it was too late."

273

"I agree. It's far too late."

"Why?" she whispered, her hand moving to stroke his face, then lower to rest upon his chest. "Why does it have to be too late?"

"Because it is, Marissa!" he cried. "Now, get your deceitful little hands off me!"

She felt his heart quicken beneath her touch, a tremor wrack his powerful body. Felt it and knew a woman's secret satisfaction. Though his words and voice said one thing, his body said another. And, for once, Marissa followed her instincts with no consideration of the consequences.

"No, I think not," she murmured, her voice purring, silky.

Her hand slipped inside his tunic to glide across the bulging planes of his chest, her fingers tangling in the crisp furring of hair. "It's never too late where there's life and love. And I intend to spend the rest of this nocte, if necessary, proving that to you."

Chapter Twelve

"It won't work, Marissa," Brace said without emotion, his voice cold and hard as stone. "I won't let myself want a woman who with one breath says she loves me and with the next betrays me."

Marissa began to unlace the front of his tunic. "Is it that simple for you, Brace? To be torn between between love and duty, and so easily choose one over the other?"

She spread open the two halves of his garment, baring his chest, and smiled, a slow, provocative smile. "Even now, I can barely remember what came between us. Even now, all I recall is how you touched me, loved me, felt inside me last nocte."

Her finger stroked a flat male nipple nestled in its dark, whorling sea of hair. Brace sucked in a breath. Marissa's eyes lifted to his.

"You're so very sensitive, my love," she murmured. "I wonder... how you'd respond... if I kissed you?"

He jerked his head aside as she lowered her mouth to his, but Marissa quickly captured it and held it in place. "There's nothing you can do, is there?" she asked, her lips a breath away from his. "I can do whatever I choose, and you can't stop me."

His hot, angry gaze slammed into hers. "You can't make me want you!"

"No, but I don't need to. You already want me. All I've got to do is make you admit it."

"And the Crystal Fires will freeze—"

Her lips, settling softly over his, silenced his furious reply. Brace stiffened against her. His mouth clamped shut.

Amusement filled Marissa. How like a stubborn little maiden he was, fighting her.

But not for long. Somehow, some way, she'd convince him of her love this nocte. The morrow was a frightening, doom-shrouded sol, but they'd at least have this nocte. A nocte no one could ever take from them, a nocte that would last through all eternity.

Marissa leaned back and stroked the tumbled hair from his forehead. "Relax, love. I won't hurt you. I'll go slow, be gentle with you."

She was mocking him, repeating some of the words he'd used in his attempts to seduce her. Brace glared back at her.

"I don't want you, Marissa!"

"Really?"

Her mouth covered his again, taking his lips in a fierce, devouring kiss. She touched her tongue to his lips, circling the sensuous fullness, then lightly, teasingly licked him. His

276

eyes clenched shut, and his mouth remained closed.

She moved to his ear, softly kissing, licking, and nibbling there. Brace shuddered, then once more stiffened, forcing his body into rigid unyieldingness. Marissa smiled as her lips trailed down his neck, lingering over the hot, throbbing pulse in his throat.

The heady, musky smell of him rose to her nostrils, and she inhaled deeply of his masculine scent. Marissa's heart began a wild, staccato rhythm, sending blood coursing through her body. She became acutely aware of every delicious aspect of the man beneath her. His warm breath, the sensuous feel of his smooth skin beneath his hairiness, the searing heat of his body. Ah, how she wanted him!

Her mouth followed her fingers as they trailed down his muscled torso until her lips captured a velvet nipple. She laved it lightly at first, then more aggressively until it puckered in arousal. Her own nipples tingled with a similar sensation. She took his now taut nipple into her mouth and sucked, long and hard.

Brace inhaled a ragged breath and moved beneath her, twisting futilely in the shackles that bound him. "Marissa," he rasped. "Stop ...it! I don't...want...this!"

"Yes, you do, my love," she purred. "You want it as badly as I."

As her mouth continued to lave first one nipple, then the other, Marissa's hand moved to his breeches. He jerked away, but not before she felt the hard swelling, stiffly straining beneath the cloth. Her hand slipped down to capture him. Brace went still.

Marissa's head lifted, her gaze meeting his. His eyes burned, hot and tormented. Beneath the fingers still resting lightly upon his chest, she felt his muscles leap reflexively, then draw taut and hard. A sensual haze engulfed Marissa and, with it, a new, primitive urgency.

Slender fingers tightened around him and she began to stroke his long, thick length, kneading, squeezing, sliding up and down. His eyelids lowered and his head fell back. A groan, low and male, escaped him.

"Marissa . . ." he breathed.

Triumph surged through her. She had power over him, a power he was helpless to resist. It filled her with joy and an immense, gut-deep satisfaction. Yet, even as Brace yielded to her, she felt her own heart and body yielding as well. And there was no defeat for either of them—only the victory of an impending, exquisite pleasure.

The pace and rhythm of her stroking quickened. Brace moved more restlessly now, writhing, his hips betraying his rising excitement by spasmodic little arches. Marissa leaned over him once more, her mouth slanting hotly, hungrily over his. This time, he responded.

His lips parted, his tongue plunged into Marissa's mouth, then slowly retreated to plunge again and again. She gasped with startled pleasure, then ardently met him, joining in a deep, savage kiss. Her fingers grew impatient. She fumbled with the fastening of Brace's breeches, freeing him. The big tip of his aroused sex sprang out against her hand.

From some distant corner of Brace's mind a tiny voice screamed that he should fight her, that no matter what she did to his body he must never surrender. She'd betrayed him and would surely do so again. And that betrayal would only hurt the more if he mated with her, allowed her to win this nocte.

But his loins ached with a fierce, burgeoning fullness, a fullness that would become agony if he didn't soon find release. And in spite of everything, he wanted her, loved her—forgave her. It was his ultimate shame, and yet, his greatest glory.

With a groan, Brace wrenched his mouth away. "Marissa," he whispered, "let me see you, kiss your body. I need it. Ah, Gods, how I need it!"

She leaned back from him and lifted her arms to slip out of her tunic. Brace had a brief glimpse of the soft mounds of her breasts straining against the tautly stretched cloth, then her upper torso was bared. His eyes narrowed to glittering slits as his gaze slid over her, hungrily taking in the smooth expanse of ivory flesh and pert, full breasts with their rose-colored, softly pouting nipples.

"Move closer, femina," he commanded. "Give me your breasts."

Marissa bent over until he could feel the heat

emanating from her, smell her fragrant feminine scent. With a soft smile, she cupped a breast and lifted it to his mouth. His lips caught her nipple, tugging it, sucking it.

Marissa whimpered. The pace of her hand, sliding up and down his straining shaft, quickened. Brace arched, his hips joining the wildly frantic rhythm. He released her nipple to nuzzle his face in the soft valley between her breasts.

"Please," he gasped, "let me see all of you! I need—I want you!"

She pulled back from Brace and slipped off her boots and breeches. Then Marissa moved to sit astride him, tugging down his breeches to below his knees. Brace's legs spread, granting her greater access. She cupped him gently there, fondling his hair-roughened sac and hardened shaft.

His breath came fast and harsh now, and a fine sheen of sweat matted his chest and torso. He groaned.

"Marissa!"

"Tell me you love me," she demanded, leaning over to rub her sensitive, swollen breasts against his face. "Tell me, even if it's a lie. I don't care. I need to hear it, to believe it, if only for just one nocte."

His tormented gaze met hers, and an aching tenderness filled his eyes. "I love you, femina. I've always loved you."

"Ah, you lie so beautifully," she whispered. "I almost believe you."

Brace sadly shook his head. "Believe, Marissa. I may be a fool, but I've never been a liar."

"Then we're both the most glorious of fools, my love."

She moved then, her white thighs straddling Brace as she lowered herself atop him. His shaft brushed against her. Brace groaned again.

Marissa reached down and grasped him, lifting his big, wet tip to slide up and down her soft woman's flesh. He jerked against his shackles and growled, the sound animal, desperate with warning.

"Marissa!"

She trembled wildly and, inhaling a deep breath, thrust him up into her.

"Gods!"

Marissa's head bent and she shuddered with the wild sensations coursing through her. She could feel him, every bit of him, all his slickness and power. And it felt good, oh so very good! If she did nothing else in her life, she could stay here just like this, impaled by his thick, deliciously hard shaft.

"Marissa . . . ?"

She glanced down at him, into dark, tender eyes, eyes burning with a barely contained need. Burning with a tormented question. She smiled.

"Yes. Oh, yes!"

With a growl Brace thrust up into her then, his hips grinding into hers with a fierce, ever increasing tempo. She moaned and pumped her own body against his, wildly, frantically. His head lifted to capture a puckered nipple and he alternately suckled then nipped at it until Marissa thought she'd go mad from the exquisite torment.

She grasped at his straining shoulders, digging her nails into his sweat-dampened flesh. The fire between her legs built to an aching, unbearable tension. All reason fled. Marissa thrashed violently, her body grinding against his. No matter how rough or deeply he plunged, she couldn't seem to get enough. The swollen length of him, sliding smoothly in and out, only increased her wildly rising need. He felt . . . so . . . wonderful!

And, all the while, Brace moved in relentless thrusts, pounding against her, hard, strong, and sure. Their harsh breaths mingled, filling the stone chamber, rising to engulf them in a heated blur of passion and sound. Engulf them until there was nothing in the universe but their damp, heated, straining bodies.

Finally it was too much to bear. As he drove into her, Marissa felt his mouth on her nipple, the sharp bite of his teeth. The delicious sensation sent her spiraling over the edge. With a keening cry she clutched Brace's head to her breast, trembling above him. Waves upon waves of ecstasy shuddered through her.

When Marissa began to rhythmically tighten around him, Brace could hold back no longer. With his own raw cry he arched up into her. Rigid with the tension of his violent release, his arms straining against his shackles, he shot his seed into her. For endless, exquisite secundae, they remained pressed together—molded, joined—body and soul as one.

Then the moment passed. Slowly they relaxed, returning to reality—and a cold, dark cell. Yet the tender comfort of each other's bodies sustained them for a time, as pounding hearts quieted and ragged breathing eased. They clung together, still hungry for the feel of the other, until the sated, heavy curtain of sleep engulfed them.

"Welcome, welcome," Ferox said the next morning, as Brace and Marissa were unceremoniously ushered into his presence. "I hope you rested well, for there's much to be accomplished this sol."

His keen glance assessed them, noting Marissa's sudden flush at the quick look Brace shot her. Ferox grinned.

"Yes, I can see you both did. Good, good. Mended hearts will only serve to further my plans." He motioned to the guards. "Escort our guest to the chair and bind him in it. Then bring in our little Traveler."

Shackled though he was, it took four men to drag Brace to the chair and force him into it. His wrists and ankles were then bound by beryllium bands fastened to the chair arms and legs. Brace soon ceased his struggles and glared at Ferox.

Kathleen Morgan

"You won't succeed in this!" he snarled. "Someone will always rise to oppose you."

"Like your father did?" He laughed. "He never had a chance, you know, even before I got to him. He dared defy the Knowing Crystal, attempted to control its powers. As if one man could ever stand alone against a force like that. I tried to convince him to join with me, that together we could contain the stone and he'd regain his sanity. But the old fool wouldn't listen."

"It seems," he sighed, "that you Crystal Masters are uniquely unwilling to key the stone for the use of others. But you'll help me, won't you, Ardane? You have a lot more to lose than just your own life."

Brace followed the blond man's mocking gaze until it came to rest upon Marissa. Ferox smiled and arched a sardonic brow. Rage surged through Brace.

"Curse you, I've no power over the Crystal! But even if I did, I'd never use it to help the likes of you!"

Ferox snickered. "Give it up, Ardane. You're no more than an insignificant pawn in this, my ultimate possession of the Knowing Crystal—and final revenge against your brother." His glance moved to Marissa. "She understands all too well what's at stake here. *She* knows how far I'll go to achieve my goal."

He pulled her to him, forcing Marissa's rigid body close to his. Ferox glanced back at Brace.

"And you wouldn't want your femina harmed now, would you?"

Barely contained fury smoldered in Brace's eyes.

Ferox chuckled. "No, I didn't think so. But then, neither do I. Unfaithful slut though she is, I still mean to have her." He cocked a dark blond brow in consideration. "Maybe I'll even let you watch. It all depends on how cooperative you are."

The door opened and Candra was escorted in. Her wide-eyed gaze found Marissa and, with a small cry, she twisted free and ran to her. Ferox released Marissa. The two sisters embraced.

"Candra," Marissa whispered. "Watch and listen. The moment of our escape is upon us."

Candra tensed, then nodded.

"Come, come," Ferox's cruel voice intruded. "Enough of this maudlin display. Guards, separate them."

The four guards moved, two to each sister, to pull them apart. Candra was dragged over to stand near Brace, while Marissa was brought to Ferox.

A hard light of anticipation gleamed in his eyes. "At last the moment has come. At last I will truly become the Crystal's master."

He moved to a small side table where a metallic-sheathed geode lay. With great care, Ferox extracted the fist-sized stone from the container.

"Quite unimpressive at first glance, is it

not,?" he asked as he turned and advanced on Brace, the stone held high before him. "Unimpressive save in the presence of a Crystal Master. You do know how to key the Crystal, don't you?"

Brace's mind raced as he scanned the fabled stone. It *was* unimpressive, a disappointingly plain piece of clear, multifaceted crystal. How could it possibly possess such fabled powers? For an instant he was tempted to commune with it and ascertain the truth for himself. But that was exactly what Ferox wanted.

He lifted his gaze. "I don't know what you're talking about."

"Don't you now?" his black-clad captor inquired. "More's the pity, for Marissa will suffer because of it. But before the torture begins, permit me to explain what I desire from you. It may motivate you to a bit more cooperation."

"There's nothing you can do to make me help you, Ferox!" Brace ground out through clenched teeth. "Nothing!"

"Ah, such brave, brave words," Ferox chuckled. "But then, you Crystal Masters are all alike."

He began to walk about the room, tossing the stone from one hand to the other, casually, carelessly. The action drew Brace's narrowed gaze.

"It's all quite simple, really," Ferox said. "I want you to key the Crystal and enable the little Traveler to mentally enter it. Then you

286

will discern the stone's inner workings, and lead her to them. Through your instructions, she will reprogram the Crystal to my psychic wavelength."

He paused before Brace and Candra. "Quite simple, really, yet the end result is most impressive. I will at last be a Crystal Master."

"And the Crystal Fires will freeze solid before that sol dawns!" Brace muttered angrily. "Even if I had the power, I'd never help you in such a thing."

"Ah, but you will, my young friend. As will our pretty little Traveler—won't you, my dear?" Ferox stepped closer to Candra, his hand capturing her chin in an iron grip. "You'll do anything to save your sister, won't you?"

"I—I don't know if I can accomplish what you ask," she quavered. "To enter the Knowing Crystal! Surely that's impossible."

"Nothing's impossible for a Crystal Master," Ferox soothed. "He'll get you in, little femina. It's all quite safe. Trust me." His grip on her tightened until she winced from the pain. "You *will* help me, won't you?"

Her tear-filled eyes turned to Marissa.

Marissa saw the question burning there and forced down the instinctive urge to protect her sister, to tell her to say yes. What Marissa needed was time, time to devise a plan, time to find a means of escape for all three of them. An escape that would ultimately also ruin Ferox's evil scheme to become a Crystal Master.

287

Marissa shook her head in reply to her sister's unspoken query, and Candra turned back to Ferox. "No, it's not possible. I cannot help you."

He released her with a growl and strode to Marissa. "So, she obeys only you, does she?"

Reaching into his pocket, he withdrew a thin laser probe. An instant later a blue-white light flared from its tip.

Ferox smirked maliciously. "How long, I wonder, will she continue to obey once I begin to slice you up with this?" He glanced back at Brace. "And how long will he conveniently forget his Crystal powers?"

Brace struggled in his bonds, a desperate urgency filling him. "I told you. I know nothing. Teran wouldn't share his powers with me!"

"Then your femina will suffer because of it." Ferox turned back to Marissa. A cold, calculating light gleamed in his eyes. "Where shall we begin, my pretty one? I'd hate to mar that lovely face of yours. Perhaps an arm instead?"

The probe lowered and a sharp, searing pain lanced through Marissa's right forearm. She bit back a cry and clenched her eyes shut against the agony. Ah, by the Crystal Fires!

"Gods!" Brace roared from across the room. "Stop! Stop it!"

"Key the Crystal," Ferox said. "Key it now or I'll move to her pretty face."

"I can't!" Brace gasped, nearly choking on the lie. "I don't know how!"

Ferox shrugged. The laser moved higher until the sickening blue light gleamed in Marissa's horror-stricken eyes. An impulse to cry out, to beg Ferox to stop, to implore Brace to do what he asked, rose within her. She twisted wildly, futilely, in the guards' iron clasp. They held her until she exhausted herself and slumped, panting, her heart pounding furiously.

A large, cruel hand entwined in her hair and pulled her head back. She gazed up into hard, glacial eyes. Eyes that were dead beyond their mesmerizing surface, as dead as the soul of the man who owned them.

Revulsion shuddered through Marissa. Not a shred of humanity remained in Ferox—his cold-hearted mother had seen to that. The only purpose left him was his single-minded obsession with the Knowing Crystal. And he was as much its slave, in his own twisted way, as were all the others over the hundreds of cycles who'd devoted their lives to its service. As were all the Crystal Masters . . .

Did Brace instinctively know that? Was that why he fought the Knowing Crystal and its seductive powers even as a fledgling Crystal Master, just as his father had? And was that, perhaps, why even now the stone was slowly turning against him, in the guise of his dreams?

"Well, Ardane?" Ferox's brutal voice intruded. "What shall it be? The Crystal or your lover?"

Brace twisted fiercely against his bonds, the

metal bands gouging into his wrists. "Curse you! If you dare touch her again, I swear I'll kill you!"

The laser rose and Marissa had a glimpse of brilliant light before the beam seared into the side of her face. She arched in soundless agony, her teeth sinking into her lower lip in an effort to stanch the scream. An anguished cry rose nonetheless, filling the room with its heart-rending sound.

A gray, swirling mist engulfed her, but even from a distance Marissa knew it hadn't been her voice. It was Candra.

"Marissa! Ah, Marissa!" her sister wailed. "Please don't hurt her anymore! I'll do whatever you ask. Just don't hurt her!"

Ferox turned to Brace. "And what about you, Ardane? How much more will it take to convince you?"

Anguished eyes riveted on Marissa as the blood welled from the cruel slash to trickle down the side of her face. Gods, what was he to do—stand by and watch as she was sliced up alive? Ferox would do it gladly, without the slightest hesitation and with the greatest of pleasure. And what would Brace's sacrifice of the woman he loved gain him in the end? Ferox would still have his purpose served, if not by Brace then by some other Crystal Master. There was always Teran, if not Alia. And if Teran were in his position, would he be able to stand by and watch his own love slowly mutilated and tortured?

No, Brace thought with a sudden surge of inspiration, Teran would play the game while formulating a plan to thwart his foe. Teran would play the game while fighting to buy time.

Brace lowered his head in apparent defeat. "No more. I'll do what you want. Just don't hurt Marissa any more."

"Good. Then we begin." Ferox held out the Knowing Crystal. "Key it, Ardane. Key the Crystal."

Brace's head lifted, and in the depths of his dark, tormented eyes a resolute light gleamed. His gaze locked with Ferox's before moving to the stone in his hand. It lay there, dull, lifeless, a challenge to his powers. Brace inhaled a fortifying breath, then closed his eyes.

From the depths of his being he called to the Crystal, summoning it to join with him. The secundae ticked by. All was silent. A moment of terror flashed through Brace. What if the stone refused to commune? What if it already knew Ferox's purpose and Brace's role in the plot? Ah, Gods, what would he do then? Ferox would never permit failure.

But, even as Brace began to despair of ever succeeding, a light began to grow in his mind, flooding him with its mesmerizing brilliance. A grim satisfaction filled him. His powers were still intact. He would succeed after all.

A low cry from Candra jerked him from his inward concentration. Brace's eyes opened, to rivet on the stone in Ferox's hand. It glowed now, its radiant, flashing light illuminating the room. Brace stared at it in wonder.

"Join with him," Ferox urged Candra. "Join with his mind and enter the Crystal."

She hesitated, glancing imploringly at Marissa. Through her pain, Marissa smiled back.

"It'll be all right, Nuggin. You can trust Brace. He'll take care of you."

Her gaze followed Candra as she obediently stepped close and touched Brace on the head. Then, for the briefest of moments, Marissa's eyes met Brace's. Intense emotion arced between them and she imagined she heard him speak. *I'll protect her*, he seemed to say. *I'll see no harm comes to her. Trust me, my love. Trust me.*

A soft smile tipped the corner of Marissa's mouth. *Come back to me*, her eyes gleamed. *No matter what happens, come back . . .*

"Enough, Ardane!" Ferox snapped impatiently. "Take the femina into the Crystal and be done with it!"

Brace shot him a savage look, then glanced up at Candra. She was pale, trembling in terror. He smiled encouragingly, then closed his eyes.

Her spirit joined with his, and for a few secundae Brace struggled to contain it. Candra's essence was like her—ethereal, elusive, unstable. Only Brace's strongest concentration maintained the mental bond between them.

Uneasiness curled within him. The task before them was difficult enough without having to expend so much energy on such a fragile, inconstant being. A being as unlike her sister in spirit as she was identical to her in flesh.

With a great mental effort Brace encompassed Candra and plummeted into the Knowing Crystal, spinning, spiraling through its myriad facets to its innermost workings. And there, deep inside, Brace let Candra go, freeing her to traverse the complex depths and seek out the Crystal's source of power.

She quickly found the computer unit and mentally touched it. Instantly Brace felt a sharp pain lance through him. He steadied his focus, maintaining his psychic grip on Candra. She touched the power source again, attempting to realign its circuits.

Blinding agony rocketed through Brace. He gasped, the sound strangled and choking. His body arched back in the chair. Frightened by the sudden weakening in their mental link, Candra backed off. Brace's pain subsided.

The Crystal knows, he thought through his tormented haze. Knows and is protecting itself. It will not be reprogrammed; it will not deviate from its own predetermined course— a course no one seems able to change—not even a Crystal Master.

But if a Crystal Master was helpless before it, how much more powerless was the entire Imperium? Powerless and in the greatest jeopardy. He *must* try to control the stone—now, in the only opportunity he might ever have.

Mentally, Brace turned to Candra. *The Crys-*

tal is fighting me. I'll try to find a chink in its defenses. Once I do, slip inside as quickly as you can and shut it down. Don't reprogram it to Ferox's bidding; just shut it down. Do you understand?

He felt her hesitate. Anger fueled his resolve.

Candra, do you understand?

Y-yes.

Brace turned from her then and focused all his concentration on the task ahead. The pain began the instant Candra touched the computer unit, searching for a way within. Brace fought back against the excruciating torment, maintaining his hold on her as he aided her in the search. The pain grew until his skull throbbed with a deafening, pounding agony. And still it burgeoned until he thought he'd go mad.

Mad.

His greatest fear, and suddenly it had shape and form. Where before it had been but a haunting specter, now it was black and heavy, touching him with icy fingers of dread. It loomed around Brace, encompassing his being, consuming him. His throat constricted. He couldn't breathe.

Brace writhed in the chair, the force of his movements contained only by the bonds that cut cruelly into his flesh. His mouth opened in a soundless cry and tears coursed down his sweat-slicked face. And still Brace fought on.

He held Candra in an iron grip, even as all around him his universe was disintegrating into bright, blinding agony. Her spirit wavered, and Brace nearly screamed aloud with frustration.

Gods, he cried to her, *don't fail me now!—Shut it down! I can't . . . hold on . . . much longer!*

The madness, like a black, flowing morass, curled around Brace, entwining him in its constricting coils, snaking into his very soul. He struggled, frantically attempting to throw it off. The blackness clung, seeping into him until he could scarce differentiate insanity from reality. The end was near. He knew it. He couldn't fight much longer.

The realization sent a stab of terror through him. For a fleeting instant, Brace's mind cleared. He was lost, but Candra could still escape. And with her life he would also assure Marissa's. It was the last thing he could do for the woman he loved.

Get out! Brace screamed. *Get out before the Crystal consumes us both! Now, Candra! Now!*

He fought to hold back the madness, to gain Candra the time to flee the Knowing Crystal. But in that last moment she hesitated, too terrified to go on without him. Then it was too late.

The last vestiges of Brace's strength shattered. Reality shredded, imploding until nothing remained but a dark, empty hole.

With a wild, despairing cry he turned. He reached back desperately for Candra, but she remained frozen with fear, immobile. Then he turned and ran, fleeing the pit yawning behind him, the madness reaching out after him. And, as he did, Candra's dying scream pierced the air.

Marissa, Brace groaned as he plummeted into anguished insensibility. *Gods, Marissa ... forgive me.*

Chapter Thirteen

The light of the Knowing Crystal wavered, sharpened. The stone began to gleam oddly and grow in size. Its voice rose, became audible, discordant.

Suddenly the Crystal seemed to explode with flashing bursts of light. It lifted from Ferox's hand to twirl wildly about the room. With a terrified cry the blond man leaped back, a frozen look of horror in his eyes.

In that instant of shock Marissa twisted free of the guards' restraining hands. She staggered to her sister, the severing of their life-link filling her with sickening, strength-sapping agony.

Candra lay slumped beside Brace's chair. Marissa sank to her knees. Gathering her sister's limp form to her, she rocked her back and forth.

It was over. Candra was gone and her own death would soon follow. She closed her eyes and waited.

"M-Marissa," a deep voice above her croaked.

Startled, Marissa lifted tear-filled eyes to Brace.

He gazed down at her, sick with despair. "Gods, Marissa. I'm sorry. I—"

The cell door slammed open, forced ajar by sheer body mass. Into the mesmerizing brightness leaped the big, hairy form of a Simian.

Recognition hit Marissa and Brace simultaneously. Rodac!

Within the glare of the rhythmic, flashing light, everything seemed to move in slow motion. A blaster appeared in the big alien's hands. One by one, Rodac eliminated the guards.

Behind Rodac, Ferox grabbed wildly for the still airborne Crystal. He missed, then grabbed again. This time the blond man captured it.

As Brace struggled futilely in his bonds, Ferox slunk across the room and out a small, half-hidden tunnel. Brace glanced at Rodac. The alien was watching the last guard sink to the floor.

"Ferox!" Brace cried. "He's getting away!"

The Simian's gaze followed Brace's to the tunnel's entrance. With a shrug, he slung his blaster over his shoulder and strode to Brace. After briefly examining the beryllium shackles, he grimaced and shook his head.

"The key control," Brace rasped. "The big guard with the beard had it around his neck."

Rodac moved to retrieve it, then quickly freed him. Brace staggered to his feet and

stumbled in the direction of the little tunnel.
Rodac jerked him back.

Where do you think you're going?

"After Ferox. He has the Knowing Crystal.
We've got to stop him!"

No, the alien motioned. *There'll be another
time for him. We've got to escape before his men
are upon us.*

Brace eyed him for a brief moment, then
sighed. "You're right. Do you know another
way out of here?"

Rodac nodded. *There's a tunnel that leads
through the mountain and I've got a skim craft.*

A grin creased Brace's haggard face. "Then
let's go."

He knelt and touched Marissa on the shoulder.

She glanced up, a confused, pained look on
her face.

"Marissa," Brace said softly, "it's time we
left this place."

"Candra ... I can't leave Candra," she mumbled. "She needs me. She'll always need me."

"She's dead, sweet femina." He gently pried
her fingers loose from her sister. "There's nothing more we can do for her. Come," he said,
pulling Marissa to her feet. "We must go."

She rose mechanically, then swayed, her
face blanching. Brace caught her, swinging
Marissa up into his arms. He turned to Rodac.
"Lead on."

The Simian led them unerringly through a
mind-boggling series of dark, twisting tunnels,

the trio pursued closely by Ferox's men. Blaster fire from the approaching guards ricocheted down the stone corridors, the resultant explosions showering them in a hail of rocky projectiles. Finally Rodac motioned Brace ahead toward a faint glimmer of light, then drew back to cover their escape.

Brace pulled Marissa more tightly to him and quickened his pace, racing toward the cave opening. Behind him, he heard Rodac's blaster fire again, then a loud cracking of rock and roar of falling stone. Dust billowed out of the cave, engulfing Brace in a choking cloud.

The Simian slid to a halt beside him. *That rock slide should slow them down for a time.*

He glanced at Marissa. *How is she?*

She lay against Brace, her arms twined around his neck, her head resting dispiritedly upon his chest. Uneasiness coiled about Brace's heart. This was not the headstrong, resolute Marissa he knew, the mouthy little spitfire.

When he'd first seen her, still alive and well with Candra in her arms, he'd thought Marissa's fears for her own death were unfounded. But now—now he was no longer so certain. Perhaps her earlier words about the twin life-link were indeed true. What else could explain her sudden lack of response? Was Marissa's soul slowly draining from her?

Grim determination welled in Brace's breast. No matter what happened, he'd never let Ferox destroy the woman he loved. Their commitment to each other *would* prevail.

He scanned the terrain. They stood upon a high plateau, the skim craft partially hidden in some nearby rocks. Bracc laid Marissa down and, with Rodac's assistance, quickly freed the craft. While the Simian warmed up the machine and programmed the appropriate commands, Brace settled Marissa between them. She snuggled against him, her pale face expressionless.

Rodac glanced over. *Where to?*

Tenderly Brace smoothed the tangled hair from Marissa's face. She needed more help than he or Rodac could give her. And, while time was lost in seeking out aid, the quest for the Knowing Crystal still beckoned. Did he truly have the right to follow his heart when the lives of millions hung in the balance? Yet hadn't Teran told him that the strength of Marissa's love was vital to the quest? If his brother's words were true, Brace couldn't hope to succeed without Marissa.

His hand fell from her face, his resolve hardening. To save Marissa, he must risk everything. They might all be lost if she died.

"Let's take her back to the only family she has left," he rasped. "The Sodalitas."

The Simian nodded. The bubble rose to encompass them, and with a surge of its powerful engines, the skim craft lifted into the air. Immediately it veered about in the direction of the distant Moracan capital.

Over sheer precipices and craggy peaks they flew, the horas slipping by as the sol slowly burned away. The beauty of the ruggedly majestic, snow-capped mountains was breathtaking, especially in light of their sudden escape and newfound freedom.

Still, the scene gave Brace little solace. A short time ago they'd been Ferox's captives, he mused bitterly, he on the verge of torture and death, Marissa and Candra facing eventual rape and worse. Now he and Marissa, at least, were free.

Yet even the relief of their escape failed to ease the pain in his heart, the growing sense of futility. To distract himself, Brace turned to Rodac.

"I thought you were dead when you fell back into that chasm," he began. "I'm sorry I left you, but there seemed little choice at the time. It was a difficult decision to make."

Rodac set the craft on auto pilot. *It was the logical thing to do. Your femina hadn't a chance if you didn't get her out of the storm. I never expected you to wait for me.*

Brace sighed. "Nonetheless, I don't deserve such understanding. I'm not in the habit of treating my friends like that."

Small, beady eyes studied him. *I've never had a Bellatorian for a friend. It's a novel idea.*

"You came after us at great risk to yourself. I'd call that an act of friendship."

The Simian shrugged. *I still needed your aid*

in relieving Ferox of all his wealth. It certainly wasn't stashed in that mountain fortress of his.

Brace smiled. "So you took a little time to search that out, did you? Well, I suppose that shouldn't surprise me. How did you manage to find us, anyway? Ferox didn't leave much of a trail."

The alien smirked. *I followed you to Tutela. In spite of Marissa's opinions to the contrary, your scent is strong enough to track.*

"In the air, following skim craft?" Brace snorted his disbelief. "I hardly think so."

Well, it was worth a try. A double row of sharp teeth gleamed at him. *Suffice it to say I made a calculated guess that Ferox was headed to the nearest transport station—and that was Tutela. Then he conveniently left behind some of his men to make sure the transport technician didn't reset the controls. It was easy enough to find one who would tell me where his leader's hideout was located.*

"Your arrival was most timely."

Was it? Rodac's glance brushed Marissa as he flipped off the auto pilot and directed his attention back to flying.

Was it indeed? Brace wondered as the horas passed and he watched Marissa slip further and further into a sleep he couldn't rouse her from. As best he could, Brace tried to quash the fears and nagging doubts.

This was not the time for introspection and self-pity. And it was certainly not the time to try to fathom what had happened in that mountain chamber with the Knowing Crystal. All that mattered was getting help for Marissa—before it was too late.

They sped through the mountains, clearing the last of the peaks about mid sol. Skimming down to the foothills, Rodac reset the coordinates to the forested area nestled on the distant horizon. Within its depths lay the fabled home of the militant Sodalitas, women shut off from the rest of the world and especially from men. Women who might not take kindly to their arrival with a dying Marissa in Brace's arms.

But whatever the consequences, Brace meant to see it through. Only other Moracans might know how to save her; only the Sodalitas would care. And he'd risk whatever it required.

Brace glanced at Rodac. There was no reason for the Simian to risk the Sodalitas's wrath. The big alien had more than fulfilled his end of the bargain in rescuing them from Ferox.

"There's no need for you to stay once we arrive at the Sodalitas's," Brace began. "Take the skim craft and head back to your people."

Rodac shot Brace a quizzical look, then once more punched in the auto pilot. *We made a deal. You promised me a share of Ferox's wealth. Are you now backing out on that?*

"That's hardly the point and you know it," Brace muttered in exasperation. "There's no way of predicting the Sodalitas's reaction when we arrive. They hate males and might only see what they want in regard to Marissa. They could well kill us on the spot."

And how is that danger any different from what we've already been through?

"This danger is mine and mine alone. Marissa is my woman."

And my partner.

"But you two hate each other!"

Rodac smirked, then returned to his flying of the skim craft. Brace eyed him a moment more, then expelled a deep breath. He hadn't the strength to argue further, especially over a subject he sensed he'd never win. Whatever his reasons, the Simian seemed determined to stay to the bitter end.

Sol set was tingeing the sky with its vibrant hues of crimson and gold before they began their descent. Brace's concern for Marissa had grown as the horas passed and she'd slid into deep insensibility. When he finally climbed out of the skim craft, she lay limply in his arms, unconscious.

His anxious gaze skimmed her. Marissa's rich chestnut tresses tumbled about her shoulders, framing her delicate little face, a face drawn and disconcertingly haggard. Her dark slash of brow and the fiery-red laser wound were the only real color in the pallid oval of skin and bone. And Marissa's breathing had become so shallow Brace could barely discern the rise and fall of her chest.

It sickened him to see her like this—and know that his own failings as a man were the

Kathleen Morgan

cause. If he'd been stronger, braver, he could have prevailed against the Knowing Crystal long enough to have gotten Candra free. But his own fears of madness had mastered him at last.

He was a coward. He'd failed. Failed when Marissa needed him most.

Yet, unworthy as he was, Brace loved her still. And that love would see her through this if it were the last thing he did. With a resolute glance at Rodac, Brace settled Marissa more solidly in his arms and set out toward the huge, timber-enclosed fortress that lay ahead through the trees.

A small band of heavily armed women awaited them outside the gate, their countenances fiercely suspicious. Brace halted before them, his gaze seeking out that of the woman who was obviously their leader.

She was tall, only half a head shorter than he, her body slender but whipcord hard. Her long hair was a deep, vibrant shade of red, her eyes a strikingly rich green, her skin fair with a disconcerting sprinkling of freckles across the bridge of her nose. A surprisingly beautiful woman—and formidable enemy—Brace thought. His eyes locked with hers.

"I need your help," he began without preamble. "Marissa is dying."

The woman's glance dipped to the limp bundle in Brace's arms. Concern momentarily softened her features, then she purposely hardened them.

"What did you do to her?"

The question was blunt and angry. Brace squared his shoulders.

"Her twin sister died. The severing of their life-link is now killing Marissa."

"And what do you expect us to do?" the Sodalitas demanded, her voice icy. "It's the ultimate fate of all twins. You should have taken more care to preserve Candra's life."

"Yes, perhaps I should have. But it's hardly the issue now." His gaze narrowed. "Are you saying there's nothing you can offer? That we should leave?"

She cocked a brow, her glance mocking. "And what good would that do? No, you'll not take Marissa anywhere. She'll die among those who love her."

The Sodalitas signaled to her followers. "You and your friend aren't leaving, either."

In the next instant Brace and Rodac were surrounded, the blasters pointed at them now aimed to kill. A low growl rumbled in the Simian's chest. Brace turned.

"Don't resist," he ordered tersely. "Marissa could be hurt, and, after all, her welfare is why we came."

The tall alien relaxed, shrugging his acquiescence. Brace swung back to the leader.

"We've no wish to leave until Marissa is well again. I'll aid you in any way I can, but her life is now in your hands. I ask only that you do your best for her."

"She is our sister!" the red-haired Sodalitas

snapped. "We will do what we can. But I assure you, if she dies, so will you." She motioned them forward. "Now come. Marissa only grows weaker while we stand idly by."

Brace nodded and stepped out, following her through the fortress gates. Inside was a small city, with a commercial section bulging with shops followed by a tract of imposing governmental-type buildings, and then a large residential area. All structures were of wood, intricately constructed and highly polished. The outer support beams and roof edgings were carved in intricate bevels and curves, then painted in bright shades of blue, green, red, and yellow. The Sodalitas leader led them through the wide avenues filled with activity and the happy laughter of women of all ages. Women who paused to stare as Brace and Rodac passed.

"They rarely see males," the Sodalitas explained. "Except in rare cases, males are forbidden within these walls."

"Then you take no husbands nor lovers?" Brace asked.

The woman laughed derisively. "Not permanently, you can be sure! Why would we wish to seek out subjugation? No fools live here, I can assure you!"

"The only fools are those who fear to love," Brace muttered.

"Is that why you brought Marissa back here?" she demanded. "Because you love her?"

"Why else?"

"Why else, needed?" The Sodalitas paused before a particularly large house. "If you've clouded her heart and mind with the mating urge, we'll find a way to free her. And with your death, Marissa will never fall victim again."

A challenging light flared in Brace's eyes. "And what if she still chooses me? What will you do then? Admit you've been wrong all along?"

She eyed him with the deepest loathing. "So like a male to think he's irresistible. Perhaps a few sols in our subterranean chamber will dampen some of your arrogance."

The Sodalitas motioned to one of her followers who immediately went inside and returned with a litter. Reluctantly, Brace surrendered Marissa to her sisters, then turned back to the red-haired leader.

The woman stepped aside and watched as Brace and Rodac were escorted through the house and down a winding passageway into the bowels of the earth. As they passed the main room, Brace caught a glimpse of gleaming wood walls decorated with intricately woven tapestries and a variety of weaponry and armor suits. The purported wealth of these warrior women really existed, Brace thought. As did their fabled animosity toward men, he added with a touch of black humor.

A heavy door slammed shut behind them the moment he and Rodac stepped inside their cell. Brace glanced around and sighed. Another dark, dank, ill-furnished prison. Of late, it seemed to be his most frequent form of lodging.

He took a seat on the stone bench placed against one wall and motioned for Rodac to do the same. "Make yourself comfortable. We could be in for a long wait."

Rodac snorted and ambled over to an opposite wall. He lowered himself to crouch on his haunches.

Do you think they'll feed us sometime in the next monate or two?

A wry grin twisted Brace's face. "Ever practical, aren't you? Well, I suppose there's no purpose served in becoming weak from hunger." His expression turned serious. "Food, though, is the least of our worries. We've been very lucky so far. Things won't go so easily from now on, *if* Marissa survives and we live to escape these female warriors."

Her sister is dead, her quest over. If she lives, we should leave her with her people.

If she lives. Even the contemplation of Marissa dying filled Brace with a heavy despair. He shook it off.

"That might be the wisest course," Brace admitted gravely. "But that decision must ultimately be Marissa's."

Long, leathery hands moved. *We'd never allow our own females such liberty We cherish them too much to let them risk their lives.*

"As I do Marissa. But you know her as well as I. If she sets her mind on going along . . ."

You need to tame her. Though I admire her courage, I grow weary of her biting tongue. It's not proper conduct for a female.

"Perhaps not." Brace grinned. "But you've got to take the good with the bad in a woman. And there's so much good about her..."

He shot Rodac a considering look. "She wept for you when I told her you were dead."

Surprise flashed across the Simian's face. *Did she now? A most surprising female.*

"Yes, a most surprising, wonderful female—and far too good for a coward like me."

As Brace sat there, the cold seeping slowly into his bones, the memories of the past sol churned up to once more mock him. The future loomed as a bleak panorama of painful decisions, haunting shame—and impending madness.

Even if fate smiled and Marissa lived, there was no hope for them and their love. There was no doubt in Brace's mind, after all that had ensued, that insanity would be his eventual fate if he continued to battle the Knowing Crystal. The stone would not be manipulated nor turned from its predetermined course. He had felt the full maliciousness and extent of the Crystal's power in those last searing moments before he lost consciousness.

The horrible reality could no longer be denied. The Knowing Crystal had meant to kill both him and Candra.

The stone, long revered for its benevolent guidance of the Imperium, had either gone awry—or, worse still, had never been what it had seemed. One way or another, its potential for further chaos and destruction grew with each passing sol. With the stone in the hands of the power-crazed, unprincipled Ferox, there was no way to anticipate what would happen next. The only certainty was that all would suffer.

With or without his two companions, Brace *had* to go after Ferox, retrieve the Knowing Crystal, and find some way to destroy it. Yet even the most fleeting contemplation of the horrendous task before him terrified Brace.

He had failed once when confronted with the Crystal. Failed miserably, turning and running like the most abject coward. Did he even possess the strength to face the stone again, much less overcome it?

It all seemed so hopeless. But what choice was there? He *had* to face his madness, fight past it, if that were indeed possible, and destroy a stone he was inextricably linked to by his inherent psychic powers. Yet what if the stone's annihilation destroyed him as well? Indeed, what would become of all Crystal Masters once the Knowing Crystal was gone?

Brace exhaled a long, weary breath. In the end, it didn't matter what became of him. Teran and Alia would also accept that fate if need be. What mattered was the welfare of the Imperium, not the petty lives of three people.

He lowered his head, his thoughts turning once again to Marissa. Gods, how was she?

Would her sister warriors be able to save her? And would he ever hold her in his arms again, make love to her?

They had mated twice now. Was it possible she was already carrying his child? He fervently hoped so. Knowing he might leave behind at least some small part of himself would make his eventual fate a little easier to bear.

The thought filled Brace with bittersweet pain. Never had he thought he'd dream of such a thing—a mate, a family. In those long cycles of his imprisonment he'd buried such needs away, never again to be resurrected. Yet now he dared hope ...

A child ... and one he'd probably never live to see. A child and its mother, alone in a cruel, uncertain world. But at least a world, Brace prayed with all the strength of his anguished heart, that would be free of the evil influence of Ferox and the Knowing Crystal.

They came for him at sol rise, rousing him from a deep, dreamless sleep. Brace staggered to his feet, instantly alert.

"Marissa? How is she? Has she wakened?"

The guards shoved him forward, their blasters pointing the way out of the room. Brace eyed them, then shot Rodac a wry grin. The Simian shrugged and promptly fell back asleep. Brace exited the cell with his female escorts, following them back to the main room. There, near a large stone hearth, sat the red-haired Sodalitas and an old, wizened woman.

313

Kathleen Morgan

Brace halted before them. "How is Marissa? I demand to know."

The leader smiled grimly. "Do you now? I'd suggest you have a care or I'll have the guards take you down where you stand. You're not in *your* world now. Remember that."

Anger surged through Brace but he fought to master it. Finally he inhaled a steadying breath.

"I was rude. Forgive me. My deep concern for Marissa harshened my words."

"Concern or possessiveness?" She motioned to the empty chair placed before them. "Well, no matter. Sit. We must talk."

Brace lowered himself to the chair. "What do you want from me?"

"Your name, young male, would be welcome," the old woman beside the leader spoke up. "We'd like to know to whom we speak."

He ran a ragged hand through his hair. "Brace. I'm Brace Ardane of the planet Bellator."

"And I am Olim." The old woman gestured toward her companion. "This is Raina, leader of the Sodalitas."

Brace inclined his head in acknowledgment. "I'm honored, Elderwoman." He glanced at the younger woman. "And equally honored to meet you, Raina."

"Enough of the false pleasantries!" Raina snapped. "While we sit here, Marissa is dying. Let's get on with it!"

Olim eyed her. "As you wish, child." She

turned to Brace. "Have you mated with Marissa?"

Startled brown eyes swung from one woman to the other. Then Brace's expression hardened. "That's a very personal question—and none of your business."

"None of our business!" Raina cried. "Why, you insolent sandwart, do you think we pry into such loathsome matters for the enjoyment of it? Why, I'd rather die than hear a single word—"

"That's quite enough, Raina," Olim interjected firmly. "For once in your life, try to put aside your personal vendetta against males. And pray, with all your heart, that Brace and Marissa truly *were* lovers. It's the only hope we have of saving her."

Brace leaned forward, instantly alert. "Then there *is* a way! Tell me what I can do!"

The weathered old face turned to him, and a soft smile touched Olim's lips. "Were you lovers, Brace Ardane?"

"Yes," Brace breathed. "Yes, we were lovers."

"If you forced yourself upon her," Raina muttered darkly, "I swear I'll cut out your—"

His eyes swung to capture hers. "She came to me willingly, out of love, not fear. And what we share is that of equals, not of master and slave."

Icy green eyes glared back. "And I'll hear that from Marissa's lips before I believe it!"

"Fine," Brace growled. "Then let's see about saving her life so she can tell you!"

Olim rose from her chair. "The truth will be revealed soon enough. If Brace speaks true, his love will be sufficient to save Marissa. If not—" she shrugged "—then you can execute him as a rapist. It matters not to me.

"But come, time grows short." She motioned them forward. "Let us go to Marissa."

As one, Brace and Raina stood, then followed the old woman from the main chamber and down a short hall to another room. Within it was a bed, and upon the bed lay Marissa. At sight of her, Brace made a move to go to her but Olim restrained him.

"Not yet," she said. "First you must understand the full implications of what you're about to do. You'll have only one chance as the act is all-consuming and life-threatening—for you as well as Marissa. Do you wish to risk that?"

Brace smiled grimly. He'd made his decision long ago when he'd decided to bring Marissa to the Sodalitas. He nodded. "I've already risked far more than my life for Marissa, Elderwoman. Tell me what I must do."

"The severing of the life-link between Marissa and Candra has left a massive psychic wound," Olim said. "In most cases there is no way to heal it and the injury eventually bleeds the life away. But in rare instances another link has been previously forged. If that can be strengthened, it might just be enough to heal the mortal wounding."

Olim paused to stare deeply into Brace's eyes. "If your love was true, you may possibly have established such a link."

"And how do you know this?" Brace demanded. "How can you be so certain?"

For a moment the old woman's eyes misted with memories of sols long past, of happiness still remembered. Then she refocused her gaze upon Brace.

"I am also a Traveler. My twin died many cycles ago when we were still young women. The only thing that saved me was my love, forbidden though it was, for a male. And that, my young friend, is how I know."

Joy flooded Brace, spilling over to glow in his eyes. Gods, was it possible? Had the solution to Marissa's plight always lain in his love for her?

"Tell me what I must do," he repeated, this time with a note of urgency in his voice.

"Take her into your arms," Olim said softly. "Hold her to your heart. Then let the love flow, your minds merge until you are bound body and soul. Then and only then can the healing begin."

"And how will I know when the healing's complete?"

The old woman smiled. "You'll know, young warrior. Believe me, you'll know."

Brace stared at her for a long moment more, then turned, shutting out the rest of the world

317

until all that mattered was the frail form of the woman dying upon the bed. The woman who had become his whole life. The woman he loved. Slowly, ever so gently, he lowered himself to sit beside Marissa and gathered her into his arms.

The laser wound on the side of Marissa's face had scabbed over, the edges neatly joined. The eventual scar would be thin, barely noticeable when fully healed. Brace breathed a silent prayer of thanks for that small blessing.

His head lowered, his lips moved to brush her forehead. He inhaled deeply of her flower-fresh scent. It stirred hauntingly sweet memories, heartfelt emotions, and suddenly tears stung Brace's eyes.

"Marissa, sweet femina," he choked. "Ah, Gods, come back to me!"

With all the strength that was in him Brace called to her, entwining Marissa's spirit with his, sustaining her faint flicker of life with the roaring conflagration of his own determination and love. Yet for a time it seemed that nothing could move her past the enormous loss of her sister.

Deep within his soul Brace saw the wound of the severed life-link, fire-red and gaping, consuming her bit by agonizing bit. He marveled that she'd survived as long as she had with such a mortal injury. It was Marissa's strength and inherent fighting spirit that had sustained her so far. But even she could not hold on much longer.

He called forth all the strength he possessed, willing it to pass to her. All his strength—and love. And, slowly, they joined.

Memories of the sols and noctes with Marissa flooded Brace, consuming him until he saw and experienced nothing else. Memories of her endearing bouts of exasperation every time he teased her, of her tears when she'd learned that Rodac had supposedly died, of the look in her eyes, so hot yet startled, when her fingers had grazed his lips while feeding him that berry. And, most of all, memories of her passionate response when they'd mated, and of her sweetly satisfying surrender.

A surrender that he felt as well, then and in this moment of exquisitely ardent joining.

She stirred in his arms, moaning softly. Elation coursed through Brace. He struggled to maintain his mental hold, terrified he'd lose her if he pulled back too soon. She moved again, slipping her hands between them to push at his chest.

"B-Brace," Marissa whispered. "It ... it's enough. Let go or you'll drain away all your life-strength. Let go."

From some place far away he heard her. Yet to relinquish this sweet, most wonderful of joinings was harder than Brace had imagined. It took everything he possessed to pull away.

For long secundae he sat there as the room spun dizzily before him. He closed his eyes in an effort to ease the disequilibrium. Still the nausea roiled in his gut until Brace feared he might vomit. He inhaled great gulps of air. Slowly the sickness passed.

Brace opened one eye a slit. The room was steady. He opened the other. Everything remained as it should. He heaved a sigh of relief and gazed down at Marissa.

She lay there upon his chest, pale but smiling. Then something passed across her face and tears flooded her eyes. Tears, then an expression of disbelief and loathing.

"Marissa?" Brace whispered, his hand moving to stroke the side of her face. "What's wrong, sweet femina?"

She jerked back, struggling to sit, then move away. Her gaze swept the room and found the leader of the Sodalitas. Her arms reached out in entreaty and Raina went to her, pulling Marissa into her arms.

"Hush, sweeting," Raina soothed. "It's but the shock of the healing experience. It will pass."

"No. It's not that at all," Marissa sobbed. "It ...it's *him*! He saved me, but killed my sister! He killed my sister, yet I want him still! Ah, what am I to do? *What am I to do?*"

Chapter Fourteen

Raina shot Brace an enraged look. "So, you lied, did you? It doesn't surprise me, coming from a male."

She turned back to Marissa, stroking her head tenderly. "Hush, hush, sweeting. It'll be all right."

"N-no," Marissa choked, sobbing as if her heart would break. "It won't. C-Candra's gone and I'm alive! Ah, how can I live with the guilt, the shame?"

"And is your shame greater than mine?" Brace rasped. "*I'm* the one who failed you both. You've done nothing to feel guilty about, unless wanting to live is now a sin!"

"I—I'm not worthy," she replied, her voice muffled against Raina's breast. "Candra was the Traveler, the twin of value, not I. My life's a waste. A waste!"

"By the five moons, Marissa!" Brace roared, his patience finally at an end. "Don't *ever* say that again! Your life has never been a waste. The ability to enter objects is insignificant in the total scheme of things. But your skills, as a warrior and a woman, are vital to this quest—a quest of Imperium magnitude. Without you, we may all be doomed. So don't *ever* let me hear you denigrate yourself again!"

"And where have you heard all this before, sweeting?" Raina prodded wryly, smiling down at her friend. "He speaks true, Marissa."

"H-he p-promised to protect Candra, to see no harm came to her. He asked me to t-trust him! And I did ... I d-did," Marissa hiccuped. "Ah, I hate him for that most of all!"

"One secundae you want him, the next you hate him," Raina muttered in exasperation. "Truly, you don't know what you really feel. You need time to clear that muddled little head of yours. You need rest."

Marissa went still and her weeping faded. After a time, she lifted her head to gaze at Raina. "You're right. I—I'm so tired," she whispered. "Please, let me sleep."

Brace made a move to help, but Raina shook her head. He restrained himself and watched as the red-haired Sodalitas assisted Marissa to lie back down, then covered her with a thick quilt. She sat beside her for a time, stroking Marissa's hair, a loving look on her face. And finally Marissa drifted off to sleep.

Raina rose, indicating they should leave. Brace shot Marissa one last look, then followed the two Sodalitas out of the room. Olim excused herself, but Raina signaled that Brace continue to accompany her.

The main chamber was empty. With a graceful sweep of her hand, Raina motioned to the chairs before the hearth. In their absence a fire had been laid and the hungry flames snapped and crackled as they devoured the pile of wood. For a long while both stared into the fire, silent and thoughtful.

"I thank you for your loyalty to Marissa," Raina began finally. "When she first came to live with us it took several cycles to get close to her, she was so afraid of rejection. And she battles still with her feelings of unworthiness." The Sodalitas sighed. "Her people left a festering wound when they cast her out to die on Mount Desolat. I fear it may never heal."

"Marissa is the most wonderful woman I have ever known," Brace said. "Brave and resourceful, intelligent, gentle, and kind."

Raina chuckled. "Gentle and kind? After how she's just treated you, are you sure we're talking about the same woman?"

"It's her pain speaking. She's devastated over Candra's death."

Reluctant admiration flared in the Sodalitas. "Yes, that she is." Raina inhaled a considering breath. "I see I was wrong to treat you so harshly, to assume you were like all the other males I've ever known." She smiled. "And I can begin to understand why Marissa loves you."

Brace grimaced. "Can you now? I only hope Marissa remembers that some sol."

"Give her time."

"There's not much of that left. I must leave

323

soon. We're all in too much danger with Ferox still in possession of the Knowing Crystal."

A delicate auburn brow lifted. "So, the criminal has the stone of power? Is that the quest you spoke of earlier?"

"Yes. He kidnapped Candra and coerced Marissa to bring me to him. Between my Crystal Master abilities and Candra's skill in traversing solid objects, he hoped to use us to manipulate the Knowing Crystal and make him a Crystal Master. But the stone must have known. It turned on me when I helped Candra enter it. I hadn't ... the strength ... to get her out in time."

"You're fortunate that even you survived." She paused, a frown wrinkling her smooth brow. "Your story explains more than you may realize. A man backed by a small, well-armed force came to us about a monate ago, demanding we give over Olim. At the time I thought it strange they found such value in an old woman. Now, it all falls into place."

Raina's glance lifted to meet Brace's. "The man was Ferox, wasn't it? And he wanted Olim's skills as a Traveler."

"It would seem so. What did you tell him," he asked, a smile tipping the corner of his mouth, "aside from 'be damned'?"

She grinned. "Oh, that neatly sums it up. He left very angry, after a protracted battle that didn't end in his favor."

Brace's expression darkened. "You must

take every precaution to protect Olim. Ferox could return at any time."

"We will. The Sodalitas always protect their own." She smiled. "You took a big chance, you know, bringing Marissa to us. We could have killed you on the spot."

"There was never any other choice. Marissa's life was at stake."

"You could have left her to die. Your quest was vital."

"She's as vital to the quest as I. The Knowing Crystal will try to destroy me before I destroy it. Marissa's love is my strength and protection."

"Fine words," Raina drawled cynically. "And so much like a male besotted with the mating urge."

Brace grinned. "You speak from experience, do you?"

A haunted look passed across her beautiful face. "What I've experienced is of no import. It's in the past. And the present reality is more than enough to deal with."

He opened his mouth to say more, then clamped it shut. Whatever the red-haired leader's personal pain, she was right. It was not his prerogative to pry, and the present reality was indeed more than enough to deal with.

"Will you talk to Marissa?" Brace asked, turning the topic to a more neutral subject. "She loves and respects you."

A soft smile lifted Raina's mouth. "I've known her for nine cycles now, ever since that sol our women found Marissa and brought her to us. I was but seventeen cycles then, she eleven. For the longest time she was so sad, so heartbroken, but over the cycles we became the closest of friends. We grew up, became women and warriors together. I love Marissa as much as she loves me."

Her glance hardened. "Yes, I'll help you, for I truly believe, beneath her pain and anger, she still cares for you. But if you ever turn from her or hurt her ..."

"That will never happen. While I have breath left in my body, that will never happen!"

"Perhaps not," Raina murmured thoughtfully as the enormity of the quest ahead of them swept through her. "But then again ..."

Later that evening Raina came for Brace. He and Rodac, now residing above stairs in more comfortable surroundings, had just finished a tasty vegetable casserole and freshly baked bread and were working their way through a plate of cerasa fruit and uva berries. Both glanced up when the Sodalitas entered.

"Marissa wants to speak with you," she stated, her gaze meeting Brace's. "She's rested well and has had time to think things through.

"So she's calmed down, has she?"

Raina's mouth twisted briefly. "After a fashion. She's still not feeling very kindly toward you. Be prepared for that."

Brace sighed and shoved back from the table. "It would be unrealistic to think otherwise."

Raina grinned and strode from the room.

Marissa was awaiting them, propped up in bed, her face pale but composed. Her eyes narrowed, however, when she saw Brace. Her lips tightened in determination.

At Marissa's look Brace hesitated, then squared his shoulders and made his way across the room. Pulling up a chair, he sat down at her bedside. He eyed her.

"How do you feel?"

"Well enough," she replied coolly. "When will we head out on the quest? I've a pressing need to spill a little of Ferox's blood."

"A pressing need to cut out his heart and feed it to a rapax would be more like it," he ventured dryly. "You've never struck me as a woman to do things in half measures."

"Whatever I do," she muttered, "Ferox will die. He'll pay for what he did to Candra!"

"Marissa, listen to me," Brace said, every word carefully measured. "As much as I need you on this quest, I'll not ask you to come, to risk yourself further. *Your* mission is over. Ferox and the Knowing Crystal are *my* problem, not yours. Stay here with the Sodalitas. Salvage what you still can of happiness."

"H-happiness?" Marissa's features mirrored her voice's mocking surprise. "Thanks to you, there's no hope of that left in my life. But I *will* see this through—and Ferox *will* pay. If you won't allow me to come along, I'll just track you anyway."

"Stubborn little elephas," Brace muttered, knowing it was pointless to argue with her further. "Fine, have it your way. We'd be *honored* if you'd accompany us."

"Fine." Marissa shot Brace a grim-eyed look. "Don't think for a moment it changes how I feel about you, though. In the end you failed me, and my sister died because of it. I can never trust you again."

He sighed. "Marissa, I may not be the bravest man in your eyes, but I tried. I truly did. Do you think, knowing how much you loved your sister—and that it meant your own life as well—I didn't care? Gods!"

Words failed as, once again, the shame flooded him. Like it or not, he'd chosen his life and his precious sanity over the lives of Marissa and Candra. He was an abject worm, a coward. It was as simple as that. Heart-twisting pain coiled within. Would there be anything of value left him by the time the Knowing Crystal was done?

Slowly his gaze met hers. "Tell me true. Can we work together, with all this between us?"

"Fear not," she said, her mouth tight with determination. "It will have no effect upon our quest. I once told you that trust was never a prerequisite for our partnership—only cooperation."

"So, we're back to 'cooperation,' are we?"

Marissa's words slashed open the old frustrations. Well, what had he expected? he asked himself angrily.

His eyes locked with hers. "That's fine with me!"

"Good." In spite of her mixed emotions, the harsh bite of Brace's words stung. "I'm ready to leave on the morrow."

From behind him, Raina made a choking sound. Brace whirled around.

"Is she ready?" he asked, struggling to master his rising irritation.

"I'm quite capable of speaking for myself," Marissa protested. "You don't have to consult her."

Brace ignored Marissa. "Well, Raina. Is Marissa ready?"

The red-haired woman chuckled. "Hardly. She'll need another sol or two, at the very least."

"Raina!" Marissa cried.

Brace turned back to her. "Just as I thought. It's two more sols then, Marissa, and not a secundae sooner. And if I see you overtaxing yourself in the meanwhile, I'll add another sol or two to that. Do you understand?"

She glowered at him.

"Well, do you?"

"Yes," she hissed. "I understand. But the longer we wait, the further Ferox gets from us. Why, he could already be halfway across the Imperium!"

"No. He's still here on Moraca."

Marissa stiffened. "And how do you know that?"

He shrugged. "How else? I'm a Crystal Master. I can sense when the Crystal is near. And it's definitely still on this planet."

She frowned. "Strange that it still communes, now that it seems to have turned against you."

"The Crystal has no control over my psychic sensitivity. That's inborn. And the stone can't hide its presence from a Crystal Master once it's within a certain distance."

"And exactly how far away is that?"

Brace shook his head. "I can't say. All I know is the closer I draw, the stronger my sense of its presence grows."

An anxious look flitted across Marissa's face. "And the more danger you're in from its power over you."

"Yes."

She leaned forward, her eyes narrowing. "You couldn't withstand it when it turned on you in Ferox's fortress. What makes you think you'll prevail this time?"

"Nothing, Marissa. Nothing makes me think that. But what other options are there? All I know is that time is of the essence. And that's exactly why I need your help."

"Really? And what good are my warrior's skills against the Knowing Crystal?"

"Your warrior's skills are next to useless," he admitted frankly.

"Well, if you're placing all your hopes on my

feelings for you, you're sadly amiss. What was between us is over—dead. As dead as my sister!"

He regarded her steadily. "Then perhaps you'd better not come along. I need your help, not your hindrance."

An anguished expression filled her eyes. Marissa swallowed and looked away.

"And my help you'll have," she whispered. "Just don't try stirring up feelings that aren't there anymore. That's not fair."

Fair, Brace thought. When had anything about this quest ever been fair? But there was no point in belaboring things. He couldn't force Marissa to return his love. He exhaled a weary breath. "No, I suppose it isn't fair."

Brace turned to Raina. "I think Marissa has had enough excitement for one sol. I know I have. With your permission, I'd like to retire."

"In a moment, if you please," the Sodalitas said. "Olim has a wish to speak with all of you. I've already sent for her and your Simian friend."

Brace glanced at Marissa. "Is that acceptable to you?"

"Quite."

He turned back to Raina. "Have at it, then."

A short while later Rodac and Olim joined them. All settled in chairs beside Marissa's bed, then looked expectantly over at the old Traveler. Her glance moved from Brace and Rodac to Marissa. She smiled.

"I called you together to speak of your

quest," Olim began. "I have knowledge about the Knowing Crystal you may not possess— knowledge of its awful purpose and secret vulnerability. Knowledge that may make the difference between success and failure."

"And how did you gain such knowledge?" Brace asked.

Olim's gaze briefly met Raina's.

Raina flushed. "While you were enjoying our subterranean hospitality, I took the liberty of going through your belongings. Your assortment of treasures was most interesting. Especially the gilded box embossed with Aranea's mutant weaving spider."

She paused to scan the trio. "Did any of you understand the significance of the scroll it contained?"

"I'm the one who found it, and no one ever looked at it but me," Marissa offered. "I couldn't read the language, though it seemed vaguely familiar."

"It was written in Antiquum, the precursor to our Imperial common language," Olim explained. "That's why it looked familiar yet still unreadable. It was the language in use when the Knowing Crystal was first created."

A rising premonition fired Brace's blood. "And this scroll contains information about the Crystal?"

Olim nodded. "It spoke about its creation as well as its flaws. And about how to destroy it."

Marissa straightened in bed. "Are you telling me that all this time we were carrying around the secret of the Knowing Crystal and didn't know it?"

"The scroll was written by Edat, the Aranean High Priest who first stole the Knowing Crystal all those hundreds of cycles ago," Olim replied. "He was also the first to learn of the stone's darker powers. Even as he penned the scroll, Edat was being slowly driven mad by the Crystal."

"So the scroll was a warning to those who followed," Marissa mused.

"Yes, a warning and a source of vital information. In all the chaos of the Crystal's theft and Edat's subsequent death, the secret must have passed from hand to hand until its potential significance was lost. Lost, until you finally found it."

"Fate," Brace muttered. "It was fate that we found it. Now, when the knowledge was needed most of all."

"No." Marissa shook her head. "An old man in white robes appeared to me and instructed me to take the box. I thought then it was just a spirit haunting the Repository, so I didn't say anything. Later, when I tried to read the scroll and couldn't, I was certain the old man had indeed been a hallucination."

Brace's brow furrowed in thought. "An old man in white robes..." Recognition flared, then joy. "Vates. It *had* to be Vates!"

His gaze met Marissa's. "His spirit is watching over us! By the five moons, with his aid and that of this scroll we are certain to succeed!"

"Perhaps," Olim agreed. "But all this knowledge is of little use in the wrong hands—or," she added meaningfully, staring over at Marissa, "by lovers torn by dissent and wounded feelings."

Marissa reddened. "We're not lovers! At least not anymore. And it's hardly wounded feelings! He failed me and I can't trust him anymore. It's just that simple!"

Olim regarded her steadily. "Nonetheless, if you two cannot work together, this knowledge is wasted."

"We'll work together," Marissa muttered. "Have no fear of that. I'm a warrior, after all. I can sublimate my personal feelings."

Rodac nearly strangled on a laugh, then glanced at Brace with a smirk.

Marissa rounded on him. "Don't start with me, you hairy bag of bones!"

The Simian's eyes widened in feigned innocence, then he shrugged.

Marissa choked down an insulting invective and forced her attention back to the old Traveler. "Time is short, Elderwoman. I'm sure we'd all like to hear what you learned from the scroll."

Olim sighed and settled more comfortably in her chair. "I fear there is no way to control the Knowing Crystal anymore, for it can infallibly anticipate and plan for any logical action. And, for that same reason, it can never be reprogrammed.".

"How reassuring," Brace muttered. "A perfect creation, infallible and indestructible, and bent on total control of the Imperium."

"Nothing created by man can ever be perfect," Olim replied, stirring Brace's memory of Teran's similar words. "As I said, it can plan for any *logical* action. You must fight it with illogic, with actions the stone has no capacity to understand or reason out."

"And what actions might those be?" Marissa asked. "We are all warriors, Elderwoman. Everything we do must be logical, coldly reasoned. To act otherwise can result in failure—if not death."

Olim smiled. "Then you've a mystery yet to be solved."

"This quest is far too full of mystery for my taste," Brace growled. "Yet what other choice is there? We must try. If we fail, the Imperium is doomed. And even failure and death are better than life as one of the Knowing Crystal's mindless slaves."

"Well said, young warrior," Olim murmured approvingly. "And despite the gravity of the situation, there is some hope. Do you recall the ancient lines of prophecy on the pedestal of power?" Her lids lowered as she reverently intoned the famous words. "*Knowing Crystal, bright and fair, secret of the richest gain. Royal quest begins the cure, for barren empire, deepest pain.*"

She paused to add further emphasis, her intent glance once more joining with Brace's. "*Begins* the cure, young warrior."

Brace frowned. "I don't understand, Elderwoman."

"That is the paradox," Olim explained. "We've misinterpreted the prophecy all these cycles, imagining that the return of the Knowing Crystal was the answer to all the Imperium's woes. But the cure was never just the return of the Crystal. It was the solution to preventing its influence from ever gaining hold again. *That* is the ultimate quest."

"Gods, it almost seems a sacrilege to destroy the stone so long revered as the benevolent friend of the Imperium! Is there no other way?"

"It seems not."

Anguish twisted his face, then Brace's jaw tightened. "Then tell me this, Elderwoman. How, when the stone is supposedly indestructible and it won't allow anyone to reprogram it, are we to destroy it?"

"The scroll speaks to that dilemma as well. The Knowing Crystal was originally formed from a rare mineral mined at the fiery pools of Cambrai. Only in the molten crystal fires of the pools, so hot they appear to all as steaming, swirling waters, can the stone be destroyed."

Brace's eyes met Marissa's. The same excitement he felt gleamed in her blue-green depths. At last, he thought. At last there was truly hope!

"Destroy the stone in the pools of Cambrai," Olim intoned, her glance suddenly far away, her voice deep and solemn as if uttering the words of yet another prophecy.

It stirred something, something that rose to swirl hotly about the room and encompass them all, inspiring the little gathering with a renewed determination and sense of purpose. Hearts pounded, breathing quickened as they contemplated the battle ahead—the final battle—for the lives and souls of their people.

"Put an end to the Knowing Crystal," Olim pleaded, her old eyes mirroring the anguished entreaty of the generations to come. "Put an end to it for the sake of the Imperium. Put an end to it at long last—for the sake of us all.

Brace watched from an upper room as Marissa wept in the winter-stripped garden. It was a bleak sol, the clouds blocking much of the weaker light of the Moracan red sun. The frigid winds blew, swirling little eddies of snow. Brace marveled at Marissa's perseverance in remaining out of doors.

The setting mirrored his own feelings. Feelings of anguish at his helpless frustration, at the part he'd played, however unwillingly, in causing Marissa such pain. Sweat dampened his brow and his fists clenched knuckle-white at his sides. But still Brace stood there, his gut twisting with the effort it took not to leave the room and seek her out in the garden.

Rodac moved to stand beside him. *Go to her*, he motioned. *She needs you.*

"You're mistaken, my friend. She *doesn't* need or want me," Brace replied stonily. "I'd only make her angry, forcing my attentions upon her. It'll never work unless she comes to me."

The Simian shook his head. *You humanoids are all alike. So caught up in self-appointed rules of conduct and misguided honor that you can't get past them to what really matters—the alleviation of another's suffering.*

Brace quirked a sardonic brow. "Oh, and you Simians do things differently, do you?"

On Arbor, when one Simian hurts another, they beg pardon in the most abject way, crawling to the offended one on hands and knees, groaning their regret and sorrow. It works every time.

"If I did that to Marissa, she'd laugh me to shame and pronounce me mad." Brace sighed. "I'm sorry, Rodac. What works on Arbor doesn't work here."

The tall alien shrugged. *Perhaps not, but there's always room for improvement.* He motioned in Marissa's direction. *Do you mind if I try?*

Brace shot him an incredulous look. "And what's this? A show of concern for Marissa?"

Rodac grinned. *She grows on you.*

"Then have at it." Brace looked back out the window, his features bleak with despair. "You're bound to have more luck than I. Anyone would."

Thanks for your vote of confidence. Rodac ambled from the room.

Brace watched until he saw the Simian enter the garden and head toward Marissa. Then he turned away.

She never heard Rodac's approach and jumped when he lowered himself to sit beside her on the bench. Marissa glanced over in surprise. She must either be getting used to his rank scent, not to have smelled him coming, or be so mired in her personal misery that her warrior's abilities had ceased to function. Either way, it boded ill. Self-disgust, then anger, filled her.

Marissa glared at him. "What do you want? Are you so bored with the inactivity that you came down to torment me? If so, you'll find me singularly disappointing. I haven't the energy nor inclination to rise to your baiting."

You're tearing him apart. He loves you.

She started, gazing at him in incredulity. For a fleeting instant anguished longing twisted within Marissa's breast, a longing for Brace's arms about her, for his mouth slanting hotly over hers.

Then she shoved it aside. It was too much to deal with—the choice of Brace over Candra. The agonizing realization of his weakness. And now, thanks to Ferox's cruel manipulations, that all-consuming hunger for revenge.

"He's a male," Marissa said bitterly. "He loves all females. But his commitment to them is as shallow as the shifting sands of Malabre. And just as dangerously unstable."

She turned to face Rodac. "He's not strong enough for this quest. He'll never be able to defeat the Knowing Crystal. He hasn't the courage nor strength of mind it will take. And I'm afraid, Rodac. So very, very afraid."

Afraid for you or for him?

Marissa stared at the Simian for a long moment. Then she sighed.

"I don't know. I truly don't know."

Brace is a good man, even for a Bellatorian. And he's one of the bravest men I have ever known. You are wrong to doubt him.

"And I say you are blind," she retorted hotly. "His night terrors alone are enough to drag anyone down. And now the Crystal's trying to drive him mad. Do you imagine those attempts will lessen the closer we draw to it?"

Rodac shrugged. *You're right, of course. He's not strong enough to defeat the Knowing Crystal. No one would be; not alone, at any rate. He needs you, Marissa.*

She rose to her feet in one angry surge. "By all that is sacred! The Knowing Crystal is Brace's problem. He's the Crystal Master, not me! I'm along on this quest solely to kill Ferox!"

A smile quivered at the corner of the Simian's mouth. *Are you, Marissa?*

"What in all the heavens do you mean by that?"

You can't turn your back on Brace any more than you could your sister.

"That's not true!"

It is true. Admit it. You still love Brace.

"No...no." She fiercely shook her head. "That's over...dead."

No, it's not, and that frightens you, doesn't it? Just as much, Rodac added, *as your lifelong battle over your worthiness to even be loved.*

She shot him a wide-eyed, wary look. "You can't know that. You can't know what's in my mind!"

I'm not without some skills of observation. I've seen your battle, a battle that finally came to a head when your sister died. Rodac grinned. *I may be a hairy bag of bones, but I'm not stupid.*

The faintest glimmer of a smile curved Marissa's lips. "No, I see that now."

Hesitantly she touched his arm. "I begin to see a lot now. *I* was the stupid one, to treat you so cruelly. I am sorry."

It's of no import. We all came into this with our biases. I despised all humanoids, saw them only as a means to further my own personal gain. You and Brace helped change that. Now, I consider you both as friends.

Marissa smile widened. "And I, you."

Then hear me now as a friend, Rodac's hands moved quickly. *You can always love and honor your sister's memory, but you cannot sacrifice your own life and happiness to her—or anyone— anymore. There's a quest to be fought and won. There's no time left to wallow in self-pity. But*

341

it's your choice, Marissa. It's always been your choice.

"My choice," she whispered. "You make it sound so simple."

It can be, if you've sufficient courage. We all have battles to fight if this quest is to succeed. Yours is to learn to trust and love—not only others, but yourself. Brace's is to face his personal demons, to heal himself.

"And yours?" Marissa asked. "What is your battle, Rodac?"

To put up with both of you while you muddle through it all, and not go mad in the process.

"Sounds like yours is the hardest battle of all," she chuckled.

My thoughts exactly. Rodac patted her hand, then rose. *I hope this has helped.*

Marissa nodded, her expression suddenly solemn. "It has. I've a lot to mull over."

And Brace. What will you do about Brace?

Her lips trembled and she looked away. "I— I don't know." Marissa's eyes met his, and the look that burned there was determined. "But I won't fail him when he needs me, that much I swear. As for the rest, I just...don't... know."

It's enough. If you stand by him as you say you will, the rest will come. He turned to go, then hesitated, glancing back at her. *Will you talk to Brace? Make peace between you?*

"Yes," Marissa whispered achingly. "I'll talk to him...soon."

Chapter Fifteen

The decision to speak with Brace did not come easily. Marissa spent the rest of the sol and into early evening in her room, agonizing over what to do. Though she knew that peace must be made if there were to be any hope of success, she found herself wavering between her fierce determination for revenge and her doubts over Brace's ability to bear up to the demands of the quest. In the end, the only surety was that Ferox must die. It was the only way to avenge her sister and assuage some of the tormenting guilt of her death.

Marissa knew this with a cold, dispassionate knowledge as she once more wound the coils of self-protection about her heart. Despite Rodac's conviction to the contrary, there was no room for love or concern for Brace on this quest. Love was too complicated an emotion for one such as she. And nothing she dared go to battle with.

What she needed now was unfeeling logic and the warrior's skills that had always stood her in good stead. Those she could trust, knew how to handle, and knew would give her strength. The other emotions, like love and tenderness, would only weaken her for the fearfully difficult task ahead.

Yet after all that had happened, after all she and Brace had shared, it was difficult to become the cold-hearted woman she'd been before—a woman she now hardly knew, or wanted to be. But someone had to be strong and sure. In the end, it could save Brace's life.

Guilt surged through Marissa as a plan formed. She shoved the uncomfortable feeling aside, centering her thoughts on the reality of the situation.

Candra would still be alive if Brace had been stronger. As painful as it was to admit, Marissa's lust for a male had clouded her judgment. Clouded it once, but never again. She must *never* allow that to happen again. It would be fatal to them all.

The plan, shameful as it was, once more insinuated itself into Marissa's mind. In the end, it mattered not what she truly felt. What mattered was what Brace *thought* she felt. And if the certainty of her love gave him strength, a strength he so desperately needed . . .

With a sigh, Marissa walked over to gaze out the window. Bright facets of light twinkled in the blackened sky. The faded crescent of Moraca's single moon glimmered in the distance . . . comforting, familiar.

She stared at it all in wonder. When had the sol fled? She must have been deep in thought for horas. It was surely time for the supper meal.

Marissa considered going down to join the others, then cast the idea aside. She couldn't face Brace just yet. She needed a little more time to gird herself for the distasteful task ahead—a task even Ferox had seemed to have sensed would eventually be hers.

His cruel, mocking voice came back to haunt Marissa, crueler now in this moment of fulfillment. "...the perfect opportunity," he'd said, a bitter, knowing look in his eyes, "...working the ageless deceit of a woman's love..."

Marissa turned from the window and the pristine, uncomplicated beauty of the nocte.

Marissa's place at the supper meal was noticeably empty. Brace's gaze met Rodac's as he took his own seat at the table. The alien merely shrugged, then dug into his mess of stewed vegetables with a gusto that belied its lack of meat.

Brace sat there for a few secundae staring at his own plate as if it had suddenly grown a face. Raina and Olim's gazes slanted in his direction, returned to their own food, then slanted again when curiosity once more got the best of them. Finally, with a low curse, Brace shoved back from the table and strode out of the room.

All eyes riveted on Rodac. He smirked, then

motioned, *He needs to talk with Marissa*, before resuming his meal.

Raina rolled her eyes and sighed. "Lovers! How illogical can one get?"

Your turn will come, Rodac's hands echoed snidely his knowing grin.

The red-haired Sodalitas grimaced. "Not likely, alien!"

Rodac laughed out loud, if a staccato series of grunts could be called laughter.

The strange sound echoed in the big room, carrying down the hall that led to Marissa's bedchamber. Brace, well aware it was the Simian version of laughter, wondered what could possibly be so amusing as to stimulate Rodac's unique sense of humor. Then he brushed further speculation aside as he stopped outside Marissa's room. More serious issues were at hand and he needed all his powers of concentration if he were to deal successfully with them.

What would he say to Marissa? What would be best received? One way or another, he meant to have the animosity between them settled. On the morrow, if Marissa felt up to it, the quest must resume. There was indeed a lot to be decided. But first they must begin to talk again, to trust.

A firm knock pulled Marissa from her thoughts. By all that was sacred, she cursed in rising irritation, why must she be interrupted now, when she'd all but gathered the necessary courage to confront Brace and put her plan into action?

She rose from her bed and headed toward the door. There was no help for it. She was just going to have to face him and let things fall where they would. Let nature, so to speak, take its course.

Marissa paused with her hand on the door handle, struggling for self-composure. Then she plastered a smile on her face for her unknown visitor and pulled open the door.

"How may I help—?" At the sight of Brace standing there, further words fled.

"May I come in?" he asked quietly. "I need to talk with you."

She stared at him a moment longer, then stepped aside. "Please." She choked out the single word. "Please, come in."

He followed her in and over to the small hearth fire that warmed the room. Marissa sat down in one of the chairs and motioned for him to take the other.

Brace shook his head. "I'd prefer to stand."

"As you wish."

Let him do what he chooses, Marissa thought. It would take more than his towering over her to sway her from what must be said— and done—this nocte. She opened her mouth to speak when Brace cut in.

"Are you well enough to set out on the morrow?"

Startled by this unexpected query, Marissa stared up at him. Inexplicably, his question angered her. Is that all he cared for, then? Whether or not she was strong enough to resume the quest? Not "How are you, Marissa?" or "Couldn't we be friends again?"

She caught herself, bemused by the illogic of her reaction. Here she was, determined to be coldly rational in her impending seduction of him, knowing it was vital to the rebuilding of his self-confidence and the outcome of *her* quest, yet at the same time expecting warmer emotions from him. Marissa brushed aside the small twinge of anxiety his coolness stirred. He'd love her again when she was through with him. There was no need to worry.

But for the moment it was better to keep things impersonal. No recriminations, no emotion-laden issues, just two warriors discussing an upcoming mission. Time enough to ease into deeper things later. She smiled and nodded slowly.

"I am quite well, thank you," Marissa said, keeping her voice carefully bland. "And have you already decided where we're headed? Where the Knowing Crystal is to be found?"

"Due north," Brace replied, unhappy with the artificially polite conversation when so much of deeper import needed to be discussed. "All I know is the Crystal lies somewhere due north of here."

"And is Ferox awaiting us there? Are we perhaps walking into a trap?"

"I don't know."

Marissa's smile thinned. "Then what exactly

do you know, Brace Ardane? Have you made any plans to ensure the success of this quest, or are we to blunder on as before?"

He shot her a smoldering glance. "All I know is Ferox is still on Moraca, perhaps awaiting another opportunity to capture Olim and use her Traveler's skills to reprogram the Crystal. That, and then recapture me to use with her. So don't start on me, Marissa."

She forced her voice to soften. Recriminations were never the way to handle him. "Brace, we have to have a plan. Have you spoken with Rodac about this?"

"No."

"Then let me fetch him and we'll talk now." She rose from her chair.

Brace's hand shot out, capturing her arm. "No, Marissa. First *we* need to talk."

Marissa lowered herself back to her chair. "Fine. Then talk."

He turned to the ornately carved mantel that sheltered the hearth, his fingers tracing the swirling pattern of the rich, red-brown robur wood. "Are we going to be able to work together?" he asked without lifting his eyes from the mantel.

"Of course we will," Marissa replied with absolute finality. "We're professionals, after all."

His eyes, dark and anguished, turned to her. "And is that all there's to be between us from now on—professionalism?"

Caught in the mesmerizing depths of his

piercing gaze, Marissa could do little more than stare, her heart leaping beneath her breast. Did he know how easy he was making it for her? Did he truly think they could ever have what they'd had before? He was a fool if he did.

And yet, a tiny voice prodded, why not allow herself to enjoy the delights of his body? Her honest response would only assure his acceptance that she loved him once more. And if he demanded to actually hear the words, what were a few lies if it would ensure Ferox's eventual defeat?

"There can be whatever you want, Brace. Do you wish to mate?" she whispered. "Is that what you want from me?"

Before he could reply, Marissa stood and began unlacing the front of her tunic. As Brace watched in amazement, she spread the garment open and, without a moment's hesitation, slipped it from her. And still he stood there, silent and staring.

Smiling, she moved to stand before him, her slender arms lifting to entwine about his neck. Brace had a brief glimpse of her tantalizingly full, white breasts and soft, rose-colored nipples before she pressed into him. Heat, unbidden, flared in his groin.

With a shuddering breath, Brace freed Marissa's hands and pulled them down to hold them at her sides. "What is this?" he demanded gruffly. "A few secundae ago you were the cold professional and now—now you're suddenly hot for me?"

Marissa arched a brow. "Are you complaining?"

"No," Brace said, "only confused. After how I failed you, after how angry you were with me, this seductive behavior is greatly out of character."

His eyes narrowed. "Are you playing some game, Marissa?"

She twisted out of his loose grip. "No games. I want you and you want me. It's as simple as that."

Her hands moved to his breeches and she began to unfasten them. As she did, Marissa glanced up at him through the thick fan of her lashes. "You *do* want me, don't you?"

"Marissa, don't." Brace stayed her hands. "Yes, I want you, but not like this. Not with so much left unsaid between us. Not with wounds still unhealed." He picked up her tunic and shoved it at her, then gestured toward the chairs. "Come, let's talk for a while."

Brace led her to her chair, then moved to sit in his. No sooner was he settled than Marissa flung aside her tunic and slipped over to hop onto his lap.

Brace glared at her. "Marissa . . ."

"We can talk just as well close as far apart," she murmured, once more entwining her arms about his neck and snuggling close. Her head lowered to lie upon his chest. "Now, what did you have to say?"

The scent of her rose to fill his nostrils—sweet, fragrant, and ripe with her womanhood. Her soft breasts pressed tightly against the hard, flat planes of his chest. Brace wished away the barrier of his tunic, yearning for the feel of her flesh upon his. Then his resolve hardened. With all his strength, he turned his attention away from the rising fullness in his groin and back to the matter at hand.

"Have you forgiven me, then?" he forced himself to ask. "Forgiven me for what happened to Candra?"

He felt her stiffen, then relax.

"The Crystal was the cause of Candra's death, not you. I see that now."

"But have you forgiven me, Marissa?" he insisted.

Had she forgiven him? Marissa lifted her head to meet him eye to eye. It was so difficult to tell. So difficult to differentiate between forgiveness and trust. *So* difficult to penetrate that wall of ice around her heart and probe the emotions that lay within.

She knew it was his lack of skill with the Crystal, his innate weakness as a man, that had been the cause of her sister's death, but could she continue to hate him for things he had little control over? If anything, he deserved her pity, not her hatred. Yet why did it anger her so to finally see him as he really was?

Marissa gazed at Brace, at the starkly etched angles and planes that merged into a strikingly handsome countenance. Gazed into deep, dark eyes gleaming with love and the most hear-trending integrity, and wanted to scream from anguish. In spite of it all, she reminded herself with ferocious desperation, he was not the man she needed, the man she could depend on, the man she dared give her heart to.

Perhaps that was why she found it so hard to forgive him. He had tantalized her with a glimpse of what life between a male and female could truly be, teased her just enough to make her crave it desperately—and then not been man enough to give it to her. And that was far crueler than never having known it at all.

The effort it took to utter the first of the lies made Marissa's stomach twist with nausea. "Yes," she rasped, "of course I forgive you. I know it wasn't your fault."

He eyed her warily. "Truly?"

She swallowed down a bitter surge of self-disgust. "Truly, Brace." Her head lowered until her mouth was a warm breath from his. "Now are you satisfied?"

"Do you love me, Marissa?"

The words prickled down her spine, making the hairs stand up on the back of her neck and her heart pound wildly. Ah, by all that was sacred, Marissa thought, here it comes now!

For the briefest instant her eyelids lowered as she struggled for the strength to answer him. But there was no solace to be found behind their shielding screen. Marissa forced her eyes to open, forced herself to face him.

"Yes, Brace," she whispered on a trembling sigh. "I love you."

An intense look of joy flared in his eyes, then Brace closed the tiny distance separating them. "Then prove it," he whispered.

He kissed her, his lips hot, insistent, frantic. Suddenly there was nothing between them—no doubts, no wounded feelings—nothing but mind-numbing, fevered desire.

With a low moan Marissa arched into him, clinging to his massive shoulders, her fingers moving to clutch wildly in his hair. He shuddered uncontrollably beneath her, his big body shaking with fierce, brutal passion. Shaking as fiercely as hers.

She tore open the front of his tunic, her fingers jerky with excitement and rising need. Her hands moved to rub his thick chest muscles, reveling in the wiry crispness that covered them, stroking the velvet flatness of his male nipples. His tongue probed for entry, teasing and tantalizing her. When she opened, he drew her tongue into his mouth, caressing it with his own.

A hot, searing need grew within Marissa. She yielded to it. Sliding off his lap, she sank to her knees before him. Her hands lifted to the band of his breeches and, with sharp little tugs, she freed the turgid swell of his manhood. For a long moment Marissa just stared, mesmerized by the thick erection jutting from its nest of dark, dense curls.

Her head lowered to nuzzle his long, hot shaft, and she kissed it.

"*M-Marissa!*" Brace arched back in his chair, thrusting himself toward her.

Her mouth opened and her wet little tongue emerged to tentatively lick him.

"Ah, Gods!" Brace cried. In one swift movement, he leaned down to grab her arms and pull her with him to the floor.

In a flurry of fevered hands and twisting bodies, their remaining clothes were shed and Brace was atop her, his big tip poised against her femininity. He kissed her then, hot, deep, and devouring. His fingers splayed, slipping intimately between her legs, sliding into the slick wetness of her womanhood. Marissa trembled wildly.

Then his hands were on her buttocks, lifting her, and he was thrusting into her hot sheath. And she was lost. With a piercing cry Marissa exploded, spiraling into a deep, dark chasm of ecstasy. A chasm free of distrust and disappointment, where only she and the man she loved could ever hope to go.

They set out early the next sol after bidding farewell to Raina, Olim, and all the other Sodalitas. Marissa and Raina embraced fiercely, tears misting their eyes.

"I wish you well, sweeting," the Sodalitas leader whispered. "The task before you is enormous."

"And when have I ever taken the easier path?" Marissa whispered back.

"Never, but still it's past time you finally did and knew a little peace and happiness." Raina's glance strayed to Brace, who was deep in discussion with Rodac. "He's nearly tolerable—for a male."

"Y-yes," Marissa mumbled, choking back a sob. "He is that."

But not for me, she thought bitterly as she stepped back from her friend and walked over to join her two companions. *Perhaps for another woman some sol, if we're fortunate enough to survive this quest, but not for me.*

At that moment Brace saw her. He strode to meet Marissa, his arm encircling her shoulders to pull her to him.

"Did you sleep well, sweet femina?" Brace asked with a smile. "You were already gone from your bed when I awoke."

"I slept quite well, thank you," Marissa replied uneasily, trying as best she could to slip away. "We should be leaving. Already the sun rises."

He pulled her back to him. "There's time enough for a moment of greeting, isn't there?"

Without waiting for her reply Brace's mouth came down on hers, taking Marissa's lips in a fiercely possessive kiss. Her hands slipped between them and she pushed at his chest in a futile attempt to break away. As the now familiar, languorous warmth began to course through her, the world around Marissa, the curious stares, the presence of others, all faded.

Brace's kiss deepened, sending silky tendrils of desire curling down her spine. Her body sprang to vibrant life in his arms and she surrendered helplessly. Then Brace stepped away. The hot, sensual haze evaporated as quickly as it had risen, leaving Marissa standing there, trembling and breathless.

He eyed her for a moment more, his glance scorching her to the tips of her toes. Then Brace inhaled a ragged breath, and grinned.

"You were right. We should be leaving."

She shot him a quelling look, exasperated at the wild excitement he'd managed to stir within her in the span of a few secundae. And even more exasperated with herself for once again lowering her guard.

This is no way to resume the quest, Marissa lectured herself as they boarded the two skim craft and began preflight procedures. Her mindlessly heated response did no one any good—least of all Brace. Somehow, someway, she must wall off her heart—once and for all.

With a whir of engines the skim craft rose and sped away, leaving behind the only real home Marissa had ever known. She never once looked back, but kept her gaze fixed firmly ahead. Beside her Brace piloted their craft, one hand clutching the control stick, the other cradling her hand. Cradling it in his big, comforting, strong hand . . .

Surreptitiously, she assessed him. Brace's

darkly handsome face appeared serene but determined, as if some newfound confidence coursed through him. It was last nocte, Marissa realized. She had managed to deceive him into thinking they had reconciled, that she loved him again. Her plan had indeed worked. She should feel very proud.

Disgust surged through her instead. Never, in all the times she'd plotted to betray Brace to Ferox, had she felt such deep and utter self-loathing. She turned away, gazing blankly out at the rolling hills and distant mountains. Brace trusted her, believed in her—loved her. And, as doubtful as she was of his ability to see the quest through, Marissa suddenly realized he was far more worthy a person than she could ever hope to be.

Tears filled her eyes. Angrily Marissa wiped them away. By the Crystal Fires, this awakening of the heart was getting to be a confusing—not to mention wet—affair.

"Femina, what is it?" Brace asked, noting the tell-tale moisture glistening on her cheeks.

"N-nothing," Marissa mumbled, hurriedly averting her face. "I'm just sorry to leave my home."

He flipped on the auto pilot, then captured Marissa's chin, turning her to face him. A troubled looked flared in Brace's eyes.

"What's *really* the matter? Was it something I did or said? Did I embarrass you back at the fort, kissing you in front of your sisters? I could've sworn you enjoyed it as much as I."

"No. I mean yes! Oh, just let it be, Brace!" She tried to twist free of his grip.

He refused to let go. "Marissa, there shouldn't be secrets between us."

The fight drained out of her and Marissa slumped in defeat. "No, there shouldn't."

She shook her head and sighed. "But our reconciliation is still so fresh, so new, and I haven't worked it all through yet. And I'm afraid of what lies ahead."

"What's this—my little warrior afraid?" He gave her a devilish grin. "I never thought I'd hear you admit to such human weaknesses. The next thing I know, you'll be confessing to a desire to give up your warlike ways and stay home and bear us children."

Marissa's mouth dropped open and a sharp pain stabbed through her. Ch-children . . . How could Brace be thinking of such a thing at a time like this? Had he guessed that she'd missed her woman's flux? But that wasn't possible. She wasn't even certain herself that her tardy menses meant anything—save that her body might be reacting to the stresses of the past half-monate.

And now was definitely not the time to worry about what was to be done if she *was* pregnant. Yet the consideration of bearing twins . . .

Despite what Raina had told her about Olim and of the manner in which Brace had saved her life, it all seemed too tenuous, this belief in the healing powers of love. And she'd never risk the life of any child of hers to such unsubstantial emotions!

For a fleeting instant, the image of a babe, plump and cuddly in her arms, flitted across Marissa's mind. What would it be like to bear Brace's children? To watch her belly ripen with his seed? To know what it meant to bring forth life?

It would make Brace very happy. She'd seen that sudden, joyous flare in his eyes when he'd spoken of a family. And, after all he'd been through of late, he deserved some small share of happiness. Happiness that she, too, could share, savor . . .

"Don't," she choked, wrenching herself back to reality. "Don't speak of a life that may never be. There's no time for dreaming, not now, not until this quest is over. It will only weaken us to the horrible things yet to come."

"Marissa, there's no harm—"

She rounded on him, glaring at Brace through a haze of wrathful tears. "Yes, there *is* harm, great harm, and if you're too blind to see it, I'm not! Now, no more of it. Do you hear me, Brace Ardane? No more of it until this is all over and we've truly a future to dream about!"

He arched a dark brow, then subjected her to a cool, appraising look. "As you wish, femina. I'm sorry to have upset you. I beg your forgiveness."

"It's of no import."

Brace eyed her for a moment longer, then

flipped off the auto pilot. He spoke no more and, as the horas passed, he guided the craft ever nearer to the mountains. Mountains that hid the Knowing Crystal—and a man called Ferox—somewhere in their craggy vastness.

"Gods! No!"

The anguished cry jerked Marissa from a deep sleep. She sat up, blinking in confusion. It was still dark, perhaps the early horas of the next sol, and the small perpetual flame box lit the cave with only a dull glow. She glanced around and met Rodac's dark, beady eyes.

A low moan came from behind her. It was Brace, writhing in his blankets, his face twisted in agony, caught in the throes of yet another dream terror. Marissa's heart leaped to her throat. She made a move to crawl over to him when a leathery hand halted her. She glanced back over her shoulder.

Is this the sleep terrors you spoke of?

"Yes. The Knowing Crystal begins again to torment him. We must try to rouse him, if we can."

Rodac released her and Marissa scooted over to Brace. For an instant she hesitated, dreading the toll the next few moments would take on both of them. And dreading even more the eventual outcome of the battle that now began in earnest with the Crystal's renewed attempts to drive Brace mad before he managed to destroy it. How much longer would she have the strength to call him back from the endless horrors of his dreams?

Long enough to at least reach Ferox?

Squaring her shoulders, Marissa bent and gathered Brace's sweat-slick, shuddering body to her. "Brace," she called. "Come back. Come away from your sleep. Come back to me."

He cried out, arching upward into her arms, his big body taut, caught in the grasp of some terrible inner torment. The powerful lunge of his body threw Marissa off balance and he toppled over on her. She struggled to slip out from beneath him, but his greater weight kept her pinned.

And then, suddenly, long, strong fingers were around Marissa's throat, choking her. "Rodac!" she gasped, fighting with all her might against Brace. "H-help me!"

The Simian was at her side in an instant, prying at hands grown superhumanly strong in the dream-induced battle with some unknown foe. As Rodac struggled with Brace, Marissa felt the breath gradually leave her body.

She gasped, choked, fought wildly, but to no avail. Brace's fingers gouged ever deeper. Whirling lights, blindingly bright, danced before Marissa's eyes. Dully, she realized she was dying.

The realization fueled her waning strength. If she died, Brace would never recover from the knowledge that her death had been at his hands, however unintentional. The quest would be over, the Knowing Crystal victorious. And Ferox would still be alive . . .

Ferox . . . still alive . . .

Never!

Her determination fought past the smothering blackness. Ferox would *not* win. And neither would the Knowing Crystal. No matter what it took, she'd never, ever, let it destroy Brace.

With the last vestiges of her strength, Marissa grasped Brace's head in both hands and willed her love to flow into him. From someplace beyond the gray mist that engulfed her, she felt the throttling fingers loosen and a heavy weight pulled off her.

She rolled away and lay there gasping. Air rushed in to fill her lungs. By all that was sacred, Marissa thought weakly, it felt so good to breathe again!

Little by little, her vision cleared and strength once more flowed through her. She rose on one elbow, weak and floppy as a babe. A meter away, a grim-faced Rodac held Brace securely in his arms.

For a long while, Brace was quiet. Then his eyelids fluttered open. He glanced up, dazed, frowning in confusion at the hairy alien leaning over him.

"Wh-what's going on here?" Brace croaked. "Got lonely in the nocte, d-did you?"

Rodac rolled his eyes and shoved away. *Not so lonely that I've yet a need for wild man like you. You nearly killed Marissa, you crazed fool!*

"K-killed Marissa?" Brace whispered hoarsely.

His eyes met hers.

She sat there, still breathing heavily, one hand at her neck. Her fingers, however, couldn't hide the angry red marks that marred the white skin of her throat.

"Gods!" Brace groaned. "The dream was bad enough, but this is beyond bearing!"

He rolled over to bury his face in his hands. "What next? Ah, what next?"

Marissa crawled over and touched him on the shoulder. "Brace, what do you mean?" she asked softly. "What happened in your dream this time?"

He stiffened when she touched him, and groaned again. "It was as before. The Crystal was chasing me, the blackness yawned up to engulf me. Then someone called and I turned. Hands appeared out of the darkness, clawing at me, drawing blood. I went mad then, striking at the unknown owner of the voice, pulling him down to me."

Brace paused for an instant, his body trembling with the remembered terrors. "I—I think I imagined it was Ferox, and a fierce joy flooded me. My fingers tightened about his throat and I began to choke the life out of him. At last, I thought, I'd have revenge—for the both of us. Then a face rose out of the blackness, white and terrifying. And it wasn't the face of Ferox."

"Who was it, Brace?" Even as she spoke, an

icy presentiment wound itself about her heart. "Who was it?"

He lifted his head then and tears glistened on his cheeks. "It was you, Marissa," Brace choked. "Gods, Marissa! It was you!"

Chapter Sixteen

Marissa stared at Brace for a long moment, her mind racing. Had it been an accident that Brace had turned on her in his sleep, that she'd been the nearest person to attack? Or had the Knowing Crystal meant for him to murder her?

His eyes met hers, and the haunted look burning there told Marissa all she needed to know. Brace was thinking the same thing. Though it had been totally out of his control, he had indeed been obeying a higher command—and that command had been to kill her.

Anger swelled within Marissa. For every step they took in this quest, the Knowing Crystal always appeared to be one step ahead of them. And now the stone seemed to realize that not only was Brace a threat to its continued power, but Marissa was a threat as well.

She doubted that the stone knew exactly why it saw her in that light. In the end, it didn't matter. The logical course of action was to destroy her—and that was precisely what it had tried to do. Marissa wondered what the Crystal would try next.

Brace crawled to a sitting position. "I think we all realize what happened here," he began wearily. "The Knowing Crystal is fighting back in every way it can."

We'll just have to anticipate its moves better, Rodac motioned. *The stone did us a favor this nocte. Forewarned is forearmed.*

"Yes," Brace agreed. "And since it influences me through my dreams, it's wisest if I don't sleep any more until we reach Ferox and the stone."

"Lack of sleep will definitely prepare you for the final confrontation," Marissa interjected sarcastically. "Perhaps you should fill us in on your ultimate plan, just in case you doze off at the last secundae."

He shot her a tight-lipped look. "I told you before. There's not much point in a plan. It all depends on what Ferox and the Knowing Crystal do."

Let me suggest that you at least let Marissa and me go in for the Crystal when we reach Ferox. There's no telling what the Crystal would do if you tried to lay hands on it. Far better that us thick-skulled, insensitive commoners give it a try.

"Speak for yourself, you hairy bag of bones," Marissa chuckled softly, the tension of the past few moments at last beginning to fade. "I am *not* thick-skulled."

The Simian grinned at her. *Be that as it may, I'm sure you see my point.*

"And what am I to do in the meanwhile?" Brace demanded. "Sit safely back and let you two risk all?"

Rodac shrugged. *Well, there's always the small matter of Ferox. You might want to finish him off while we're busy stealing the stone. His death would simplify things greatly.*

"Ferox is mine!" Marissa's voice slashed through the air.

Two pairs of masculine eyes turned to her.

"Does it really matter who kills him, as long as he dies?" Brace asked.

"It matters to me!"

Well, what you desire in this is of no import, Rodac motioned. *You are a warrior and know better than to allow personal needs to cloud things.* He arched a speculative brow. *You do know that, don't you?*

"Of course I do," she muttered. "But if the opportunity arises—"

"*If* the opportunity arises," Brace said, "I'll save him for you."

He paused. "After we take care of Ferox and regain possession of the Crystal, we must set out immediately for Cambrai and the pools. The stone *must* be destroyed as quickly as possible."

"Yes, yes," Marissa waved him on. "Tell us something we don't already know. If not, I'm ready to get some rest. We've a long journey ahead on the morrow." She arched an inquisitive brow at Brace. "I *assume* we've still a ways to go?"

"Another sol or two, I'd guess," Brace agreed grimly, "from the faintness of the Crystal transmissions I'm picking up."

He frowned. "Strange, that ever since we escaped Ferox, the Knowing Crystal's transmissions have varied so greatly. Sometimes its signals are quite strong, and other times I can barely pick them up."

"And do you have an explanation?" Marissa asked.

"I think it's the box Ferox carries the Knowing Crystal in. Teran's research spoke of some container capable of blocking Crystal transmission. I think Ferox is using that box at times."

"But why?"

Brace shrugged. "Perhaps he doesn't want us on his trail just yet. His plan, whatever it is, isn't working, though. Even when it's in its box, I can still pick up faint signals from the Crystal."

"So there's a chance we can reach Ferox before he realizes it?" There was an edge of rising excitement in Marissa's voice. "Perhaps take him by surprise?"

"Perhaps, if nothing else enters in to complicate matters." Brace paused, motioning to Marissa's and Rodac's bedding. "No matter what lies ahead, you'll need your rest. Go to sleep, both of you."

"Are you serious about not sleeping until we

reach Ferox and the Crystal?" Marissa asked, concern darkening her eyes. "I didn't mean to sound so flippant about what you said earlier."

His mouth drew into a ruthlessly determined line. "Yes, I was serious."

"Brace, I'm not so sure—"

"I meant what I said, Marissa," Brace repeated gently. "Now, no more of it. Please."

She stifled the impulse to go to him and take him in her arms. Marissa had seen the look of anguish that had passed across his face when she'd just questioned his decision not to go back to sleep. Seen it and known that to argue further would only increase his personal torment. But to leave him to fight his demons alone . . .

"As you wish," she murmured and went back to her bed. If Brace insisted on staying awake, a good nocte's rest was even more vital for her. She must maintain her strength and alertness if she were to be of any help.

"He means you, too, you hairy bag of bones." Marissa pointedly glanced at Rodac.

The Simian's rows of tiny teeth gleamed in the firelight. He then climbed back into his squat of repose and promptly began to snore.

For a time Marissa lay there, quietly watching Brace. He sat propped against the stone wall, his gaze never meeting hers, his face a mask. A mask of taut anguish and haunted questions. She wondered what his questions were. Did he doubt his ability to continue, much less see the quest through to a successful completion? Did Brace even dare consider such possibilities? And yet, how could he not?

Watching him, Marissa tried to steel herself to his plight. Time and again, however, a woman's compassion filled her and she had to fight mightily against the impulse to go to him. Finally the interior battle exhausted her. She drifted off to sleep.

Brace heard Marissa's breathing slow to a deep, even rhythm. He at last dared a glance in her direction. She lay curled in unguarded slumber, her mouth soft and sweetly beguiling. Remorse twisted into a painful knot beneath his breast. He had almost killed her, the woman he loved. Gods, what else would he subject her to before all this was over?

Doubts and fears, like the snaking tendrils of the mists of Cygnus, wended their way around his heart. They pervaded him until his entire body felt damp and hollow. Wracking tremors began to shake him, and it was all he could do to contain the movements, fearing the sounds would once more waken his companions.

He didn't want them to see him like this, shaking like some frightened child. So weak, so uncertain, so cowardly. He, the Imperium's only hope, its savior! Ah, what a ludicrous thought!

A sound—half sob, half groan—rose in his throat. Brace flung back his head, pressing it into the unyielding stone. His eyes clenched shut and his strong throat worked with barely suppressed emotion. Had it come to this, then? Was he gradually succumbing to the influence of the Knowing Crystal? And where would it all end—in the murder of Marissa?

He would kill himself before he'd let that happen. Not even for the sake of the Imperium would he allow the stone to manipulate him to ever again harm the woman he loved! But if the Crystal seemed determined to force it, how could he fight back?

Rodac. Rodac would help him. He'd take the Simian aside on the morrow and speak to him. Make him promise to guard Marissa, protect her from anything Brace might do under the Crystal's influence.

The decision filled Brace with a sense of relief. Gratitude surged through him. He was fortunate to have found such a loyal friend in Rodac.

Brace's glance strayed once more to Marissa. His gaze softened. He was even more fortunate to have found such a wonderful woman to love. Now one final obstacle lay between them and the hope of a life together. With a determined set of his jaw, Brace turned his thoughts to the coming sols—and the culmination of the quest.

They were deep into the mountains the next sol when the skim craft's fuel finally gave out. They headed down to a relatively flat spot near the summit of one rock-strewn mountain, gliding to a sputtering landing.

Brace was the first to disembark. He shook his head.

"Well, it's on foot from here on out," he muttered wryly. "Hope you're both ready for some strenuous exercise."

Marissa grinned. "I was beginning to get stiff with the inactivity. A nice long walk about now couldn't be more welcome."

Rodac merely grunted and gathered up their supplies, slinging a blaster over his shoulder. *Enough talk. Let's get on with it!*

A bitterly cold wind blew through the mountains, hampering their progress as fingers and limbs began to numb despite the heavy winter clothing. After a time, however, Brace had more pressing problems to deal with. As the sol wore on, a low ringing in his ears intensified to a dull, rhythmic pounding. For a while he thought it was the effect of the rising altitude. Gradually, as the sound assumed the character of harmonic vibrations, he realized it was the Knowing Crystal. Ferox must have discovered they were hot on his trail and decided once again to unleash its powers.

Brace tried as best he could to close his mind to the Crystal's transmissions. For short periods it seemed to work, but the mental effort required could not be maintained indefinitely. Brace's head began to throb. His eyes watered.

His reddened eyes and the taut set to his jaw finally drew Marissa's attention. "Brace," she asked, moving to his side, "what's wrong? Are you in pain?"

He refused to look at her, continuing to plow doggedly onward. "It's nothing I can't deal with."

She pulled him to a halt. "You look as if your head is splitting. If so, I've a mild narcotic I thought to bring along. Let me give—"

"It *won't* help! Gods, Marissa, let it be! It's hard enough to concentrate past it as it is."

Her eyes narrowed. "It's the Knowing Crystal, isn't it? It's beginning to affect you while you're awake. Isn't it, Brace?"

He wheeled about and strode on, attempting to close the gap between them and Rodac up ahead. Marissa stood there for an instant, frustration and fear welling inside her. Her purpose on this quest was to help him reach Ferox and the Knowing Crystal. So far there hadn't been anything she could do, save watch Brace slowly be worn down by lack of sleep and the now seemingly incessant mental hammering of the stone. How much longer could he keep on?

Well, she resolved, as long as he persevered, so would she. With renewed determination, Marissa hurried to catch up with Brace. Never once breaking stride, he glanced at her as she drew to his side. The look was strained and wary, but nonetheless resolute. She smiled at him, then matched him stride for stride.

At mid sol they reached an impasse. The mountain before them could either be scaled, or they could waste an extra sol or two in skirting its wide girth. Brace glanced at Rodac.

"Well, what do you think? Is it climbable?"

For me, easily. For you two, with great difficulty.

"Then what do you suggest?"

If we tie ourselves together and you follow carefully in my stead, I think it can be done. It will be dangerous, but quite possible.

Brace turned to Marissa. "I know you don't like heights. Are you up to it?"

Her glance lifted to scan the sheer mountain face. It rose sharply upward, dotted here and there by jagged outcroppings of rock. The climb would be treacherous. By the time they reached the summit they'd be thousands of meters above the ground. Marissa's stomach took a sickening plunge.

She swallowed hard and turned back to Brace. Time was of the essence, especially in light of the Knowing Crystal's now-active attack upon Brace's mind. She nodded grimly.

"Of course I'm up to it. I've never imagined this was some leisurely jaunt through the mountains to pick wildflowers. Just tell me what you want me to do."

For an instant the tight, strained look fell from his face and his features softened. Brace stroked her cheek, trailing downward to the curve of her mouth. Then he turned to Rodac.

"Let's get on with it."

The ascent began easily enough, with Rodac skillfully leading the way, Marissa in the middle, and Brace bringing up the rear. But when they reached the halfway point, the rock outcroppings that had initially simplified the climb grew fewer and farther apart and decidedly less stable. Several times Rodac's greater weight loosened stones that came tumbling down upon Brace and Marissa's heads. The gusts of wind that buffeted the mountain did nothing to make the trek any easier.

Despite the chill, sweat began to bead their brows and their limbs soon quivered with fatigue. The lack of sleep, combined with his painfully throbbing headache from fighting the relentless mental sounds, began to tell on Brace. He made several slips that almost cost him his hold on the mountain. After a time, it was sheer force of will that kept him going.

With the few sporadic glances she dared cast downward, Marissa saw him gradually weaken. Finally she tried to call to Rodac, but the winds had increased to a low howl and whipped the sound of her voice away. Frustration filled her. They *had* to take a rest.

Marissa glanced down at the large, flat outcropping of rock they'd passed a short while ago. It lay about five meters below them. Though she hated losing ground, it was the closest place to rest. There was nothing above them but the summit, and that was over a hundred meters farther.

She slowed her climb until Brace drew even with her. He glanced over in surprise, unaware of Marissa's presence until he joined her. One glance at his haggard face solidified her resolve.

He was exhausted, his eyes bloodshot, his features tight with pain. "Brace," Marissa shouted to him above the wind's loud wail, "we need to rest."

Dark, bleary eyes scanned her, then he shook his head. "We've got to get to the top before darkness. There's no time for rest."

Brace continued his climb, muscles trembling with fatigue pulling him relentlessly upward. Marissa rejoined him.

"Brace, please. You've got to rest or you'll soon make a mistake and fall."

He ignored her and kept on. She didn't understand, he thought. It was nearly automatic now, the placement of hand and foot in this seemingly endless ascent. As long as he kept himself moving and didn't think about the pain...

At that instant a bright light exploded before him. From its center burst a bolt of sheer, blinding energy. It shot straight toward him and into his right eye. Pain, excruciating in its suddenness and intensity, vibrated through him. His skull rang with a horrible sound. He felt his eye swell, thought it would burst. A nauseating dizziness engulfed him, and suddenly Brace couldn't see.

"M-Marissa!" he cried, and then his fingers loosened.

She saw him begin to fall and screamed. Blessedly, this time Rodac heard her. Realizing what had happened, he flung himself against the mountain and hung on with all his might, awaiting the instant of full impact as Brace's weight hurtled downward.

Marissa also held on, her eyes clenched shut in rising terror, but the momentum of Brace's falling body was too great for her. With a breath-grabbing jerk, her fingers tore loose and she joined him, dangling in the air.

A sense of weightlessness engulfed her. A momentary sense of disorientation, then nausea and light-headedness. For a horrible instant Marissa thought she'd pass out.

Then reason returned. She was a warrior, not some weak-kneed, helpless female. She must open her eyes and face the situation before she could ever hope to do something about it. But to have her worst fears assume reality! Marissa swallowed hard, forcing down the gorge that rose in her throat, and slowly opened her eyes. She looked up.

High above, Rodac was still firmly plastered to the mountainside. Relief flooded Marissa. At least for the moment they were in no danger of falling. Gathering all her remaining courage, she swung her gaze downward. Brace, several meters below, swayed in the blue expanse of sky, flailing blindly.

"Brace," Marissa shouted down to him. "Are you all right?"

He glanced up at her, his face contorted in agony, and forced one eye open. "Your dagger," he cried. "Throw down your dagger!"

She knew why Brace wanted it. As powerful as Rodac was, he couldn't hold on much longer, burdened with the weight of two people hanging in the air below him. Brace meant to ease the Simian's load by cutting himself free. To save her and Rodac, Brace was willing to sacrifice his life.

"*No!*" Marissa cried. "There's got to be some other way! I won't do it! I can't!"

"There isn't any other way. And it's only a short drop to that ledge beneath us. I—I can make it."

His dark, beautiful gaze locked with hers. One hand lifted, open and waiting.

"Throw me your dagger, Marissa."

She glanced down to the ledge that lay below him. It looked so very far away. If a gust of wind should blow at the wrong secundae or Brace misjudge his trajectory, he could easily miss the outcropping and continue to fall—all the way down the mountain.

Marissa choked back a sob. To lose Brace . . . Still, there was no other recourse.

Twisting around, Marissa freed the dagger from her thigh. Nimbly flipping it over to grasp it by the blade, she tossed it carefully down to Brace. He caught it with a quick movement of his hand.

For one last, lingering instant he gazed up at her. Then his features hardened. With a quick flick of his wrist, Brace sliced through the rope binding him about the waist. He fell, the dagger still clutched in his hand.

Marissa watched, her breath solidifying in her throat, and saw Brace strike the ledge below. At the last moment he twisted and his hands went out to break his fall. His left arm hit first, bending at the shoulder in a grotesque angle. Then Brace toppled over onto his back, slamming into a small, jagged pile of rocks. He lay there, unmoving.

She glanced up at Rodac to see him already beginning the climb downward. His movements sent her to swinging wildly in the air, and Marissa closed her eyes for a brief moment, then forced them open again. She riveted her gaze on Brace. The nearer she drew, the more worried she became.

He was bleeding from a gash in his forehead, and blood trickled down the rocks from some wound in his back. His left arm was twisted awkwardly at the shoulder, and, from the shape of the deformity, Marissa knew it was dislocated. Her eagerness to reach him grew with each passing moment. The last few meters before her feet touched down were agonizing.

Quickly she untied the rope about her waist and ran to Brace. First, her fingers probed for a pulse in his throat. It beat there, strong and reassuringly steady. Relief flooded her. Brace was alive.

Next, Marissa examined the gash in his forehead. It was bleeding freely, but when she blotted away the majority of the blood she found the wound was superficial. A tight pressure

380

dressing fashioned from one of her tunic sleeves dispensed with that injury. She then proceeded to examine him for broken bones. Aside from the shoulder, he seemed reasonably intact.

Rodac landed behind her on the ledge. Marissa turned, glancing up at him.

"Help me," she demanded. "Brace is bleeding from somewhere in his back and, with his dislocated shoulder, I need help turning him over."

Together they managed to get Brace on his stomach. A sharp rock protruded from just below his right shoulder blade. Marissa's glance met Rodac's. She ripped off the remaining sleeve of her tunic, then slipped out of her backpack.

She handed it to Rodac. "We'll need water to cleanse Brace's wounds, and I've a small vial of healing powder, plus an extra tunic in my pack."

As Rodac rummaged through her backpack, Marissa ripped her sleeve into several long strips.

The Simian handed her a water flask, the vial of powder, and the clean tunic. Marissa turned, slipped off her tunic and donned the fresh one, then proceeded to use half of the old garment for bandages and the other half for additional long strips of cloth.

What are you planning to do? Rodac motioned.

"First, we'll take care of his back wound,

dress it and bind it with these strips," she explained, indicating the first pile of long bandages. "Then, before he regains consciousness, we'll reset his shoulder."

Have you ever done that before?

Marissa shook her head. "No, but I've seen it done. Besides, you're going to do it. I haven't the strength to reset the shoulder of a man Brace's size and muscle mass."

Rodac's eyes widened. *I'm no healer. That sort of thing makes me ill.*

She smiled and patted his hand. "You'd be surprised what you're capable of when you've no other choice. And I'll help you. We're partners, remember?"

You pick the worst times to remind me of that.

The stone was quickly removed from Brace's back, the wound treated and dressed. Then they turned to the more gruesome issue of his shoulder. Despite his initial reluctance, Rodac's great strength made the resetting a surprisingly easy task. Afterwards, Marissa bound Brace's affected arm in a sling to his side.

"The muscles and tendons of his shoulder have been severely strained," Marissa explained, noting the alien's questioning look. "Binding it will force him to rest it and allow the arm to heal."

He can't climb very well with one arm.

"I know," she sighed. "I guess we're back to carrying him."

It'll cost you extra.

Marissa shot him a startled look. Rodac

smirked down at her, a teasing light gleaming in his beady eyes. She smiled, then shook her head ruefully.

"Here, if you help me turn him over so I can clean and treat his head wound, I'll even throw in a hot meal. Somehow, I doubt we're going any further this sol."

Rodac glanced up at the sun. It was just beginning its downward descent. *We've only another three horas of climb ahead. We could reach the summit by sol set, if we hurry. I could carry Brace—tie him to my back. I've certainly done it before.*

"Yes, that you have," Marissa agreed softly, her thoughts flitting back to that sol, now over a monate ago, when they'd first found Brace in prison.

So much had changed in so short a span of time. Brace and she had been lovers, Rodac had become her friend, and Candra had died.

That realization wrenched Marissa back to reality. There was no time for tender recollections. They were perched on a ledge on the side of a mountain, in danger of freezing to death if they spent the nocte here. Brace was badly injured, and there were still Ferox and the Knowing Crystal to deal with. A decision must be made—and now!

She gathered up her supplies and shoved them back into her pack. "Let's get on with it, then. I don't know how long Brace will remain unconscious, but the sooner we get him to a sheltered area, the better."

With Marissa's assistance, Brace was lashed securely to Rodac's back and the climbing rope retied about their waists. She then shouldered the extra backpacks and blasters. At the last moment, Marissa remembered to retrieve her dagger from the rocks where Brace had fallen, and shoved it back into her thigh sheath. If something happened to her during the climb and it endangered the others, she'd use the dagger just as ruthlessly as Brace had done.

But nothing was going to happen, Marissa assured herself as they resumed the climb up the mountain. There was too much at stake to dwell a moment more on some minor fear of heights. As powerful a climber as Rodac was, the additional burden of Brace's inert form would greatly increase the difficulty of the ascent. And if Brace awoke and began to struggle from the pain and confusion, he could very easily throw Rodac off balance.

No, Marissa thought as she followed as closely as possible behind Rodac, she must stay near to assist the Simian with Brace. Her touch and the sound of her voice might be all that kept them from falling to a certain death.

The climb was arduous, but Marissa managed to keep up. Blessedly, Brace didn't waken. As the final rays of the sun disappeared behind the distant peaks, Rodac reached the summit. Several secundae later, Marissa heaved herself over the top. They both lay there, panting and exhausted, until the frigid wind roused them once more.

Marissa propped herself on one elbow and looked around. Thick stands of shaggy sempervivus fir grew here and there between large outcroppings of boulders. At least there'd be wood for a fire, if they could find a windbreak or cave among the rocks. Wearily she climbed to her feet.

"I'll go scout those rocks over there," Marissa said, glancing down at Rodac. "Stay with Brace. I'll return soon."

Ignoring the protesting muscles that quivered with exhaustion, Marissa forced herself into a slow jog. Time was of the essence if they were to find shelter before darkness. A half hora, no more, and full nocte would be upon them. She scrambled up into the rocks, searching for a protected spot from the winter winds. At last she found an adequate windbreak, then signaled Rodac to join her.

While she awaited his arrival, she gathered several armfuls of dead wood. By the time Rodac arrived, Marissa had a small pile of firewood stacked and was digging through her backpack for her tinder box. She paused to assist the Simian in unlashing Brace from his back. Together they carefully laid him in the most sheltered part of the windbreak. While Rodac took over starting the fire, Marissa reexamined Brace.

He was still unconscious, his face pale, his skin cool. That worried Marissa. Had he suffered internal damage, a head injury they had no way of knowing, much less doing anything about? If so, Brace could well die before they'd be able to get him to civilization and a healer.

A helpless, frightened feeling crept into Marissa's heart. If Brace should die . . .

Anger flooded her. Anger and a growing realization that, despite everything that had torn them apart, she would not let him die. She'd called him back from his dream terrors and the edge of madness several times before. How much different could this time be?

With resolution made desperate by Brace's rapidly deteriorating condition, Marissa first moved him closer to the fire, then extracted two blankets from their packs. Next, she unfastened Brace's phoca coat and the front of his tunic, then quickly did the same to herself. Covering them both with the blankets, Marissa scooted close to Brace and pressed her bare flesh against his.

He was so cold, so still, his breathing shallow and erratic. She probed for a pulse in his throat. It still throbbed beneath her fingers. Marissa pulled him closer, flattening the soft mounds of her breasts into his hard, hair-roughened planes. Her head lowered to lie beneath his and she inhaled deeply of his musky, masculine scent.

It might well be the last time she held him in her arms, Marissa realized. A painful, aching emptiness filled her. Never to see his dark, dancing eyes glinting with devilish glee as he teased her. Never to hear the soft murmur of his deep voice, telling her he loved her. Never to feel his strong arms around her, or taste or smell him!

He had given her so much in such a short time, shared his life, his love with her. Yet what had she given him in return? Nothing but lies ... and pain ... and betrayal.

Marissa choked back a sob. She'd been convinced he was unworthy of her, that he was weak, a coward. She'd been a fool, trying to protect her heart, lessening his value by denigrating him. In the end, it was she who was the weak one, she who was the coward.

Brace Ardane was the most courageous, most valiant man Marissa had ever known. He had *never* given up, not in all those cycles of his imprisonment, not in the battle against his madness, not in the face of her betrayal or the vicious onslaught of the Knowing Crystal in its attempts to destroy him. He would fight until his dying breath—he was that strong, that brave.

If he died now, Brace would never know how sorry she was for distrusting him, for belittling him. He would never know that she truly loved him. And never know of the two little lives she was now certain she carried deep within her. Anguish welled in Marissa's heart.

"Brace," she whispered. "Brace, come back to me. I love you. I need you. Please, Brace, don't leave me."

He lay there, limp and oh, so very cold. Marissa clutched him to her, her hands gliding over him in frantic, urgent strokes. And still he didn't respond.

A tiny spark of resolve, fanned by her fear and rising anger, flared to life within Marissa's breast. She *wouldn't* let him die! If it required the sacrifice of her life to save him, she'd give it. Marissa squeezed her eyes shut and, from someplace deep within, willed her heart and soul to flow into him.

Love swirled about them, encompassing both in a glowing aura of heated energy. Rodac, watching through the fire, saw it and marveled. Watched, and prayed that Marissa's love was strong enough to call Brace back from the land of the dead.

And somewhere within the soothing, healing mists Marissa found Brace. Touched, spirit to spirit. Pain arced between them. Fear coursed through her.

He was so weak, she realized. He'd drain her of everything. An impulse to flee, an instinctive urge toward self-preservation, flooded her. Yet Marissa fought past it, her spirit resolutely moving back to join with his.

If it required the sacrifice of her life ...

Their spirits merged, and for an instant in eternity, she touched the essence of him. A strange sensation coursed through Marissa. She heard a voice, haunting and lovely, saw a radiant light and, within that light, a sparkling stone. Then Brace groaned and moved in her arms.

The light and voice faded.

"M-Marissa?" Brace whispered.

Her eyelids lifted. Brace stared up at her, white as death but quite alive. She smiled.

He glanced around, confused. "Wh-where am I? I remember falling, striking hard . . . then great pain and blackness . . ."

"I patched you up as best I could, then Rodac carried you up the rest of the mountain."

A shadow passed across his face, as if a sudden realization had assailed him. "You saved me, Marissa," Brace murmured. "Once again our spirits joined and, this time, *your* strength brought *me* back. The strength of your love . . ."

She looked away.

"Marissa, sweet femina," Brace whispered hoarsely. "What's wrong? What did I say?"

Her tear-filled eyes met his. "I—I almost loved you too little and too late. Not until you were lying here, dying in my arms, did I finally realize how much you meant to me."

She inhaled a sobbing breath. "Ah, Brace. I—I've never been worthy of you. Never!"

Aching tenderness warmed his beautiful eyes. "You're all the woman I'll ever want or need, femina. No one else could have saved me. No one, Marissa, but you."

His glance strayed to where Rodac sat before the fire. Their gazes locked.

"Well, old friend," Brace rasped. "Had your fill of this quest yet?"

Are we rich yet?

Brace chuckled weakly. "Not quite, but soon. I promise."

He attempted to prop himself up, and grimaced. "Gods, I feel as if a herd of wild equs just stampeded over me."

He tried to move his left arm and found it bound tightly to his side. "What's this?" Brace asked, glancing down.

"You dislocated your shoulder," Marissa was quick to explain. "Plus suffered a gash on your forehead and puncture wound to your back. Anything else you'll have to tell us about."

Gingerly Brace moved his body. "Well, I can't see very well out of my right eye. Aside from that, everything else seems intact. I think I'll live."

"What happened, back there on the mountain?" she asked.

He shook his head. "I'm not sure, but I'd guess the Knowing Crystal decided the moment was right to take a more active part in my destruction. We're very close to the Crystal now." Brace paused, his glance moving from Marissa to Rodac. "Thanks to Marissa's healing link, I'll be ready to set out on the morrow."

"You're mad!" Marissa exclaimed in outrage.

Brace studied her, a smile hovering on his lips. "My wounds aren't incapacitating. I've an eye left to see out of, and I can use my shoulder if I must.

"And, as far as my mind goes—" he paused,

a wondering light in his eyes "—somehow, in our linking, I think you gave me something I've never had before. A greater strength, perhaps ...and confidence."

His jaw tightened. "At any rate, we *must* head out on the morrow."

"You're the most stubborn male ..." Marissa sighed and shook her head. "But why should that surprise me?"

She rolled away and sat up, refastening her tunic and fur coat.

"Where are you going?"

Marissa leaned over and tucked the blankets more snugly about him. "Nowhere. I'm just going to start supper. You can rest until it's ready."

A sudden look of interest flared in his eyes. "A stew perhaps? With meat?"

"Meat?" Marissa couldn't help a small grimace. "Well, considering your weakened state, I suppose I could throw in a few scraps of meat. But only to hasten your recovery, no more."

A weak grin tipped the corner of Brace's mouth. "Thank you, Marissa."

"Don't ever thank me for helping poison your body," she muttered as she dug through her back pack.

Brace smiled and lay back, watching for a time as Marissa began preparations for the meal. Gradually his eyes closed and he dozed.

A short while later, Rodac roused him. With Marissa's assistance Brace hungrily consumed a bowl of stew, then fell back in exhaustion. A half hora later, despite his best efforts to the contrary, he was sound asleep.

He'd rest for horas now, Marissa thought as she eyed him through the fire's smoky haze. Well into the next sol, if she and the narcotic she'd mixed in his food had anything to do with it. Marissa hoped the combination of his sheer exhaustion and the narcotic's drugging effects would put him in so deep a sleep that even the Knowing Crystal couldn't reach him.

Still, to guard against the possibility, she watched him far into the nocte. One way or another, Marissa meant for Brace to have at least another sol's rest before reembarking upon the quest. Ferox and the Knowing Crystal could wait a while longer. Finally convinced that Brace would have his uninterrupted sleep, Marissa dozed off.

It seemed, however, that Brace had other ideas. He was gone when Marissa and Rodac awoke the next morning.

Chapter Seventeen

Sol rise found Brace several horas due north into the mountains. For a time as he slogged awkwardly along, his multitude of aches and pains kept his mind off other, more unsettling things. With one arm useless at his side, an eye still painfully swollen shut, not to mention the condition of his bruised, wounded body, it required all of Brace's powers of concentration just to traverse the snow-covered terrain.

As the horas passed, however, he grew numb to the stiff joints and protesting muscles. His forward momentum became automatic, freeing his mind. And then the memory of last nocte's dream terror once again returned.

For some reason it hadn't been as powerful as the others, as if the influence of the Knowing Crystal had struggled through additional barriers. Perhaps Ferox had chosen to place the Crystal back in its box for a short while. It seemed the only explanation for the episodes of respite Brace had experienced so far. The geode box at least seemed to prevent the stone's more active, painful effects—even in his dreams.

Though the dream had been identical to the last one—the murder of Marissa—this time Brace had managed to fight past it and waken on his own. Wakened, panting and dripping with sweat, to find Marissa and Rodac both asleep.

He had lain there for a long while, willing his pounding heart to slow and his breathing to even. Lain there, watching Marissa. And, as he'd watched her, once again felt the inexplicable urge to kill rise within. Brace fought against it until he trembled with the effort—and the realization that the Knowing Crystal was once more influencing his conscious mind.

Finally he could bear it no longer. The sound of his movements muted by the howling winter winds, Brace rose and stealthily gathered up his backpack and blaster. With one last, tender glance at Marissa, sleeping so cozily before the fire, he left the windbreak and headed north.

They'd find him gone in the morning. Even with several horas' lead, however, Brace knew that Marissa and Rodac would quickly be on his trail. It was to be expected—they were now as committed to the quest as he. And in his weakened state, he would soon need their help.

In the meanwhile, Brace meant to confront the Knowing Crystal alone. Marissa had given him everything she could. He'd not risk her further. To do so would play right into the Crystal's plans.

The stone's attempts to influence him to kill Marissa had a twofold advantage if they succeeded. Brace saw that clearly now. Not only would her death eliminate her potential threat, but it would also destroy Brace's abilities as a Crystal Master. That realization had come to him as he'd set out in the dark, lonely horas before sol rise.

Teran's words had teased his memory, finally forcing their way back to conscious recognition. *Once your powers come to fruition, you can never kill again without destroying forever your ability to commune with the Knowing Crystal.*

Angry frustration filled Brace. The Knowing Crystal was a crafty foe, always seemingly one step ahead. It had been that way from the start, from the first time he and Teran had attempted a joint communing. Both had thought it strange even then, that the Crystal refused to permit Teran's entry. Now, the malevolent intent was obvious.

Two Crystal Masters would have been more than the stone could have handled. It had simply manipulated them, and the events, to separate them. Alia's vision of the monastery at Exsul had been but another part of the Knowing Crystal's plan. The stone hadn't accidentally gone awry—it had deliberately planted the scene in Alia's mind to lure Brace there. Lure him there to a father dying of the same malady Brace so desperately feared.

Divide and conquer. Undermine your foe's self-confidence. Two of the most elementary military tactics. Tactics that now pitted Brace as a solitary warrior against the might of a nearly omnipotent stone.

Despair welled within. How could he possibly hope to defeat a foe with a computer-like mind capable of analyzing and choosing from hundreds of logical outcomes, then plan for every action Brace might take? To outguess the stone seemed impossible.

Yet outguess it he must. His leaving the others was but one attempt to do so. It wasn't logical to split forces at a time like this. The Crystal had to know he was hurt and needed his friends. The Crystal had probably also reasoned that Brace had realized by now how vital Marissa was to the success of his quest. Brace hoped that, for once, his highly unorthodox plan would take the stone by surprise.

It seemed to work for a time, gaining him valuable ground. But the mental link could not long be ignored. The humming began anew, rising to a pounding, harmonic intensity. Brace fought it, gritting his teeth against the throbbing agony, but his weary, battered body could not hold out for long.

The sun rose to gild the sol in a golden glory. The frigid winds died, soothed to a gentle, nearly warm breeze that wafted through the mountains. Sunlight glinted off the fallen snow like tiny, twinkling stars. Beauty, serene and silent, surrounded Brace, mocking him with an illusion of the peace he craved so desperately.

And still the cacophony in his mind continued, until he thought his skull would explode. Finally he could go on no longer. Brace sank to his knees, his head clutched in his one good hand, and groaned out his agony.

Time lumbered by as he fought to master the pain, fought against the awful fear that he'd either soon die or at last go mad. Voices rose through the tumult, to shriek and wail in his head. Brace fell to the ground. Gods, he couldn't take much more!

Then, suddenly, the noise and excruciating pain were gone. Brace lay there, tense with anticipation, not daring to hope the onslaught wouldn't return. And, as he waited, footsteps drew near, then halted around him.

With his last bit of strength he raised himself to one elbow—and gazed up into the triumphantly grinning face of Ferox. Behind Ferox was his usual entourage of armed men.

In his hand, the black-clad man held the metallic-sheathed geode. "It doesn't like you anymore, does it?" he inquired slyly. "And you'll obey me at last, or I'll turn the stone upon you again. You wouldn't like that, would you, Ardane?"

Despair welled in the pit of Brace's stomach. He squelched it quickly. This was not the time for weakness or indecision. This was the time for action.

The situation seemed virtually hopeless, but there might never be another chance. For the moment the Crystal was contained. If Brace killed Ferox, he'd lose his Crystal powers if not his life, but it was worth the sacrifice. Teran would just have to finish the quest. But at least Ferox's more immediate threat would be over.

Brace eyed the blasters pointed at him, mentally calculating the odds. They were very poor, but he had to gamble that Ferox still needed his Crystal powers and wouldn't harm him. He climbed to his feet.

Then, with a wild cry, Brace sprang at Ferox.

"Curse his arrogant, stubborn male hide!" Marissa cried as she shoved her bedding into her backpack. "That ignorant sandwart is determined to get himself killed, sneaking off and leaving us behind! Why did he do it, Rodac? Why?"

The Simian glanced up from his banking of the fire. *Brace has his reasons.*

"But he's badly hurt, weak and exhausted!" Marissa protested, fiercely blinking back the tears. "He may not have been thinking clearly."

Then all the more reason to catch up with him as soon as possible. Rodac rose and slung his backpack and blaster over his shoulder. *In his weakened condition, he can't travel fast and his trail will be easy to follow. We'll catch up with him soon enough.*

"Yes, you're right, of course."

Marissa clamped down on her emotions and climbed to her feet. She graced him with a grim smile, then shouldered her own backpack and blaster.

"Lead on, partner."

Two horas later they reached the spot where Brace had been captured. Signs of a large troop of men and a brief struggle were evident in the windblown snow. Rodac glanced at Marissa.

Ferox has Brace.

Marissa's eyes hardened. "Then we've not a secundae to waste. There's no telling what he plans to do to Brace this time."

They followed the trail all sol, taking care to avoid sites of possible ambush. The going was arduous, both mentally and physically, as Marissa fought to maintain a dispassionate warrior's perspective. Near sol set, they found Ferox's camp.

Brace's captors had taken haven for the nocte in a large cave, guarded heavily from the outside. Nearby sat several large skim crafts. Extra men must have arrived later, bringing the crafts with them.

More reinforcements, Marissa thought as she scanned the discouraging scene from the shelter of the distant rocks. Just what they needed. Finally she sighed and glanced at Rodac.

"There's nothing easy about this quest, is there?"

He shrugged. *Acquiring wealth beyond your wildest dreams never is.*

Marissa eyed him consideringly. "You know, I seriously doubt that Ferox carries all his ill-gotten gains around with him. And if we take him out, who's to say we'll ever find the secret

399

hideout where he's stashed all his loot. Your dreams of great riches may be just that, Rodac. Dreams."

This long ago ceased to be a treasure hunt, Marissa.

She started at his use of her name, then at the realization of what his words implied. Tender regard for the tall alien filled her. By the Crystal Fires, how rapidly things had changed!

Marissa had never imagined it was possible to develop such feelings of trust and affection for Brace, much less Rodac. Yet here she stood, her heart torn with fear and concern for the man held captive in the cave, while she marveled over her newfound feelings for a Simian. It was all so very amazing—and wonderful.

"Well, treasure hunt or no," she muttered, taking herself firmly in hand, "we've got to find some way to get to Brace. Preferably," she added wryly, "with minimal physical damage to either one of us."

Stay here while I scout the backside of their hideout. I'll return soon.

Marissa nodded her acquiescence and watched as Rodac stole away. An hora later, he returned.

"Find anything?" she demanded immediately. "If not, we'll have to make a frontal assault."

Personally, my choice is the smoke hole atop the cave.

"By the Crystal Fires, not another smoke

hole!" Marissa grimaced. "Well, it's not the most thrilling thing to contemplate, climbing down into another choking chimney of smoke, but I suppose it *is* the best of all options. Did you get a glimpse of Brace when you looked down the hole?"

Rodac gaze shifted from hers. "He's alive."

Unease fluttered through Marissa. "Why doesn't that sound overly encouraging?"

It seems he's the nocte's entertainment.

"You mean they're torturing him."

The Simian nodded.

Anger hardened her resolve. "Then let's go. I've had about all I can take of Ferox!"

Under cover of darkness, they made their stealthy way to the smoke hole. As they neared the opening, the sounds of raucous male laughter and cruel taunts floated up to their ears. Marissa choked down her fury, willing her emotions into icy determination. It was the only way to save Brace, she reminded herself repeatedly. The only way.

The smoke hole was wide, affording them a full view below. The cave held about twenty men standing in groupings of three or four in a rough circle around Brace and Ferox. Brace knelt in the center, bare-chested, his hands bound tightly behind him. His head was bowed and sweat glistened on the corded planes of his back and shoulders. Nausea coiled in the pit of Marissa's stomach.

Rodac tapped her on the shoulder. She glanced over to see him secure their rope around a large boulder and then unfurl it carefully. The rope fell, dangling to almost reach the nearest rocky outcropping.

Let's head on down for a closer look.

She nodded and watched as the Simian lowered himself over the side and slid down the rope. Marissa followed quickly. They paused at the ledge, about seven meters above the gathering. The position afforded them a view of the faces of the two men in the circle.

"Well, what'll it be, Ardane?" Brace's captor was mockingly demanding.

Casually Ferox tossed the geode box from one hand to the other. "Will you obey me or shall I turn the Crystal upon you again? For a time longer it's still your choice, but you and I both know you can't take much more."

Brace's head lifted slowly. "I—I've told you before," he rasped in a pain-constricted voice. "The Crystal will no longer obey me. It—it's gone awry. To tamper with it further is destruction for us all."

"Liar!" Ferox snarled. "Thanks to you and that little Traveler's manipulations, however incomplete they were, I gained an even greater ability to commune with the Crystal."

At Brace's look of surprise, a grin of evil triumph spread across Ferox's face. "You're so stupid, so easily manipulated. Both you and your brother."

His grin became pitying. "And you've never known, have you? Never been told the full story?"

"Wh-what story?" Brace croaked. "What are you talking about?"

"Why, the story of how I gained my partial Crystal powers. How I always knew your location no matter how far you were from me, how I tracked you to that hut in the mountains, and why at times I turned the Crystal upon you and at other times chose not to."

Ferox arched a dark blond brow. "Didn't you *ever* stop to wonder about that, Ardane?"

"How do you have powers?" Brace demanded. "It's not possible, save through inheritance..." He paused. "Who were your parents?"

"My parents?" Ferox smirked. "Ah, so at last you care. It warms my heart, this sudden interest, this—"

"Cut the barsa dung, Ferox. Just tell me!"

The blond man's expression hardened. "And tell you I will. My mother was of no consequence, save for her glorious beauty," he began, "a simple serving woman in the House Ardane. But she was also a woman who longed for better things. As beautiful women are wont to do, she used her body to obtain her desires and seduced a young lord. I was the fruit of their love."

"Go on," Brace growled.

"There's little more to tell. The young lord kept my mother as his mistress until he was compelled to life mate with his betrothed, then he set my mother aside. Though he never came to my mother after that, nor claimed me as his son, he always saw to our support. At least until I was nine cycles old. Then the payments stopped."

Brace stared up at him in silence, knowing there would be more.

"No curiosity, Ardane, about why my father suddenly stopped supporting us? No concern over the fate of a fatherless boy and his impoverished mother?"

"Somehow I don't doubt you'll tell me anyway."

Ferox chuckled. "Ah, you know me all too well. Of course, I'll tell you. You *need* to know."

He licked his lips like some predator considering its prey, savoring the moment to come. "The payments stopped because my father left on a military mission. When he returned, he was mad."

The color drained from Brace's face.

"I see you're finally catching on, Ardane."

"No." Brace shook his head fiercely. "It—it can't be. I would have known, someone would've told me!"

"Told you what?" Ferox prodded softly. "That your father had shamed himself with a serving woman? That you had a bastard brother? That, by all rights, *I* came first, should have been the heir?"

He threw back his head and howled with laughter. "You're such a stupid, trusting fool! There was never concern for love or fairness in any of this. House Ardane wanted a purer, nobler bloodline than my mother could ever produce. So they inbred our father to a third cousin, in the process inadvertently strengthening the Crystal powers in you and Teran, while I received only the diluted leavings."

Ferox's handsome features twisted into a look of pure hatred. "So, do you finally understand? Begin to comprehend the enmity between us, and most especially for Teran? He took it all—my inheritance, the full Crystal powers, the Academy honors, and, finally, my mother's love...

"Yes, even my mother's love..." His voice faded, then it rose in volume and intensity. "But I'll soon have my revenge upon Teran. And you'll help me, *brother dear*—or die!"

"Be damned!" Brace snarled, his mind whirling with this newest, most unnerving turn of events. "Blood or no, you ceased to be any kin to me when you turned against us all. I told you before. I won't help you!"

"Now, now, brother dear," Ferox chided mockingly. "Don't let your jealousy blind you. As long as Teran lives, you're little better than I. Help me with the Knowing Crystal and I swear there'll be a place for you in my kingdom."

"And you're a greater fool than I," Brace cried, "if you think the Crystal will ever allow itself to be controlled. Just as you used it to manipulate me, it has surely used *you* in the same manner. In the end, who do you think is *really* in command—you or the Knowing Crystal?"

Kathleen Morgan

"Liar! Madman!" Ferox spat, his face purpling with rage. "*I* control the Crystal. Never doubt that. It can be no other way. It—it's my destiny!"

"Is it, Ferox?" Brace countered softly. "Then why do you need me?"

Ferox trembled violently, fighting to master himself. "Your powers are stronger than you realize," he finally forced himself to reply. "That's why the stone is so determined to destroy you; you're its greatest threat. But together, our combined abilities will be enough to vanquish it, to become its ultimate master. So make your choice, dearest brother. Either join with me and key it to my bidding, or be driven mad like our father."

"As mad as *you* already are?"

Disbelief flitted across Ferox's face, then his handsome features hardened with resolve. "So you've made your choice, have you?"

He began to open the geode box. "Well, I've yet to turn mad," he said grimly, "but you will certainly soon be. And when your mind is finally gone, I'll still rework it to my bidding and make you my abject slave. How will you like that, brother dear? Hmmm?"

Brace barely heard him. His eyes were riveted on the box, his big body already trembling in anticipation of the torment to come. Twice this nocte Ferox had turned the Crystal upon him. And each time the agony had nearly driven Brace over the edge. He didn't think he could withstand another encounter.

The lid opened fully and a blinding light flooded the chamber. Brace cried out, arching backward at the first onslaught of mental joining. With all his strength, he attempted to block the Crystal's psychic probing, but its attack was like fingers clawing their way through his defenses, inexorably gouging into his mind.

He was spent, ground away to exhaustion by his endless battle with the Knowing Crystal, the demands of the quest, his battered, wounded body. And now, by this newest, most horrible of revelations that his half-brother was the Imperium's vilest criminal! Gods, would the tragedies of his family never cease?

It was all too much. He hadn't any more to give. Yet still Brace girded himself, loath to surrender without one final struggle. The stone would win, would take his sanity at last, but he would fight it all the way.

The mental fingers ripped through his skull, his brain, then melted into a black, burning liquid to inundate his nerves. The fluid oozed into every screaming fiber until Brace jerked helplessly in a numbed, dreamlike horror. His mind bellowed, twisted in despair against his utter helplessness. His mouth opened, his face contorted in frozen agony, and choking sounds tore out of him.

And all the while Ferox chuckled softly. "Had enough yet, brother? It's your last chance."

Gods, the pain was tearing him to pieces!

Brace doubled over as the ooze reached his gut, twisting it into knot after agonizing knot. He retched, then dry-heaved, gagging so badly he thought he'd die from lack of air. Then Brace caught his breath, gasping and sobbing. Tears coursed down his face.

Ferox kicked him squarely in his injured right shoulder. Sharp, fresh pain rocketed through Brace and he nearly passed out. He fell, sprawling at Ferox's feet. Fingers entwined in his hair and his head was jerked back.

"Fool!"

Through swollen, bleary eyes, Brace stared up into a pitiless face, a face suddenly so like his own. His brother, he thought through a pain-reddened haze. Gods, *his brother!*

Ferox squatted before him, the shining stone in his hand. "Stupid, stubborn fool."

A sense of déjà vu swept through Brace. He had heard those same words before, in a similarly painful situation, that sol his jailer Mardoc had last tortured him.

The irony of the moment mocked him cruelly. He'd escaped that last time only to find himself once again a captive, teetering precariously on the brink of madness. Had it been the Knowing Crystal even then that had beckoned him in that prison cell?

It didn't matter. There was nothing left to fight with.

Before, the battle had been to preserve his honor, his pride—and to survive. But none of that was of consequence in light of this awful, reckless, doomed quest. His pride and honor were gone, drowned in his defeated tears, beaten out of his twisted, tormented mind and body. And survival'? Gods, all he wanted was to die, to end the agony at last!

The madness called to him ... haunting, seductive. Brace moved toward it with desperate abandon. Then something stayed him. A memory, faint but lovely, of a woman ... his love.

Marissa ...

From someplace outside her mind Marissa heard his call. A fierce joy surged through her.

Brace. I am coming. I am here, my love.

With all the power within her, Marissa strove to join with him, willing Brace all the strength of her body, all the force of her love. She felt him hesitate, waver, then his resolve harden.

Marissa turned to Rodac. "It's time," she whispered. "We've got to rescue Brace now or we may lose him forever."

The Simian nodded and unslung his blaster, signaling for Marissa to do the same. *Try to take out as large a group of men as you can with one blast. It will be our first and only opportunity for the element of surprise. Then, while I see to the others, try to get to Brace as fast as possible. Finish Ferox. It's the only way to save Brace.*

Finish Ferox.

The words had a wonderful ring. Marissa

nodded grimly. Her finger moved to the firing mechanism on her blaster.

In those last moments as they waited for Ferox's men to move into the most advantageous groupings for maximum use of the blasters, time slowed for Marissa. Everything faded save the scene of the two men in the center of the circle.

Two brothers. One blond and strikingly handsome, clever and ambitious. And the other, equally talented and darkly attractive. But in their souls as stark a contrast as there ever was.

Despite the tragedy of his illegitimate birth, so much had been given Ferox—his great abilities, his physical attributes. Yet he'd allowed one terrible loss to poison him until he'd squandered everything. Brace's life had taken a similar course of familial betrayal when his uncle had turned against him and Teran. Yet, though he'd had to struggle against overwhelming adversity time and again, he'd never lost that shining essence that made him the man he was.

A good man. A strong yet gentle man. A man of courage and integrity. A man who'd had to choose between right and wrong, and who had always made the more difficult but better choice ...

The movement of the guards called Marissa back to the reality of the moment. Her concentration sharpened. With a low grunt Rodac fired. A split secundae later, Marissa's finger clamped down on her own blaster's firing mechanism.

Pandemonium filled the cave as they methodically dispatched two large groupings of Ferox's men. Bursts of blue light exploded about the chamber as their opponents found their own weapons and returned fire. Three guards toppled over, seared by Rodac's weapon's superheated blast. Marissa managed to finish off two more, then ducked barely in time to avoid being scorched alive herself.

Momentarily her eyes sought Brace. Ferox had dragged him over to a small alcove where both were safely out of the line of fire. The Knowing Crystal still clenched in his hand, Ferox hovered over Brace's writhing body. He seemed determined to complete the task of driving Brace mad before making good his escape. There would be no rival for the Crystal left behind this time.

More guards rushing in from the outside diverted her attention. There was no choice, Marissa thought, forcing herself back into the fray. For a time longer, Brace would have to hang on as best he could.

"I'll take care of them," she shouted, motioning to the men entering the cave. "You finish the ones in here."

Rodac nodded and concentrated on the guards already in the chamber. And, one by one, Marissa blasted down the new arrivals.

Gradually the cacophony lessened as the battle drew to a close. Leaving Rodac to eliminate the remaining combatants, Marissa slipped down to the floor and around toward the alcove that held Ferox and Brace. Seemingly aware the battle had not gone in his favor, Ferox had moved to the more expedient act of strangling Brace. The still glowing Crystal lay beside him, now in its open box.

Marissa considered finishing Ferox with the blaster but feared hitting Brace as well. Slinging the weapon over her shoulder, she pulled her dagger out of its sheath and worked her way over to the two men.

With his hands tied behind his back, Brace could do little to resist the choking grip about his neck. He bucked and twisted to free himself, but his waning strength, combined with the Crystal's continued mental hammering, soon left him incapable of further resistance. The life ebbed from his body and a roiling mist darkened his vision.

Gods, he was dying! he thought in despair. Dying at the hands of his own brother! Dying with the Knowing Crystal lying so close he could have reached out and touched it. So close at last—and he could do nothing!

Utter anguish filled him, anguish and a terrible fear of what was to come. What would happen to the Imperium, to Teran and Alia, to Marissa? Whatever still lay ahead, he had to be there to fight it with them! He *had* to.

With a strangled cry Brace heaved up and threw himself into Ferox. It was enough to knock the criminal aside. Ferox's grip about Brace's throat loosened. Brace jerked away.

In that instant Marissa reached them, flinging herself onto Ferox's back. Her dagger slipped around to the front of his throat and she slashed. Thrown off balance, Ferox fell back into her and the blade left only a superficial cut.

Bellowing in rage and pain, Ferox twisted about in Marissa's grasp. He shoved the full weight of his big body into her. She tumbled backwards, her blade hand slamming into the rocks as she fell.

The dagger flew out of her grasp, and Ferox caught it. Her head hit the ground, the impact hard and jarring. Marissa saw stars and frantically fought past them, struggling back to full awareness.

Ferox stood there, the geode box clutched to his chest, staring up at the brilliant stone now hovering above him. His expression was intent and horror-stricken—as if the Crystal were speaking to him. The blood drained from his face. He shook his head slowly, his lips moving.

"No," he whispered piteously. "Please, Mother. No!"

With a wild cry Ferox grabbed at the stone, capturing it and shoving it quickly into its container. Then he ran, panicked and unthinking, straight toward the cave's entrance.

Straight toward Rodac.

In that awful instant Marissa saw the blond

man raise her dagger as he barreled directly at the Simian. She leaped to her feet as Rodac lifted his blaster in a threatening motion. Ferox, crazed with fear and haunting memories, didn't see, didn't hesitate—didn't stop.

"No! He's mine!" Marissa screamed, even as she knew it was too late.

Rodac fired, hitting Ferox full in the chest. The blond man shrieked, an awful, piercing sound of agonized despair, then toppled to the ground.

Marissa met Rodac's gaze, battling her anger at being denied the pleasure of killing Ferox—even as the relief that his life was finally over washed through her. With a mighty effort she mastered both. Emotions were a luxury yet to be savored. Brace was still in the gravest danger.

Squaring her shoulders, Marissa strode to Ferox's prone form and retrieved her dagger. Without a backward glance, she turned and made her way to Brace's side.

His eyes were clenched shut, his features contorted in pain as he fought to regain his breath. Marissa knelt and tenderly stroked the sweat-damp hair from his face.

"Brace," she said softly. "It's over. We have the Knowing Crystal."

He inhaled a ragged breath and forced his eyes open. Agony burned in their dark depths. "It's not over, sweet femina. Not while the Crystal still exists."

Brace levered himself to one elbow and glanced around. "Ferox? Is he dead?"

"I'd assume so," Marissa replied dryly. "He took a direct blast to the chest."

He frowned in puzzlement, as if suddenly remembering something. "At the end I heard him cry out to his mother. What did it mean?"

She sighed as the memories flooded back. "It's a long story, but suffice it to say that Ferox lacked the strength to fight past his personal demons. He let his bitterness destroy him."

"And the Knowing Crystal. Did he have it? Was it in its box?"

Marissa nodded. "I saw him clutch the container to his chest just before he rushed Rodac."

Brace groaned and fell back. "The box. Only when the stone is contained am I safe from its mental assault."

Gently she shoved at his shoulder. "Well, first things first. Turn over and let me cut you loose. Then we'll see what became of the Knowing Crystal."

The faintest glimmer of one of his old, devilish smiles touched Brace's lips. Then he rolled over. With a quick slash of her dagger, his bonds fell free.

Marissa resheathed her blade, then helped him to his feet. Brace swayed precariously. She could barely keep him upright.

"Rodac!" Marissa cried. "Help me!"

The Simian halted his careful inspection of

the cave's lifeless occupants and strode over to them. *They all seem quite dead*, he motioned, indicating Ferox's men.

"Rodac! Please!"

Need help, do you? He scanned Marissa and her heavily leaning companion.

"You know I do, you hairy bag of bones!" she gasped, struggling to keep Brace upright. "Now help me before I drop him!"

Rodac took Brace from her, pulling him to stand firmly against his side. Marissa, relieved at last of her unwieldy burden, ran to where Ferox lay. With her booted foot, she shoved him over onto his back.

He was quite dead, a large, gaping hole burnt into his chest. Once again Marissa experienced a fleeting regret that she hadn't been the one to kill him. Yet, even if she had, she doubted that the emptiness of the victory would have been any less. Even the end of his cruel life could never begin to compensate for all the pain and destruction he'd wrought. One man, and so many innocent lives lost because of him . . .

And still the danger wasn't over. The Knowing Crystal yet remained. Marissa's glance scanned Ferox's lifeless form, searching for the box he'd carried. Just as she'd feared, the blaster had struck the container, melting it away in the superheated fire.

The stone, however, had not been damaged. It lay where it had fallen when its box was destroyed, at Ferox's side. Lay there intact,

416

glowing as brightly as ever. Glowing brightly, functioning fully, as it continued to work its powers upon Brace's mind.

And there was no way to protect him from the terrible stone as they began the final, desperate journey to the pools of Cambrai.

Chapter Eighteen

They appropriated a skim craft and quickly helped Brace in. As Rodac readied the vehicle for takeoff, Marissa secured the Knowing Crystal in a backpack, then slung all the gear into the skim craft's rear storage compartment. Climbing in beside Brace, she glanced at him.

His head was bent and his breath came in ragged gasps. Though drenched with sweat, he shivered uncontrollably. Uncertain whether the shivering was due to the frigid nocte air or the effects of the Knowing Crystal, Marissa drew a phoca-fur coat over his shoulders and tucked it snugly around him. As the engines rose to full force and they lifted into the air, she pulled his head down to lie upon her breast.

He lay there as the horas passed, his hands about her waist, silent and suffering. As best she could, Marissa willed him her strength to bolster his struggles against the Crystal's assault. It helped for a time. He was even able to doze in fitful intervals, but as her energy waned, Brace's pain once more returned.

"Ah, Gods, Marissa," he groaned softly. "How much . . . longer?"

She bent and tenderly kissed his clammy forehead. "Soon, my love. We'll be there soon."

Marissa's eyes lifted and she shot Rodac a questioning glance. His expression, in the light of the new dawn, was grim. He shook his head.

Cambrai is at least another two or three horas from here. Can he make it?

"I don't know," she mouthed silently. "I just don't know."

Then find out if we can destroy the stone in the pools of Cambrai, or if it requires the powers of a Crystal Master.

The horrible implication behind Rodac's words sent a prickling chill down Marissa's spine. The moment had come to face reality, the reality that Brace might soon lose his mind, if not actually die. To admit such a possibility, much less consider a plan that dealt with that contingency, was almost more than she could bear.

Yet consider it she would. If Brace was willing to give his life to save the Imperium from the Knowing Crystal, then she must accept his sacrifice and carry on. He'd expect that of her, of their love.

With a shuddering sigh, Marissa leaned close to whisper in his ear. "Brace. If we reach Cambrai and you're not able to . . . to function, what should we do? Can Rodac or I toss the stone into the pools?"

"I—I don't know," he moaned. "Gods, Marissa. I just . . . don't know!"

"It's all right, my love," she soothed softly. "Don't distress yourself over it. Time enough to discover the answer when we arrive."

"But what . . . if it requires a Crystal Master?" he persisted desperately. "And what if . . . I'm not able? Gods, M-Marissa. What will we do then?"

"We'll send for Teran," she said. "And somehow, someway, hold the stone at Cambrai until he arrives."

Brace glanced up weakly. "You won't fail me, will you, sweet femina? No matter what happens, you'll carry out the quest?"

She smiled down at him through a sudden mist of tears. Though the need for revenge had been a driving force, Marissa realized now that somehow, along the way, her determination to see the quest through had grown. Grown, until now Brace *was* the quest and all that counted—no matter the outcome.

"You know I'd never fail you, not *ever* again," Marissa whispered. "But rest now, take your strength from me, and we'll yet prevail. It's not over. The Knowing Crystal hasn't beaten us."

"I—I don't dare take too much more from you," he mumbled, his head settling once more upon her breast. "We can't both be weak when the time comes."

"Hush," Marissa murmured. "Rest. My love for you is an endless source of strength." *For as long as I live*, she continued silently. *For as long as my heart beats in my body*.

But even the force of one's will required the body's sustenance. And Marissa's energy was indeed waning. No one, no matter how determined, could maintain such psychic energy indefinitely. And she was so tired, so emotionally drained.

The parallel between this moment and that of her past life suddenly struck her. She, too, had once been as discouraged, as beaten as Brace. She, too, had lost nearly everything. And she, too, had ultimately prevailed.

She had more than prevailed. Somehow, someway, she had also earned the love of a man like Brace Ardane. And in that realization Marissa at last found the secret of her own worth—and a renewed determination to fight for the man she loved.

She had not *earned* his love—she deserved it! Her choices had been equally as hard as Brace's, yet she had never let herself give up or turn to evil. And, just as she loved Brace for the wonderful man he was, he loved her for the woman *she* was. Loved her for her courage, her intelligence, her passionate nature, and for all her unlimited potential still awaiting the right moment for fruition. Loved her, most of all, for the depth of caring and commitment he'd always known she possessed.

Fierce resolve filled Marissa. She was free at last of the bonds of her shame—and Brace had shown her the way to that freedom. It was now her turn to help liberate him, not only from the Knowing Crystal's domination, but from his own self-doubts and bitterness. Only then, at long last, could they follow the course of their newfound love. Only then could they deal with their twin babies—babies Marissa now knew she wanted as much for herself as for Brace. Babies that would survive and thrive on the love between father and mother, parent and child ...

Yet was she not an idealistic fool, an insidious little voice intruded, to believe all the pious mouthings, to place such mystical power in a nebulous, albeit wonderful, emotion? It was one thing to use love as the underpinnings of a relationship between a man and woman, and quite another to trust it to overcome a physical menace such as the Knowing Crystal. Warrior's skills were what counted in battle. They had ultimately defeated Ferox.

The stakes were even higher now. Far safer, Marissa resolved, to confront the Crystal in the same manner. Love had its place when the fighting was done, but it didn't belong in battle. If Brace, when the time came, was too spent to face the stone of power, then she would face it in his stead. But face it as a warrior—not as a woman in love.

Through the journey out of the mountains and over undulating, winter-yellowed farm lands toward the distant, famed volcanic pools, Marissa and Brace clung to each other. Clung for physical solace as well as emotional support, the burning intensity of their love the only thing that kept alive the now guttering flame that had become their lives.

As the horas passed, the mental effort to control the Knowing Crystal ground Brace down. He began to have periods of uncontrollable seizures. His jaws would clench shut. His big body would jerk in Marissa's arms. Drained as she was, it was all Marissa could do to hold him until the grotesque spasms passed. Each one left Brace a little weaker, a little less alert until, gradually, he slid into a deep coma.

Despair filled Marissa. She glanced at Rodac in desperation.

Soon, he motioned. *We're almost there*.

Several secundae later, they glimpsed Cambrai.

For a time, Rodac tried to bring the skim craft in low enough to attempt dropping the Knowing Crystal into one of the pools, but the heavy mists that enshrouded the area precluded that. They were forced to land and approach on foot.

There was no one about, as the pools were closed to visitors in the winter. Tall stone gates barred the way, but beyond them, high up in the mass of volcanic rock, steam from the molten pools could be seen rising. It was a lonely, desolate spot, mirroring not only their emotions but the gloomy, cloud-covered winter sol.

The Simian barely paused at the gates before pulling the laser probe out of a backpack and going to work on the locks. Marissa awaited his return in the skim craft, Brace clasped in her arms.

With a weary sigh, she lifted her head at the Simian's approach. "What now, partner?" Marissa asked, her gaze shifting to Brace's bowed head. "He's done all he can do."

It's as good a time as any to take on the Crystal, Rodac motioned, his face set in a grim mask. *I only hope Brace weakened it enough for me to get it to the pools and toss it in.*

He strode around to the storage compartment and pulled out the backpack that held the stone.

Marissa laid Brace gently down on the skim craft seat, tucking his coat and the extra blankets around him. Then she glanced back at the Simian.

"I'm coming with you. It may take more than just one of us to handle the Crystal."

He shouldered the pack. *Your concern for my welfare is quite moving.*

Marissa smiled sadly. "It's long past time for concern for any of us. For the sake of this quest, we are all quite expendable."

Her fingers traced a tender, lingering trail down the side of Brace's beard-stubbled face, as if memorizing it one last time. "All quite expendable," she murmured, "though I don't know what I'll do if I lose him."

A leathery grip settled on her arm. Slowly, reluctantly, Marissa's gaze lifted.

Leave him, Marissa. It's the only chance we have of saving him.

She sighed, then forced herself to climb out of the skim craft. After a moment of light-headedness that caused her to grip the side of the craft, Marissa straightened. She grabbed one of the blasters and slung it over her shoulder. A determined light in her eye, she motioned Rodac forward.

"Lead on."

The path to the pools sloped gently upward as it wound its well-worn, sinuous way. They heard the pools long before they saw them, a rumbling noise akin to that of churning water. As they drew near, the sibilant hiss of steam mingled with the sound of the swirling, molten maelstrom, and the sweltering air became damp with moisture.

The reason for the dampness became evident as they rounded the last rocky obstacle. Above the volcanic pools, a small waterfall cascaded downward. Upon contact with the molten rock, the water condensed into a thick blanket of steam that engulfed the area. Only the rising sounds led them through it all to the glowing, wildly churning pools.

Marissa halted at the edge of the largest of the pools and turned to Rodac. "It's time. Remove the stone."

He slipped the backpack off his shoulder and dug into it, withdrawing the Knowing Crystal. Brightness exploded before them. The Crystal rose from Rodac's hand to spin wildly, throwing off sharp, blinding beams of light. An eerie, high-pitched whine assaulted them.

425

"Catch it!" Marissa screamed, realizing they were too late, that the Knowing Crystal had managed to recharge itself.

She slammed her hands over her ears in a futile attempt to dampen the sound. "Catch it and throw it into the pools!"

Rodac leaped for the stone, but it easily slipped away, hovering just out of reach. He leaped again, wildly, and lost his balance, tumbling down a steep embankment that led to a neighboring pool. His head struck hard on a sharp, rocky outcropping. Rodac fell the last few meters in the limp state of unconsciousness, landing just millimeters from the edge of a seething, molten pool.

"Rodac!" Heedless of the shrieking Crystal hovering overhead, Marissa scrambled down the embankment to where the Simian lay. With frantic jerks, she managed to pull his massive form away from the edge of the pool. A quick examination showed nothing broken, his skull intact save for a small, rising bulge on the back of his head. But, try as she might, he could not be roused.

The scream of the Knowing Crystal heightened until Marissa thought her head would split. It had moved to hover overhead once more, its aura malevolent and lethal. She knew in that moment that it possessed the ability not only to destroy a Crystal Master, but anyone else who stood in its way.

There was no choice. She was the only one left to fight it.

Marissa rose in one fluid move, her body tense with the passion of battle, and shot the Crystal a fierce glance. "You won't win," she cried, her fist raised in defiance. "Not this time, not *ever* again!"

Whirling wildly, the Knowing Crystal shot downward, straight toward her. Marissa dodged it, hen twisted around, blaster in hand. The stone halted, spinning in the air. The blaster began to glow. Searing heat scorched through her. Marissa jerked back, dropping the weapon.

She clutched her burnt hands to her chest as the horrible realization flooded her. The Knowing Crystal was even able to affect inanimate objects!

Marissa glanced around, searching for the backpack Rodac had dropped. Her only hope lay in capturing the stone and flinging it, backpack and all, into the pools. The Crystal moved toward her again, shrieking through the air as it plummeted downward. Marissa threw herself onto the rough, lava rock floor, rolling over and over as the stone followed.

The noise! The pain of it was unbearable! She clamped her hands over her ears, suddenly unable to move further. There was nowhere else to go—save into a molten pool.

Marissa crawled to her knees, her head lifting to the Crystal. It spun erratically, emanating beams of light that sent shards of bright, blinding agony through her. Marissa staggered to her feet. Where was that cursed backpack?

She found it at last, lying beside a black volcanic boulder. She stumbled toward the bag, the Crystal screaming, wailing, following relentlessly. The air began to pulsate and pound at her. Marissa sank to her knees, crawling the last few, agonizing meters.

Her fingers clenched in the backpack's coarse cloth. For a fleeting moment, hope flickered in her breast. She rolled over, shoved herself to a sitting position, and flailed wildly with the bag, trying to capture the stone. The Knowing Crystal remained just out of reach.

With a wild, frustrated cry, Marissa climbed to her feet. She swung again and again with the bag, fighting past the excruciating agony of the howling stone, the tears streaming down her face. Swung, and missed, as the Crystal dodged the backpack easily.

Her desperation grew. She couldn't hold on much longer . . . couldn't take much more pain. And still the light and noise intensified.

The brightness was her undoing. Marissa lashed out, tripped, lost her balance and fell, skidding down a gravel-strewn incline that dropped off into yet another molten pool. She heard rather than saw the liquefied rock, churning and bubbling with loud, sickening plops.

Terror welled in her. She rolled over, clawing frantically at the slanting ground. The razor-sharp bits of volcanic stone sliced her fingers. Her nails tore as she gouged for some sort of hold in the hard, unyielding rock. And still she slid inexorably down.

Her feet slipped over the edge. In the last instant, Marissa's desperately groping hands caught hold of a gnarled outcropping of rock. For what seemed an eternity she hung, dangling on the edge of oblivion, before swinging up and onto the ledge.

She lay there panting while the Knowing Crystal halted above her, poised in its evil intent, bearing down in a mind-numbing cacophony of sound.

There was nothing Marissa could do. The stone had won. It would soon drive her mad with pain, and she would end it all by falling into the pools.

Next the Crystal would turn on Rodac, then Brace. There was no one who could save any of them. The realization filled her with a gut-deep, heartrending despair. It was over. Over.

Brace. Ah, my love, Marissa cried to him in those final moments. *I tried. I tried for you but it was not enough—neither the strength of our love nor all the warrior's skills we brought to this quest. There is* nothing *that can defeat the Knowing Crystal!*

A sob rose in her throat, bitter as gall. She had finally found love and happiness and now must lose it. Had experienced that special joy of conceiving life, and that, too, would soon die with her. Defeat pressed down on Marissa, mocking her. Death hovered overhead.

Then anger flared once more to life, surging

past the pain and light and noise. It flamed brightly, firing the dying embers of her being.

Fierce determination rose in Marissa's breast. There was still too much to live for, too much so dearly won to give up without the fiercest of battles. A battle that had never been hers alone.

Brace, Marissa called mentally, her thoughts flitting past the scene of horror to an unconscious man in a skim craft. A man who had become her whole life—and was now her only hope.

Brace, I can't do it without you! I need the strength of your love!

"Yes, child," a gentle voice whispered. "That is the answer. You've learned at last . . ."

Marissa flipped over onto her back. For a moment, the harsh intensity of the Knowing Crystal seemed to dim. Through its muted glow she made out the form of a white-robed old man.

Her heart stopped. But only for an instant. Then it commenced a wild pounding.

The old man of the Repository. The apparition . . .

"Wh-who are you?" she cried. "Tell me who you are!"

"Does it matter?"

"Yes!"

He smiled. "Vates. My name is Vates."

Vates. The name of Brace and Teran's old teacher. *But he was dead!*

She quashed the surge of fear. This was not

the time for superstitious sniveling. If he were truly who he said he was, ghost or no, he might be able to help. And she was just that desperate.

"Can . . . can you aid us against the Knowing Crystal?"

He shook his head. "There is no need, child. You have already discovered the answer. It was within you all the time."

Even as he spoke, Vates's form began to glow softly, the outlines of his body to blur. "Give my love to Brace," he whispered as he shimmered and faded. "Tell him my thoughts will always be with him . . ."

As if his presence had been the only thing that kept the Knowing Crystal at bay, Vates's disappearance seemed to signal the stone to renew its onslaught against Marissa. Bright light exploded, the ear-splitting noise resumed. With a cry, Marissa rolled over and covered her ears.

Brace, she called, fighting desperately against the agony that consumed her like some maddened, howling pack of demons. *Brace, come to me! Now, before it's too late!*

Please!

The word teased the edges of Brace's consciousness, a consciousness rapidly returning to full awareness in the absence of the Crystal's relentless hammering. His eyes opened. He blinked blearily.

His head lifted to scan the area. "M-Marissa?"

She was nowhere to be found.

Brace groaned, then shoved himself to a sitting position, shrugging out of the coat and blankets. "Gods," he muttered, cradling his head in his hands, "I feel as if a herd of elephas pounded me into the ground."

Brace. Help me!

His head jerked up and he once more scanned the terrain. Where was she?

The hiss of steam caught his ear. Brace twisted in the craft seat—and saw the mists rising from behind the tall lava rooks. The pools of Cambrai! Fear rocketed through him.

"Marissa!"

Crawling, half-falling out of the skim craft, Brace headed for the pools. He stumbled, fell, then dragged himself back up again, relentless in his resolve. He *must* get to Marissa before it was too late. Before he lost her forever.

The climb to the pools took everything Brace had. Sweat beaded his brow, trickling down the sides of his face and into his eyes. His breath came in long, painful gulps, his muscles screamed in agony. And the doubts, the fears!

What if Marissa were already dead? And even if she weren't, how could he hope to prevail against the Crystal? It had all but killed him before. He had nothing left to fight with.

Nothing—save the knowledge he couldn't desert the woman he loved, no matter the cost.

The roar of the pools intensified. The humid touch of the mists reached him. Gods, it was

432

so hot! Then he was there, engulfed in the heat, the dampness—and the light.

The Knowing Crystal whirled crazily over an outcropping of rock at the base of an incline, spinning as if its inner gyrostabilizing mechanisms had gone awry. Discordant humming permeated the air. Brace halted, his muscles bunching, tightening.

Marissa lay there, a helpless victim of the Crystal's vicious mental attack. Rage filled him. Brace summoned all his strength and forged on. He *had* to get to her!

The full power of the Crystal struck Brace as he reached the top of the incline, in a vicious, blinding, excruciating onslaught. He staggered backward, nearly sinking to his knees.

"Gods!"

The muscles of Brace's neck bulged with the effort to keep his spine from snapping under the force of the Crystal's psychic assault. His face twisted in agony.

A black, swirling morass consumed him, heavy, rank, and smothering. The madness! he thought in rising panic. Gods, not the madness!

Terror engulfed him. Brace turned from the Crystal, flailing wildly, fighting to find a way out of the clinging, sticky ooze that drenched him, seeping into his skin, his bones, his very being. He couldn't take it. He had to run, to get away!

The attempt was futile.

He screamed, his entrails knotting, suddenly sick to the marrow of his bones, gagging, retching. And all the while the madness continued its inexorable progress, taking Brace bit by agonizing bit.

Despair lanced through him. He hadn't the strength to fight it! No man did . . . not alone.

But he was no longer alone.

Marissa, Brace cried. *Gods, Marissa, help me! Help me!*

Yes, she answered, her words piercing the deafening blanket of sound. Her spirit rose to meet his. Her love reached him through the madness and the pain.

Yes, my love. I am here, am here with you to the end.

With a superhuman wrench of body and soul, Brace turned back to the Knowing Crystal. And, as he did, another voice, gentle and beloved, whispered through his mind.

Face what you fear most. Accept it, take it within you. It is the final secret. The final secret . . .

For a brief moment everything cleared. Brace saw the madness in a different light—suddenly familiar, as if it were a part of himself.

The realization confused, yet intrigued him. A part of himself?

Face what you fear most. Accept it, take it within you. It is the final secret.

The final secret.

Was that secret his *fear* of madness, rather

than an inevitable consequence of his blood? Was it but a weakness of character, a choice to flee rather than fight, that ultimately determined if the insanity of the Ardanes prevailed? If so, the only way to defeat it was to do as the voice suggested—accept it, take it within himself. Allow the madness to overcome him and, once and for all, discover its true essence. But what if, once he allowed it in, it never let him go?

Fear burgeoned, clouding his mind, draining his courage. Gods, Brace thought. He'd face anything, but not that horrible, mind-sucking madness!

Yet, what choice had he? He couldn't run away as he had with Candra. He'd die before he'd suffer *that* shame again. He *had* to go forward, fight through it to reach Marissa. There was no other way.

Marissa, help me, Brace once more cried. *Give me your strength, your love for but a few moments more. Sustain me in what I must do and, if I don't return, remember that I loved you!*

You have it, she replied achingly. *Now and always.*

He smiled, then turned inward. This time Brace willed his body to relax and open to the blackness. To open and take in the madness.

A moment of sheer panic engulfed him. Of icy fear. Of fingers clawing their way through all his defenses, digging inexorably into his mind. Then they calmed. The black, burning liquid became a gentle, soothing balm, inundating his soul with peace, knowledge.

"Brace!"

His eyes opened.

Marissa lifted her arms to him. "Brace, I'm down here!"

He scrabbled down the incline in a flurry of choking dust and gravel, then crawled over to take Marissa in his arms. "Ah, femina, you're still alive. Thank the holy ones for that!"

She came to him, her arms entwining around his neck. Her head lowered to rest upon the broad expanse of his bare chest. It was *so* good to hold him, to be with him one last time.

"We can't fight it," she mumbled. "Our warrior's skills are useless against it. The Crystal's too strong, Brace. Too strong."

"Too strong for any one being," he rasped, "but not for two joined as we are. Our love will see us through this, as it has all along."

"No," Marissa moaned, clasping him all the tighter. "It's too late. Too late."

Two callused hands grasped her face, lifting it to his. Dark, beautiful eyes stared down at her.

"Listen to me, Marissa. I've beaten the madness. We've only to face the Crystal together and it will all be over. You'll not desert me now, will you?"

Tears stung her eyes. Her throat constricted. How could he ever think such a thing? To turn from Brace, to let him face the Knowing Crystal without her?

"Never!" Marissa breathed, her hands capturing his to hold them tightly. "We are one, until death separates us!"

They turned then, clinging to each other—and faced the famous stone of power. It lurched erratically above them, its light flickering, its hum harsh, jarring, but suddenly lacking in power. Almost as if...Marissa thought...as if it were confused. Defeated.

Fierce, triumphant joy filled her. She smiled up at Brace. "Call the Knowing Crystal. You are truly its master now. Call it to you—for your father, for Vates. For us all."

He glanced down at her, and for a fleeting moment his eyes misted with memories. Then his jaw hardened. Brace turned, back to the hovering stone.

His hand lifted, opening. *Come.*

With a harsh grating sound, the stone hesitated in its wavering gyrations, then obeyed, moving through the air until it came to rest in Brace's outstretched palm. He turned to Marissa then, the light of victory gleaming in his eyes.

"The quest. Our quest. We've won."

She nodded, smiling. "Yes, my love. We've won."

They climbed to their feet, then made their way to the edge of the pool. With a powerful backward coil of his arm, Brace flung the Knowing Crystal into the churning crystal fires. It sank, disappearing from view.

The swirling liquid never changed. The hissing steam continued unabated. Brace felt a fleeting stab of disappointment. The famous stone of power had sunk away like some common bit of refuse.

Then the ground began to shake. Shards of rock tumbled loose from the cliffs rising around them. Brace was thrown backward, nearly falling. Quickly regaining his balance, he turned to Marissa, taking her into his arms.

"Brace," she cried, clinging to him as the earth shuddered beneath them. "What's happening?"

"Gods, Marissa, I don't know!"

The rumbling heightened to a dull roar. The ground heaved. With a frightening cracking sound, the far edge of the pool split in two. The swirling liquid sank lower and lower into the crevice that slowly formed. The chasm then spread to all the pools in a series of tremendous, shuddering cracks.

As Brace and Marissa watched in fascinated horror, the molten crystal fires drained away deep within the center of the planet. Bursts of flame shot up to explode in a shattering of sparks and glowing liquid stone, then sank back into the chasm from which they had come. Water mingled with the superheated lava, evaporating in a sibilant hiss. The heavy mist intensified.

Then, suddenly, there was nothing left. No pools. No Knowing Crystal.

With a sound like the clap of thunder, the crevices closed. The sun slipped out from behind the clouds, bathing Brace and Marissa in a weak, golden light. Save for the waterfall high overhead, it was silent. As they watched, the pools filled again, this time with clear, sparkling water.

"It's over then," Brace's deep voice finally rumbled.

Marissa turned. "Yes, I suppose it is."

Their gazes locked, a look of relief mingling with the heated intensity of their love. Brace's hand moved, threading through Marissa's tumbled hair to clasp her head to his breast. She came to him, molding tightly to his hard-muscled body, clinging to Brace as if still afraid she might lose him. His head lowered to rest atop hers.

She inhaled deeply of his heady scent, her fingers stroking his broad, hair-roughened chest. Would she ever get her fill of him, sate the desire that smoldered even now for the passionate ecstasy of their matings? It was so good to be his woman. To know he was her man.

Yes, it was indeed over, yet Marissa struggled still with the newness of it. The sudden absence of strife, of pain and fear, was too fresh to accept. The only reality was the warm touch of Brace's body, the reassuring beat of his heart—and the knowledge that they were alive and together.

It was enough for a time, but finally Brace stirred. He glanced down at her, and there was a glimmer of his old devilish smile in the look he gave her.

"About that partnership," he began. "For future quests, I think a sixty-forty split would be fair."

She arched a slender brow. "Oh, and who gets the larger portion?"

"Why, you. Provided, of course, you do all the cooking. A good trail cook is well worth the extra expense. Interested?"

"Perhaps." Marissa stroked the strong line of Brace's jaw. "Does this offer also include the commitment of a life mating?"

He grinned. "Most assuredly, sweet femina. Most assuredly."

"Good. I'd hate for our twin girls to be fatherless."

Brace gaped in open-mouthed surprise, speechless for once in his life.

She smiled and gently crooked him under the chin to close his mouth. "You *did* say you wanted children, didn't you?"

"Y-yes," he agreed carefully, "but one at a time is the usual way to begin."

Marissa shrugged. "We'll manage. We may have to put off further quests for a time, though."

Brace managed a wan smile. "Yes . . . I suppose so."

She chuckled, amused at his lingering befuddlement. "Good, then that's settled."

Marissa paused, a tiny frown puckering the smooth expanse of her brow. "Just one final question."

"Yes?"

"Your madness. What did you find when you faced it?"

Brace hesitated. "Myself."

"I don't understand."

"I found myself, sweet femina. My madness was nothing more than my own self-doubts and fears, my lack of trust that the human spirit could overcome anything if it just had the courage of heart and mind. Once I faced that, it made all the difference."

A fleeting look of sadness crossed his face. "If only Father—and my brother Ferox—had done that. Things might have been different..."

"They weren't strong enough, my love," Marissa murmured. "They weren't like you and Teran."

"Perhaps. I don't know." Brace inhaled a shuddering breath, a wondering light gleaming in his eyes. "Strange, but I feel healed, whole again. And the bitterness is gone."

He paused, a smile of remembrance quirking his lips. "Vates tried to pound that truth into both Teran's and my head all the cycles of our youth. I think it has finally gotten through to the both of us."

"He came to me again," Marissa said, "when I lay here on this ledge with the Knowing Crystal trying to kill me."

"Vates? Did he now?"

"Yes, he did, Brace Ardane," she muttered, stung by his teasing note of skepticism. "He came to me when I needed him most, and told me I'd finally learned the answer."

"And that answer?"

"The answer was that I couldn't succeed without you and the strength of our love."

"Indeed?" He thoughtfully stroked his jaw. "And where have I heard that before?"

Marissa shot him an exasperated glance. "Well, it worked, didn't it?"

"Yes, sweet femina," Brace chuckled, deciding it was time to soothe her ruffled feelings. "It did indeed. In the end, that's all that matters."

She eyed him steadily. By the Crystal Fires, how she loved him! Yet at times he could be so aggravating, so typically male!

"He also said to tell you his thoughts would always be with you," Marissa persisted stubbornly.

The words sent a shiver down Brace's spine. Vates's thoughts had indeed been with him. The voice that had spoken to him during his final battle against his madness had been the old white-robe's. He recognized that now. And, in retrospect, his teacher's words had been so prophetic—and so like Vates.

Perhaps Marissa *had* seen the old man after all. Brace found a strange comfort in the thought.

He pulled Marissa back to him, clasping her tightly. The wind gusted in frigid blasts to swirl around the pools. Marissa shivered. For a moment longer, Brace held her close.

It was time to go.

His glance scanned the area one last time and alighted on the form of Rodac, still sprawled beside one of the smaller pools. Brace smiled, gently pushing Marissa back from him.

She glanced up.

He extended a hand. "Come, sweet femina," he said huskily, motioning to where Rodac lay. "There's a long quest called life ahead, but first we've a friend who needs us."

Eyes shining with love, Marissa took his hand.

Their First Noel

DON'T MISS THESE FOUR HISTORICAL ROMANCE STORIES THAT CELEBRATE THE JOY OF CHRISTMAS AND THE MIRACLE OF BIRTH.

LEIGH GREENWOOD
"Father Christmas"

Arizona Territory, 1880. Delivering a young widow's baby during the holiday season transforms the heart of a lonely drifter.

BOBBY HUTCHINSON
"Lantern In The Window"

Alberta, 1886. After losing his wife and infant son, a bereaved farmer vows not to love again—until a fiery beauty helps him bury the ghosts of Christmases past.

CONNIE MASON
"A Christmas Miracle"

New York, 1867. A Yuletide birth brings a wealthy businessman and a penniless immigrant the happiness they have always desired.

THERESA SCOTT
"The Treasure"

Washington Territory, 1825. A childless Indian couple receives the greatest gift of all: the son they never thought they'd have.

__3865-X(Four Christmas stories in one volume)$5.99 US/$7.99 CAN

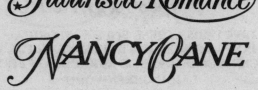

★ Futuristic Romance

NANCY CANE

"Nancy Cane has proven herself a master of the genre!"
                                    —*Rendezvous*

Starlight Child. From the moment Mara boards his starship, Deke Sage knows she is going to be trouble. He refuses to open himself, body and soul, to the raven-haired temptress until he realizes that without Mara's extrasensory powers he'll never defeat his enemies—or savor the sweet delight of her love.

_52019-2 $4.99 US/$5.99 CAN

Moonlight Rhapsody. Like the sirens of old, Ilyssa can cast a spell with her voice, but she will lose the power forever if she succumbs to a lover's touch. Forced to use her gift for merciless enemies, she will do anything to be free. Yet does she dare trust Lord Rolf Cam'brii to help her when his mere presence arouses her beyond reason and threatens to leave her defenseless?

_51987-9 $4.99 US/$5.99 CAN

Dorchester Publishing Co., Inc.
65 Commerce Road
Stamford, CT 06902

Please add $1.75 for shipping and handling for the first book and $.50 for each book thereafter. NY, NYC, PA and CT residents, please add appropriate sales tax. No cash, stamps, or C.O.D.s. All orders shipped within 6 weeks via postal service book rate. Canadian orders require $2.00 extra postage and must be paid in U.S. dollars through a U.S. banking facility.

Name_____
Address_____
City _____ State_____Zip_____
I have enclosed $_____in payment for the checked book(s).
Payment <u>must</u> accompany all orders.☐ Please send a free catalog.